MOONLIGHT DRAGON
BOOK ONE

Dragon's Deception

NICOLETTE ANDREWS

Dedicated to all my Kickstarter backers who made this book possible! Thanks for believing in me.

This Novel Is Made Possible By

Andrew Trushinski ☾ Cheryl Isaac
Sam ☾ Jacqueline Pal ☾ Katie Wasley
Emma Radovich ☾ Marcia Esders ☾ Brenda Z
Therena Carlin ☾ Megyn "Crimson" MacDougall
Kellie Lopez ☾ Deborah Hedges ☾ Sherry Mock
Jennifer Roberge ☾ Cynthia Offman ☾ Ember Nox
Samantha Landström ☾ Emmy Zdgiebloski
Alison Fertig ☾ Rebecca N Young ☾ Susan Simko
Cynthia Anne Ofer ☾ Billye Herndon
Barbara Sawyer ☾ Melissa Wiliams ☾ S. Meredith
Jessica Philips ☾ Michelle Huang ☾ Jax Pierson
Alicia T. Stoesser/Kiwri/Nattwinged
Rebecca Naomi ☾ Shannon Pemrick ☾ Seamus Sands
Brittany Saunders ☾ Richard Cailanan
☾ Juliana F. ☾

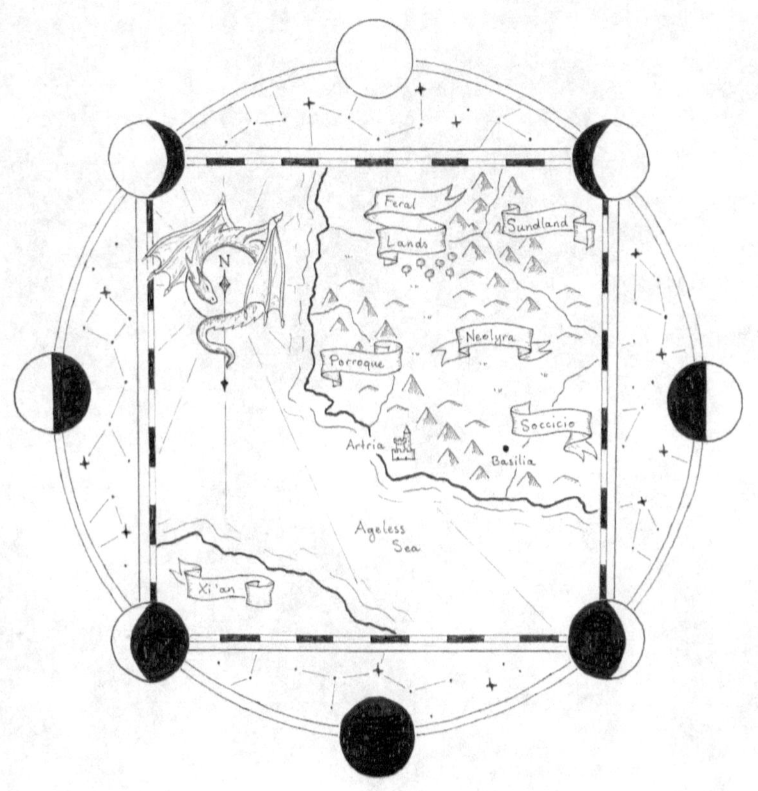

N
Feral Lands
Sundland
Porroque
Neolyra
Soccicio
Artria
Basilia
Ageless Sea
Xi'an

I

Erich gripped the pommel of his dagger, lengthening his stride as the Midnight Guards' elongated shadows chased him. They didn't move from their positions at the temple steps, but he felt their eyes following him just the same. A sliver of moon burned defiantly against a twilight sky. Few precious hours remained before curfew, and he couldn't waste a second. If he didn't make it back to the Wind Maiden by then, not only would they leave on the morning tide without him, taking all his geld and belongings, but they'd strand him in Artria for weeks, long past the next full moon. That was assuming the Midnight Guard didn't discover him first.

Head down, he joined the crowds spilling out of over-crowded inns lining Temple Street, as they sought enter-tainment in cheap theaters and gambling houses the next district over. Market-type stalls popped up to line the street and take advantage of the influx of pilgrims swarming Artria. The scent of meat pies wafted on the air, commingling unpleasantly with the fetid stench of the city, and each brush of a stranger made his skin twitch. He couldn't have picked a worse time to visit with the solstice looming, the city bursting at the seams, and him fresh off a long stint in a hermit's cottage in the wilds of Soccicio. Erich had grown accustomed to the company of shamans and wisewomen and had forgotten what it was like to walk amongst the unwashed masses.

Despite his instinct to break from the pack, he let the crowd pull him along like the current of a river, flowing downhill, and as they did, barkers lured pilgrims into their brightly-painted establishments, thinning the crowds, drip by drip. The road curved, and those that remained kept their heads down and walked with purposeful strides; unlike the wide-eyed ambling pilgrims, they didn't need someone to direct them to where they were going.

The street was dirtier there; putrid puddles collected between cracked stone and buildings leaned against each other as if they'd collapse without their support. Erich consulted a street post at a four-way intersection, and its dangling faded sign indicated he'd arrived in the Velvet District. A rather sumptuous name for a seedy district of the city. The corner where he stood stank of boiled vomit, and a few feet away, a tree-sized man leaned against the greasy wall of a tavern picking his teeth with the tip of his pocketknife. Erich removed a piece of parchment from his pocket, squinting at ink-splotched letters, to check the name of the tavern where his contact waited: The Gilded Weasel.

He'd found the place, though it wasn't what he'd imagined when the Soccicio sailor had told him about the Miracle Worker of Artria. A potential cure had been an irresistible temptation and lured him off the boat despite the risks. In the past, he'd scaled a mountain to find a healer with a gift for herbs, and crossed a desert seeking a man who still spoke the language of stars; what was a quick jaunt into the city to meet this supposed miracle worker? Maybe he'd be different than the rest, and they'd free him of this dragon corruption.

Plastered on the wall outside was a poster promising geld for information about the corrupted, and his hand twitched, wishing to grasp his dagger for comfort. A blow struck his shoulder, and spinning, Erich drew his blade from under his coat and pressed it against the neck of his assailant. The man paled to the color of milk, and his wide, dark eyes darted between the dagger and Erich.

"Please, I have nothing," he stuttered, hands held up helplessly as the sleeves of his overlarge jacket slid down his thin wrists.

Judging by his moderate attire, a clerk or something similar and no threat to him. Sighing, Erich sheathed his dagger. The tree-trunk man grasped his comically small pocketknife in his beefy fist and eyed Erich, as if looking for a fight.

This was why he hated the cities; in less than an hour, he was assaulting innocents.

"No harm. I overreacted. Guess, I'm jumpy since the war," Erich said with a smile and a pat on his shoulder.

Both nodded their heads. Everyone on the continent could sympathize; war had scarred them all. It made for a convenient cover because no one asked questions, and though he might not have fought in any war, he'd fought his fair share of battles.

"Let me buy you a drink." The clerk gestured toward the pub.

Tree man hadn't let go of his pocketknife, and his beady eyes shifted from the poster then to Erich. Had Erich moved too quickly or in some way appeared inhuman? He was always careful to keep a tight rein on his reactions and movements to not give away his unusual strength and senses. But mistakes happened, as the past had shown. Best to get what he came for and leave before he aroused any more suspicion.

With a forced smile, he slung an arm around the clerk's shoulder, who buckled beneath the weight of him as Erich ushered him into the tavern. Inside, dark panels lined the walls, a familiar hazy, sweet-smelling cloud of smoke choked the air and obscured the faces of the patrons crowding the battered tables throughout the room. Beneath the stench of sweat, smoke, and cheap ale, something tugged at his senses, a thread of magic. A tingle raised the hairs on the back of his neck, faint and hardly noticeable to anyone who wasn't trained to.

The clerk slid out from under his arm and found them seats at the bar. It, too, pulsed faintly with live magic. Running a finger against the lip of the bar, Erich discovered runes carved there that responded to his touch and sent a jolt up his arm. They were everywhere in the pub, hidden along ceiling beams and in decorative flourishes on archways. His ability to read runes was academic at best, meaning educated guesswork, but they seemed to be wards of protection. Who'd carved them here, in a city that outlawed magic? For the first time in a long time, he felt hopeful.

After The Corruption, the language and practice of rune spells had been lost. Sometimes, in small remote villages, he stumbled across them carved into a tree or rock, remnants of the past, more superstitious ritual than real magic, never flickering or giving any indication of power even when he actively tried to awaken them. They'd lost their power ages ago, and those villagers that remained wouldn't say who'd created them, and no one remembered where they'd originated before that. Except perhaps the Church of Sol, who hoarded knowledge of the age before The Corruption, keeping those last fragments of magic for themselves.

"An ale for me and my comrade," the clerk said, when the bartender came over.

Grasping two tankards in one hand, the bartender filled them both from a golden stream of ale pouring out of a dusty barrel before plopping them down onto the counter in front of them. Erich tossed a few kupfer to the bartender, a small penance for drawing a dagger on the clerk, and the bartender caught them midair, revealing a black circle tattoo, encircled by half a dozen stars. A cold chill ran down his spine; now, he understood the runes throughout the establishment.

Each star on his wrist represented a successful hunt. Dead corrupted. Men and women like him. Were there other dragon-corrupted among his trophies? The bartender caught his stare and brushed a hand against his wrist as he pulled down the sleeve of his shirt.

"I'm retired now," he said, to answer his unasked question.

Bad enough he'd recognized it. The Church of Sol didn't want civilians hunting corrupted; that was the Midnight Guards' job. But desperate men and women risked it all to hunt and kill corrupted, harvesting valuable horns, claws, and fangs to be sold on the black market. Retired hunters were rare, as most died in pursuit of their next bounty or were caught by the church and punished. Erich took a swig of the bitter ale and scanned the room, suddenly aware he might have stumbled into a trap. The bartender moved on, and most of the patrons were absorbed in their own glasses, but for one sandy blond-haired man standing by the door, arms crossed, and eyes narrowed. Erich sought the comfort of his pommel.

"You seem young to have fought in the war," the clerk said.

"You're one to talk. What are you, seventeen?" Erich replied without looking away from the man at the door. His eyes were following someone, but it was difficult to say who amongst the crowd.

"I'm older than I look," he said.

Erich ignored him as he'd found who the blond was watching. A fiery redhead sauntered over toward him, and he tensed. Sometimes hunters worked together in a group: the bartender, the woman, and the man at the door could be attempting to entrap him. She squeezed between him and the man on his left, leaning against the bar. She flagged the bartender over, whose face lit up as he hurried over to take her order. While the bartender filled her drink, he studied her profile, full lips, pale skin, and smooth hands that didn't fit her homespun. The lack of scars and callouses told him she wasn't a sword for hire, but that didn't mean she wasn't a hunter's lure.

Her blue eyes slid toward him, and a smile curled her rouge lips.

"You gonna sit here all night staring into that tankard?" she asked.

Lure or not, he wasn't going to take the bait. After chugging his drink, he slammed the empty tankard down onto the counter. It was possible he was being paranoid, but he hadn't come this far to not at least try. Besides, at this moon phase, he wasn't worth anything to a hunter, and he'd fought against worse odds and lived.

"All yours," Erich said, sweeping an arm to his now-empty seat.

She flashed him a brilliant smile before taking it.

"My thanks."

Without looking back, Erich walked to the back of the tavern, seeking the man the sailor had described. The tables here by the back door were mostly empty but for a man leaning back in his chair, alternating rolling a coin over his knuckles and tossing it in the air. Limp, greasy brown hair covered a ragged hole where an ear used to be. He'd found his guy. A quick glance over his shoulder, and he confirmed he wasn't being watched.

According to the sailor, no one spoke to the miracle worker without speaking to their representative first. Erich snatched the man's coin in midair. Glowering, the man rose from his seat, scarred hands splayed against the tabletop.

"The stars are bright tonight," Erich recited the code.

"And the moon fades." The man spat onto the floor and jerked his head toward a set of stairs leading up to a second floor.

Resting his palm against the hilt of his dagger, Erich followed him up the stairs, and the din of the tavern faded. At the top, a narrow landing greeted him, and his escort's shadow stretched out over threadbare rugs as he marched down the hall. It ended at a single door that he opened and gestured for Erich to enter.

Inside, a man with half a pointer finger counted geld and silbern coins without looking up at Erich even as the door closed behind him. A man, a head taller than Erich, a cudgel strapped to his belt, stepped in front of it, blocking any potential exit. Not exactly the way he pictured a meeting with a miracle worker, but perhaps this was his representative. After all, if the Church of Sol knew what they were doing, they'd be arrested for breaking laws against unauthorized magic. Relaxing his posture, he reluctantly released his grip on his dagger.

"Evening, gentlemen," Erich said as he took a seat uninvited at the table.

The man swept away his coins into a pouch, then shoved it into a pocket inside his coat before finally glancing up at Erich.

"Did your mother raise you in a cow pen?" Half-finger asked.

"Never knew my mother."

The man scoffed. "You've got some nerve, foreigner."

He hadn't thought his accent was that bad, but it'd been ages since he'd spoken Neolyrian.

"I hear you're the man I need to talk to to find a healer."

"If you want a healer, go to the temple."

"The sort of healing I'm looking for the temple cannot provide."

The thug's gaze flicked to the guard, and a slow smile crept over his face. "I might have something; if you have the coin."

Erich reached for his belt, and Half-finger's eyes narrowed onto his dagger before he nodded at the big man, who shuffled, presumably grasping his cudgel. Erich removed his sheathed weapon and set it on the table slowly, then raising his hands in a gesture of good faith; he waited on Half-finger's signal before making another move.

"Any other weapons on you?" the thug asked.

Many. "That's it. Can I show you what I'm offering?"

The thug nodded curtly.

"Is this enough?" Erich asked as he dumped out his purse of geld coins onto the table.

Half-finger's eyes lit up as he reached for the geld, but Erich swatted his hand away. "First, let me see the Miracle Worker of Artria. If he's not a fraud, then I'll pay you this and more."

The thug threw his head back and laughed. "Miracle Worker of Artria? That's just a myth."

"There's no need to play games. I'll pay you this and more. I'm good for it. Name your price." He'd empty Father's coffers if that's what it took to be free of this curse.

Half-finger must have scented his desperation

because the wicked curve of his mouth and the twinkle in his eye screamed greed.

"I'm the Miracle Worker of Artria; whatever ails you, I've got the remedy." He pulled out a small bag from his waistband and dropped it onto the table.

Erich plucked it off the table and felt the pulse of magic inside, tugging at him and reaching out like a thousand tiny tentacles attempting to take hold. Inside, burnt sugar-scented golden powder shimmered, and Erich dropped it, letting it spill across the scarred table. Stardust. A potent, highly addictive drug that reduced pain along with a euphoric high. For some, one taste was enough to create a powerful enough craving that they were driven mad with want, and withdrawals caused greater and greater pain with each dose. It wasn't a remedy, but a sickness.

Lurching forward, the thug scraped up golden granules with surprising reverence.

"Careful with the product. This is a rare commodity." He glared at Erich.

"I think there's been a mistake." Erich rose, reaching for his dagger and bag of geld, but before he could, the thug stabbed it through, and coins spilled from the torn fabric.

"I don't think you understand. You're not leaving here without paying for what you've spilled."

Blood pounded in his ears as he considered his options, and as there was no use reasoning with them, it left him with only one: fighting his way out. Fortunately for him, his dragon curse made him faster and stronger than most humans. Erich lunged for his dagger, had a hold of it, and turned as the big man swung his cudgel at Erich's head, barely missing by a mere hair's length. Twisting around, he jabbed at the big man as the cudgel came back down, striking him in the shoulder and knocking him back into Half-finger, who poked a knife into his lower back.

"No one gets away without paying," he snarled.

Then the door burst open, and all eyes turned toward the redhead from the bar standing in the doorway.

"City Watch, no one move!" she said in a commanding voice.

Something told him he wasn't leaving Artria with the morning tide after all.

2

Raucous laughter roared in Liane's ear as she passed a table of gamblers. The winner scooped up geld and silbern coin, whooping triumphantly as his companions groaned. The tavern was hot, smoky, and crowded, which made the rough-spun clothes even more unbearable. Commoner's clothing was ideal for these sorts of operations; no one gave her a second glance as she worked her way through the crowd. If only they weren't so Nameless damned itchy. Did common women really wear them, or had Ludwig bought her a dress made of itching nettles?

She rolled her shoulders, attempting to relieve the itching scar on her back to little avail, and glanced at Ludwig, who leaned against the wall by the door, his sharp gaze scanning the room conspicuously. He'd been against her plan from the start, and it had taken days of cajoling to get him to agree. Never mind him. There were already too many distractions, pulling her in a thousand directions when she needed to focus. The handsome man, whose seat she'd taken, had gone upstairs with one of Niklas Ehrle's lackeys, and she'd gotten up to follow them.

For months she'd been hunting the Onyx Gang, trying to link them to stardust, and tonight she'd witnessed a deal in progress. Niklas couldn't slip out of her grip this time. Not paying attention to where she was going, a drunk jabbed his elbow into her rib and knocked her into a nearby patron who spilled their drink onto the table and over everyone's cards. Stumbling back, she watched as a drunk man rose up and jabbed his finger into the chest of the man she'd collided with.

"You great oaf!" shouted the man she'd run into, glaring at the drunk who'd knocked into her.

"It wasn't me. It was her." The drunk pointed at Liane.

"Pardon me." Liane bobbed her head and turned to follow her mark.

But the man grasped her shoulder, spinning her around to face him.

"I was winning that game. How are you going to repay me?" he said, his gaze lowering to the neck of her gown. Liane's hand reached up to cover herself from his unwanted stare.

Over his shoulder, she spotted Ludwig making his way over. If he reached her, he'd separate the man's hand from his wrist and then force her to retreat. There wasn't time for sweet-talking or attempting a negotiation. Instead, she stamped hard on the man's foot and the shock forced him to release her shoulder, and she scurried across the room and out of reach.

It was an inelegant solution, but an expedient one, and she couldn't lose sight of the buyer for long. Darting between patrons, she evaded capture and headed up to the second floor, where the buyer and lackey had disappeared. As soon as her foot hit the first step, she heard Ludwig shout out after her.

"Liane!" But she ignored him.

She'd ask him for forgiveness later, he always gave it, and it was easier than waiting or trying to convince him. The hall at the top of the stairs was empty until the door at the end opened, and the one-eared lackey stepped out. When he saw her, a grin spread across his pockmarked face.

"What's this? Little bird, is you lost?" He strode toward her.

"I'm looking for someone," Liane said, wringing her hands in a pitiful display of a lost and helpless damsel. She fumbled for the dagger she'd hidden in the waistband of her skirt.

"And who's that?"

"I've heard you could help me. You see, my ma is sick..." saying those words turned her stomach, thinking of all the poor innocents who'd been lured in by the Onyx Gang on the promise of a miracle cure only to get hooked on a drug so potent and expensive it would bankrupt them before robbing them of their loved ones.

His smile widened, and he stepped closer, attempting to wrap an arm around her shoulder, and the putrid scent of his rotten breath made her want to gag. But she fought against the urge to recoil and clenched a fist around the dagger hidden in the waistband of her skirt.

"Come with me, little bird; I can help you."

Liane drew her dagger and pressed it against his chin, and his eyes widened as realization dawned upon him.

"Tell me, is Niklas in there?" She nodded toward the back door.

Throat bobbing, his lips turned into a sneer.

"You think I'm afraid of a little needle like that?" He grasped her wrist and squeezed, twisting her arm backward and forcing her to drop the dagger.

It fell to the ground a moment before she twisted in his grip and thrust an elbow into his gut. Doubled over, he gasped for breath as he fell to his knees. Liane darted past him, eyes focused on the door, but he grasped the hem of her dress, tripping her. Crashing to the ground, she wriggled onto her back, hands fumbling for her fallen dagger just out of reach as he crawled over to her, pinning her hands to the ground, leering down at her.

"You Nameless blighted whore. I'll make you pay for that." He raised a hand to strike her.

Behind him, Ludwig's florid face popped up at the top of the stairs, and she must say, he had impeccable timing.

"A little help?" she said, interrupting the swing of the lackey's hand.

He turned a second too late, as the hilt of Ludwig's rapier struck him on the top of the skull, and he crumpled like a rag doll on top of Liane. With his dead weight on her, she shoved him aside, wiping away the dirt and imaginary stains he'd left behind. Repulsive. But all in all, that had gone smoother than she'd anticipated. Back on her feet, she turned to head for the door, but Ludwig caught her by her arm, stopping her in her tracks.

"You've had your fun; now let's alert the City Watch and be done with it."

"And tell them what? That you've knocked a man unconscious? By the time they get here, the buyer and stardust will be gone. Without proof, he'll get away like last time."

"It's nearly curfew. Do you want to spend the night in a jail cell?"

As if to emphasize his point, the eleventh bell tolled. One hour left. At the twelfth bell, the palace guards closed the gates, and the City Watch rounded up and arrested anyone caught out after hours. From the Velvet District to the palace, it took twenty minutes on foot, less if by some miracle they caught a carriage, but few were out this late, and there'd be even less available with all the pilgrims in the city. That didn't leave her much time to catch Niklas and drag him to the magistrate's office, but she liked a challenge.

"You worry too much." She shrugged free of his grip.

"It's my job to worry about you."

"Then I take it back; you're doing an excellent job. Let's not waste time arguing, when you know I'm going to do as I like." She flashed him a smile and scurried down the hall before he could try and convince her otherwise.

Pressing her ear against the rough wooden door, she heard two men talking. Their words were indiscernible, but at least they were easily matched. Liane held up two fingers to indicate two people, and Ludwig nodded stiffly as he unsheathed his rapier. Though he was slower to action, he wanted Niklas and the Onyx Gang to pay as much as her. Their eyes met, and he nodded. *For Elias*, she thought.

Weapons at the ready, she grasped the doorknob and threw it open. It slammed into a broad back, less dramatic than she'd hoped. The man blocking the door moved out of the way, and the door swung fully open, and three confused men stared back at her. Niklas, behind the handsome man from the bar, narrowed his eyes as he looked her up and down. She recognized him by his portrait and reputation. He reached up to stroke his close-cut beard, and a smile curled his dastardly lips. She should say something or do something, shouldn't she?

"City Watch, no one move!" Liane shouted and pointed her dagger at him.

Her battle cry had the opposite effect, however, and Niklas flipped the table between them, rushing toward her. Swerving to avoid him, she crashed into the big man who pinned her arms to her side, and she rocked her head back, slamming her cranium into his jaw. It stung the top of her head, and blood dripped onto her forehead. Hers or his? No time to check because Niklas had a knife in hand that he swiped at her but missed when the buyer kicked out his legs from beneath him.

Amidst the chaos, their eyes met; his were a deep brown, and the edges bordered in liquid gold.

"Are you hurt?" he asked.

Liane reached up to touch the blood dripping down her scalp and shook her head, though she couldn't be certain. Her scar pulsed, not the painful itch from before, something deeper, a pleasant warmth that seeped out from deep in her bones, flushing her skin.

Footsteps pounded down the hall, and she tore her eyes away, seeking Ludwig. He'd knocked the big man flat onto his back and headed for her, ready to retreat, and for once, they agreed.

But Niklas blocked the exit, eyes blazing. His mouth formed a word that she couldn't hear because of the chaos behind him. People wearing gold and black uniforms of the Midnight Guard swarmed in, filling the space. Hands grasping, fists flying, and her lungs closed in. Ludwig tried to reach her, but a Midnight Guard yanked him back, and she was jostled between bodies. Voices turned to buzzing in her ears, and she was flung forward, colliding with someone's chest. Glancing up, she met the startling brown eyes of the buyer, moments before someone's elbow caught him in the chin.

Had he taken a blow for her?

They were yanked apart and dragged out into the hall, where they forced her to kneel. Head buzzing, and shocked beyond words, she stared mutely as a female Midnight Guard lined her up amongst the criminals. What were they doing there? Smuggling and other such crimes were outside their jurisdiction; they dealt with corrupted and stopping the spread of corruption magic. Unless...

"I am a member of the Royal Guard, and you will unhand me this instant," Ludwig said as he struggled against the pair of Midnight Guards.

"You can speak to the magistrate, like the rest," said a burly male guard, forcing him to kneel beside Liane.

"If you'd just look at the documents in my pocket, you'll see I'm telling the truth," Ludwig said.

Fortunately, he was willing to humor Ludwig and allowed him to retrieve papers from his pocket. The burly guard scanned them, then looked to Ludwig and then to Liane and did a double take. His face paled, and he signaled for the female guard holding her to let her go. She helped Liane to her feet much gentler than before, but as soon as they were free, Ludwig stepped in front of her assuming the role of protector and guard.

"I assume we're free to go then?" Ludwig asked, glaring at the guards as if they'd greatly inconvenienced him.

"Take an escort with you. This part of the city isn't safe," the burly guard said as he handed Ludwig his documents, and looked sidelong at Liane, probably wondering what she was doing so far from the palace.

"That won't be necessary, thank you," Ludwig said, shoving them into his pocket.

Then with one hand against the small of her back, Ludwig ushered her down the hall. She'd rather stay and see Niklas brought to the magistrate's office but knew by Ludwig's grim expression it wasn't a good idea to argue. Before they left, she glanced back one last time at Niklas and the buyer. The latter kept his gaze lowered to the ground. *Who was he*, she wondered and couldn't help but compare him to Elias, even though they looked nothing alike. She hoped he'd never used stardust, and this night would deter him from ever trying again. Then she might have spared one person from Elias' fate at least.

They walked in silence up the narrow streets from the Velvet District and toward the bright lantern lights of Imperial Square. Pilgrims hurried back to their lodgings, even outsiders knew to be back indoors before midnight, but outside the palace walls, such rules were a matter of life and death. Thanks to the Midnight Guard, the city had been free of corrupted for decades, but in the country, without walls and guards, chimera attacks and the like were much more common.

The northern road leading away from Imperial Square led back to the palace. Braziers glowed in the courtyard, illuminating the palace façade against the inky-black sky. Ludwig hadn't said a word for several long minutes, and his silence was beginning to trouble her. He might be really angry this time.

"I'll admit that could have gone better," Liane said, trying to cut the tension.

Ludwig spun to face her. "Better! That was a disaster. Liane, you promised me you wouldn't take chances this time," he said, thrusting his arms out to punctuate his point.

"They were calculated risks."

"If the Midnight Guard hadn't intervened…" He growled and ran his hands through his ash-blond hair as he paced in circles beneath the glow of the flickering lanterns.

"Did you alert them?"

He stopped pacing and frowned. "No. Why would I?"

Liane's entire body felt electrified. Five years ago, stardust had arrived in Artria and swept through the city like a plague. No one knew where it came from, but scum like Niklas grew rich by peddling it to the desperate and unsuspecting. If her hunch was correct, the Midnight

Guard was onto something, perhaps a magical or corruption origin.

"They must know where stardust comes from. Perhaps it's a form of corruption magic? It would explain why it's so addictive. How it destroys its users!" Liane's mind whirred with possibilities.

"Enough." Ludwig held up his hands. "Let the Midnight Guard handle it from here. Niklas has been arrested; you've gotten your revenge."

Liane's excitement deflated as she stopped in her tracks. Niklas was one dealer among many; there were stardust dens all over the city. Catching him wasn't going to solve the problem, and she couldn't rest until it was all gone.

"Are you satisfied? Does this feel like enough to you?"

A shadow passed over Ludwig's face, and he turned away from her. "No. But I know he wouldn't want you getting yourself killed over his memory."

Liane balled her hand into a fist. Ludwig was right; he usually was. But she wished she could find a counterargument that could justify this burning need to do something. If only she'd seen the signs sooner, if she'd acted quicker, maybe Elias would still be here with them...

A single clear bell rang. Half-past eleventh hour. A warning to get inside before curfew. By the stars, where did the time go?

"We should go," Ludwig said.

They raced through the streets, dodging late-night laborers hurrying home and the City Watch out ushering stragglers into their homes before curfew. The palace was in sight, and lungs burning, stamina waning, she lagged as the twelfth hour chimed. Each bong urged her to move faster, but she couldn't get her exhausted body to cooperate. The guards were closing the gate, and Ludwig, several paces ahead of her, would make it in time, but he slowed to keep pace with her, a sympathetic look on his face. She hated that look. Pity had been flung at her most of her life, reminding her she wasn't as capable as others, too weak, too sickly to keep up. Knowing she'd regret it tomorrow, she pushed past the fatigue, and urged her heavy feet to keep pace and then outrun Ludwig.

"Hold the gate!" Ludwig shouted.

And thank Cyra, they recognized them and held the door even as the last bell chimed. As Liane and Ludwig stumbled through the gates, they slammed them closed behind them.

"Another late night, Princess?" said the gate guard.

"Something... like... that." She panted as she attempted to catch her breath.

A stitch in her side sent needles of pain through her lungs as she bent over, gasping for breath. She still had two flights of stairs between her and her bedroom and hoped she wasn't seen by courtiers, or worse, her family, wearing commoner's clothes. When she'd caught her breath enough to walk, they took the long way back to her room, taking servants' stairwells to avoid any awkward run-ins.

They exited onto her hall, and Ludwig checked to make sure it was empty before they darted the last bit to her room. Throwing open her bedroom doors, she strode into the sitting room while Ludwig took his post outside. Alone, at last, she tore off the itchy garments and tossed them onto the floor. Luzie, her maid, had laid out her nightgown on her bed, and she pulled that on, luxuriating in the feel of soft silk against her irritated skin. Tomorrow, she'd ask Luzie to apply cream to her back to soothe the rash on her spine, but in that moment, she was too tired to even care about that. Her bed was calling her, and she pulled back the covers.

"You were out late again," Aristea said.

Startling, Liane spun to see Aristea, her older sister, sitting on the sofa, one blond brow perfectly arched. She'd been caught after all.

"What are you doing sitting here in the near dark? For a moment, I thought a chimera was in my room," Liane said, grasping her chest as her pulse pounded against her palm.

Aristea's blue eyes scanned her up and down. "Where this time?"

"A tavern in the Velvet District."

"Really, Liane?" In her best disapproving older sister tone.

"Really, Aristea," Liane said, sticking out her tongue, using her right as a younger sister to tease her.

Aristea wouldn't be here in her room this late without reason, and so sleep would have to wait a little while longer. Luzie, ever the gracious hostess, had served Aristea tea and cakes. Liane took a seat on the sofa across from Aristea, her legs crossed under her as she reached for one of the cakes.

"Aren't you too old to be galivanting late at night?"

"First of all, I'm nearly twenty-six, practically a shriveled-up old maid, and second of all, I'm not galivanting. I caught the head of the Onyx Gang tonight." Liane plopped a powdered cake into her mouth.

The buttery, flakey pastry melted against her tongue, and Liane sighed with pleasure. Now that she was home, her hunger caught up with her. She'd missed dinner...

Liane's eyes widened. The Soccicio ambassador's gala! With a groan, she slammed her palm against her forehead. How could she have forgotten? Mother must be furious she'd missed another function.

"Now you remember," Aristea said before picking up her teacup and taking a delicate sip.

"How angry is she?"

"I managed to smooth things over by lying and saying you weren't feeling well."

She was fortunate Mother hadn't sent the Vice Premier and a physician to tend to her. Any time the sun flushed her skin, Mother thought the fevers had returned.

"What do you want for your silence?" Liane asked.

"Remember when I asked you about dancing at the Masquerade?"

Liane groaned again. Even if she weren't a terrible dancer, the Masquerade was the next day; she couldn't learn the steps in time.

"Are you trying to ruin your performance? Because there are easier ways to do it."

"I have no choice; Lady Carmen twisted her ankle today at practice, and we'll be uneven."

"Can't have that."

"If you prefer, I can tell Mother the truth, and I'm certain she'd have you make up for it by having you join her at all her luncheons and dinners. There's lots of dignitaries and dukes visiting for the Sun Ceremony that she'd love for you to meet…"

"No. No. No. Let's not be hasty now. I'd love to dance with you," Liane said, waving away the very thought.

Mother had been trying to get her to wed for years, but she'd resisted until her vow to Elias was fulfilled. She wouldn't marry, she never would, and she liked it that way.

3

Metal bars separating the prison cells provided no shelter from the chill breeze, which stole what little warmth Erich's coat provided. Pulling it tighter around him, he tried to get comfortable on the cold, hard ground, but that was impossible. Not that he could sleep in this place, not surrounded by snoring drunks and filthy, petty criminals. His palms itched to take hold of his dagger, but they'd taken his one source of comfort, along with his other personal effects. All that remained was his mother's ring, which they'd somehow overlooked when they searched him. Reaching into his pocket, he ran a thumb against it. A fine mess he'd gotten into. For six years, he'd run away from the man he'd been, thought he'd shed that persona entirely, but here in this stinking cell, all he had left was her last relic and the curse she'd laid upon him.

Removing his hand from his pocket, Erich sighed and leaned his head back against the bars. It shouldn't have been surprising that the miracle worker was another fraud. Another charlatan and failure among many setbacks, and disappointments. It was more foolish of him to keep hoping. No one had ever healed corruption, and yet he kept looking. Perhaps it was for the best he'd missed his ship to Xi'an, rumor had it their alchemists could bottle lightning and transmute metals, and some whispered they sought to heal corruption as well. But knowing his luck, it would have been another dead end.

"Psst," his cellmate whispered.

Erich ignored him by closing his eyes and pretending to sleep. He wasn't in the mood for prison cell chit-chat.

"Hey, pretty boy." He jabbed him in the shoulder.

If he wasn't going to take a hint, perhaps he should make himself clearer.

"I'm flattered, but you're not my type," Erich replied, not bothering to open his eyes.

Straw scratched on the floor as he slid closer to Erich. Rolling his head to the side, Erich glared at the one-eared thug from the tavern who smiled back at him, revealing his blackened, rotted teeth.

"You got a patron?" One-ear asked.

"Do I look like a painter or poet to you?"

"Not that sort. You'll need someone to get you out of here." One-ear peered at the prison guard who snoozed in his chair, head drooping onto his chest and drool wetting his shirt.

Erich wasn't familiar with the Neolyra legal system, but he was fairly sure a patron wasn't necessary. In Sund-land, a magistrate heard evidence of the crime before passing judgment, and since Erich hadn't committed a crime, he assumed come morning, they'd let him go.

"You're not from here, so you might not know." One-ear picked at a sore on his pockmarked chin.

"Know what?" Erich said with a sigh. Maybe if he humored him, he'd get to the point and then leave him be.

"This time of year, you'll be lucky to be out of here in a month."

Panic made him sit up straight, and on instinct, he looked out the window. Even though a cloud blocked it from view, he remembered distinctly it was a crescent moon tonight. One night since the last new moon and thirteen days until the next full moon and the change. He'd planned after his release to find some way out of the city, fleeing to the remote mountains to wait out the transformation before moving on. But if One-ear was telling the truth, then he'd die in here. As soon as symptoms presented, they'd kill him. Fear gripped his chest, and Erich steadied his breath to not let real panic set in. Think. This dealer of death wouldn't have told him this out of the kindness of his own heart.

"What do you want from me?" Erich asked, keeping his tone neutral.

"Then you're not just a pretty face. Boss is looking for another big guy to help with some new business ventures."

"Quiet in there." The dozing guard roused just long enough to shout at them before his head slumped back onto his chest.

One-ear pressed a greasy piece of paper into Erich's

hand. "Give the morning guard the code, and you'll walk out of here a free man."

A free man indentured to thugs. Even as desperate as he was, and he was pretty desperate, he wouldn't work with scum like him. Erich crumpled up the paper and tossed it into the nearby shit bucket.

"No, thanks," Erich said, before rolling over and turning his back to One-ear.

Arms crossed over his chest; he reached into his pocket and grasped his mother's ring in a tight fist. There was one way he could walk out of this cell without selling his soul, but it was nearly as bad. Back in Soccicio, he'd gone to see an old friend at the Sundland Embassy, and a servant at the gate informed him that Ivar had been transferred to the Sundland Embassy in Neolyra. If it were true, and he had no way of knowing for certain, then he might get out of here without undoing six years of work. If he was wrong, then he'd start over, go as far away as he could. Father would never find him if he could help it.

His mind made up; he stood up and approached the bars and knocked on them, trying to get the guard's attention.

"Stop that, or I'll give you a beating," he snarled, not even bothering to look up.

"I need to send a message to the Sundland Embassy," Erich said.

"There's no messages. You wait for the magistrate to hear your case when it's your turn."

"That doesn't work for me. I don't have time to waste, you see?"

Growling, the guard stood up and grasping his cudgel;

he stomped over to where Erich stood and slammed it against the bars, rattling them and sending a sharp ringing sound echoing across the prison cells. Erich didn't flinch, meeting the guard's gaze with defiance.

"Now, look here. I told you once to be quiet," the guard said, pointing his cudgel at Erich's face.

Erich thrust out his flat palm, revealing the ring with the golden three-headed dragon, eyes made of rubies and topaz flames bursting from the center dragon's mouth, flickering with life as if the dragon might lift off the ring and take flight.

"Are you familiar with this emblem?"

The guard's eyes widened before narrowing in suspicion. "Where did you get that?"

"From my father." Technically true, he'd stolen it from him when he was a teenager, but the guard didn't need to know that.

The guard snatched it from him. "If you're lying to me, you'll be flogged."

"And if you keep a prince captive, what will happen to you?" Erich pitched his voice low as to not alert his cellmates.

The guard swallowed, and either the obvious opulence of the ring or the tone of his voice convinced him. His gaze darted down the hall. "It doesn't change the fact that I can't get you out before sunrise."

"Then I'll wait until morning." Erich settled back down onto the cold ground.

He'd missed his ship anyway. What was one night in a cell if it meant escaping with his life? Across from him, Erich caught the flash of golden eyes watching him. One of the corrupted, here? The Neolyrian curfew was meant to keep the corrupted from roaming the streets at night and protect the citizens. But the guards had hardly given him a second glance, but what happened after weeks of being locked in a cage? Eventually, they'd realize Erich wasn't entirely human. With his knees drawn up to his chest, he looked small and vulnerable, and for a moment, Erich considered reaching out to offer what, comfort? Those were empty words, and he was hopefully leaving by morning; attempting kindness was pointless. Besides those few corrupted that remained knew survival was easiest alone.

Between the cold, the stench, and a cramp in his leg, sleep evaded him. Gray streams of light poured in through the grime-covered window looking into his cell. The Wind Maiden would be casting off, along with his few meager possessions and the geld he'd spent on an expensive cabin. Best not to think about that. He could make more geld, and clothes and objects weren't worth much to him. Better to worry about getting out of this prison cell and hope Ivar was the current ambassador.

A pair of guards in crisp gray and blue uniforms marched down the hall, stopping in front of his cell. One of them thrust a key into the lock, and the door creaked as it swung open. All eyes turned to the open door, but no one moved; even Erich held his breath, waiting.

"You!" the guard barked, pointing at Erich. "Warden, wants to speak with ya."

Guards flanked him front and back as soon as he exited the cell before slamming the door closed behind him. Prisoners pressed against the bars, howling and jeering at him as he passed. Erich avoided looking at them, keeping his head high.

Beyond the prison cells was a wide, flat prison yard, where guards milled about. A few curious glances were cast his way as he and his escorts mounted the wooden staircase leading to an office. Inside, a man with snow-white hair wrote in small, neat rows upon a piece of parchment, and when Erich entered, his shrewd gaze flicked up, assessing him.

"Your majesty, a pleasure to meet you," he said, though his tone said otherwise. In fact, he seemed annoyed to be meeting with Erich. "I'm Warden Oswald. Take a seat." He jutted his chin toward the straight-backed wooden chair across from his desk.

"I believe I requested to send a message to the Sundland ambassador. Is there a reason I've been summoned to your office?" Erich said, using an imperious tone that made him hate himself.

Warden Oswald steepled his fingers and studied Erich for a beat.

"It is my job as warden to keep dangerous elements out of the city. All those who are found out past curfew must spend a night in our cells, per the empress' decree."

"Understandable. I myself, being new to the city, got lost and couldn't make it back in time, an honest mistake to make."

"I've looked at your arrest documents." He tapped a paper on his desk. "It says you were caught purchasing stardust."

"Another mistake, I'm afraid. I thought your government would be more organized than this."

"Indeed." He pursed his lips, as if he were biting back saying more.

"Have you contacted the ambassador then?" Erich asked.

"I have, and he has vouched for your identity. But there is still the matter of paying the fines for your arrest..."

Erich's nostril flared. A bribe, then. There couldn't be another explanation as to why he would be here.

"How much?"

A slow smile spread across Warden Oswald's face. "A hundred geld, and I burn this document." He picked up the paper, holding it over the flame of a candle.

"Done."

The malfeasance made his stomach turn, as it reminded him too much of home and the corruption he'd run from. Their business concluded, guards escorted Erich out of the prison yard and out the prison gates to where Ivar paced, mangling his velvet hat.

"Your majesty!" Ivar shouted as he rushed over to greet him.

"Hello, Ivar," Erich replied.

Ivar's eyes flicked from the prison yard to Erich, a question in his gaze, but he shook his head, apparently deciding against asking. That's what he'd liked about Ivar; he didn't ask unnecessary questions. "Come, your majesty. I've a carriage awaiting us to take you back to the embassy."

Sweeping his arm out in front of him, Ivar guided Erich down the narrow alleyway away from the prison yard.

"Forgive the walk; the carriage didn't fit in the alley-way. I cannot understand how these people live like this, stacked on top of one another." Ivar tutted.

Erich spotted the carriage and driver at the end of the alleyway, but he had no intention of going with Ivar back to the embassy. He'd try to convince Erich to return to Sundland. Reaching for his dagger, his hand came up empty. He'd nearly forgotten they'd taken his weapons and coin purse.

"Do you have my things?"

Sighing, Ivar handed him his dagger and signet ring. "Thank the Trinity you held onto it after all this time. Had I not seen it, I wouldn't have believed it was you. Have you heard the rumor you're dead?"

"Good."

Maybe Father would stop looking for him then.

Ivar shook his head and strode toward the carriage; Erich fell behind, pretending to strap his dagger onto his hip while he looked for an escape route. A man entered the alleyway, walking toward them with his head down. Erich attempted to move out of his way, but the man collided with his shoulder, knocking him back a step. Spinning, Erich reached for his dagger, but drew a stick from the holster instead.

He blinked at it in confusion, then looked to the ground and then up to see the man running back down the alleyway. He'd stolen his dagger. But why steal it of all things? He didn't bother to question it, and chased after him, as Ivar shouted his name.

On the main street, early morning vendors pulling carts of produce blocked the road, and Erich had to weave around them. Then a woman with her baby strapped to her back, pulling a cart full of fresh-baked pastries, stepped into his path, and he slid to a stop to prevent a collision. Craning his neck, Erich kept his eyes on the man, tall and thin and walking at a half jog. The thief darted down another alleyway and out of sight.

The city was like a labyrinth; if he didn't keep up, he'd lose the dagger forever. After apologizing to the woman, he leapt over her cart to continue his pursuit. He couldn't lose that dagger. Lucky for him the alley narrowed into a dead end, and there was nowhere for the thief to escape. Erich stalked closer as the thief turned to face him, the clerk.

Somehow, he'd escaped the prison. Perhaps he was working with those thugs. Were they angry that he'd turned him down and taken the dagger to lure him into a trap?

"Give me back what you stole, and I won't pummel you," Erich said, holding out his hand for the dagger.

The clerk held it loosely at his side, and his demeanor shifted. Gone was the timid, shy clerk and in his place was a confident creature staring at him with uncanny golden eyes. Erich glanced over his shoulder, expecting someone to be closing in from behind, but they were alone. What made him suddenly sure?

"It's thrice we've met now. Surely, it's time we exchanged names. I'm Fritz. And you are?"

"In no mood for games."

"Strange name." A mischievous smile curved his lips.

Growling, Erich lunged for the dagger but grasped nothing. The clerk blinked in and out—there and gone in an instant. Not anticipating his sudden disappearance, Erich stumbled and caught himself on a brick wall.

"Seeing as you drew a dagger on me the first time we met, I thought it was safer to approach you unarmed. Hear me out, and I promise to return your weapon to you," the clerk said.

Erich turned to face him, hand clenched into a fist.

"And what is it you want?" Erich hated to admit it, but he was intrigued; he rarely met other corrupted, and none were faster or stronger than him.

"I need a way into the palace." He nodded in its direction, to where the tips of its spires were just barely visible over the city skyline.

"I can't get you in. Now I've heard you out; give me my dagger."

"Then did I hear wrong? You weren't looking for the Miracle Worker of Artria?"

"Listen, I imagine you had to sell your soul to get out of that hell hole. But I'm not interested in stardust. There was a misunderstanding."

"And I'm not selling false hope. I'm authentic."

He was too young for a healer; the healing arts took decades to master. But while he held his dagger, Erich would play along.

"Prove it."

"Very well."

Grabbing his chin, the clerk's flesh spread like clay in a potter's hands, forming a cleft. Then he pinched his cheeks, and they swelled rosy and plump. A subtle stroke across his eyelids and his eyes changed from brown to a startling green.

Mouth agape, Erich stared at a stranger's face. Magic, real magic. Not the fractured remnants hoarded by the Church of Sol, or poisoned corruption. After years of searching, had he found it, a cure?

Erich shook his head. After six years of living as a ghost, he couldn't just stroll into the heart of the most powerful empire without Father finding out.

"I'll do anything else; name your price. Do you want geld? I have plenty."

Fritz shook his head. "I have no use for coin. What I need is the Golden Blade."

The Golden Blade, a powerful magic sword, brought kingdoms to their knees. And was currently in the possession of Empress Eveline, ruler of Neolyra and champion of light. She'd made it her mission to eradicate corrupted like him. Even if he were willing to enter the palace, stealing that sword would be a suicide mission.

"I can't help you." Erich shook his head.

"You won't find a cure for your dragon curse without my help."

"How do you know about that?" The hairs on the back of his neck stood on end, and he lunged forward, fueled by fear, and grasped Fritz by the collar.

"I know more about you than you realize," Fritz said.

Fritz ran a hand over his face, and it transformed once more, this time thinning and paler, cheeks sharper, ears pointed—an elf outside the feral lands. Erich dropped him as if he'd been burned and took a step back. Should he run, even if it meant losing the dagger? Better than having his entrails ripped out of his gut and feasted upon...

"I wish you no harm; I need you, Erich."

Icy hands grasped him by the nape, and he swallowed hard, choking on the lump in his throat. They said The Corruption sprang from elven dark magic, and the elves were its master. No human could cure him, but what if an elf could?

"Can you really cure the dragon curse?"

Fritz smiled and nodded.

Trinity help him; he must have lost his mind. "Then you've got a deal."

4

Bees, unbothered by the thick, sticky heat, bounced between wilting flowers, buzzing merrily about the garden. The gurgling fountain mocked Liane as sweat rolled down her brow and stung her eyes. If only she could dunk her head in that cool water. Even beneath the canopy of a maple tree, sweltering temperatures left her stumbling to keep up with the tempo of Dance Mistress Eleanor's tapping foot. Wiping the sweat from her brow, Liane paused to catch her breath. She should be at the magistrate's office watching Niklas' sentencing. Instead, she was flouncing around like a wilted flower in this heatwave.

"Again," Mistress Eleanor said, clapping her hands together.

Their accompaniment started over, but even their notes drooped and sagged in the heat. Groaning, Liane returned to first position. When would practice end? They'd rehearsed all morning, but even a lifetime of practicing wouldn't improve Liane's abilities; she was too inflexible to be a dancer. Court ladies flanked her on both sides and moved into position on Mistress Eleanor's count. They swept in from the wings of their mock stage, forming a line behind Aristea, who was the principal dancer. As was the case all morning, Liane struggled to keep time and misjudged the space between her and the next dancer, and when they twirled, Liane, a beat behind, accidentally struck the dancer.

"Sorry," Liane said, and backing up to give her space, she collided with another dancer behind her.

She attempted to salvage the rest of the performance, but Mistress Eleanor's glare made her forget the next step, and she floundered out of time behind the rest of the group. As the music rose to its crescendo, they surged around Aristea for the final pose. Panting for breath and on the wrong side of the stage, Liane looked forlornly at her fellow dancers, as the last notes of the song faded. Tonight would be a disaster. As if her lackluster performance wasn't enough, all this exertion was making her scar throb.

"No. No. This isn't right. Princess Liane, you must float delicately like a cloud on the breeze," Mistress Eleanor said, extending her hand outward to show the motion.

"I wish a breeze would blow," Liane grumbled as she fanned herself.

"Please, Princess Aristea, show us again," Mistress Eleanor said.

Delicate pink splotches colored Aristea's cheeks, and the sweat glistening on her brow made her glow, rather than look like a bedraggled, drowned rat like Liane. The harpist plucked a few notes, and Aristea twirled in time with the music, arms arched upward and back bent. The silk ribbons tied to her wrists trembled with each movement, capturing the essence of the breeze, effortlessly. Everything was effortless for Aristea. Everyone loved her, and how could they not? She was perfect.

If she were petty and spiteful, Liane might have hated her. But instead, it made her love her more. Aristea's dance concluded, and as the last lingering notes hummed on the air, Mistress Eleanor clapped uproariously.

"See, Princess Liane. That is the way it's done."

"Yes, Mistress."

Then when she turned her back, Liane muttered under her breath, "Why does it even matter? The Avatheos won't be able to see me from past his veil."

"Liane!" Aristea gasped, covering her mouth to disguise her heretic giggles.

Mistress Eleanor spun around and narrowed her eyes at them, reminding Liane of the same disappointed look she bestowed on her as a child.

"Why don't we take a short intermission for some refreshments?" Aristea said to Mistress Eleanor, saving them from being scolded. Her savior.

"As you wish, your majesty," Mistress Eleanor said with a sour expression.

Linking arms with Aristea, Liane dragged her from their practice stage and toward a shaded bench at the edge of the garden. When they were children, Aristea, Mathias, their younger brother, and she used to climb it. That was before the fevers left her bedbound, and by the time she'd recovered, she was too old for climbing trees. Leaning back, she closed her eyes, enjoying the feel of the breeze on her face.

"I've missed this," Liane remarked.

"I thought you hated dancing," Aristea teased.

"I meant us, the three of us. Remember when we used to sneak around in the servants' passageways to get away from that odious nurse we had?"

"I don't remember doing such a thing." Aristea sniffed primly.

Liane shook her head. They used to always be together; before Aristea married Heinrich and Elias died, they were inseparable. Now there never seemed to be a time when they were together. Aristea had her duties, and Liane focused on ridding the city of stardust. Even their little brother, Mathias, had joined the royal army two years ago and hadn't been home since.

"Today would be perfect if Mathias were here," Liane said, stretching her arms above her head.

"I am pretty perfect," said a rumbling voice behind her.

Liane tilted her head backward, and for a moment, she thought her eyes were deceiving her. They and the shape of the mouth were her brother's, but he'd matured since she'd last seen him.

"Mathias!" Liane shrieked and leapt from her seat to throw her arms around his neck.

Mathias' arms crushed her in his embrace with enough force to crack a rib.

"Good to see you, sis," he said, tussling her hair.

"I hardly recognized you. You grew a proper beard."

She tugged on the ends of his thick black beard. When he'd left, his mustache had been a shadow on his upper lip, and the hard angles of a man had melted the plump cheeks she remembered.

Aristea stood and said formally, "Mathias."

"Don't be so stuffy, Artie, come here." He opened his arms, welcoming her into his embrace.

When Aristea hugged him, he picked her up, twirling her around and eliciting a giggle from her. After setting her back down on the ground, he slung his arms around both their shoulders, and they took their seats back on the bench beneath the tree.

"How are you here? Your last letter said you were headed for the Soccicio border," Liane said.

"First company captured elvish raiders in the north, which were attacking a mining town near the northern border. Mother rewarded our valor with a promotion and a month's leave."

Jealousy pricked at Liane, but she stifled the feeling, not wanting to ruin the happy reunion.

"You would've heard had you been at dinner last night. Mother announced it then," Aristea said, flattening the imaginary wrinkles in her gown.

Mathias' lips curled in a knowing smile. "You missed a family dinner? And why is that, dear sister?"

Liane shrugged her shoulders. "That's my business."

He caught her in a headlock before she could squirm away. "What were you doing? Were you with a man? Were you sneaking out to meet your lover?"

"You think now that you're a soldier, I won't pound

you into mush?" Liane said, grasping onto his forearm as she wriggled in his grip to no avail.

"I'm not that scrawny kid anymore," Mathias teased.

"Could have fooled me." Liane threw a playful punch against his arm, and he pretended to be wounded and let her go, feigning cries of pain as Liane crowed at his imaginary agony.

"Mathias, Liane, you're acting like children." Aristea sighed.

"And you're acting like a stuck-up princess," Mathias taunted, ruffling Aristea's perfectly coifed hair.

What ensued was a three-way tussle; hair was pulled, sides were pinched, and it ended with Liane's arm twisted behind her back by Mathias.

"Ouch, ouch, ouch," Liane whined. "You're hurting me."

"Tell me what happened last night, and I'll think about letting you go."

"I, too, would like to know what Liane deemed more important than meeting the ambassadors." Their mother's calm voice silenced their playful banter.

Mathias let her go, and Liane smoothed out her ruffled hair, avoiding her mother's gaze. But she couldn't avoid it forever. Slowly, she looked up at her, and her mother's serene expression gave nothing away about her real feelings.

"Mother!" Mathias boomed and swept over to her, and pulled her into an embrace. "You look more radiant than when I last saw you. Cyra's light pales compared to your beauty."

"Don't even try it," Mother said, patting his cheek

with an indulgent smile. Mathias had always had the charm to soothe Mother when she was upset.

Liane looked to Aristea, pleading with her eyes to intervene.

"I'll do anything," Liane mouthed.

Aristea shook her head. They couldn't save her this time.

"Liane? We need to talk," Mother said.

"Yes, Mother."

Following her mother in the hedge maze, Liane's shoulders drooped as she trailed behind. Along the winding path lined with manicured hedges that led to a small fountain, a statue of Cyra sat at its center, pouring water from an endless jug, just as Cyra had poured out water to form the Ageless Sea. Spray from the fountain was a refreshing reprieve from the heat and her burning back as she turned to face her mother, who sat down on a white marble bench. Mother's guards stayed behind, blocking the exits so no one could interrupt them. Shoulders bunched and her scar throbbing, Liane took a seat.

"I'm not that angry. So, unclench your shoulders," Mother said.

"For the record, Ludwig didn't want to go, but I forced him to. Don't punish him. Please," Liane said, raising her voice loud enough for Falko, Mother's head of the guard, to hear. She was just glad he wasn't here to get scolded as well; instead, one of her secondary guards was on duty.

"Poor Ludwig. Even when you were a child, he'd come to me in tears."

"He always was a tattle." Liane shook her head.

"And thank the stars above, he's sensible. I thought he

could balance out your recklessness. But perhaps I was wrong."

"I wasn't being reckless. I had a plan. I caught the leader of the Onyx Gang! Well, technically, the Midnight Guard did the arrest, but..."

"Liane. Look at me."

Liane turned to her mother with hesitation. She grasped both sides of her face, her palms cool against her flushed skin. And as much as she feared her mother's disappointment, she craved her approval. She wasn't perfect and poised like Aristea or strong and accomplished like Mathias, but she was trying her best to be more than an invalid.

"Your heart is in the right place. But you should have alerted the City Watch. What if they'd hurt you?"

When Elias died, she'd begged her mother to do something about stardust, and while she had increased funding to the City Watch in hopes of stopping the gangs who were smuggling and selling stardust, it continued to proliferate, and people kept dying.

"I have, many times. They're not doing enough."

"Regardless, it's not your place to solve it."

"If not mine, then whose?" Liane's voice rose, and her skin flushed.

Mother sighed. "I'm one woman, torn in many directions. But, for your sake, I will give the problem more attention."

"Truly?"

Mother nodded.

"Thank you, Mother." Liane flung her arms around

her mother's neck, pulling her into a tight embrace and inhaling her lavender perfume.

"Perhaps, once this is sorted, you might think of marriage..."

An icy chill ran down her spine, and Liane let go of her. "I see." She should have known help came with strings attached.

"You can't waste your life chasing ghosts, Liane."

"And you think marriage will make me happy? Look at how it's treated Aristea."

"Henrich made a mistake."

"You call three different mistresses a mistake?"

"He has repented to both Cyra and Aristea. And both have forgiven him. Besides, no marriage is perfect."

"Not everyone has the marriage you and Father have."

Mother laid her hand over Liane's, and some of her temper cooled. "But it still takes work. I just want you to be happy."

Aristea was an excuse, as was stardust, and everything else she said. No matter how many lords, dukes, and princes her mother introduced her to, none of them were Elias...

"You promised to let me choose," Liane said. That same old refrain she'd used as a shield.

"And I stand by my word. But the Vice Premier has read the bones and stars, and she says you'll have a fated encounter soon. Does it really hurt to open yourself to the possibility?"

Mother trusted the Vice Premier's omens too much. Liane didn't have Aristea's skill for diplomacy, but she knew that if she wanted her mother to take the stardust problem seriously, she'd have to give a little.

"Who is it you want me to meet?"

"You know me too well." Mother smiled. "Duke Licht has just arrived for the Sun Ceremony. I thought you could get to know one another tonight at the masquerade."

"I'll talk with him, but I won't make any promises."

"That's all I ask." Mother grasped her hand and squeezed.

Their chat finished, Liane and Mother walked out of the garden to where her siblings waited with curious expressions. Liane forced a smile to keep them from worrying. It wasn't the first time her mother had tried to play matchmaker, and it wouldn't be the last. And she didn't want to waste this precious time with her siblings worrying about that. She was headed toward them when Ludwig entered the garden, scanning for her. And when she saw him stride toward her with a scowl on his face, her stomach sank. Bad news.

She excused herself and walked off into a secluded corner with Ludwig.

"Don't tell me," Liane said, hoping she'd read his expression wrong.

"They released Niklas. He didn't even stand before the magistrate." Ludwig's fisted hand trembled.

Kicking a helpless bush, she shouted, "Nameless blighted darkness!" She thought she had him this time.

"There is a single ray of hope, however. I followed Niklas and his thugs to their hideout, and I overheard them talking about a meeting with their supplier tonight."

The hairs on the back of her neck stood on end. This was what they needed. If they intercepted the supply, they could find out where it was coming from. It could be the break they'd been waiting for all along.

"I know that look. I'm planning on handing this information over to the Midnight Guard. We should let them handle it."

"That's pointless. Niklas has connections. Who's to say he doesn't know someone inside the guard? If we find out who's bringing it into the city, we can eliminate the problem, yank the infection out by the root."

"This is too dangerous."

"Hasn't stopped me before."

"What about the masquerade?"

"I can do both."

"They're meeting in the ruins just outside the city."

"We'll take the tunnels; I know the way."

"That's not what I meant, and you know it."

The ruins were forbidden. According to the church, they were a source of corruption, and everyone heard stories about some hapless fool who wandered there and ended up with the withering, a wasting sickness that blackened the body before killing them. But her mind was made up.

"I'm doing this whether you come or not."

"I was afraid you'd say that." Ludwig sighed and ran his hands through his hair, searching the garden as if seeking support amongst the trees. After a few minutes, he seemed to come to a decision. "If at any point I feel your life is in danger, we retreat, got it?"

"You worry too much," Liane said, hitting him playfully.

She knew Ludwig wouldn't let her down. *Don't worry, Elias. I'll get them this time.*

5

Rich, dark Sundland wine cascaded into Erich's silver goblet. As he envisioned the tart and sweet taste of Gauldeen grapes, his mouth watered. The valley province was renowned for winemaking, and in fact, none other could compare. It'd been too long since he'd partaken of such an extravagance. Along with the wine, the maid set down a platter of biscuits and the fragrant cheeses from Porroque. Erich pierced a soft slice of cheese and smeared it over a biscuit before shoving it whole into his mouth. It melted on his tongue in a symphony of buttery, savory ecstasy. Though he hated to admit it, he'd missed this part of royal life. Lifting his overflowing glass, precious drops spilled, rolling down the side as he brought it to his lips. Because he didn't know when he'd have wine again, he'd intended to relish it, but one taste, and he was gulping it down like a man dying of thirst. After draining the cup, he set it back down with a satisfied smack.

"Is everything to your satisfaction, my prince?" the doe-eyed young woman, his hostess, asked. Hearing the words "my prince" in his mother tongue turned the wine sour in his stomach.

"It is," he replied, as he waved away the second glass the maid offered.

When he'd come to Ivar's townhome looking to call in his favor, he hadn't considered the unpleasant memories being around his people would invoke.

"It's been so long since I've seen you. I hope the Trinity has kept you in their care," she said, fluttering her long eyelashes at him.

Squinting, he studied her features, but he was terrible at remembering faces. Either they'd met before, and he didn't recognize her, or they'd never met, and she was attempting to ingratiate herself to him with false familiarity.

"Remind me again, of your name."

"Don't you remember me?" Her face crumpled with momentary disappointment, then she scooted closer to him, invading his personal space. "Don't tease me! How could you have forgotten? You used to bring me sweets when I visited the palace with Papa."

He remembered now. Ivar's daughter, a child last he'd seen her, now a woman. No wonder he didn't recognize her. What was her name? Gertrude? Gilda... it definitely started with a G...

"Greta!"

"I knew you hadn't forgotten." She lowered her eyes in a failed, sultry stare as her hand slid across his thigh.

It was impossible to untangle the child he'd known

from the woman she'd become, and he gently pushed her hand away.

"You've grown well. And you joined your father in Neolyra, I see. I thought you'd be married by now." She looked about that age.

Her nose crinkled, and she turned away, crossing her arms over her chest. "There's been plenty of offers, I'll have you know. But I told Papa one day you'd return for me as you'd promised me. And here you are. You haven't forgotten your promise, have you?"

Erich looked at his empty wine glass, wishing he hadn't refused a second as he tried to wrack his brain for a promise he'd made and forgotten. Surely, he hadn't promised to marry her, had he? But looking back, back then, he'd been eager to please, and as he remembered, Greta used to cry ceaselessly. Might he have agreed to marry her to stop her crying? He seemed to remember something like that. But vows between children couldn't be taken seriously.

When he met Greta's gaze once more, she looked at him ardently. Whatever she believed he'd promised her hadn't been left discarded in her childhood. He needed Ivar's help, and upsetting his daughter wouldn't exactly win him any favors. But he couldn't let her live under the delusion that he'd marry her or anyone and the least he could do was let her down gently. Grasping her small pale hands, he sandwiched them between his.

"Forgive me, Greta. I cannot honor the promise I made. The Trinity has called me into her service, and as part of my mission, I have sworn to take no wife and father no children," he said, hoping his hunch was correct.

"You've become a monk?" Tears welled in her eyes.

"It is her will." Erich wiped the tears from her eyes with his thumb.

"No, this can't be. We promised one another." Her bottom lip wobbled.

"It is the Trinity's will," Erich said solemnly.

"What is going on here?" Ivar said.

Erich turned to see the ambassador's flushed face and dark gaze bouncing between Erich and his daughter sitting much too close together. Erich let go of Greta and put as much space between him and her as possible. But the damage had already been done.

"Papa. My life is ruined!" Greta shouted

"What did you do to my daughter?" Ivar's furious gaze landed on Erich, his mustache bristling.

"I told her I've dedicated my life to service to the Trinity." Erich held up his hands in surrender.

"You what?" Anger defused from his expression, and puzzlement replaced it. "Is that where you've been? In some monastery?"

Sobbing loudly, Greta fled the room, slamming the parlor door on the way out. Both stared after her before sharing a look. Ivar no longer looked angry; he just looked weary as he sunk into the seat across from Erich and pinched the bridge of his nose.

"She's refused eighteen proposals, and most recently one from a very wealthy Neolyrian merchant. I thought bringing her here would help her forget this childish nonsense, but she's persisted in this delusion that you'll make her Queen of Sundland." Ivar rubbed his palm over his face.

"She's welcome to become Father's heir. I've no intention of filling that role."

"I suppose I was naïve thinking you came here because you're ready to return home."

"Afraid not, Ivar. I came to call in that favor."

"This is your favor? Then what was freeing you from prison?" His eyes shot up, narrowing once more at Erich.

"Doing your duty to your prince?"

"I'm afraid to ask what you want. First, you need me to release you from prison, and then you break my daughter's heart..."

"I guess Soccicio meant nothing to you..." Erich half rose from his seat.

"Now, let's not be hasty. I didn't say I wouldn't help. What is it you want exactly?"

"Nothing too hard. I need you to get my friend and me into the palace... unofficially."

Tugging on the ends of his drooping mustache, Ivar considered his proposal as echoes of Greta's sobs rippled through the townhouse. If he refused, Erich would have to find another way in, but that meant presenting himself at court as Prince Erich, and he hadn't claimed that title in six years and wasn't about to give up anonymity, not even for a cure.

"Who is this friend?" Ivar shook his head. "Actually, don't tell me. The less I know, the better. I owe you a great deal, your majesty, but I cannot put my neck on the line for any illicit dealings. You must know it would be in my best interest to send you back to Sundland."

"Hasn't he gotten a new son from that young woman yet?" Erich said to change the subject.

"Queen Freya. And no, he hasn't. The king hasn't been... well..." Ivar's bushy blond eyebrows drew together.

The briefest twinge of sadness passed over Erich. But it was short-lived. When Father died, his cruel legacy went with him, as did Erich's responsibilities to the throne. In his absence, his uncles would squabble over the throne, and Erich would be free at last.

"Pity." Erich examined his nail beds.

"I know the king isn't the most nurturing."

Erich scoffed.

"But Sundland needs you. Duke Mattison and Duke Ericson are gathering allies. You must return, before they plunge the kingdom into a civil war."

"Let them fight for supremacy. Isn't that the law of Sundland, only the strongest survive?" The words left a bitter taste in his mouth, as he envisioned Father looming above him as the cane fell over and over onto his backside.

"Then convince me otherwise. What are you after in the palace?"

Grasping the stem of his empty goblet, he twisted it between thumb and forefinger. Few knew of his dragon curse, and even if Ivar were one of them, he couldn't tell him he'd made a deal with an elf. Ivar wouldn't turn him over to Father, at least not straight away. He owed him that much, but Ivar wouldn't tolerate an elf.

"You owe me, Ivar."

"I repaid your favor when I released you from jail. And

I will not be informing your father of that fact. That's two favors, but out of my love for you, I'm willing to do one more."

Erich tapped his foot on the ground.

"What do you want, to send me home?"

Ivar shook his head. "That is your decision to make. I want to see my daughter happy. Be her escort to the ball, and I will not ask questions, and I will allow you and your companion to join us at the masquerade tonight."

"Hoping I'll change my mind and make your daughter my queen, Ivar?"

"I can't say I wouldn't be pleased with that outcome. But I know you well enough not to raise my hopes too high. If she's seen with someone unknown, it will intrigue others. Perhaps enough to talk to her and find her a suitable replacement for you."

"A pragmatic plan; I shouldn't have expected less from you."

"Thank you, my prince. But there is one other obstacle, I'm afraid."

"And what's that?"

"Prince Consort Heinrich, will be attending the masquerade as well."

"Who?" Erich asked.

Ivar cleared his throat. "During a diplomatic dinner in Sundland, you, um, punched him in the nose."

"Did I?" Ah. Now he remembered. Prince Consort Heinrich, a fledgling duke who didn't know how to keep his hands to himself. Erich caught him harassing a maid, and when she'd tried to push him away, and then Duke

Heinrich had persisted, Erich made the point clear for him.

"Well, in any case, I'm sure he remembers you, because he's made it impossible for me to see the empress despite all my best efforts. If the two of you cross paths, I fear the repercussions."

He never wanted to hurt Ivar. If there were any other way, he wouldn't have asked for a favor. But he had no choice.

"I'll be as silent as a grim."

Ivar frowned.

"Remember Soccicio?" Erich touched his nose.

"Do not make me regret helping you..." Ivar sighed.

6

Heart rattling in her chest, Liane peeked around the curtain. The loose, glimmering layers of Aristea's gown fluttered as she glided across the stage. With the audience's rapt attention upon her, no one would notice Liane fumbling in the background. Inhale and then exhale; she could do this. Pacing, she shook out her hands, hoping it would ease her nerves. On the opposite end of the stage wing, Mistress Eleanor gave the signal, and the dancers dutifully trotted out, followed by Liane, a fake smile plastered on her face. She could do it. She could do it...

Stage lights blinded her as she stepped out and froze in place as her scar throbbed. She couldn't remember the steps, and her soul vacated her body, leaving her to watch from above as a casual observer while dancers flowed around her, parting as water moved around a boulder dropped into a river. Beyond the dazzling light, she could see a sea of masked courtiers, cold and uncaring expressions watching her failure.

Then a warm hand grasped hers, and the ice around her limbs thawed. Liane slammed back into her body, suddenly aware of all the dancers turned to face her, and Aristea, who stood with her back to the crowd smiling at Liane.

Liane mouthed, "What are you doing?"

"Keep your eyes on me," Aristea whispered before tugging her after her.

As young children, she and Aristea used to dance in the nursery together, spinning around and around, their limbs moving seemingly without reason. But they knew each step by heart and had painstakingly memorized their childish choreography to perform for their parents. Grasping onto Aristea's hands and whirling together, her body remembered that dance and took over, impossibly falling into sync with Aristea. Accompanied by orchestral music, Liane in midnight blue and silver, the shadow to Aristea's golden sun, the dance felt more sophisticated and refined than it had in those days, or perhaps it was the childlike joy that bubbled up within Liane to replace her fear.

Their song reached its climax, and hand in hand, they struck the final pose to uproarious applause. Panting for breath and her back aching, Liane wiped her sweat-plastered hair from her forehead and cheeks but couldn't keep the smile from her face. Thank the stars above for Aristea's quick thinking, or the performance would've been ruined. The curtains closed, and dancers rushed over, chittering about the change in choreography, words dripping with praise. Even Mistress Eleanor didn't seem entirely displeased.

"Thanks for that," Liane said, when they were alone again.

"Don't mention it. I know you'd do the same for me," Aristea said as she accepted a towel from a servant and delicately dabbed at her brow.

"That is if you ever made a mistake."

Aristea laughed. "I make plenty of them."

Just one, Liane thought, but she wouldn't mention it and ruin the mood. Luzie arrived to usher Liane into a dressing room to change into her masquerade outfit: a simple emerald gown with a rose mask and matching flower crown. Futzing over her headpiece and the fall of her curls, Luzie met her eyes in the mirror.

"I have a good feeling about tonight," she said.

"Me too," Liane replied while her stomach did somersaults.

The plan was simple: meet Duke Licht before slipping away to the ruins, catch the criminals, and return before the masquerade ended. With a squeeze of her shoulders, Luzie left, and Liane went to join her family for the grand entrance.

Father turned his fanged dragon mask toward her as she approached; the hollowed eyes and sharp pointed teeth made him look ferocious.

"There you are, darling; once Aristea and Heinrich arrive, we can start."

"It's getting late," Mother said, fingers tapping

against the hilt of the Golden Blade as she looked down the hall. When she was a girl, Liane used to beg her mother to retell the story of her quest to obtain the sword and how the goddess herself had gifted it to her to vanquish dark forces that threatened to destroy the land.

Once, she dreamed the blade chose her instead of Aristea to rule, and the sword had enveloped her in bright blinding light. The goddess had spoken to her in the dream, but she couldn't remember the words anymore.

"I enjoyed your performance," Mathias said, pulling her from her thoughts, and she narrowed her eyes at his mischievous grin beneath his golden satyr mask.

"I'd love to see your performance next, Mat," Liane said in a sickly-sweet tone.

"Children, please. Mathias could never be that graceful." Father smirked.

Liane groaned at his terrible joke and shook her head.

"Speaking of, where is Aristea?" Mathias asked as he searched the hall for her.

As if summoned by his words, Aristea and Heinrich turned a corner, coming into view. Aristea's sun mask couldn't disguise the wrinkle on her forehead, or her mouth thinned in displeasure. They'd fought again, or better put, were in the midst of a fight.

"Forgive us for being late," Aristea said.

"My darling wife couldn't decide on what accessory to wear, even though I thought we agreed to go as a pair," Heinrich tutted, gesturing to the star-shaped buttons on his inky-black doublet.

Aristea's nostrils flared, and Liane contemplated the

merits of punching him on her behalf. Not that it would do any good. Aristea would only come to his defense if she did. But she couldn't stop herself from fantasizing of a day where Aristea realized she was better off without Heinrich, political alliance or not.

"Shall we, then?" Mother said, forcing levity into her voice.

They entered the grand hall: Mother and Father at the front, followed by Aristea and Heinrich, and Liane and Mathias at the rear. Across the crowded ballroom, the Avatheos, the guest of honor, sat on a gilded throne. Normally important guests would enter along with the rest of the family, but she'd never seen the Avatheos walk. For all she knew, beneath his floor-length robe, there was nothing but mist and magic allowing him to glide from place to place or appear wherever he intended to be. Like all priests, a hood covered his eyes, representing the veil between the divine world and the mundane. Little magic remained since The Corruption, and to save themselves from impure sights, and thoughts, they wore hoods to preserve themselves and their magic. It was fortunate the Avatheos didn't visit Artria often. Every time she saw him, a strange twisting feeling churned in her gut, and despite his hooded veil, she felt his stare across the room, and it sent a tingle up her spine. She'd be glad to be away from him and the masquerade as soon as possible.

They took their seats at the head of the room, the Avatheos behind her. Liane focused on the crowded ballroom, plotting her escape route. The orchestra, which had accompanied her dance performance, played a waltz, inviting the courtiers onto the dance floor. Father stood and bowed with a flourish to Mother, who giggled like a girl half her age. It was an unofficial tradition for them to dance first. She took his hand and walked onto the dance floor, where they were quickly lost in one another's gazes. Over thirty years of marriage and still madly in love. Before Aristea married Heinrich, Liane thought all marriages were like her parents': passionate, devoted, and enduring.

Next to Liane, Aristea rested her hand on Heinrich's arm as she whispered in his ear, asking him to dance with her. Liane tried to imagine Aristea as empress and her and Heinrich taking on the tradition their parents had started, but couldn't picture it. As if proving her point, Heinrich shook his head, refusing to dance, and instead abandoned Aristea to go greet some lordling across the room as other dancers joined her parents. Hurt flashed across Aristea's face, and she glanced around the room, checking to see if she'd been noticed. Their eyes met, and Aristea's skin flushed. Liane resisted the urge to follow Heinrich and give him an earful, but it wouldn't make a difference other than to cause a scene, which would ultimately delay her and embarrass Aristea.

But she didn't need to anyway because Mathias offered to dance with her instead. With a bow, he offered his hand, mirroring Father's gesture, and when Aristea shook her head, trying to refuse, he tugged her onto the dance floor anyway. Mathias always had a knack for improving their moods. Once, when Liane had been bedbound, he'd danced outside her window for her amusement.

Ludwig materialized at her shoulder in a plain, black

domino mask, the same uniform as the other Royal Guards scattered about the room. With a sidelong glance at the Avatheos, who seemed to be focused on the dancing, she inclined her head toward Ludwig.

"Did you get it?" she asked him from the corner of her mouth.

"I'm beginning to wonder if I'm your accomplice or your tailor."

"Perhaps a bit of both." She smirked.

"It's not too late. You could dance, and I could alert the guard instead."

"I'd rather choke on hors d'oeuvres," she said a little too loudly, and the Avatheos turned ever so slightly in her direction.

Ludwig shook his head, and Liane smiled and bobbed her head in his direction, though she wasn't sure he noticed. His attention seemed to be elsewhere, or at least she thought it was. It was impossible to tell past the veil. From the corner of her eye, Liane noticed Heinrich returning, and he wasn't alone this time. Though she longed to leave the ball and get on with more important work, she still had to meet Duke Licht.

"I'll meet you in the passageway after I've finished business here," Liane said.

Without further comment, Ludwig slipped back into the shadows, and Liane pretended to be very engaged in watching courtiers as they danced while Heinrich drew closer and closer, his eyes trained on her. He couldn't be coming to talk to her, could he? Liane tried to ignore him until he and his friend were standing right next to her.

"Princess Liane," Heinrich said with a slimy smile. Did he think that was charming?

"Prince Consort," she said with a stiff bob of her head.

Over his shoulder, a man with greasy, brown hair leered at her through his merlot mask festooned with grape leaves.

"This is Duke Licht; the empress asked me to introduce you." He jabbed a thumb toward the greasy man.

Liane did a double take. This was her fortuitous encounter? Either Mother had never met the man, or she thought little of her tastes. Why had it not occurred to her that he'd be arranging this meeting? If she could call it that. Knowing Heinrich, he owed this man a gambling debt, and an introduction would lessen it.

"Your majesty, it is a pleasure to meet you." Duke Licht bowed, his gaze lingering on her chest.

Delightful. At least she could make this quick.

"The pleasure is all yours," Liane said with a false laugh.

The man frowned and laughed along as if he got the joke.

"I'll leave the two of you to get acquainted then." Heinrich nodded and faded back into the crowd.

Standing side by side, neither of them spoke as the music thrummed in her ears, and the crowd flowed around them. Liane fidgeted with the hem of her sleeve and looked anywhere but at Duke Licht. If he didn't say anything soon, when the song ended, she would excuse herself and go find Ludwig.

"A lovely evening..." he said.

"It is."

A long, painful pause stretched out

"Have you ever been to Greadorf?"

"No. I haven't."

"That is where I am from. We grow grapes for wine." He gestured toward his mask.

"I see."

The first song ended, and Aristea and Mathias stepped off the dance floor, but Mother and Father were still dancing. Heinrich approached Aristea, but she wouldn't look at him. *Good, give him the cold shoulder*, she thought. Time to make her exit.

"It was a pleasure meeting you, Duke Licht, but if you'd excuse me." Liane made a move to walk away, but he caught her by her upper arm.

"Shall we go outside where we might speak more freely?" Duke Licht leaned into her personal space to whisper into her ear.

"I'd rather not." Liane reeled back, yanking her arm from his grip, and turned to weave through the crowd.

He followed. She felt his hot, sour breath on her neck, and she quickened her pace, but the press of bodies forced her into a darkened corner, and he blocked her escape.

"You don't have to be coy with me. I know you're not a maiden," he said, inching toward her with a lascivious smile.

It was true; she'd taken lovers: courtiers and commoners. It wasn't a secret, and she knew courtiers loved to gossip about her, but no one dared say it to her directly.

"How dare you." Liane seethed and raised her hand to

slap him, but he grabbed her wrist stopping her mid-swing.

But instead of being angry, he looked pleased. No, not pleased, eager...

"He said you'd be difficult, but I like a challenge," he said, taking another step toward her.

"I think you're forgetting whom you're addressing," Liane said, yanking her arm free.

"You should be grateful for my interest. What man would have you at your age and reputation... But I don't care if you're as barren as your sister. I already have three sons."

Seeing red, she slapped him across his disgusting face. "Say what you will about me. But you may never speak ill of my sister."

The slap drew the attention of nearby courtiers, who didn't move to intervene but whispered behind their hands, turning sad gazes to her. Chest heaving, she sought an escape, but he grabbed her as she struggled against him. They turned away as if they didn't see. There was nothing to gain from Liane, so they didn't care.

"I wasn't finished speaking," Duke Licht said against her neck, making her want to retch.

"Get your hands off me, you greasy weasel." She shoved an elbow into his gut and spun to get away, but he caught her again, keeping her from escaping.

"You think you're something special? You're nothing but a trumped-up whore." He raised his hand to strike her, and she flinched in expectation.

Before it could land, someone yanked them apart, and

Liane glanced up to see a broad back between her and Duke Licht.

"Is something wrong?" her rescuer said with the faintest unfamiliar accent.

"Who are you?" Duke Licht glared at him.

"Her dance partner," he said, turning to face her.

She'd never seen him in her life, but she jumped at the chance to escape and linked arms with him.

"There you are. I've been looking for you all evening!"

"What is the meaning of this?" Duke Licht stuttered.

"I suppose you haven't heard; I'm being courted. I would say it was lovely meeting you, but it wasn't." With a toss of her head, she strolled arm in arm with her rescuer away from a sputtering Duke Licht.

When they were far enough away, she dared a glance to make sure he hadn't followed them, and certain of her safety, she untangled from the masked stranger.

"Thank you for stepping in," Liane said.

"If you're thankful, why not dance with me?" He offered her his broad, calloused hand. Not soft and milky like most lords.

Gaze flicking up, she met the smoldering intensity of his golden-brown eyes behind his pearlescent white-blue mask. Gooseflesh pebbled on her skin. If she didn't already have plans, she'd have accepted without question. Even so, she was drawn to him in ways she couldn't explain. Who was he, and why had he stepped in when everyone else had turned their back?

"I'm a terrible dancer."

"I'm excellent at leading." He smirked, and butterflies took flight in her chest.

"Then save a dance for me," Liane said. When she was finished, she needed a way to slip naturally back into the masquerade.

Before he could reply or ask her to stay, she ducked between revelers and escaped out of the ballroom. With any luck, she'd return in time to claim that dance.

Striding briskly, she headed away from the grand hall and toward her apartment. The distant hum of the masquerade faded, and the sound of her hurried footsteps filled the silence. When she returned to her room, Luzie was waiting for her with the change of clothes Ludwig had procured. Stripping down quickly, Liane shed her gown and mask in favor of a pair of black trousers and a shirt. After changing clothes, she approached the tapestry on the far wall and pulled it back to reveal a decorative knob. Pressing on it released a mechanism that opened a hidden doorway.

The palace was filled with such passageways, hidden throughout as a security measure to protect palace residents in an emergency. Beyond the flickering light of the candle Luzie held aloft, the stairwell descended into a black abyss. Liane took the candle and headed down the stairs, with just enough light to illuminate the next step in front of her, not that she needed it; she'd taken this same passageway a thousand times and could traverse it in total darkness. At the bottom of the stairs, the faintest orange light flickered on the rough-hewn wall and revealed Ludwig pacing, torch in hand.

"I was hoping you'd changed your mind," he said.

"Don't you know me better than that?"

"Call it wishful thinking."

"Mother says I shall have a fateful meeting. I think it means we'll find out the supplier tonight."

"I don't think that's what your mother meant."

Liane snatched the torch out of his hand and ignored him to walk down the roughhewn hall. Despite Ludwig's pessimism, she had a good feeling that tonight everything would change.

7

Erich's eyes followed her path as she weaved through the crowd, her vibrant red tresses burning like a beacon against a sea of beads and brocade. When he'd seen the cold indifference of the courtiers while the red-haired woman was harassed, he'd intervened, knowing it was reckless. There in the viper's den, drawing attention onto himself, was a dangerous gamble. He'd spotted guards hiding in alcoves like gray sentinels, eyes scanning, ever watchful. Erich had already decided if the elf were discovered, he'd abandon him. His own survival was paramount.

"You're more chivalrous than I thought," Fritz remarked, materializing at his shoulder without a sound.

He hadn't noticed his approach, and the elf moved liked a shadow. Hand twitching, he sought the comfort of his blade, but Ivar insisted he come unarmed. And then gate guards had taken the one he'd hidden in his boot. The empress was paranoid, as most rulers were, but it didn't make him feel any easier, especially with an elf for an uneasy ally.

"I'm not made of stone. Any man would've done the same," Erich replied.

"You're surprisingly optimistic; I've seen little good in men."

"Shh, do you want to get us both killed?"

A quick survey of their surroundings indicated no one had heard. Much like the Sundland courtiers, they were too absorbed in their own petty ambitions to notice much beyond their own noses, unless it benefited them.

"Nervous?" Fritz teased.

"Did I risk my neck just so you could taunt me?" He hadn't asked the elf what he'd come for, and he didn't want to know.

"That was an added benefit." With a pat on Erich's shoulder, he melted back into the crowd.

A passing servant offered Erich a glass of wine, and he took it, sipping on the too-sweet vintage. Stalking the perimeter of the dance floor, he watched the empress and emperor consort as they danced, the Golden Blade glittering at her hip. Empress Eveline, the first Empress of Neolyra, the great reformer, who overturned a centuries-old rule forbidding women from roles in the military and government. Erich was a babe in the nursery when she claimed her throne by blood and magic. But he'd heard tales of her all his life. Throughout the Neolyrian Empire, she was their goddess Cyra's avatar, made in her image and sent to save the empire from darkness.

According to Father, she'd manipulated the people, using their faith against them, to centralize power between the empire and the church. Though, by his very nature, Erich did not like the Church of Sol for their stance on corrupted, he did not see what the empress had done wrong compared to someone like Father, whose people suffered under his tyrannical rule. He'd traveled to many provinces throughout the empire, and everywhere flourished. Erich suspected Father's thoughts were born of jealousy, because his ambitions of grandeur were stymied by the might of Neolyra.

Erich shook his head and turned his attention away from politics. None of that mattered to him anymore. As he weaved his way through the crowd, seeking Ivar once more, the gooseflesh on his arm raised at a prickle of magic in the air. Glancing up, he met the golden-veiled stare of the Avatheos, the head of the Church of Sol. According to them, the Avatheos' light magic was the antithesis to his dark corruption, and they'd made it their goal to eradicate people like Erich from existence. Sounds faded away, and his vision focused on glowing light that haloed the Avatheos. A sound whispered against his ear, growing louder until it thundered, roaring in his skull.

Someone grasped his shoulder, and Erich jerked backward, expecting to see someone from the Midnight Guard arriving to arrest him.

"Forgive me, I didn't mean to startle you..." Ivar's frowning mouth was oddly juxtaposed with the bulbous eyes of his frog mask.

Sounds rushed in as revelers moved between Erich and the Avatheos, blocking him from view. The prickle of magic faded but left a sour taste on his tongue.

"You're forgiven," Erich said before gulping down the rest of his wine to wash away the taste.

"Where's your friend?"

"You promised not to ask." Erich tutted, resisting the urge to seek out Fritz from the crowd.

"Indeed, I did. And I believe you made a promise to me as well." He stepped aside, revealing Greta.

Her feathered peacock mask made her blue eyes appear wider and more childlike. He hoped Ivar was right, and tonight he introduced her to a more suitable partner.

"Shall we?" Erich offered her his bent arm.

The orchestra started a new waltz, a familiar tune that transported him back to forgotten days. For a moment, Erich stood transfixed, listening to the notes back at Lord Endland's manor during the solstice. Boughs of winter-green perfumed the air, and the wine flowed freely as the laughter of his household echoed to the rafters.

Greta grabbed ahold of him, bringing him back to the present as she urged him onto the dance floor. They took positions across from one another, and men and women who made up rows on each side took turns twirling down the center aisle. Empress Eveline promenaded first, hands interlinked with her husband, and rosy-cheeked. Not far behind them, he noticed Fritz opposite a young court lady, but his eyes were trained on the empress with a strange hunger gleaming in his dark gaze. What was he doing?

"You know I've been thinking," Greta said as they joined in the center for their turn.

The war between the elves and the Neolyrian Empire was legendary. It was Empress Eveline's father, the former emperor, who'd driven the last of them into the feral lands. Had Fritz used him to get close enough to assassinate her? Not that he cared who ruled over Neolyra, but it was bad enough to be linked to an elf. A would-be killer meant a death sentence for not only him but Greta and Ivar, who brought him here.

"Are you listening?" Greta fumed.

"What's that?" Erich asked as they linked arms to promenade down the line.

He'd lost sight of Fritz in the crowd, but he could clearly see the empress at the front of the line laughing and clapping in tune with the music. Then he spotted him at the empress' shoulder.

"You said that you couldn't take a wife. But many priests keep a mistress..." Greta said.

Erich's head jerked toward her, noticing her for the first time as they, too, reached the end of the line. He had to get her away before it was too late.

"Shall we get some refreshments?" Erich asked; pressing a hand to her lower back, he guided her off the dance floor.

"The song isn't over; I wanted to dance longer," Greta pouted, trying to pull away and go back to the dance floor.

But by grabbing her by the upper arm, he guided her through the crowd, searching for Ivar among the revelers. There were too many people. Their masks blurred together into an amorphous mass. Snaking their way through the crowd, he kept glancing over his shoulder, waiting for a scream, or worse, the guards to come and arrest him.

Then two men stepped in his way: one he recognized as the magenta lord he'd rescued the redhead from, but the other he didn't know. Erich attempted to navigate himself and Greta around them, but they stepped in his way once more.

"And who's this? I find you with another woman already?" The magenta tsked.

"What is he talking about?" Greta asked with confusion.

"Go and find your father; tell him we must leave right away."

Greta's brows furrowed as she glanced between Erich and the two men.

"Yes, run along, girl. We need to have a chat with our friend here," the man in the starry mask said, with a cold sneer.

Taking the hint, Greta scurried away, leaving him alone with the two men. He hadn't anticipated the magenta lord returning with backup, but he wasn't afraid of them. Erich's eyes flicked past them to the dance floor, where the empress and her consort were still twirling about without a care in the world. What was Fritz doing...

"I've been asking around, and no one seems to know who you are." Star-mask sneered.

"Isn't that the point of a masquerade: anonymity?"

A hand grasped his shoulder, and Erich pivoted, hands up and ready to fight, but he held back just in case.

"Let's talk, shall we?"

Then, grabbing him by the elbow, the lord escorted Erich out into the hall. He calculated knocking them both down and making a run for it. As far as he could tell, they weren't with the Midnight Guard, but if he fought them, it would alert the guards. Better to play along until an opportunity to escape presented itself.

"You had something to say?" Erich crossed his arms and squared his stance.

There was no one in the hall but the three of them, and he scanned it for exits; the best way out was behind them.

"Duke Licht informs me you're Princess Liane's suitor. I wasn't aware she was being courted," Star-mask said.

Princess? Trinity help him; of course it'd be a princess he crossed paths with.

"And you are?" Erich gestured toward him.

"You've an ill manner of speaking that displeases me. You are clearly a foreigner to not recognize your future emperor."

"Emperor consort."

"Pardon?"

"You wouldn't be the emperor. I may be a foreigner, but I know that Princess Aristea is the future empress, and you must be her consort."

Ivar warned him to stay away, but trouble had a way of finding him, it seemed.

Prince Consort Heinrich cleared his throat. "Enough. I order you to reveal yourself." Spoken in a tone that was not accustomed to disobedience.

"I'd rather not." Erich backed up a step, a cold chill swept over him, and the hairs on his arms stood on end.

Though it was faint, he felt a twinge of magic in the air. Had Fritz made his move? If so, the entire palace was about to erupt into chaos, and he'd rather not be here when it happened.

"Remove that mask, or I will remove it for you." Heinrich seethed, and as he jabbed a finger into Erich's chest, he smelled his sickly-sweet breath.

Erich took another step back, but the magenta lord got behind him and grasped onto his shoulders, holding him as Prince Consort Heinrich inched closer to tear the mask from his face. Erich clenched a fist, ready to swing, when a guard stepped out into the hallway, and he hesitated. They looked both ways, noticed the three of them, and strode over. His entire body tensed; Erich prepared to run, but the guard did not glance at him for more than a second before addressing Heinrich.

"Your majesty," the guard said.

"What is it?" Heinrich asked, with an impatient scowl as he lowered his hand to his side.

The guard leaned in to whisper in his ear, and the lines around Heinrich's mouth deepened. Because his expression was calm and Erich didn't hear any screams coming from the ballroom, he assumed Fritz hadn't attacked yet.

"We shall finish this later. Licht, keep him here." Then Prince Consort Heinrich strode away past the ballroom and down the hall.

When Prince Consort Heinrich walked away, Erich jabbed his elbow into Duke Licht's stomach, and he crumpled onto the floor, gasping. The quickest way out was the way Prince Consort Heinrich had gone, and so he went the opposite way, hoping to find another exit. He passed a few meandering guests on the way, turned at a darkened corner, and that's when Fritz stepped out of the shadows and into his path.

"We need to get out, now," Fritz said. His enlarged pupils darted around erratically.

"What did you do?" Erich asked.

Shouts proceeded the thundering of booted feet as the Midnight Guards rushed toward them, blocking the end of the hall. They'd been seen together. Rather than risk questioning, Erich ran. But as he retreated the way he came, he was blocked by more guards who pinned him between their two forces. To his left, there was an open window looking out onto the roof. Signaling to Fritz, he jumped through it onto the rooftop.

Howling wind tore at his clothes and hair as he teetered on the apex. Mistakenly, he looked over the edge, and the ground spun beneath him, threatening his balance. Erich closed his eyes, taking a deep breath, then, with a gulp, he focused on putting one foot in front of the other to reach the edge of the roof. When it ran out, the next ledge was out of reach. Arrows whizzed past his ear, causing his foot to slip on a roof tile. The tile broke loose and cascaded down the side before smashing onto the ground. That would be him if he wasn't careful.

"What now?" Erich asked.

"We jump," Fritz said, pointing over the edge.

"Are you crazy? The fall will kill us."

Behind them Midnight Guards followed, balanced on the roof peak, while even more of them aimed arrows at them. It was jump or be impaled and then fall to his death. He wasn't sure which was worse. Then Fritz leapt over the edge, and Erich looked down after him, expecting to find a splattered mess of blood and brain matter on the cobble. But the Trinity smiled upon them because they were near the stables, and just below them, a pile of manure broke Fritz's fall.

Closing his eyes, Erich jumped. Rolling as he fell, he landed on his hip, and it sent a jolt of pain shooting through his leg. Through gritted teeth, he climbed out of the pile of straw and manure to find a pair of stable hands staring at them in wide-eyed horror. There wasn't time to explain as arrows rained down from the rooftop.

A few feet from where he landed, a water channel sloped downward and out of view. If they were lucky, it would lead out of the palace. Or it could lead to certain death. One way to find out. They sprinted for the channel and dove into the water, which only came up to mid-thigh. Water filled his boots, and he gagged on the stench of manure that embedded itself in the fibers of his clothes. He pressed on, sloshing downhill, heading for the palace walls where water trickled out through a hole and to the sea. When they reached the wall, however, they discovered thick iron bars with gaps too narrow to squeeze between.

"Watch my back," Fritz said, kneeling in the murky water. His hands glowed with faint, white-blue light as he grasped onto the bars.

"What are you doing? We need to run!"

"Just trust me."

"I trusted you, and look where it got me," Erich said, turning to search for something he might use as a weapon, but the best thing he could find was a fist-sized stone.

"Capture them alive," a woman shouted.

"How kind of them. They're going spare our lives, probably long enough to torture us for information," Erich commented, as he gripped the stone tighter.

The rock wouldn't be enough; if he wanted to live, he'd have to unleash the dragon. Even the thought of it made the dragon stir within him, pressing against the chains that bound him.

"One more second..." Fritz said, his voice strained.

One bar snapped, the metal ringing, then the second, and then a third. Somehow, he'd made a space for them to slip through, but it was small. Fritz went first and just barely managed to wriggle out. When Erich tried, his broader shoulders caught on the edge, and fear gripped his throat as he heard water splash behind him. The guards were on top of them, and someone grasped him by the ankle and pulled. Kicking backward, he landed a blow to their chest, giving him enough time to readjust and break through. As soon as he slithered onto the other side, he heard a pop, and then the bars buckled inward, preventing pursuit.

Outside the palace, the channel flowed further down-hill, reaching the ocean. His instinct was to follow it, but Fritz raced up the hill toward the forest through an open plain, leaving him exposed to archer's arrows along the wall. But seeing as Fritz hadn't led him astray this far, he might as well follow. Sprinting up the hill, he resisted the urge to look back, and by some miracle or elf magic, clouds moved over the moon, blocking the moonlight and obscuring them in darkness. By the time they reached the grove of pines, Erich was panting for breath.

"Mind telling me what happened back there?" Erich asked as he collapsed onto a fallen log.

"An unforeseen complication." Fritz gasped, clutching his side.

"Were you trying to kill the empress?"

"What? Of course not; I'm not a mad man. I simply was trying to steal her sword."

"Her sword? You attempted to steal the enchanted blade off her person? In the middle of a ball?"

"It seemed like a good plan at the time... well that is before I realized she was wearing a fake. Sensible really, she can't risk just anyone stealing the divine blade while she's dancing."

"This is madness. I've made a deal with a mad elf." Erich shook his head. "Well, I've done my part; I got you into the palace. Now heal me as you promised."

"But I can't. Not without the sword's power."

Erich's shoulders slumped; it had happened again. He'd risked his life for nothing. For another false hope.

"Then this is where our paths diverge," Erich said and turned to walk away, picking hay and manure off his clothes. He'd need to change, no, burn it all. After he retrieved his dagger and lay low for a few days, he'd travel on foot to Porroque and catch a ship from there across the Ageless Sea.

"Wait!" Fritz shouted.

Erich kept walking.

"I can't do this without you."

"With or without me, this plan is doomed to fail."

"I saw you in my dream; together we steal the sword, and I heal you. You must believe me."

"Unlucky for you, I'm not—" He froze as he turned to look at Fritz.

The elf had changed in the sliver of moonlight peeking from between the clouds: his eyes golden, eternal as if they contained the cosmos within them. Magic warmed the air, vibrating between them. Here in the woods, away from the pollution of stone and human filth, he could sense the power in him in a way he hadn't before.

Along his travels, he'd met charlatans a plenty, and in rare instances, he felt real power. Those times before paled in comparison to what he felt rolling off Fritz in waves. Magic knew magic. It spoke in a forgotten ancient language that even Erich didn't understand, but he felt it instinctively. The dragon within him raised its head curiously, nostrils flaring as if it might scent the enchantments in the air. Whether it was fate or dumb luck that brought them together, his gut told him this was it. A wordless promise stirred in him; this was it, the answer he'd been looking for all along.

But if he were to stay in the city and help Fritz steal the sword, he couldn't do it as a nameless vagabond. He'd have to resume the role of Prince Erich once more.

8

A twig snapped, and Liane's eyes darted across the shadowy detritus as a chill wind sent a shiver down her spine. Vine-covered crumbling columns framed the waxing crescent moon hanging against the inky-black sky, lending little light. Long grass pushing through cracks in the decomposing cobble swayed as a rat skittered out, leaping from stone to stone before diving into a nearby hole. Liane exhaled in relief. There was nothing there but rubble and weeds.

Nature had reclaimed this citadel of the ancients, turning it to rubble over the past hundred years since corruption wiped out the city. Those same forgotten ancients who'd built it had also carved the stone tunnels beneath the palace. Most knew of the higher tunnels, which were used as escape routes for the royal family or as storerooms for wine and cheese. Most didn't know about the lower rooms and passageways.

She'd discovered the tangled thread of tunnels quite

by accident. As a girl, she and Elias used to hide amongst the barrels of wine they stored in the upper tunnels and jump out to scare servants, but once when they were caught, they retreated deeper, discovering a labyrinth that soon became their underground playground. Before long, their exploration took them deeper and farther from the palace, and together with Ludwig, they'd mapped out the many winding passageways. Beyond collapses they discovered rooms filled with mosaics and ancient store-rooms with collapsed shelves and empty sacks of dust.

One tunnel led away from the city and to the ruins. She and Elias used to stand upon the precipice of it, taunting one another to enter. Despite their boasting, neither of them ever did. The fear of The Corruption held them back.

Ludwig stepped out of the cave first, and despite her fears, no tendrils of magic burst forth, nor did chimera leap out of the shadows to devour him. After a quick inspection, he beckoned her to follow, and she crept out after him. Gravel crunched beneath her boots as they explored the ruined city. There was an unnatural stillness to the place, and each sound they made was swallowed up as if falling into a void of silence. It made the hairs stand on the back of her neck and her stomach twist with uncertainty. *What if the church was right, and this place was a fountain of corruption?* Liane pushed these thoughts aside as they continued on.

They passed through what might have once been a city square, and she wondered, not for the first time, who were the people that once lived here. Were they human, elves, or some strange forgotten race...? If only

Elias were alive, he would have marveled at the carvings in the stone facades, and spun theories about the people who'd carved them, what their lives were like. Liane stopped to examine a purple flower blooming in what appeared to be a community fountain; its velvety petals unfurled and swayed gently in the evening breeze. She reached out to touch it, then froze when she heard footsteps nearby.

"They're late." A man's voice accompanied the footsteps.

"You can never trust an elf to keep their word," a second man replied.

Liane's heart leapt into her throat, and tingles rippled out from her spine, reaching the top of her head to the tips of her fingers. Elves? What were elves doing this far south of the feral lands? After they'd tried to conquer the continent generations ago, they'd become humanity's mortal enemies.

Ludwig pressed his finger to his lips and nodded toward a gap in a nearby collapsed wall. Taking care to move silently, they positioned themselves inside the building, to peer between a curtain of vines onto the street below. One smuggler paced while the other leaned against a wall.

"I thought you were getting us some extra muscle," the pacing man said.

"I tried; the arrogant prick thought he was too good for us," replied the one-eared man.

"Those pale bastards make me uneasy."

"Don't worry 'bout them. I can handle 'em." One-ear opened his jacket to reveal the dagger strapped to his hip.

"I thought we agreed to no weapons," an elf said as she emerged from the shadows.

Liane had blinked, and four pale and lithe creatures stood in a half circle around the smugglers. The tales described them as if they were ten feet tall with fangs dripping in venom, but apart from their pointed ears, they looked human and otherworldly beautiful. How could something so horrid be this beautiful? Her mind struggled to comprehend the two contradicting facts.

"It's a dangerous world, and besides, you outnumber us by two. That ain't fair now, is it?" One-ear said.

"I assume you have what we asked for." The elf woman's lips curled with disdain.

One-ear jerked his head at his companion, who removed a rolled-up piece of parchment from his satchel and handed it to the elf. As she unfurled it, her dark, pupilless eyes scoured it. When she finished, she rolled it back up, and with a twist of her wrist, it disappeared into thin air. Liane's jaw dropped. Then it was true; the elves still possessed magic.

"Your price." The elf handed him a small satchel.

He opened it, and golden stardust glimmered like fallen stars. This was it, the missing piece of the puzzle. Stardust must be corrupted magic, and the elves were delivering it to scum like the Onyx Gang to sicken the population. But why risk their own lives, for geld? It seemed unlikely. Perhaps this was part of some bigger scheme to destroy humanity...

"We agreed to twice as much," One-ear said.

"As we said last time. We cannot provide what you are asking; the harvest cannot be rushed."

"If you don't deliver, perhaps I pay a visit to the royal army?"

"The deal does not change. No matter what threats you make."

"Are you trying to con us?"

"We have what we want. If you are unsatisfied, then our business can end here." The elf turned to walk away.

Dagger in hand, One-ear rushed the elf woman. But before he reached her, a bloody gash opened his stomach, and a crimson stain spread across his greasy tunic. Liane hadn't seen her move. One-ear staggered to his knees; his dagger slid uselessly from his fingers. Meanwhile, his companion turned to run, but two elves blocked his path. He turned to run in the other direction, but a shadow pierced him through his back to the front, blood dripping from the ebony tip. Jerking her hand backward, the elf removed the shadow blade, which dissipated like mist. The smuggler collapsed onto the ground, and a dark pool of blood spread out around him. Gasping, Liane clapped her hand over her mouth, and an elf peered in their direction. Ludwig yanked her down beneath the windowsill, clamping his hand over her mouth and his own. She dared not move, dared not breathe.

"It isn't wise to spill blood on sacred ground," an elf said.

"He broke our accords first; it had to be done," the elf woman said.

"Did you hear something? I don't think they were alone..." a third elf said.

Footsteps approached, and her heart thundered in her ears. Liane feared it would betray them. With shaking hands, she fumbled for the small dagger strapped to her thigh. After seeing their speed and precision, she felt less confident in her ability. Gravel skittered as Ludwig crouched, rapier drawn and a determined glint in his eyes.

"Leave it, Elyon. We should be away before sunrise."

The steps retreated.

They sat frozen for a long while, neither moving nor talking. After a while, Ludwig stood up enough to peek past the vines and then went to investigate, leaving Liane alone in the shadows. Her knees were drawn up to her chest, and she shook uncontrollably. A few minutes later, Ludwig returned, his fingers bloody. Liane stared at his stained digits in mute horror.

"Are you hurt?" she croaked.

Ludwig shook his head. "They're both dead."

He'd gone to check for survivors, while she trembled in fear. Shamed at her own cowardice, Liane stood without taking the hand Ludwig offered, partially because the thought of touching blood made her skin crawl. A stone settled in the pit of her stomach. She thought finding the smugglers would solve all her problems, but instead, she'd uncovered something much more dangerous.

"What do you think the Onyx Gang gave them?" Liane asked in a hushed tone. The elves might still be nearby.

"Nothing good. We need to tell the Midnight Guard."

"And how do we explain it to them?" Liane asked.

"Elves are in the heart of Neolyra; I think that's more important than being caught where we don't belong." Ludwig's voice was harsh and echoed off the stone. The torch he held cast long shadows across his face and turned his expression menacing.

They'd been through a lot in the years since Elias passed, and he'd never once raised his voice. But she knew Ludwig, and he was as scared as she was. These weren't petty criminals. These were elves, a threat to life as they knew it. Whatever they were plotting, it went beyond them; it was bigger than her vengeance. But thinking of handing information over to the Midnight Guard and doing nothing felt wrong as well. Elias deserved justice, and if she let go, she feared he'd be forgotten.

"We can fig—"

Shadows moved at the periphery of her vision, and Ludwig stood in front of her, rapier drawn and his stance wide. Grasping her dagger tighter, she watched as half a dozen figures stepped closer. Gold bands on their arms flashed in the crescent of moonlight: Midnight Guards.

"Stand down," they ordered Ludwig.

Ludwig lowered his weapon and looked at her. It seemed the choice had been made for her.

"You'll need to come with us, Princess," the guard said and gestured to the tunnel they'd exited from.

Panic spiked in her veins, but she went willingly, through the twisting corridors all the way back to the palace. As they marched two in front and two behind, she tried to think up an excuse for why they'd been there and what they'd been doing, but as they exited the tunnel, passing by barrels of wine and out a servants' entrance, she knew she had no choice but, to tell the truth.

Mother would be furious when she found out she'd

snuck out of the masquerade to hunt smugglers, but there was no escaping punishment now. The midnight tower loomed against the night sky, and her throat tightened. She'd never entered it before but often envisioned what secrets it held. The Midnight Guards operated in secret, hunting the corrupted and keeping the city free of magical corruption. She should have known when they'd raided the tavern that they were onto the same trail as her.

The first floor of the tower was a large, circular room, the mosaic floor embossed with the blazing sun crest of the Church of Sol. At the back of the room, a locked door presumably led down into the dungeons, and she might have imagined it, but she swore she heard a roar come up from the ground. Her escorts led her toward the spiral staircase that led up to the officers' quarters.

By the time they reached their destination, Liane was panting for breath, and her back was aching. They knocked on the door, and a muffled voice answered. Inside, a crackling fire cast a warm glow upon sumptuous stuffed chairs and a plush burgundy carpet. Captain Rosen, head of the Midnight Guard, sat at her mahogany desk and rose as they entered.

"Please make yourself comfortable, Princess Liane. And your guard can wait outside with Fynn and Arne." She gestured to the chairs beside the fire.

"I'll stay with the princess," Ludwig said.

"I assure you she is safe with me." Her smile was stiff, as if she were unused to it.

"I'll be fine," Liane assured him. Typically, when she was being punished, she wasn't told to make herself comfortable, nor was she taken to what appeared to be the captain's personal quarters.

Ludwig scowled, clearly unconvinced, but he followed the guards out. Liane took a seat in one of the squishy chairs as her back pounded.

"Comfortable?" Captain Rosen asked with an arched brow.

"Am I in trouble?"

"You're a princess; I don't think I have the rank to punish you."

Liane's face burned. They'd never spoken before, but she'd been watching her career with interest. Captain Rosen was the first woman to rise to the rank of captain of the Midnight Guard, and to say she admired her was an understatement. Had illness not stolen her stamina and ability to join the Midnight Guard, Liane would have liked to be someone like her. Now, the first time they'd spoke, she would be scolded for wandering around the forbidden ruins like a wayward child. Straightening her shoulders, she met her gaze, trying to muster what little dignity she had left.

"Then I would like to know why you brought me here," Liane said.

"You're direct. I admire that. I'll get straight to the point then. An elf got into the palace tonight. We don't know how. But while searching for them, my men found you and your guard wandering in the tunnels and out into the ruins."

An icy chill swept through her. The elves had gotten into the palace. It was worse than she thought.

"I saw four elves in the ruins, and they were

exchanging information with members of the Onyx Gang for stardust." The words poured out of Liane. Even if she couldn't be the one who made the arrests, at least she could provide valuable information.

"We know," Captain Rosen said, drumming her long fingers onto the arm of her chair as she stared into her empty fire.

Liane's shoulders sagged. Then she'd done nothing but get in the way again.

"What I want to know is how did you find that tunnel?" Captain Rosen asked, turning her hawk-like gaze back on Liane.

Liane blinked. "I discovered it when I was a girl. My friend and I used to play in it all the time. Surely you were aware of it?"

"My men have combed every inch of those tunnels. We thought we had found every entrance and exit. And somehow, you found one even we could not detect."

Liane leaped at the chance to be of help. "I can help you find more. There's many underground tunnels and rooms, perhaps hundreds of them. I could take a map maker down to help them draw a map."

"That isn't why I wanted to speak with you. I know you were there the night we attempted an arrest upon Niklas Ehrle, and as you must have noticed, City Watch continues to turn a blind eye as the problem grows. I have petitioned the palace multiple times to no avail." Captain Rosen frowned as the pace of her drumming fingers increased.

"Surely you have enough power to arrest him and bring him into the midnight tower?" Liane said.

She'd gladly see Niklas and his ilk locked away in the dark for the rest of their days.

"If only it were that easy. I suspect someone at court is supporting the gangs, to keep the stardust flowing into the city."

"But why? It's killing people. Who would do such a thing?"

Captain Rosen turned back to look at her, gaze assessing.

"Why have you been hunting down gang leaders?"

This was a test; she was sure of it. Liane met her gaze, unflinching. "Someone I cared about died because of stardust. It was earlier on when we knew less about it. I want to stop its spread before more people are hurt."

Captain Rosen stood up and paced around Liane, who followed her path with her eyes, waiting for her to speak.

"What do you know about stardust?"

"The same as you: a drug with potent attributes, superior senses, euphoria in users, then it degrades after multiple uses," Liane said, frowning. Why quiz her on stardust...

"In most cases," Captain Rosen amended.

"What do you mean most cases?" She couldn't think of anyone who'd gotten hooked and hadn't been hollowed out like an old gourd by it.

"There wouldn't be business in it if everyone who took it died," Captain Rosen said. She was staring intently at Liane now, making her want to squirm in her seat, but she held her gaze. She considered her words. There were whispers, rumors mostly, of people who took stardust and got stronger, that could do things no normal human could. But she'd dismissed it as gang lies, trying to hook the unwary.

"Are you saying..."

Captain Rosen's eyes flicked to the door, then back to Liane before she nodded. "I believe someone at court wants to create powerful soldiers capable of rising up against the empress."

Liane sank back into her chair as she processed those words. Mother had come to power amidst blood and civil war. The threat of it had seemed far away all her life, but even Aristea remained in an arranged marriage to maintain that tenuous peace.

"Heinrich." His name escaped from her lips.

"You'd accuse your sister's husband without a second thought?" Captain Rosen's expression was a blank wall. Whether she was judging her or impressed, Liane couldn't say.

Heinrich was fourth in line to the throne, after Liane and her siblings. But before they'd been born, his father had tried to make him emperor. When his coup failed, he was executed, and Mother appeased those who supported him by betrothing Heinrich to Aristea. Captain Rosen knew this as well as her and must have come to the same conclusion.

"Do you disagree?" Liane asked.

"I could say the same of you. If your sister was out of the way, then you'd be the next empress or your younger brother... Some would rather not see another woman rule."

The very thought made her stomach churn, and she would never betray Aristea, nor would Mathias.

"I know my brother; he wouldn't do something like that."

"And yet, I cannot arrest the prince consort based on words alone. I need proof. The rich and powerful do not play by the same rules as commoners."

And that meant her as well. She hadn't brought her here for her help; Liane was a suspect.

"What if I brought you proof?" Liane asked.

"How do I know I can trust you? Even telling you this much, I could be putting my entire investigation and the kingdom, in jeopardy."

She'd revealed more than she intended, Liane suspected. If she truly suspected her of plotting against Aristea, she wouldn't have exposed her hand this way.

"What has conspired here will not leave this room. I swear not to tell a soul. Not my mother, nor my sister, or the rest of my family."

"Even your guard?" Captain Rosen arched a brow.

Liane's throat tightened. She shared everything with Ludwig. There were no secrets between them, but if she wanted Captain Rosen's help, she needed her to trust her.

"I swear to the stars above, I will not tell another living soul."

The corner of Captain Rosen's mouth quirked up in the shadow of a smile.

"We shall see," Captain Rosen said.

9

The morning after the Masquerade, Ludwig was off duty, and Liane used the opportunity to go straight to Aristea and Heinrich's to look for evidence. He knew her too well, and he'd draw the truth out of her. It wasn't as if she didn't trust him; in fact, there wasn't anyone she trusted more. But she had to do this alone, without Ludwig's help. As soon as she had proof of Heinrich's treasonous plotting, she'd tell Ludwig everything. Ludwig would forgive her in the end; he always did. At least that's what she told herself as she rapped on their chamber door. A maid answered.

"Princess Liane." She bobbed her head in greeting.

"I'm here for Princess Aristea," Liane said.

"I'm afraid her majesty isn't here. She's in the garden for luncheon."

It was just as she'd hoped. With the glut of visiting nobles and dignitaries arriving daily for the coming Sun Ceremony, Aristea and Heinrich were preoccupied entertaining and wouldn't be back to their apartment for a long while. Giving her plenty of time to search their rooms uninterrupted.

"Yes, I know. She sent me to fetch something from the prince consort's study," Liane replied.

"What is it? Perhaps, I can get it for you." The maid frowned skeptically.

"Well, it's long, or was it short. No, it was thick, or perhaps thin..." Liane trialed off. "Actually, don't trouble yourself. Aristea described it to me, and I'll know it when I see it. May I?" Without waiting on the maid's response, Liane pushed the door open.

The maid had no choice but to step aside and allow her into the main sitting room. It had been months since she'd visited Aristea's personal chambers, and everything was as pristine and orderly as she remembered. A bouquet sat atop a polished table between two velvet couches adorned with starched pillows facing the cold fireplace. Above the mantel hung a portrait of them. The artists had captured Aristea's golden radiance, and they'd softened the edges of Heinrich's slimy, smirking face but hadn't failed to miss the possessive grip Heinrich had on Aristea's shoulder. Once she found proof of Heinrich's treachery, Aristea would be free of him.

"The study is this way, your majesty." The servant directed her to the double doors which adjoined the room.

Liane stepped inside and scanned the room, skimming past dark, paneled walls to let her gaze rest on the cluttered oak desk. Fortunately, Heinrich had always been a slob. Rolls of parchment, leather-bound ledgers, and broken quills were scattered about yet to be tidied by servants. She could add to it, and he'd never notice, she suspected. Before she could start her search, however, she had to get rid of the servant hovering in the doorway.

"If I have need of anything, I'll call upon you," Liane said.

With a bob of her head, the maid retreated, closing the door after her. Alone, at last, Liane pounced on the desk and picked up a ledger to thumb through its pages. It contained nothing but an accounting of crops and live-stock from his duchy in the west. Moving on, she shook out other books on his desk, hoping to find a secret letter shoved between pages, or a hidden account book. When she found nothing, she turned her attention to the draw-ers, only to find spare quills, loose pieces of scrap parch-ment, a spare inkwell, and empty ledgers. With growing frustration, Liane opened the final drawer on the desk and discovered it empty.

The grandfather clock in the corner ticked, mocking her efforts. If Heinrich wasn't hiding evidence in his study, then where else could she look? In his bedroom? It would be harder to make an excuse to enter there. What if her hunch was wrong and Heinrich wasn't the plotter, but surely it couldn't be Mathias... there were other distant relatives, but their claims to the throne were much weaker than Heinrich's.

In anger, Liane kicked the empty drawer closed, and as she did, something rattled around inside it. With a frown, she opened it again, still empty. Under closer examination, she spotted a gap along the edge of the drawer. Then, comparing it to its companion drawer on the opposite side, she noticed it was shallower.

After grabbing a letter opener from the desktop, she stabbed it into the gap and wriggled it around until the false bottom popped and revealed a stack of letters bundled up in red thread. Pulse pounding in her ears, she removed them with shaking hands before carefully untying the ribbon. As she unfolded the first letter, a woman's perfume wafted off it. She expected letters about stardust, gangs, war, and elves, but instead, she discovered insipid love notes between Heinrich and his mistress. It took all her self-control to not crumple them up into a ball.

As deplorable as infidelity was, it wasn't proof of treason. And Aristea had forgiven him in the past for being unfaithful. If she brought these letters to Aristea, she was certain she'd forgive him again. Though the letters made her stomach turn, she kept reading, hoping somewhere in their contents he'd slipped up and revealed he was behind the stardust plot. She knew him well enough to know he wasn't sentimental enough to keep mementos. There had to be something here.

The writer was besotted, and her vivid descriptions of intimate acts made even Liane blush. The woman, whoever she was, seemed to be married as well, as she made many a vague reference to a husband. That's why Heinrich had kept the letters, to blackmail her. Liane was about to give up in disgust when she discovered a fragment of a letter caught between pages. The edges were singed, and the writing almost indiscernible. But she could make out one chilling phrase.

"... I have given you an heir."

Liane's blood ran cold. Heinrich had a child, perhaps a son? For five years, Aristea and Heinrich had tried and failed to conceive. Rumors swirled that Aristea was infertile, but after numerous examinations by the Vice Premier, they'd found no reason she couldn't. But gossip persisted. If Heinrich had gotten his mistress pregnant, then it proved Aristea was barren, but more importantly, it would destabilize her position as future empress. Those dukes that chafed of female rule might be willing to risk another coup if Heinrich had an heir.

But who was the woman in these letters? Liane sifted through them again, but whoever she was, she'd been careful not to sign her name. Even if she found the woman and Heinrich's bastard child, it merely proved motive, not guilt. She needed something more, something more concrete...

Footsteps approached, and Liane froze in place, letters clutched in her fist. Thinking fast, she shoved the letters back into the false bottomed drawer and slammed it shut as Heinrich strode in. He paused in the doorway with a scowl, dark gaze darting from her to the desk and back again. Behind her back, Liane clutched the letter opener.

"What are you doing here?" He stalked toward her.

"I was looking for something for Aristea," Liane lied.

"You were snooping," he said. Only the desk stood between them.

The bottom drawer was ajar. If he came around, he'd see she'd found the letters. Not that he needed confirmation, he'd already figured her out. What would he do to her? Strike her? He'd never raised a hand to her before, but she was certain unleashing the vile Duke Licht upon her had been his idea of petty revenge. Heart racing, she tightened her grip on the letter opener. If he made a move, she wouldn't hesitate to strike back.

"Why would I waste my time on you, unless you have something to hide?"

"You seem to think I do. Disappointed you haven't found anything?"

He thought she was bluffing. Good. Let him underestimate her.

"I don't need evidence to know you're scum."

"It doesn't have to be like this; I'm a changed man." He held out his hand, as if she were foolish enough to believe him. Her skin prickled with unease, as it often did when they were alone together.

"You don't deserve forgiveness." Liane spat.

Malice carved his features as he raised a hand to strike her, and Liane brought out the letter opener, poised to strike. She faltered when she noticed Aristea walk in behind Heinrich.

"Heinrich—Oh, Liane, you're here?" Aristea said, smile faltering.

All the animosity evaporated from him in an instant, as he turned to pounce upon Aristea. "Darling, I thought you were preparing for the luncheon."

Aristea frowned as her blue eyes flicked from Liane to Heinrich. "I was... what's going on?"

Liane set down the letter opener and walked over to link arms with Aristea in their usual companionable way.

"Nothing. We were having a talk," Liane said.

"Liane came to ask me where the luncheon was being

held. She wants to join you," Heinrich said, leering at her with a devilish smile. Perhaps he thought he'd caught her in a clever trap.

"Really? But, Liane, you hate luncheons. You said you'd rather have your nose hairs plucked out one by one," Aristea said with an accusatory stare.

Liane couldn't look Aristea in the eye, let alone come up with an adequate excuse to explain herself. "Heinrich has a child with another woman," she wanted to scream, but as gratifying as it would be to expose his infidelity, it would only give Heinrich an opportunity to hide the mother and child until he made his move. Until she had proof, she'd have to bite her tongue and search in secret.

"Did I? I don't recall," Liane said lamely.

Aristea's frown deepened. "Is something going on? You're both acting strange."

"Are you saying you don't trust me?" Heinrich asked. On the opposite side of Aristea from Liane, he squeezed her shoulder.

Aristea's posture slumped. "Of course, I trust you."

"Well then, why don't you and Liane run along and enjoy your luncheon." He turned Aristea and Liane around, shooing them out the door.

As they walked away, she felt Heinrich's stare burning a hole into the back of her head. Outside their apartment, and away from Heinrich's oppressive presence, she tried to change the mood.

"Who's going to be at this luncheon?" Liane asked.

"The usual court ladies," Aristea replied, then with a sideways glance, she said. "Are you sure you want to come?"

"Definitely. I'm starving," she lied. If enduring the idle gossip and chatter of court ladies would cheer up Aristea, she'd go. Besides, maybe amid their vapid chittering, she might glean information about Heinrich's latest mistress.

When they arrived at the garden, a flutter of court ladies descended upon them like a flock of birds. They pulled Aristea out of Liane's grip, and began lavishing her with praises, complimenting everything about her, from her hair to the embroidering upon her slippers. Little by little, the bright and animated Aristea returned as she greeted each lady in turn. With the ritual compliments and greetings finished, everyone took their seats, and Liane, a late addition to their party, was sandwiched between two middle-aged ladies. Duchess Hirsch and her hanger-on Lady Keisel.

"Wonderful to have you join us for lunch," said Duchess Hirsch on Liane's right.

"I thought we'd been visited by a forest spirit," laughed Lady Keisel behind her fan.

"I hope Her light has shined upon you since last we met," Liane said with a false smile.

"She blesses me in all things," Duchess Hirsch said as she sipped her chilled wine.

"Blessed be Her light," Lady Keisel said, making the shape of the star against her brow.

She resisted the urge to roll her eyes. She hated these sorts of gatherings for three reasons: fake smiles, trite conversation, and gossip.

"I very much enjoyed your performance at the ball," Duchess Hirsch said with a sideways glance at Liane.

"It was unexpected," Lady Keisel said, sniggering.

"I'm glad you enjoyed it," Liane said, feigning ignorance.

"I hear you're being courted. Has the wild princess finally found her match or...?" Duchess Hirsch asked.

Ah, and there was the third. Nothing was more fascinating than budding romance. Unfortunately, the ball had ended before she could meet with the masked stranger. Not that it mattered, she had more important things to worry about than those casual flirtations.

"Your sources are wrong; I have no intentions of marrying any time soon," Liane said, trying to keep her tone neutral.

"Well, don't wait too long. You're not getting younger, and it will be harder to conceive if you're too old. Then they'll think both Starweber sisters are barren." Duchess Hirsch tsked.

Liane clenched her napkin in her hand and exhaled through her nose. Ladies stared at her, their eyes burning against her skin like a brand. The empress' curse, the unfortunate fate of the Starweber sisters. She'd heard variations of the same insults: broken, sad, hollow, blighted by their mother's ambitions. Before Mother became empress, no woman had dared take the throne. Even more audacious, she had surpassed a living son and declared her oldest daughter her heir. The rumors had been created to discredit Aristea and Mother both, and Liane's own illness and refusal to marry was another blotch on Mother's otherwise idyllic rule.

Perhaps if she hadn't just learned about Heinrich's bastard, she might have held her tongue. Instead, the words spilled out.

"And how is your husband, Lady Keisel, still a drunk?" Liane asked, meeting Lady Keisel's eyes.

Her face flushed, and she looked away without response.

"Indeed, he is," Duchess Hirsch chuckled.

"And you, Duchess Hirsch, I'm surprised you can wear such fancy jewels. Just last week, your husband came to the emperor consort begging him for another loan. If you're not careful, the debtors will come and rip those rubies from around your wrinkled neck."

They both gasped, as several ladies around them looked at Liane in horror. It wasn't princess behavior, but she wasn't trapped the way Aristea was: unable to speak her mind, or bite back at their venomous slander. They already saw her as the lesser, broken sister. Why not use her position to defend Aristea? Slamming her hands onto the table, she drew attention from everyone in the garden, and they gawked at her as her scar throbbed.

"Would anyone else like to voice their opinions about my sister and my ability to breed?"

Silence stretched out as the women around the room avoided her gaze.

"Liane," Aristea said in a warning tone.

"You all love to make your snide remarks, and we pretend not to hear them. But whether we can bear children or not, it doesn't mean Aristea isn't the rightful heir to the throne. Nor does it change the fact that she would be the best damn empress we've ever seen!" Liane shouted as a flush burned her cheeks.

Silence met her proclamation, and she shoved away from the table, too disgusted with them to spend another moment in their presence. As she strode away, Aristea soothed their indignant chatter, making excuses for her outburst. She might have thought Aristea a fool for mollifying them, but they were the wives of the most powerful men in the kingdom. The Dukes of Parliament decided the fate of the kingdom as much as Mother. Someone had to appease them, but it didn't make Liane any less angry at them.

As her anger pulsed, her back itched, and a rash spread out from her spine, but for once, she didn't care. It was worth it to make her point. Absorbed in her own thoughts, she didn't watch where she was going and collided with a wall of male flesh. Propelled backward, he saved her from landing on her rear by catching her in his powerful arms. As Liane glanced up to thank her rescuer, she met the grinning face of a stranger. Or was he? Why did that smile feel so familiar?

"It's becoming a habit to run into you like this," he said in a rich baritone. She knew that voice; it was the man from the masquerade.

"Forgive me. I wasn't watching where I was going," she said, clearing her throat. Painfully aware of the stares of the court, she untangled from his grip and put adequate distance between them.

"It's no trouble at all." His words wrapped around her, brushing against her like a caress. Had they run into one another at any other time, she might have stopped to talk to him.

"If you'll excuse me." She bowed and strode away from him.

"It was you, that night at the tavern. Wasn't it?"

Liane stopped in her tracks and turned to face him as the pieces of the puzzle fell into place. The stardust buyer, it had been him. A shiver of warning raced up her spine.

"I don't know what you're talking about," she said before striding away without another word.

There wasn't time for investigating mysterious lords, but they'd run into one another three times now. Was it fate or coincidence? She didn't know, but she must admit she hoped to see him again.

10

Sunlight burned through Liane's eyelids as Luzie unceremoniously yanked away her blanket. Groaning, Liane rolled over, pulling it back over her head.

"Luzie, let me sleep," Liane grumbled.

"I cannot, your majesty. The empress has ordered you dressed and ready for the sunrise rites," Luzie said as she yanked the blankets out of reach.

"Why does it have to be early?" Liane said, draping an arm over her face to block out the sun.

"Then they wouldn't call it sunrise rites, would they?"

Tugging on her arm, Luzie coaxed her into a seated position. Her stiff muscles protested, and her scar pulsed faintly. Luzie pressed a water bottle against her back, and warmth suffused her body, making her groggy, and her head sagged forward into her chest. Just a few more minutes of sleep...

With a clatter, Luzie set down Liane's breakfast tray

on her lap, and her eyes snapped back open. The plain oatmeal, crusty bread, and sliced apricots weren't appetizing, but eating was the last thing on her mind when her back ached. Rest improved her condition, but that also meant admitting she wasn't feeling well. Which would mean a visit from the Vice Premier and another round of treatments that might leave her bedbound for weeks. Time she had precious little of. She'd already wasted an afternoon searching in vain for Heinrich's mistress. Because of her outburst at the luncheon, many a court lady had given her the cold shoulder. It was reckless to shout at them, but she still maintained that they deserved it.

Tearing off a small piece of bread, she nibbled upon it, but even small morsels made her stomach churn. If the ladies of court wouldn't help her, she'd have to find another way to uncover his mistress. But how?

"Are you still in bed?" Mathias bellowed as he barged into her room.

"Keep your voice down; my head is throbbing." Liane pressed her fingers to her temple. Had he always been this loud, or had military service increased his volume?

Without invitation, he plopped down on the edge of her bed, rocking her breakfast tray. A glob of oatmeal spilled out onto her comforter.

"You've been busy. I've hardly seen you since the masquerade," Mathias said as he used her fork to spear a piece of apricot.

"I've been busy," Liane said as she ripped up pieces of bread and dropped them onto her plate. Captain Rosen's words came back to her, casting doubt upon Mathias as she watched him polish off her apricots.

In previous generations, Mathias would have been the logical successor to the throne, but not long after his birth, Mother had fought to change the law. Mathias had never been the ambitious type, and she couldn't imagine him betraying Aristea out of greed. She shook her head. Better to cast those sorts of thoughts far from her mind.

"So, who is he?" Mathias said, drawing her attention back to him.

"I have no idea what you're talking about." Liane frowned, puzzled at the non sequitur.

"Don't play coy with me. The palace is buzzing with rumors about your mysterious suitor."

"My suitor?" Liane yelped. The masked stranger at the masquerade. Those damned court ladies had gotten their revenge by helping spread that rumor.

"When is the wedding? If we hurry, you can wed before my leave's over. I'd love to be in attendance on the happy day." Mathias gently elbowed her in the ribs, grinning mischievously.

Liane tossed a pillow at his head, which he dodged with ease.

"There is no suitor. I'll never marry."

"If that's what you say," Mathias drawled.

Brandishing a pillow, she threatened to strike Mathias with it, but he scampered out of the room before she could follow through on her threat. After he left, Liane pushed aside her breakfast tray, giving up on the pretense of eating. Her chamber maids spirited it away while Luzie helped her dress. Dressing was slow and painful because

Liane couldn't raise her arms higher than her shoulders. Too much activity without enough rest had left a toll on her body, and today she paid the price. By the time they were finished, a thin sheen of sweat gleamed on Liane's forehead. She tried to catch her breath as she leaned on a bedpost, while Luzie looked on with concern.

"Perhaps I should call the Vice Premier..."

"No. I'm fine," Liane said, standing up straight and rolling her shoulders back. If she couldn't do something as simple as attending morning rights, how could she hope to expose Heinrich's treason?

Composed again, Liane stepped out into the hall and exhaled with relief when she saw Isaak on duty as her morning guard. She'd managed to dodge Ludwig the previous day, but she couldn't avoid him forever. The longer she kept this secret, the more the truth burned in her chest. Putting aside secrets for now, Liane headed down the hall, but as she rounded a corner, she discovered her father pacing. Normally, he'd be with Mother as her escort.

When he saw Liane, a smile illuminated his face, and he strode over. "Morning, my starlight. Did you sleep well?"

"I did..." Liane studied him for a moment; he was acting suspiciously. Why come greet her when they'd meet in the courtyard with the rest of the family, and why had Mathias come to her bedroom early in the morning, for that matter? Liane frowned.

"Why the sour face? Can't I escort my beloved second-born?"

"This is about the suitor rumor, isn't it?"

Father cleared his throat. "I might have heard something about that, yes."

Was there nothing else to keep wagging tongues occupied? She groaned to think of the whispers and stares of the courtiers when she entered the temple. Then sudden panic gripped her.

"Does Mother know?"

If her mother caught wind, she'd take it too far and start planning a wedding.

"Not yet. I wanted to confirm with you first before word reaches her."

Liane exhaled with relief.

"I'm sorry to tell you this, but there is no suitor. A man at the masquerade intervened to help me escape that wretched Duke Licht..."

"What did he do? I'll have him pulled apart by wild horses if he laid a finger on you..." Father said, turning as if he would hunt the man down that instant.

Grabbing his arm, she slid her hand into the crook of his arm, and he instantly relaxed. "It wasn't anything I couldn't handle. You don't need to try the man for treason..." *Yet.* She added silently to herself.

"Ah, I see. Well, it was one unsuitable match. There will be others."

"I'd rather there weren't." That wasn't the first poor match, and she knew it wouldn't be the last either. Until the Sun Ceremony passed, Liane would likely have to dodge even more "fortuitous encounters," as her mother put it.

"We just want you to be happy, that's all."

"I am happy," Liane said.

Liane knew they worried, but she was happier without a husband to hold her back. Besides, after Elias, she wasn't sure she could.

"Then I suppose I can rest easy then." But there was uncertainty in his gaze.

They went to join their family in the courtyard and climbed into the waiting carriages. Once they were settled, guards opened the gates. Two rows of guards marched out in front of the carriage, clearing the way through the crowd of gawkers gathered outside the gates. They crowded them, hands grasping, reaching out to brush against the carriages. There were more than usual, with a flood of pilgrims coming to the city for the Sun Ceremony. Artria was usually densely packed during the festivals, but the arrival of the Avatheos had brought even more pilgrims to visit.

They waved and tossed coins to them as they made their slow progress down the Temple Street. Premature summer humidity drenched Liane in sweat and plastered her hair to her brow even before the sun had risen. On the seat across from her, Mathias looked cool and comfortable. Unbothered as he waved to the citizens and pilgrims. Neither of her siblings seemed to wilt in the heat as she did. At times it felt as if she absorbed it into her body, storing it up, a theory she'd posited to the Vice Premier as her fevers were worst in the summer months. But there was no explanation for whatever illness Liane suffered. It had never been seen before.

They were nearing the temple, and the guards had to push back more crowds at the temple steps. It was over-flowing with worshippers coming to participate, as was their weekly duty. Those that could not fit inside would give reverence to the sunrise outside. When a path was cleared, they pulled up against the steps, and servants rushed over to open the carriage doors. Mother stepped out first, and the crowd roared when they saw her.

She mounted the temple steps and stopped at the top to turn and wave to the crowd. Sunlight reflected off her golden sunbeam crown, and the people upturned their hands as if they might capture the rays of light she cast. To them, she had ascended to near goddess. No ruler before had harnessed the power of Cyra's Golden Blade.

Attention given to the common people, they headed into the temple proper. The statue of Cyra greeted them as they entered, standing twenty feet tall, her golden sunbeam crown brushed against the painted arched ceilings of the temple. Distant and serene, her marble face gazed down at Liane. In her hand, she grasped a giant replica of the Golden Blade, with which she had vanquished the Nameless Goddess, sending her beyond the veil. At her feet, the Avatheos waited, and Cyra's imposing figure loomed over him like a gilded shadow.

Each member of her family knelt before him in turn, receiving the oil anointment and murmured blessing.

"May Her light shine upon you," the Avatheos intoned as Mathias received his blessing.

"And banish the darkness from within," Mathias replied by rote.

Then it was her turn, and Liane bowed her head, awaiting the blessing. When the Avatheos touched her forehead, a small jolt ran down her spine, strange, electric. Though it wasn't appropriate, Liane glanced up and caught a glimpse of his face beneath his veil and saw his storm-gray eyes. Had he sensed her discomfort and eased her pain? A priest could soothe injuries and sickness, but even the Vice Premier couldn't take her pain away. A brief touch from the Avatheos and it was gone completely; she felt lighter than she had in a long time.

"May Her light shine upon you," the Avatheos said after an overlong pause.

Dropping her gaze, she scolded herself for her blasphemy, none but Cyra could look into the eyes of her chosen. To do so in her temple must be a terrible sin.

"And banish the darkness from within," Liane replied before getting up to scurry away as quickly as possible.

She joined Mathias in the front pew and felt the Avatheos' stare follow her across the room. He must be angry at her for daring to look at his face, but it was impossible to read his expression under the veil. Liane lowered her gaze, chastely, to not draw any more of his ire.

With the blessing finished, the Avatheos held up his hands, and a hush fell over the temple.

"Darkness gathers." He paused, letting the echoing reverberance of his voice fill the room. And it seemed to come from all directions, as if spoken by multiple mouths at once.

The hairs on the back of her arms stood on end. The threat of death and destruction were often on priests' and priestesses' lips, but after seeing the elves in the ruins, the danger felt palpable and near.

"A dragon star rises in the evening sky, and the Nameless One is closer than ever." Another dramatic pause.

Then with a sharp inhalation of breath, he continued, "If we are not vigilant, darkness will return to our world!" The Avatheos' head tilted toward the heavens, and his voice cracked of thunder.

Audible gasps rippled around the room.

"Every thirteen years, the Nameless Goddess gets another chance to escape from beyond the veil, and the Sun Ceremony is not merely a celebration of light. No." He turned ever so slightly in Liane's direction, and she felt that allover body shiver once more, and her stomach twisted. "We must protect the light, or else the darkness will consume us..."

The rising sun was at the bottom edge of the circular window before Cyra. Sunrise rites wouldn't be over until it was fully illuminated. Liane fidgeted in her seat as the Avatheos' sermon carried on, transitioning from prophecies of doom to more mundane topics: the love of the goddess, her glorious light...

And the longer he droned on, the more her mind wandered, and she gazed around the room, searching the faces of the gathered courtiers hoping to find Heinrich's mistress among them. Some fanned themselves and tried to keep cool, while others whispered behind their hands with pointed looks in her direction. She didn't shy away from their stares; that only gave them more fuel.

But then, among the crowd, she saw a familiar face grinning back at her. When their eyes met, her cheeks flamed at being caught staring, and she turned back to the front, to pretend to be listening to the Avatheos. It shouldn't have been surprising to see him in the church; everyone came for sunrise rights. But had he been staring at her all this time? Just to confirm, she turned to check a second time, and he was still staring. Liane whipped her head back around, her entire body flushed. It must be a coincidence that she saw him again, but this was the fourth time they'd run into one another. Could she really call it that? And if he was following her, what did he want from her? Unless he'd been sent here by Niklas and his gang. He was trying to buy stardust, after all... She'd have to be on her guard.

When the Avatheos finished his sermon, everyone rose and shuffled over to greet the royal family as was tradition. As she took her place in line with her family, she craned her neck, searching the crowd for the stranger, but he was gone. Then surely, it was all in her imagination. She had enough to worry about without having to worry about Niklas sending one of his addict lackeys after her. A few courtiers trickled by to greet her, before moving on to the rest of her family, where they lingered. Then he appeared in front of her, smirking down at her, and her stomach lurched.

"We meet again, Princess," he said.

"My lord," She greeted coldly, hoping he'd move along.

His posture was relaxed, and he made no move to greet the rest of the royal family, instead lingering in front of her.

"There's a rumor going around that I'm courting you, have you heard?" he asked.

Liane gasped and covered her mouth, before looking sidelong to make sure her family hadn't heard. Was he perpetuating that rumor? Perhaps he'd come to court with the intention of wooing her, and he had no nefarious intent at all. Whatever his motive, she couldn't let her mother hear him.

Before Mother noticed them together, Liane grasped him by the wrist and pulled him between pews and out a side door into an adjoining garden outside the temple. An ancient ash tree with drooping untrimmed branches provided a small measure of privacy. Liane's eyes swept their surroundings before she felt safe to speak.

"You're rather direct. But if you asked, I would have followed you somewhere private," he said.

"What do you want?" she asked.

"You were the one who kept looking back at me, remember?"

Her face flushed. She didn't have time for flirting. They could be discovered at any moment.

"If you're trying to seduce me, it won't work."

"Oh? What makes you so certain that's what I'm trying to do?"

He chuckled under his breath as he reached out, grasping a stray strand of hair to tuck it behind her ear. Liquid heat coiled in her belly as he closed the space between him. She'd be lying if she said she wasn't attracted. But she could never be with someone who was using stardust. She didn't need another reminder of her pain. Instead, she hitched up her skirt, and his eyes widened just before she drew out her dagger strapped to her thigh and pressed it against his chin.

"Enough games; tell me who sent you."

His golden-brown eyes flicked from the dagger to her face, but he made no move to escape her.

"I think there's been a misunderstanding…"

"Liane, there you are," Mother said.

Dropping the dagger, she hid it behind her back as she turned to greet Mother, who wasn't alone. Behind her was some ruddy-faced lord she'd never seen before.

"There was someone I wanted to introduce you to, but it seems you're preoccupied." Mother raised her brows, looking slowly away from Liane, and a slow smile spread across her face as she misinterpreted what she was seeing.

"We're finished here. Who was it you wanted me to meet?" Liane asked, waving away the stranger. Hopefully, he'd think twice before approaching her again.

"Liane, don't be rude. You haven't introduced me to your friend," Mother said, putting emphasis on friend. Like a hound on the scent, she wasn't going to give up until she caught her prey.

"Prince Erich of Sundland. And your radiant reputation is understated, your majesty." Prince Erich bowed to Mother, and taking her hand in his, he planted a kiss.

"Prince Erich!" Mother said with a gasp. "I didn't know you would be coming to Artria, now isn't this a fortuitous arrival," she emphasized, with a pointed look at Liane.

A prince! Mother must be hearing wedding bells. But what would she say if Liane told her she'd caught him buying stardust? She might not sound so gleeful then.

"The visit was unplanned. Though I am planning on making my introductions at court soon."

"Then you must join us for the hunt this afternoon. I insist."

"It would be my pleasure. And might I be so bold as to say, I look forward to getting to know you and your lovely daughter better." He shot Liane a smoldering look that Mother couldn't have missed. Liane's face burned. The wheels were in motion, and they couldn't be stopped.

II

Liane inhaled the smell of pine and the crisp mountain air blowing through the trees. It reminded her of those precious summer days, before her fevers started, that they spent at the hunting lodge. Their mother had taught her how to shoot, and Father taught her to ride. That's where the fevers started as well, the first time had been at the lodge. They'd found her burning up and gripped by hallucinations, wandering the lodge halls, rambling about talking animals and other such nonsense. Liane frowned to remember it; those memories were painful and better left in the past, unexamined.

The baying of hounds brought her back to the present. A kennel master's apprentice struggled to keep his charges under control as they tugged on their leashes, lunging at the cool and impassive Prince Erich, who rode beside Mother and Father. They chatted together like old friends. Liane scowled at the back of his head. He wasn't any different than the others before him; they all thought the same way: win the heart of the mother and get the girl. But unlike most monarchs, Mother had given Liane the right to choose. And much to Mother's chagrin, none had met her standards. As tempting as it was to expose him, and be rid of him, she held back. It was better if Mother's matchmaking had a target; otherwise, her next one might be another Duke Licht.

Liane couldn't risk distractions. There was a pattern to Heinrich's cheating, he knew Aristea despised hunting, and he used that for clandestine meetings. If Liane knew who the mistress was, then she could hopefully find the child and proof of Heinrich's plotting.

Behind her, someone chortled, and Liane pivoted in her saddle to see a gaggle of Heinrich's favorites, including Duke Licht, casting sidelong glances in her direction.

"You see what I mean?" Duke Licht proclaimed.

They were likely making some joke at her expense, but she wouldn't give them the satisfaction and instead smiled in their direction. But it only seemed to fuel their amusement because they laughed harder.

"I told you she was an attention-seeking harlot," Duke Licht said with a leering grin.

A flush burned her cheeks, and she was tempted to snap back a cutting remark, but their laughter had caught another's attention. Mother looked back at her with a small nod of warning. It wasn't princess-like behavior to engage; better to rise above. She clenched her reins tighter in her hand, and her horse tossed its head in agitation.

"They're not worth the trouble," Ludwig said sagely. Of course, he would agree with Mother.

Without warning, Erich's horse reared, turned, and charged toward her. Ludwig grabbed onto her reins, pulling her out of the way, but it wouldn't have mattered because he swerved past her before straightening again to crash through her tormentors and startling their horses. In their panic to regain control of their mounts, Duke Licht was thrown from his saddle and into a thorny bush. Servants rushed over to rescue him, but he tottered unsteadily and fell back down, howling in pain at the thorns stabbing his rear. By the time they got him onto his feet, there was a hole torn in his breeches that exposed his pale, pasty flesh.

Laughter burst out of Liane, and she clamped her hand over her mouth, but the entire hunting party was snickering behind their hands at the spectacle. Erich, seemingly having gotten control of his horse, looped back around and stopped in front of Duke Licht. He held out a hand to him.

"Pardon me, I lost control of my horse for some reason. You weren't hurt, were you?" Erich asked while looking down at him.

"Don't you know how to ride!" Duke Licht seethed.

Erich shrugged. "Forgive me; I am a foreigner who doesn't understand your Neolyrian horses."

Duke Licht's face turned purple as he sputtered something unintelligible before stomping off; servants scuttled behind him, trying to stop him from exposing himself to the entire group and failing.

"Princess," Erich said as he trotted past her.

"You didn't have to do that," Liane said.

"I have no idea what you're talking about. I merely lost control of my horse." The corner of his mouth twitched into a smile, and he cantered ahead.

Despite her better judgment, her stomach fluttered.

Their procession moved forward and arrived at a tented area set up by servants earlier that morning. Beneath shaded awnings, servants arrayed platters of sandwiches and chilled wine. Some came to the hunt, others for the festivities. The former, mostly women, drifted over to cushioned seats and accepted glasses of wine and refreshment. The hounds had lost interest in Erich and were howling excitedly, eager to be let loose. Then on Mother's signal, the kennel master blew his whistle, and they shot off into the forest, startling birds from their roosts and rabbits from their dens. Eager hunters raced after them. Between dogs, courtiers, their servants, and guards, they'd be lucky to catch anything at all. Smart hunters moved toward the fringes of the hunting ground, deeper into the forest where the bigger prey waited and watched.

Smaller groups broke off, heading in different directions. Mathias went to the left, as did Mother and Father. Liane expected Heinrich to lounge about with his goons and let someone else do the hunting for him while he flirted with the court ladies, but instead, he rode off to the right into the forest. She could stay behind and try talking to the ladies and see if any of them would yield the information she needed, or she could try and follow him and try to spy.

"Which way?" Ludwig asked.

She hadn't thought he'd be here today, but there'd been a sudden change in guards, and she couldn't protest without drawing suspicion. Her secret burned in her chest, threatening to burst out of her. They shared everything about stardust. But while he shadowed her every move, she couldn't investigate without arousing suspicion. She had to follow Heinrich and hope for the best.

"To the right."

A STAG's antlers brushed the tree's canopy, and as Erich met its noble gaze, something ancient and feral stirred inside him. Hunger gnawed at his insides, like an itch he couldn't scratch. At this phase of the moon, he could tame the dragon, but during the full moon, the seals broke, and he was a monster consumed by hunger, impulse, and need. Before he'd learned to control it, he'd often wake up covered in dried blood, regardless of the moon phase. If Lord Endland hadn't recognized his affliction, the hunger would have destroyed him. Most would've killed him on sight, but Endland taught him to fight, gave him the discipline to control the dragon, even during the full moon, though nothing could prevent the change. It came sure as the changes of the monthly moon cycle.

The stag's ears flicked as he stamped the ground, issuing a challenge to him as a trespasser in his kingdom. He had no intention of ending his rule. For Erich killing was a means of survival, not sport. He was only there to get close enough to Empress Eveline and steal the sword, but she'd disappointed him by not bringing it. She didn't have it that morning at the temple either, though he was certain she'd bring it for ceremonial purposes. He didn't have time to waste. He needed to get the sword and get out of Artria.

Sinister laughter startled the stag, and it bounded away. Erich turned slowly in the saddle to Prince Consort Heinrich and his cronies slinking out of the forest to surround him. Grasping the hilt of his dagger, he did not draw it. Even though he was outnumbered six to one, he wasn't afraid. With his dragon strength, they were no match, but victory came at a price. If he won that fight, he was an anomaly, something to fear, one of the corrupted. Dropping the reins of his horse, he relaxed his shoulders as to not appear as a threat. If they didn't engage him, then he didn't need to defend himself.

"Well, look who we found," Heinrich said.

His cronies guffawed as if he had said something hilarious.

"My lords." Erich bobbed his head

"These woods are dangerous. Chimeras lurk in the shadows. Why not join us on our merry hunt? We can keep you safe," Heinrich said, gesturing to their group.

They nodded with malevolent smiles, convincing no one.

"I prefer to hunt alone," Erich said as they circled him like vultures, moving closer and closer.

"I insist. We never got to finish our chat from the masquerade after all," Heinrich said.

Two men closed in from both sides. Instinct said to run, but that was prey mindset. It only gave them a reason to chase, and he'd already figured out that Erich was the man from the masquerade. Better to wait and watch.

"Drink?" The man to his right offered Erich a skin of wine.

Erich grasped it, not taking his eyes from Heinrich. Sniffing it, his nose wrinkled. Oaky notes of bad wine couldn't disguise the acrid scent of a mild poison, not enough to kill a man but make him very sick. One of the few advantages of his dragon curse was resistance to toxins. It would have little to no effect on him, and so he gulped it down. A waste of wine.

Sniggering, the men jabbed one another with their elbows thinking themselves clever.

"Will you share a drink with me?" Erich offered Heinrich the wine skin.

"I'm not thirsty," Heinrich replied with a smirk.

"A clever poisoner can drink from his own poisoned cup," Erich replied.

Heinrich's eyes widened. "You insult me by insinuating foul play. I merely wished to welcome you to court, even after your rude arrival, Prince Erich." The way he said his name was like a curse. "We've met before, haven't we? You were that arrogant boy who tried to punch me."

"As I remember it, I did punch you, and you bled quite profusely."

"You're not in Sundland, Prince. It is I who rule here." With a snap of his fingers, his men rushed forward, grasping ahold of his legs as they attempted to pull him from the saddle.

Kicking one in the chest on instinct, it sent him flying backward to collide with the man behind him, and they fell into a heap on the ground. Another he caught in the nose, and a fount of blood poured down his face.

Then three more men grabbed hold of him, and he let them yank him out of the seat, though he could have fought them off with ease. He didn't want Heinrich to see. He wouldn't hesitate to turn him over to the guard. They forced him to kneel by kicking him in the back of the knees, and then Heinrich strode over, looking down his nose at him.

They held onto him, though he didn't struggle. With one quick twist of his arm, he could rip his captors' arms from their sockets and be gone into the woods, never to be seen again, but he'd also lose his chance at the sword. With a self-satisfied smirk on his face, Heinrich punched him. Blood filled his mouth, and he spat it out onto the grass.

"You've got a weak punch," Erich said.

The dragon stirred, uncoiling like a massive serpent, tail whipping back and forth. Erich focused on his breathing, calming the dragon within. The scent of blood and fear had awakened him, but he wouldn't lose control here, not now.

"You should know your place," Heinrich growled.

Heinrich struck him in the gut, and Erich grunted as he doubled over, the wind knocked out of him, and the dragon roared. One of the chains holding back the dragon snapped, and phantom wings unfurled as his skin prickled, threatening a change. Erich tensed, trying to hold back, but if he was hit again, he'd lose control.

Heinrich pulled back his leg as if to kick Erich, and he bit back the rage threatening to boil over.

"What are you doing?" Princess Liane's voice snapped like a whip crack, and Heinrich let his leg fall to his side.

The men holding him let go, but Erich remained kneeling, while panting and shaking slightly.

"We were having a little chat between men, nothing to worry about."

"It doesn't look like that to me." Princess Liane placed her hands on her hips. Over her shoulder, her guard gripped the pommel of his sword.

Heinrich seemed to calculate his next move as he studied Liane; his gaze lingered on her glowering guard.

"Come, there's no game to be found here."

One by one, they backed away and mounted their horses, leaving him alone with Princess Liane.

"Thank you," Erich said.

"We're even now," she said, without any hint of kindness in her expression.

Somewhere along the way, she'd gotten the wrong impression of him, but that didn't matter. It was her mother he needed, not her. With a polite incline of his head, he turned away from her. When he reached for his horse's reins, it skittered away, nostrils flaring and tossing its head. Animals could sense what the human eye could not. The dragon remained too close to the surface, rolling under his skin. It took some coaxing, but he got back astride. But by the time he did, Princess Liane was gone.

Before he rejoined the hunt, he needed to collect his thoughts and calm his nerves. He wouldn't charm anyone in this state of mind. The forest soothed him, and he headed deeper into it, away from humanity. Wind blew against his face and cooled his flushed skin, and the musky scent of plant decay and mountain air soothed his rattled nerves. The dragon calmed, and he tightened the chains around it, but its shadow lingered, a reminder of what lay beneath his human facade. Six days until his next change.

DISCOURAGED AND FRUSTRATED, Liane headed deeper into the forest, trying and failing to find Heinrich and his goons again. By intervening, she'd given herself away and lost her chance to spy on him, but at least she could hunt to try and cool her head and plan for next time. Debris crunched under their horses' hooves, and birds called to one another from treetops. She loved the stillness and silence of the forest. When she listened closely, she swore she heard the beating pulse of magic in the woods. Before The Corruption, magic had flowed in the wild places, and creatures of myth ruled. How glorious it would have been to see a dragon take flight or a unicorn prance in the autumnal leaves.

"Why were you spying on Prince Consort Heinrich?" Ludwig asked.

"I wasn't spying; he was beating up poor Prince Erich. If I hadn't intervened, they would have left him bruised and bloody," Liane replied without looking at Ludwig. If he met her eye, he'd know she was lying.

"You were following him long before that, or did you think I wouldn't notice?"

She didn't have an answer for him, so she didn't speak at all. And instead nudged her horse to follow an animal track that led to a creek. Horse hooves plopped in the soft, muddy banks filling the lengthening silence.

"Are you going to tell me what's going on?" Ludwig asked.

"You're worrying over nothing again."

"You've been acting strange since the night of the masquerade."

"I've been distracted. Mother is very keen on Prince Erich."

"As she's been with many men before him, what makes him different?"

"Well, I think she's serious this time."

"And you didn't tell her he was trying to buy stardust?"

Liane flinched. She'd hoped Ludwig wouldn't notice or remember.

"After all she lets Heinrich get away with, do you think she'd care? He's a prince and that's all she cares about."

"Empress Eveline, I can understand. You've been seen together, multiple times."

"Courtiers love to talk." Liane forced a laugh and hoped Ludwig would drop it, but his frown deepened instead.

"I have a bad feeling about him. I don't trust him."

"You don't even know him."

"Why are you defending him?" Ludwig's voice rose and echoed back at them.

A bird startled and squawked indignantly as it took to the sky.

"What's gotten into you?" she asked. It wasn't like

him to raise his voice with her, but he'd done it twice in the past few days.

Ludwig ran a hand across his face and wouldn't meet her gaze. "It's nothing…"

"Clearly, it's not, if you're upset." Liane reached to touch his hand, but he jerked it away.

"Are you seriously letting Prince Erich court you?" Ludwig asked.

The question startled her, and on impulse, she replied in a joking tone, "I can't put my life on hold for a dead man. We couldn't be together, anyway," Liane said.

But even making light of it, the truth sliced at her, and raw emotion threatened to bubble up, swallow her whole, and leave her in a sobbing mess on the floor. Move forward and get revenge; that's all that mattered. That was the only way to run from the feelings she dared not speak.

"Did you even love him?" Ludwig tossed back with a hurt tone.

It shocked her to silence for several long minutes.

"I didn't know you knew…"

She and Ludwig never talked about her love for Elias out loud, because even they had never said it to each other. Not until it was too late. But she loved Elias, and he loved her. She knew because he left her bunches of wild-flowers on her pillow, clasped her hand when no one was looking, and kissed her beneath the stars. They'd kept it a secret from everyone, including Ludwig. Not that it mattered now. Even if he'd lived, they could have never been together. He was a servant's son, and she was a princess.

"How could I not? His eyes were always watching you. His smile only for you." Ludwig clenched his reins in his fist. "Maybe it's time we stopped this futile quest for revenge. Marry your prince and live your life, and I will too."

"I haven't given up on justice. Why would you think that?" Her temper rose; it wasn't like Ludwig to act this way. Was it because she hadn't told him about what Captain Rosen said?

"Because I swore to him, I would protect you; as he lay dying, he begged me to keep you safe. I thought…" His throat bobbed as he swallowed. Hurt, loneliness, and emptiness shone in his eyes; she recognized them because Elias' death had gutted her to the point she knew she'd never love again.

"Thought what?"

"If I couldn't be by his side, then at least his love lived on in you, and seeing you move on, it reminds me that he's dead and no amount of vengeance will ever bring him back."

Guilt and shame struck her like a blow to the chest. Why hadn't she seen it before or thought to ask? She'd assumed his love for Elias was like a brother, but it had been as deep and painful as hers. They could have comforted one another; instead, he'd been suffering in silence alone. Liane reached for him, but Ludwig turned away.

"Forget I said anything." Ludwig dug in his heels, leaping across the creek.

"Ludwig, wait!" Liane cried out, her voice echoing through the forest.

Beside her, brush rustled, and a black boar stepped out. Its sharp tusks curled up, covered in dried blood and its dark beady eyes fixed on Liane as its nostrils flared. She stood very still, boars were dangerous man killers, and any sudden move might frighten it. Beneath her, the horse trembled, and then the boar screamed.

A heartbeat and a breath, and then it tore through the mud, tusks lowered. Pulling hard on the reins, her horse reared, kicking at the boar. It slashed at its foreleg, tearing the flesh, and sending it into a panic. The horse bolted, and all she could do was grasp a fist full of his mane and hold on.

Hair whipped her face, hers and the horse's, as they weaved between trees. Branches caught her sleeves, tearing them to shreds. One snapped back, hitting her eye, which watered. The shock of it made her lose her grip. She couldn't grasp back on as the saddle slid out from beneath her.

For a moment, she floated mid-air, suspended and caught between earth and sky. Then she was falling. Greenery spun around her. She collided hard with the ground. Pain like a bolt of lightning raced up the elbow she landed on.

Stunned, she lay in the undergrowth, staring at the dabbled sky beyond the canopy of trees. Then slowly, she took stock of her injuries, flexing her legs and finding no pain, then moving up to bend her knees and wriggle her ankle and shuffle her leg. Then she tried sitting, wincing at the stabbing pain in her elbow, broken. Bushes rustled, and she floundered for her bow, but she'd lost it in the chaos. One lone arrow remained in her quiver. Grasping it like a dagger, she got to her feet.

"Ludwig?" Liane called.

The whistle of wind answered.

A white flash darted past her periphery, and a tingling sensation flowed out from the scar on her back, like the feeling of a sleeping limb. Instead of feeling heavy and numb, like usual, she felt weightless and aware. Perhaps she'd hit her head in the fall. Liane pressed her fingers to her temple and was relieved to not find a lump or blood.

Then a stag, one half jet black, the other side pure white, stepped out of the shadows. It pinned her with its dual-colored eyes, evoking a memory that floated just out of reach. Liane stumbled backward, and her back collided with the trunk of a tree as the stag dipped its head, pressing its black and white nose against her elbow. When it did, her pain disappeared. Flexing her previously broken arm, she marveled at the complete recovery.

"How did you do this...No, better yet, what are you?"

It said nothing but blinked at her with an intelligent expression, before bounding away to the edge of a clearing. What did she expect from a magic deer? It looked back at her, as if waiting for her to follow. That wasn't possible. Pressing her hand against her forehead, she checked for a fever. Maybe this was another hallucination? But her skin was cool to the touch.

"Do you want me to follow you?" Liane said.

Saying it out loud only made her feel crazier, but crazier still, the deer seemed to nod almost imperceptibly. She took a faltering step in its direction, gaining confidence with each step. When she was almost close enough to touch, it leapt forward again, before waiting for her between a pair of oak trees.

Then, like a woman possessed, she ran to catch up, but it merely bounded again out of reach. She chased it through the woods unthinking, flashes of memory running through her mind: a moonlight forest, the feel of cold metal in her hand, and a place... she could not recall. While the stag was nimble and spirit-like in its quick movements through the forest, she struggled against thick undergrowth as brambles ripped her trousers and scratched her flesh. But deeper and deeper they went until the stag disappeared.

Liane stopped, turning in a circle looking for the stag, but it was gone. A few yards away, she spotted a half-buried moss-covered column and scattered along the forest floor, crumbled bits of stone. Had the stag taken her to the ruins? No. This place was much too wooded. But it must have been built by the same people because it inexplicably felt the same. The air felt heavy, making it harder to breathe. Her skin itched, twitched, trembled, and her scar throbbed, pulsating, pushing, urging her to do what?

The stag stepped out from beneath a broken archway, carved with an emblem she'd never seen before, but it felt familiar somehow. Sun and moon intertwined, insepa-rable halves of a greater whole, and their division aligned with the stags' markings.

"Was this what you wanted to show me?" Liane wondered aloud. "What does it mean?"

"You've forgotten," a voice whispered through her mind.

"You can talk?" It should have terrified her, but there

was a strange comfort in it as if she were greeting an old friend. "What have I forgotten?"

"Look." The stag's voice seemed to ripple through her, reverberating, as it lowered its antlers down to a pool of water she hadn't noticed before.

A starless sky reflected on the surface, though it was mid-day. *Strange*, she thought, but she couldn't tear her eyes away from it. Peaking over the edge, she didn't see her reflection, but a black, endless void, and at its center, a pinpoint of light growing bigger and bigger. As it got closer, her back started to burn. She remembered this feeling from the first fever, overwhelming consuming heat. It felt as if her back would split apart and lay her broken in two pieces on the ground. She tried to look away but could not. The darkness had her, and it was pulling her down into oblivion.

12

"Hello? Is someone there?" a voice called out, and Erich drew his weapon. He'd thought he was alone.

He scanned the forest, thinking it was another one of Heinrich's traps, until Princess Liane's guard limped into view, a bloody gash torn into his thigh. One inch lower, and it would've severed an artery, and he'd have bled out. He still might if he didn't see a healer soon. Erich jumped down from his saddle and offered him a shoulder to lean on as they hobbled together toward Erich's horse.

"You're fortunate I came by when I did. The rest of the hunters are chasing a boar."

"I know; the boar is what tore into me. I've been shouting for help for a while, but no one came. Did Princess Liane send you to find me?" he asked.

"I haven't seen her. We should get you a healer; you look pale."

The man swayed a bit in his arms, like a drunkard, and his eyelids fluttered.

But suddenly, he snapped to attention. "Stars. I'd hoped she'd made it back; I lost sight of her when her horse spooked. I have to find her." He tugged against Erich as if he'd stumble off into the woods himself and look for her.

Erich held him tight. "You're no use to her in this condition. Do you think you can ride?"

"I think so."

"Get on." Erich helped him into the saddle, and the man winced when he put weight on his bad leg.

"Someone needs to alert the guards, and you need a healer. Go back, ring the alarm, and I'll find the princess."

The guard studied him for a moment, as if debating his willingness to trust him. Then with a nod, he dug his heels into the horse and rode off back toward camp, while Erich turned his attention to the forest. A shaman in Porroque taught him how to track, and he'd found he had a knack for it. With the dragon close to the surface, his senses were heightened more than usual. He could smell the pungent musk of boar and deer contrasted with the fainter scent of humans. The creek where the guard and Princess Liane had been attacked was close by, and from there, he spotted the trail of broken branches and trampled foliage and followed it.

Her horse was grazing alone in a meadow. He caught it and searched the surrounding area for signs of her, fearing he'd find her lying battered and unconscious in the tall grass. Instead, he detected the faint scent of magic on the wind. His skin prickled with it, and his stomach roiled. When Prince Consort Heinrich had said there were corrupted in the woods, he thought he was taunting him, but now he saw hints of them everywhere, marks on the trees from claws too big for a bear or wild cat. He had to find her before it was too late.

After catching her horse, he noticed a soft shoe print on the ground, surrounded by magic, leading deeper into an old grove forest. He'd found places like it before and never lingered long in them. Thin threads of magic coursed through the trees and soil, and their invisible tendrils tugged upon his bindings, threatening to unravel his control over the dragon. But his concern for Princess Liane urged him forward, following the path she'd taken through the old growth.

Eventually, it grew so thick, he had to leave the horse tied to a tree and continue on, fighting against the bramble which reached up to tear at his clothes. The forest didn't want him here, or worse, it wanted him to stay forever. Hacking at the plants with his dagger, he cut his way through until the forest opened onto a grouping of moss-covered ruins.

He recognized the sleeping magic; it coated his tongue with a sweet and sour taste. Then he noticed the dead runes carved into stone, weathered to the point of obliteration. He thought the old temples were a myth, a legend passed on from The Corruption, but he knew what it was by the dual sun and moon carved into the archway. Many of the old places were forbidden because they seeped corruption magic. Already cursed, he didn't want to risk becoming a chimera. But seeing the temple, he understood why it hunted in these old woods, why those thin strains of magic remained. Those that worshipped the Nameless Goddess might be gone, but the trees and earth remembered.

A faint, golden glow shined out from behind vine-covered pillars, and the pulse of magic grew stronger. Dagger held out in front of him; Erich came around the corner to discover Liane kneeling beside a pool of water, her eyes unfocused, as if in a trance.

"Princess Liane, are you hurt?" he asked, taking a step closer.

Then a stag stepped into his path. Unlike any animal he had seen before: split down the middle, one-half white, and one-half black. It fixed Erich with its ageless stare. Ancient magic older than time itself unfurled from it, tugging at the fibers of Erich's being and eroding the chains which held the dragon back. Recoiling, Erich pulled the chains tighter, doubling them to keep the dragon in check, but the call of ancient magic couldn't be denied, and he stepped closer.

"Will you protect her, or will you run?" the stag said inside his mind.

"I'm not fit to protect anyone," Erich said with naked honesty, surprising even himself.

"And yet you came here, knowing the risks."

He didn't have a reply to give, and the stag didn't seem to need one because it turned to stand over Liane once more at the water's edge. Her skin glowed faintly, as if illuminated from within, the strongest light burning like a rod along her back. Behind her, the shadows shifted. He heard the twinge of a bow string seconds before it flew. Grabbing hold of Liane, he yanked her away from the pool's edge and caught the arrow with his shoulder. The dragon roared as warm blood trickled down his shoulder blade and dripped into the water.

"You've made your choice then." Then in a cloud of mist, magic fizzled in the air, and the stag disappeared.

Holding Liane, he scanned the ruins to look for the shooter. Someone ran through the brush, and he debated chasing after them, but her eyes fluttered open, glassy and unfocused.

"What happened?" she murmured.

How did he explain what he had witnessed when he wasn't even sure himself? What did the ancient mean when it said he'd made his choice?

"I found your guard injured, and he told me you were missing." Better to start with the concrete facts.

A faint sheen lingered on her skin, and heat radiated off her. She was burning up with a fever. Had corruption already started to take hold? He suddenly felt very protective of her, but if she were infected, he couldn't reverse it. Would her family kill her if she were? Perhaps he could take her with him? He shook his head; that was foolishness. His best chance at survival was alone.

"You're hurt!" she said, and very gently, her hand brushed over his wound.

The dragon stirred again, lifting a curious head, sniffing in her direction, and Erich pulled away. With it this close to the surface, it made his moods unpredictable. He didn't want to do something he would regret.

"It's nothing."

"I think I can get it out for you, if you'll let me stand."

He set her on her feet, but his hands lingered too long

on her hips, and he felt a spark of desire shoot through him. Her eyes flicked up to meet his and held. It was reckless to desire something; he'd learned that the hard way. But in that moment, he wanted her, badly. Erich turned his head away, breaking their stare.

"Go ahead," he said.

"This will likely hurt."

"I can handle it."

She grasped the arrow with both hands, and he braced for the pain. Though the dragon curse allowed him to heal quickly, he felt pain like any man. She pulled it out with a wet pop and then gasped.

He didn't have a chance to ask her what had surprised her because horse hooves thundered toward them, and he positioned himself between her and the oncoming riders. Prince Mathias, flanked by several Midnight Guards, approached. Irrational panic clawed at his throat. But when Prince Mathias dismounted, he walked straight over to Liane and grasped her by the shoulders.

"Liane, are you hurt?" Prince Mathias said, scanning her up and down.

"I'm fine, but someone shot Prince Erich," Liane said, gesturing behind her.

With a nod from Mathias, the guards dismounted and went to investigate. Erich couldn't help but notice how Liane took the arrow and hid it in the band of her pants, beneath her loose tunic shirt. Their eyes met, and he pretended to not have seen.

"You're burning up with fever," Mathias said, pressing his the back of his hand to Liane's forehead. "We should have a healer see you both."

"I don't—" she said, then shouting cut her off.

Clenching a fist, Erich held his breath. Metal rang, and grunts followed. Then minutes dragged by, and silence settled over the forest. They waited for what felt like an eternity before the Midnight Guard emerged from the forest, hauling a man with shorn black hair and a mottled black splotch across his face and neck between them. The withering. It'd started to creep over the tips of his fingers, shriveling them up like dried fruit. Erich was surprised the man had been able to hold a bow, but despite the advanced stage of his corruption, he struggled against four guards with the strength of ten men.

He broke free suddenly and came charging toward Liane, hands outstretched and grasping, but before he could reach her, an arrow pierced him through the eye, and he slumped to the ground in a heap.

Liane half screamed and covered her mouth with her hand.

"Mathias."

"It had to be done. This is more kindness than he deserved. Better the withering slowly kills him for trying to kill you." Then he turned to Erich and clamped him on his good shoulder. "Thank you for protecting my sister."

Erich shouldn't, but his eyes went to the dead man on the ground. This was what happened to his kind. Corruption could not be allowed to exist, and so it was stamped out. His mouth felt suddenly very dry.

"It was nothing," he said.

No one spoke as they rode back. Liane looked as pale as fresh milk, and her brother kept shooting furtive glances in her direction, as if he wanted to say something but thought better of it. When they returned to the hunter's party, priests were waiting with a litter for Liane, and they'd already strapped in her guard. And though Erich insisted his injuries were minor, they insisted he see a healer at the temple.

As they made a slow, arduous return to the city, he tried to plot his escape. But with guards surrounding him on all sides, that was impossible. By the time they arrived, his wound would have knitted back together. If he didn't get away before then, he'd have a difficult time explaining it to the healer, and he feared he'd end up like the withered man.

They reached the temple without an opportunity for escape, and priests and priestesses greeted them at the temple steps before whisking Liane inside to the women's wing of the temple. Erich and Liane's guard were taken to the men's. The guard's injuries were more severe, and he was given a short reprieve when they sat him down on a cot in the infirmary.

As he waited, Erich glanced around the infirmary. There was one exit next to the bed where the guard was being treated. At the opposite end of the room was a big window, and next to it, an old man being tended by another priest hacked into a stained handkerchief, his body convulsing as he wheezed for each breath. Erich wasn't a healer, but he knew a death rattle when he heard one. When he caught his breath, the acolyte handed him a steaming cup from which the man took small sips.

"You'll need to drink if you want to heal," said a familiar voice.

Erich did a double take. He hadn't recognized Fritz

beneath the veil, nor would he have expected an elf inside the temple. Fritz must have a death wish to come here. Even more shocking, Fritz tended to the old man with gentle hands, and when he placed them on his back, they glowed. Erich half rose from his seat, afraid the elf would kill the man in broad daylight with the same power which broke the iron bars.

"Now, breathe in for me," Fritz said.

The old man inhaled sharply, then sputtered. Fritz's hands grew brighter before the light sunk into his back and the shadow of death hanging over the old man dissipated. Even the best healers couldn't perform such miracles, but Fritz brought him back from the brink. How could corrupt magic do this?

"How does that feel?" Fritz asked.

The old man inhaled, and visible relief spread over his wrinkled face.

"No more pain! Oh, thank you, priest, thank you. The goddess has blessed you with Her light." He grasped Fritz's hands, shaking them up and down as Fritz smiled.

Then he escorted him out the door. When he was gone, Fritz turned his attention to Erich, but when the elf reached to pull back Erich's sleeve, he reeled back, scowling at Fritz.

"I heard you were shot during the hunt. May I inspect your wound?" Fritz said with a curl of his lips.

Erich glared. Surely the elf knew his wounds healed on their own. Was he trying to get them both killed, perhaps?

"You're staring," Fritz said

"I'm wondering what you're doing here," Erich replied.

"Healing the sick and injured."

"This isn't a game. This is life or death."

"Isn't it always?"

The guard groaned, and the priest tending him soothed him with nonsense words. Erich clenched a fist.

"I trusted you, but you're taking a dangerous risk," Erich hissed under his breath.

"I came here to help you. You're welcome, by the way." Fritz grasped his arm and rolled back his sleeve.

He felt Fritz poke around the wound before he cleaned away dried blood with a damp cloth. Though his methods were questionable, it was a relief to see Fritz here.

"Making any progress?" Fritz asked.

"Hardly."

Fritz set aside the bloody clothes and bound up the healed wound in bandages. "Anything you want to tell me?"

He thought of the stag and its cryptic words, but he couldn't see how that was any of Fritz's business.

"No."

"Well, if that changes, come find me. All done." He stepped back.

"Thanks," Erich said, shaking his head as he pulled his shirt back into place. "But where do I find you? You never told me—"

But when he looked up, Fritz was gone and on the bed next to him was a torn piece of parchment with the words: Moonlight Tavern.

13

Liane glared at the white plastered ceiling, as the acrid scent of incense burned her nostrils. The wet cloth on her brow dripped rivulets of water that ran down her cheek. Her fever broke hours ago, but the Vice Premier insisted she stay overnight for observation. It'd been years since her last delirious fever, and she feared Liane was relapsing. Rationally, she knew the talking deer wasn't real, but that didn't explain the very real arrow she hid under her pillow or the corrupted man who'd shot it. Whoever he was, he'd come for her. She'd seen the look in his eyes moments before Mathias shot him.

If only he wasn't dead, she might have asked him why. Had Heinrich been trying to assassinate her? Then why bother luring her into the ruins? It would be simpler to make it look like a hunting accident. And those ruins were real, even if the deer wasn't. But how had she stumbled upon it, then? Trying to make sense of it all made her head throb.

Reaching under her pillow, her fist closed around the strange arrow. When she'd first drawn it out of Erich, it had been warm to the touch, but it was cool now. He'd taken the arrow for her, but how was he there right on time? Did he follow her? Erich, ruins, stag, stardust, were any of them related?

Footsteps approached, and Liane let go of the arrow to pretend to sleep. The Vice Premier was doing her evening rounds early, and if she saw her awake, she'd make her drink a bitter sleeping draft. Two sets of footsteps approached, one shuffling slightly. Vice Premier pulled the blanket up to Liane's chin, before smoothing it out in an affectionate gesture, then she removed the damp cloth from Liane's forehead.

"As I said, the princess is resting. As should you," the Vice Premier said.

"May I sit with her a while at least?" Ludwig asked.

"You're not on duty. You should focus on healing."

"I know."

Liane imagined the look the Vice Premier gave Ludwig, the same she'd given her hundreds of times: one of disapproval tempered by compassion.

The Vice Premier sighed. "Drink your tonic, and when it's finished, off to bed with you."

"Yes, your grace."

As the Vice Premier padded away, the bed beside hers creaked. Not ready to confront Ludwig, Liane lay still, eyes shut. In truth, she was ashamed of herself. She called herself his friend, and yet she never knew how he felt about Elias. And if she was being honest, she felt a small twinge of jealousy as well. That potent combination made it difficult to look at Ludwig. She thought she knew him, but perhaps she didn't know him as well as she thought.

"You don't have to pretend. I know you're awake," Ludwig said.

"How'd you know?" she asked, opening her eyes to stare at the ceiling.

"When you're asleep, you drool," he said in a deadpan tone.

"I do not!" She flipped over to face him. Crutches rested against the edge of the bed, and Ludwig's bandaged leg extended out in front of him. The Vice Premier told her he'd been wounded but seeing it in person was worse. Ludwig wasn't as infallible as she thought; even her steadfast rock could crack.

"How's your leg?" she asked.

"It'll heal, but I'm off duty until further notice," he said as he absently rubbed the top of his thigh, not meeting her gaze.

Liane sat up. "But you'll be back when it heals, won't you?"

Ludwig cleared his throat. "To be determined."

"This isn't fair. It's not your fault I was hurt." Kicking off her blankets, Liane shimmied to the edge of her bed. Mother and Falko couldn't blame Ludwig. She'd startled the boar with her shouting, and she'd followed the mystical deer into the forest. She would go straight to Captain Falko and plead for Ludwig's reinstatement, explain everything to them. Leaning forward on his good leg, Ludwig stopped her by jutting out his arm.

"Don't worry about me. I need the rest after everything you've put me through." Wincing, he sat back.

Liane sank down. Ludwig meant to tease, but the words cut deeper today. He was right; she'd always taken advantage of his willingness. Each time he followed her out of the palace in disguise, he risked dismissal or worse. The near-death experience today made her painfully aware of the effects of her actions. She couldn't keep putting him in danger, not because of Elias' promise. If Elias had truly loved her, he wouldn't have left her alone. The thought made her feel cold and hollow, so she stuffed it back down.

"I'm sorry for everything," she said as she grasped the hem of her sleeve, running it between thumb and forefinger.

"Don't be. I shouldn't have let my personal feelings impede me from protecting you."

"Not that, Elias. I claim to be your best friend, but I never knew how you felt about him."

"Forget I said anything." Ludwig rubbed the back of his neck. "I spoke out of anger. I should be happy if you're escaping the ghosts of the past, even if I'm still trapped by them. It's reassuring to see you moving on. It gives me hope for myself." Glancing up, he smiled at her.

Ludwig deserved the truth, but if she told him, he'd want to help. And it was better if he focused on healing instead of galivanting around the city looking for answers with her.

"Still friends?" he asked sheepishly.

Leaping across the gap between beds, Liane wrapped her arms around Ludwig's neck. "No matter what happens, you will always be my best friend. And nothing will get between me and vengeance for Elias."

At first, his arms hung at his sides, then cautiously, he embraced her. When they broke apart, Ludwig cleared his throat awkwardly.

"I should let you get your rest." Ludwig stood and, leaning on his crutch, hobbled out.

As the door closed, she removed the arrow from under her pillow. She ran her fingers along the shaft, tracing the carved runes while wondering at their meanings. Everything about it was unlike anything she'd seen before, from the carvings to the dabbled feathers of the fletching. It seemed to weigh almost nothing, but it seemed to have been much heavier when she first grasped hold of it. Dragging her thumb across the arrow tip, a jolt coursed down her arm, and she dropped it with a yelp.

She eyed it dubiously. For all she knew, it was imbued with corruption, and no amount of studying was going to reveal any of its secrets. Perhaps taking the arrow was a mistake. Climbing out of bed, she carried it over to a refuse bin but hesitated to throw it away. What if one of the acolytes found it and was stricken with the withering like that man? His crazed eyes and mottled skin flashed before her eyes, and Liane shook her head to dispel the image.

Arrow grasped in her hand, she climbed back in bed and shoved it beneath her pillow once more. She'd dispose of it when she was out of the temple. Liane pulled the blankets up to her chin and tried to go to sleep—the sooner she did, the sooner she could leave the temple— but sleep evaded her. As she closed her eyes, the starless void filled the space behind her eyelids, and her restless thoughts returned to the stag, the pool, glowing runes, and the elves that moved like shadows. All of it forbidden, treacherous, and alluring. She had to know more to make sense of these half-forgotten memories the ruins had evoked.

The temple held an archive of many tomes of corruption magic, including the language of runes. If she could decipher the runes on the arrow's shaft, perhaps she could make sense of the would-be killer's motives. Tossing off her covers, she leapt out of bed and retrieved it once more, and headed for the door, where she stopped short. Books about corruption and runes were forbidden to everyone but senior librarians. They'd never let her stroll in and read their books, and if she dared to ask questions, they'd simply wave her off, saying it was better not to meddle with corruption.

No one would be in the library at night, however. And if she snuck in unnoticed, then she might find answers under the cover of night. Decision made, she crept to the door and peered outside; two guards stood watch. After the attack, Mother had doubled Liane's guard. Without asking, she knew they'd refuse to escort her to the library. The Vice Premier would have given orders to keep her in bed. Instead, she'd have to sneak past them.

Tip-toeing back to her bed, she arranged her pillows to look like she was still sleeping. Satisfied it served at a casual glance, she padded back, picking up a clay cup on her way. Their backs were to her, more concerned with keeping people from getting in than what might come out. One guard's head bobbed, as if he were about to fall asleep. The second guard was pacing at the opposite end of the hall, presumably trying to keep himself awake. When the closer guard stretched and yawned, Liane tossed the cup out into the hall, where it shattered on the ground.

Both men jumped to attention, rushing over to investigate the broken cup, and while they weren't looking, she darted out of her room and around the corner. Then with her back against the wall, she held her breath and waited. If she moved too quickly, they'd hear her footsteps and come looking.

"Did something come out of the infirmary?" the further guard asked.

"I'll check," replied the closer.

Heart in her throat, she listened as the door creaked.

"Princess is sleeping," the guard whispered.

"Don't know where this cup came from, though."

"You must have kicked it over while you were pacing; they leave trays all over."

Which was what Liane had been counting on. During the midnight change over, acolytes collected various vessels for washing, which were left out by the previous shift in the hallway. She waited for a few more breaths before moving silently down the hall and toward the library.

Pale light from a quarter moon illuminated the vacant hallway, giving it an eerie glow, and without the bustle of priests and priestesses filling it, each breath echoed off the cold marble walls. At the end of the hall, marble columns arched over a pair of double spruce doors. Testing the doorknob, she discovered it was unlocked, and thanked the stars for that. It swung open with a small groan, and she froze on the threshold, fearing the sound would alert the guards. But when no one came to investigate, she stepped inside.

Silver beams of moonlight illuminated an unlit oil lamp sitting atop a tidy desk where the chief librarian typically sat. Opening drawers, she sought a match to light the lamp. After a short search, she found one, and she struck it. Its meager flame flickered against her palm as she led it to the wick. It caught, and while she fumbled with the glass cover, she accidentally spilled oil onto the desk. Using her sleeve, she wiped up the mess the best she could. But by the time she'd finished, her heart was pounding against her ribcage. The librarians would be horrified to see her now.

Liane headed down a nearby row and wandered the aisles, scanning the shelves of leather-bound tomes, unsure where to start. As a girl, she'd spent hours in the library reading through illuminated manuscripts about all manner of things. One kind archivist once let her peek at a very old book, said to be one of the few that remained from before The Corruption. It was that book she sought.

As she remembered, there was a door in the far back corner of the library, but when she tested it, it was locked. This had to be where it was, and so she returned to the desk and hunted for a key. She rummaged through drawers, finding quills, ink, and loose pieces of parchment with splotches of ink. Just as she was about to give up, a tingle raced up her spine, and instinct told her to press the ornate molding placed between two drawers. If this worked to reveal secret passages in the palace, why not hidden drawers in the temple? She pushed hard against it and felt the click of a hidden mechanism. The molding jutted out like a handle, and when she turned it, she heard another metallic click as a second thin drawer slid out. Inside, a pewter key rested on the velvet interior.

Liane rushed back over to jam the key into the lock, and when it swung open, the smell of old paper and ink overwhelmed her with pleasant memories. Being bedbound in her youth wasn't all bad; at least it had given her plenty of time to read.

There were no windows into the room, as to better preserve the ancient books, but she feared accidentally setting the thousand-year-old tomes on fire, so she left her lamp at the entry before moving on to peruse the shelves. As she scanned titles written in dead languages, a prickle raced up her spine. Instinct told her to take a left, and she always trusted her gut.

At the end of the row, she discovered a book lying open upon a pedestal, its illuminated pages seemingly glowing in the dark. Though it was difficult to see, she recognized the scrawled runes running across the page. Hands shaking, she turned one brittle page slowly. If she moved too fast, the entire thing might crumble. Eyes devouring the unfamiliar characters, she compared them to the markings on the arrow but couldn't make heads or tails of it.

Though she didn't understand the words written, she recognized the creatures illustrated along the margins: mermaids flapping their fishy tales, unicorns rearing, and dragons soaring. They reminded her of picture books she'd read as a girl, but though they were the same creatures, they were markedly different. They lacked menace, she realized. Now they called them chimera, as they'd been so horrifically changed by corruption, and were said to be dangerous. The illustrator had captured their likeness in such exquisite detail it seemed they might leap off the page, and stranger yet, they looked friendly, beautiful even.

Liane turned to the next page, and her heart stopped.

A golden sun cut in half by the moon hung in a twilight sky, and beneath it, staring out at the viewer, was the two-toned stag. A shiver ran down her spine. She'd never seen such a creature before in any book, and thought it was a product of her hallucinations.

"Have you come seeking as well, child of light?" the Avatheos said in his sonorous voice.

Spinning, Liane turned to face him. "I couldn't sleep." Liane stammered the first thing she could think of.

"Something troubling you?" he asked, standing unnervingly still, back lit by her lantern, which cast him in sharp relief.

There were many things troubling her, but somehow she thought confessing to the Avatheos would condemn her to an afterlife wandering the void. Especially considering just that morning, she'd dared to gaze upon his veiled face. But was lying to him any better?

Swallowing past the lump in her throat, she stepped aside to reveal the page with the two-toned stag. Though the Avatheos terrified her, he was best qualified to answer her questions.

"Do you know what this is?" she asked, pointing to the illustration.

He moved closer, and then his veiled face snapped back to her.

"Where did you see it?" He took a step toward her.

Liane backed away, frightened by his intensity and the crackle of power that emanated from him. "In a dream," she lied on impulse. Or was it a lie? She wasn't sure what was real and fake anymore.

"Dreams are powerful portents. What you saw is the ancient being of twilight and dawn, master of balance. What else did you see in your dream; did it speak to you?"

Mouth dry, her throat clenched tight on her words. Her back thrummed like the beat of a drum as she started to shake her head. Every instinct was telling her to run, to get as far away as possible.

"I don't remember. It was nothing but a fever dream. Forget I said anything." Liane turned to run, but he grasped her forearm, stopping her.

Shock burned through her as it had when she touched the arrow, but this time it was accompanied by images flashing through her mind, moving too fast to absorb: a child's hand grasping a golden sword, a moonlight forest, black and white antlers and then a sudden bright flash of light obscured her vision. Liane gasped and pulled away from the Avatheos.

That burst of light had darkened her vision, and for a moment, she was disoriented and fumbling. Her chest heaved with panic, while her scar burned that same searing pain she'd felt in the forest as if her back might split open.

"What did you see?" the Avatheos asked, grabbing hold of her shoulder, squeezing much too tight.

"Please, you're hurting me." Liane gasped.

And then, suddenly, he let her go, and the pain subsided. The Avatheos took a step back from her.

"Forgive me; I shouldn't have pushed you when you were unwell. Let me escort you back to your room."

She had no choice but to go with him, but she noted the Avatheos was careful not to brush against her even casually. The guards were surprised when she arrived with the Avatheos but didn't ask questions as she went back to bed. As she lay down to sleep once more, her thoughts raced, trying to make sense of what had happened. She felt as if she were going insane. Perhaps she'd pushed herself too hard too soon after a fever, but a niggling thought at the back of her mind refused to agree.

14

Erich's hand lingered on his dagger as the guard took it from his unwilling grip.

"If I find one scratch on its hilt, I'll open the veil and unleash darkness, I swear," Erich said.

The guard rolled his eyes before motioning him through the gate, and simultaneously ushering the next in line, Ivar, forward.

"Is this necessary?" Ivar asked as a guard turned his velvet hat inside out.

"Empress' orders," the guard said as he handed back Ivar's crumpled hat.

"They can't risk letting you sneak weapons in that voluminous hat of yours, Ivar," Erich said.

"I'm glad you're amused, your majesty," Ivar grumbled as he adjusted the feather on his hat.

Erich craned his neck to watch as his beloved dagger was handed off and then placed into a back room. *I'll be back for you soon*, he thought. There'd been too many close calls lately, and he'd brought it unthinking to the palace, forgetting the strict no-weapons policy. Running his thumb across the bottom of his heavy signet ring, he debated if reclaiming his identity, no matter how temporary, was a mistake. His plan, already fraught with uncertainty, was taking too long. And he had precious little time left before the full moon.

But getting into the palace to search for the sword was harder than he realized. Few were allowed in without invitation, even princes, and had he not been the one to find Liane at the ruins, he might not have gotten an invitation inside again. A stroke of good luck. But before they met for his luncheon with the empress, he had to find where she kept the sword.

Invitation presented and their persons searched, Ivar and Erich were allowed at last into the palace courtyard by the guards. Ivar stomped ahead, muttering about indignity as he smoothed out his hat. Erich fell behind, scanning the palace grounds. He noted the four defense towers, one at each corner of the palace. The closest one to him appeared to house the Royal Guards, a defensible place to hide a precious object like the Golden Blade, but Erich also knew Empress Eveline wasn't so careless as to leave the sword with mere palace guards.

"Years I've spent trying to get an audience with the empress, years. And in the span of an afternoon, you've been invited personally," Ivar said, grumbling, as he looked at Erich sidelong.

When Erich had returned to the embassy the night of

the masquerade covered in manure, Ivar didn't ask questions. When Erich asked to go to the sunrise rites, despite not worshipping their sun goddess, Cyra, he said nothing. Ivar must suspect Erich was plotting something, but he wasn't a fool.

"What can I say? I'm rather charming," Erich replied distractedly.

A cloud moved over the sun, and the air suddenly crackled with the threat of a summer storm as a company of Midnight Guards marched past him. Erich's jaw clenched as he watched them march over to their tower, opposite the Royal Guard tower. If he were Empress Eveline, he'd hide the sword there with the most elite guards in the capital. But walking in there was a suicide mission.

Five days before the next full moon. Five days left to steal the sword. No time to waste, but before he did something reckless, he was going to search for an alternative.

"Go ahead, Ivar, and mingle. I've got something to do."

Ivar didn't try to stop him but marched over to a cluster of nearby lords and made his introductions as Erich strode across the palace courtyard. The humidity was stifling, and he unbuttoned his top few buttons seeking relief, but it caught the appraising glances of passing court ladies. They whispered behind their decorative fans, their hunger palpable as he passed them by. One woman accidentally dropped her kerchief in his path, and on long-ingrained instinct, he stopped to pick it up and handed it back to her with a smile.

These habits resurfaced like the ghosts of his past life, and he suddenly felt more stifled than before. In Sundland, he'd wielded sexual appeal like a weapon, honed like a knife to pierce the heart of his targets. Because, as Father would say: attractive people were impossible to hate. At the time, he'd perfected his skills as a means of survival, but it wasn't long before his hunger for more started to take over. Shaking away the specters of the past, he went to work.

The first thing he did was walk the perimeter of the palace, taking special care to seek out hidden alcoves, disguised doors, or seemingly abandoned buildings. But he quickly realized it was filled with them. Servants emerged from behind bushes or descended stairs into cellars beneath small structures.

Investigating one such doorway, he discovered a well-lit underground labyrinth that would take years to map out. He followed one passage that passed beneath salons, apartments, and gaming. Doorways opened out onto them so servants might enter and exit without being seen. He backtracked, thinking of going deeper into the tunnels, when he heard footsteps behind him. While he'd been investigating, he'd been careful not to be seen by the servants who'd realize he was a nobleman at a glance.

"Have you gotten lost, sir?" said a female voice.

Erich turned with a charming smile. When their eyes met, her breath caught, and she clutched at her throat, already in his thrall. And he hated himself for it. It was his father who'd first recognized it, one of the abilities given to him by the dragon curse. A magic sort of persuasion that made the willing highly suggestible.

"I'm afraid I have. I must have made a wrong turn somewhere as I've been fumbling in the dark for much too long," he said, lacing the words with his own magic: allure.

"Who are you?" she asked breathlessly.

"Prince Erich," he said, taking a step closer to her and reaching out as if to cup her cheek.

But as he did, the smallest frown wrinkled her brow and her gaze sharpened with sudden recognition.

"Your majesty." She bowed, lowering her head and breaking his controlling gaze.

Was it a coincidence, or had she broken herself free of his spell?

"Perhaps you could show me the way out of here?" he asked.

"My pleasure, your majesty," she said, again a bit breathlessly.

A prickling sense of unease crawled up the back of his neck as she led him through the tunnels. They ascended a stairwell, and Erich's hand itched to take hold of his dagger. At the top of a darkened stairwell, she opened a door onto a bedchamber where Princess Liane paced. She turned as they entered.

"Luzie, I'm glad you're back—"

She froze, staring wide-eyed at him.

The maid bowed. "I ran into Prince Erich, who seems to have gotten lost wandering in the underground tunnels."

Whatever shock she might have felt was erased from her face. Erich looked from the maid to Princess Liane. Why had she brought him here? More importantly, how did he explain why he'd been caught wandering where he did not belong? Rather than let the silence linger, he cleared his throat.

"Princess, am I wrong in thinking you were looking for me?" Erich remarked, keeping his tone bland

"I wasn't—What were you—?" She stopped to collect herself. A touch of pink kissed the apples of her cheeks. He'd noticed she blushed when she was flustered. It was rather endearing. Then she shook her head.

"I hope this time we can speak without blades."

"I, too, wanted to finish our conversation from before."

"The one where you accused me of buying stardust? Or the one where I took an arrow for you?" Erich asked. It was a gamble to bring up the stardust, but while he'd been spinning his wheels trying to get an invitation into the palace, he'd done a little digging into Princess Liane. Apparently, she'd made it her vendetta to eradicate stardust from the city. Which explained her point weapons first, ask questions later approach. But if he could use what happened in the woods to his advantage, she might be an ally. If not, she could make his job much harder.

"You're always around. How did you find me in the woods that day?"

"You were the one who saved me first, remember? I was just paying back a debt."

"And the stardust?"

"I was led there under false promises, and when I realized what they were selling, I tried to leave. Happy?"

She nodded thoughtfully, as if considering what he was saying. Her stance wasn't hostile, but not welcoming either, not yet. If he used this opening, he might win her over. A bit of fluff landed on her cheek, and on impulse, he reached up to brush it away. That bare sweep of her soft skin jolted him. Liane's eyes widened; she'd felt it, too, the spark. It flashed like an ember in the dark, rippling down his arm and awakening the dragon inside him. It stirred restlessly, pushing against its bindings, and he pulled the chains tighter. Not until the full moon, until then, he would smother this animalistic hunger.

Instead of pulling away, he let his hand linger, cupping her cheek and tilting her head up. Eyes soft and lips parted, she inched closer to him. Without trying, he had her under his spell, and it made him sick. He thought he could stomach it, but his conscience wouldn't let him. Letting her go, he turned his back, breaking eye contact and the spell.

"Say I believe you, then tell me, why did you come to Artria?" she asked, breathless.

"Why does anyone of royal blood visit another king-dom?" Courting was the perfect disguise, one that no one would question.

"Too bad for you, I've vowed never to marry," she said with a smirk.

"Perhaps I could change your mind," he said with swaggering confidence he didn't feel. From the defiant tilt of her chin, he knew Princess Liane wasn't easily swayed, but he needed her to think of him as an arrogant prince seeking a marital alliance.

"Are you the one spreading rumors of our courtship then?"

Erich scoffed. "I don't need such petty tricks."

She scanned him up and down again, assessing.

"I can ruin all your ambitions with a single word, you know. Aren't you afraid?"

Not at all. But he'd play along. "And what's that?"

"If I tell my mother about the stardust, you'll never be welcomed at court again."

"You said you believed me," Erich said, trying to keep his voice calm.

"I said if I were to believe you. I never said I actually did."

She'd caught him there, entangled him without realizing it. He must admit, he was impressed.

"What's stopping you then?"

"I need you."

Three words, but his body's reaction was visceral. A tight, squeezing sensation filled his chest. When he'd shed his old life, he swore never to let anyone else in again. More for their protection than his. Erich licked his dry lips. But like it or not, he needed Liane.

"Is that so?" he said, voice husky and raw. Unpleasant thoughts floated too close to the surface: memories of blood and shards of bone. He closed his eyes for a moment, willing them to leave.

"Pretend to court me."

His eyes flung open. "Come again?"

"Mother keeps trying to match me with men, and I can't afford the distractions. If she thinks I'm seriously considering you as a suitor, she'll let me be."

And under the guise of courting the princess, he'd have access to the palace without misleading her. If he moved quickly, then he could steal the sword before word reached Father, and he'd avert political entanglement. But he couldn't seem too eager, or else she might grow suspicious.

"I'll agree on one condition," Erich said.

"I don't know if you have leverage for such a thing."

"Humor me."

She crossed her arms and gestured for him to speak.

"We don't make our courtship public. If word reaches my father…" he trailed off.

"Deal. We'll be seen together, let the courtiers speculate, but nothing official. And while we're at it, let's establish some ground rules. No hugging, no kissing, and no sleeping together." She ticked them off one by one on her fingers.

"I'll fight the temptation." He winked.

She sauntered over to him, swinging her hips and a sultry smile on her lips. Grabbing the front of his shirt, she pulled him close, her lips brushing against his ear.

"See that you do. I can be dangerous when I'm crossed." She patted his chin before letting him go.

As perilous as this arrangement was, he couldn't help but be impressed. She had fire in her, and he didn't doubt she would make good on that threat.

"I'll keep that in mind."

"Luzie." Liane signaled the maid, who watched this all transpire. She stepped forward with a piece of paper, a golden wax seal pressed into it.

"What's this?"

"An invitation to tonight's opera. I thought we should get started straight away."

Liane didn't realize it yet, but she'd given him exactly what he needed: that night, he would find the sword.

OPERA INVITATIONS WERE rare and coveted. Much to Ivar's chagrin, Erich was attending solo. If something went wrong, he didn't want Ivar to get hurt. Joining the throng of guests, Erich kept his head down as they entered the grand entrance hall. A chandelier hung from the ceiling and cast yellow-orange light over the crowd as Erich scanned the room for Princess Liane. Before sneaking off to search for the sword, he had to hold up his end of the bargain.

A man in sky-blue and gold livery stepped out onto a balcony that overlooked the crowd and, in a booming voice, declared, "Presenting their majesties, Empress Eveline and Emperor Consort Alexander."

Heads swiveled toward the stairs as the Starweber royal family descended downward. When he'd first arrived at Sundland's court a young, naïve boy, he'd been enthralled by the pageantry of court life. But now, returning to it after years away, he saw it for the hollow spectacle it was. Royalty thrived on such practice, drawing the line between them and everyone else.

Erich was about to turn away in disgust when he noticed Princess Liane trailing behind her family. Her fiery-red hair was twisted up but for a few loose tendrils which brushed her freckled shoulders, exposed by her plunging neckline. When she tossed her head back, laughing at some joke Prince Mathias told, he couldn't tear his eyes away from her.

The dragon rolled, tugging at his chains, its leathery wings extending, threatening to push free as it had been all afternoon since their talk. She must have felt his stare because she caught his gaze from across the room and held it. Heat suffused his skin, spreading out, stoking the flames of desire he must smother if he hoped to get out of here alive. When her ruby lips curled into a mischievous smile, it felt as if she knew what she was doing to him and enjoyed it. No. Breaking their eye contact, he turned away and loosened his collar, feeling as if it were tightening around him like a noose. No distractions tonight; even a seemingly harmless attraction could ruin everything.

Someone grabbed him from behind, spinning him around to face them. On instinct, he reached for his dagger but came up empty. Instead, he knocked Heinrich's hand away, and they glared at one another.

"We meet again, Prince Erich," Prince Consort Heinrich inclined his head slightly, but his posture was too stiff and defensive to be considered anything but offensive.

For his part, it took all of Erich's self-control to not punch him in the nose again. Heinrich was lucky there were witnesses around. Opera guests fluttered past them, some watching with undisguised curiosity. Maybe that's why he'd confronted him in public.

"Do you have something you wanted to say to me?" Erich said, relaxing his shoulders, though every instinct was telling him to fight.

"A friendly warning. You're a foreigner, so you likely haven't heard. The empress' daughters are paying the price for her greed. They call it the Starweber curse. Princess Liane might look normal, but she's often struck by fevers and horrific rashes. As a future king, you need a wife who can bear you healthy sons."

A muscle ticked in Erich's jaw as he envisioned his father saying those same words to him. They were cut from the same cloth. Erich had heard the rumors about both sisters; Aristea was supposedly barren, Liane plagued by fevers. But while he had a low opinion of Heinrich before, he hadn't thought he'd go so far as to insult his wife to a stranger.

"I pity your wife," Erich said, unable to hold his tongue.

Heinrich grasped a handful of Erich's doublet and leaned in close.

"You don't want to make an enemy out of me."

"I'll take my chances." Erich grabbed his shoulders and squeezed hard, his fingers digging into his flesh. If he wanted, he could snap his clavicle, but he held back.

Pain flashed in Heinrich's eyes, and Erich hated that he liked it. He wanted to see him suffer, watch him squirm under his boot as he squashed him like a worm. Erich let go before he gave in to impulse. The dragon wanted that, not him. It hungered for blood, and that feral madness would overcome him one day if he didn't find a cure...

"Prince Erich, I presume," Princess Aristea said, smoothly stepping between them, with a diplomat's smile that didn't reach her eyes.

"And you are Princess Aristea? You're the spitting image of your mother."

"So, I'm told." A small smile curled the corner of her lips.

He needed to get away. Petty small talk made his skin crawl. But as he turned to walk away, he found Liane standing behind him.

"Prince Erich, lovely to see you again." She bowed in greeting.

"This is him, isn't it? Your would-be suitor?" Prince Mathias joined them, and though his tone was light, his eyes raked Erich up and down with the same shrewd assessment he'd cast over him before.

"Surely I'm one of many," Erich replied.

"You'd be surprised." Prince Consort Heinrich cleared his throat, and Erich glared in his direction.

Liane walked over to stand toe to toe with him. A head shorter than him, she had to tilt her head back to meet his gaze. She'd draw a dagger on him; he was sure of it. And a part of him wanted to stand back and let her. But he couldn't risk a spectacle. To search for the sword, he needed the court to be calm.

"Shocking, Princess Liane is an exceptional beauty," Erich said, ignoring the war brewing between the two of them.

She spun to face him, a pink blush coloring her cheeks. She looked from Heinrich to Erich and seemed to reconsider their fight.

"You're too generous with your praise. If your majesty would like, perhaps you could join us in our box this evening."

He couldn't join her because he intended to spend the night searching for the sword, but he couldn't refuse either or risk suspicion.

"Liane, you shock me. Mother will be delighted when she hears about this," Prince Mathias said, then turning to Erich, continued, "though I feel obligated to warn you, she's a lot to handle." Mathias winked.

"I think I'm up to the challenge," Erich replied, offering his bent arm to Liane. Better to play the part of a suitor for now and wait for a chance to sneak away.

She took his proffered arm, and her proximity awakened all his senses. Her scent, her heat, even the casual brush of her hips against his as they walked. His dragon wanted her. For days it'd been too close to the surface: restless and unwieldy. But now, it was intent on Liane. Just another reason to leave as soon as possible, a dragon's obsession was a danger to them both.

Courtiers passing by cast curious glances at them. Their buzzing whispers followed them all the way up the stairs to the second floor leading to the opera boxes. If Artria's court was anything like Sundland, by tomorrow, everyone would be gossiping about a potential royal engagement.

The others went into the box before them, and Liane held him back so they could talk alone in the hall. After the curtain fell behind her siblings, she turned to Erich.

"Thanks for your help back there. I didn't mean for you to get caught up in a family squabble..." Her skin was flushed red, and her fists clenched at her sides. Heinrich's comments, however seemingly mild, had affected her deeply.

"Don't apologize; he deserves worse. Can I tell you a secret?"

She nodded her head warily.

Erich leaned in to whisper in her ear and inhaled the scent of her lavender soap. "The first time we met, I sucker punched him."

Gasping, she pulled back and covered her mouth, but her eyes danced with mirth. "You didn't."

Erich nodded. "I did. Perhaps I'll tell you the story sometime."

"I'd like that." She smiled.

Guards parted the curtains to allow them entry onto the balcony, and then they took their seats. Down on the first floor, the audience shuffled into place, murmuring. When everyone was settled, the house lights were doused, and the spotlights lit to illuminate the red velvet curtains on the stage. They rolled back to reveal a blond opera singer wearing a shimmering golden gown, sewn with some other reflective material that caught the light and cast small beams of light around the stage. When she sang in a mournful soprano, Liane gasped.

From the corner of his eye, he watched her as she leaned forward, eyes transfixed upon the stage. Though he should be plotting his exit, he found himself enraptured by her. Looking at the opera through Liane's eyes, he could see the way the prima donna wove magic with her words, spinning out a tale of love and loss, a struggle between light and dark. But while he tried to focus on the music, she continually drew his gaze. Her every movement entranced him, the way her hands brushed stray hairs behind her ears, or how her brow crinkled when she was concentrating. During sad scenes, her lips parted slightly, as if she wished to sing along. Then, without realizing it, the first half finished, and the curtain closed for intermission.

Liane turned then, catching him staring, and he cleared his throat.

"You enjoy the opera?" he asked.

"Mmm. Very much. Isabella's talent is well renowned, and I've always wanted to hear her sing, but she's never come to Artria before, and I've never left it…" she trailed off.

"You look as if you wanted to say more; why did you stop?

She shook her head. "It's silly."

"Your passion is infectious; I find myself interested in opera for the first time in my life."

She laughed, and the dragon preened at her attentions. This was his doing, distracting him from more important matters. With the arrival of intermission, Erich had a reasonable excuse to step out. He stood up.

"I'm going to step out for some fresh air," Erich said, jabbing a thumb toward the door.

"Don't be too long, or you'll miss the second act," she said.

With a nod, he slipped out the door past the bored guards, then down the stairs and out into the twilight garden before heading straight for the Midnight Tower. There wasn't time to waste. While he'd tried to convince himself otherwise, instinct told him that's where it would be. Now the problem was getting inside.

The tower rose against the starry sky like a pale

monolith. Smooth white limestone without windows meant climbing in was impossible. That was ignoring the two guards standing at the tower's only entrance. If he unleashed the dragon, he could fight his way past them at the risk of exposure, and that was without knowing how many guards were inside. He imagined the inside like an ant hill, thousands of guards swarming, tearing him apart for daring to enter their nest. Alternatively, he could wait until the changing of guards, corner one of them alone and put on their uniform and attempt to sneak in that way. It was still risky, but less so than charging in. A nearby garden provided cover to hide out and wait for his opportunity, and it was there he took shelter.

It wasn't long after he'd settled into the shadows between shrubbery that he heard multiple footsteps crunching on the gravel path in the garden. Tensed and hand aching for his dagger, he waited for them to pass. Two Royal Guards marched past, closely followed by Empress Eveline in her opera gown, alongside the Avatheos, followed by a half a dozen Midnight Guards.

"We weren't expecting your visit, your divinity. Had I known, I would have better prepared," Empress Eveline said.

"The signs are ominous tonight, and I knew it couldn't wait," the Avatheos replied, his sonorous voice echoing through the still garden.

"What did you see?" she asked.

"The Golden Blade is at risk of corruption..." His voice faded as they moved away toward the tower.

Silence stretched out, and they moved out of earshot. He noted how the normally composed Empress Eveline fidgeted, twisting her hands together and gazing anywhere but at the Avatheos. Though it was dangerous, he moved out of his hiding spot to follow at a distance to eavesdrop on their conversation.

"As I told you before, I have seen no changes in the sword. We cannot be certain the wielder has been born." Her voice rose in opposition of her usual calm and collected demeanor.

A guard at the back of the line turned around, and Erich leapt behind a tree to avoid being seen and missed a portion of their conversation. They kept walking, and he waited for a few heartbeats before following again.

"... If we are to stop the rise of darkness, they must have the sword. Have the sword brought to the temple tomorrow night; I would like to examine it myself before the Sun Ceremony," the Avatheos said.

Trinity's blessings. They'd given him a gift. A transport would be easier to steal from than breaking into a fortified tower alone. Erich retreated before he was caught spying, thanking the stars and any goddess who was listening for his good fortune. One more day, and then he'd be free of this wretched city.

When he was certain he wouldn't be spotted, Erich stepped out onto the path and headed back for the theater. The second act had likely already begun, but at least he'd managed to gather information without arousing suspicion.

Then, as Erich mounted the stairs heading back to the second floor, an ear-piercing scream brought him to a halt.

The theater seemed to hold its collective breath before

chaos erupted. Behind him, doors flooded open, and a panicked crowd flooded out. Logic told him to run and save himself, but inside, the dragon roared, nostrils flaring, scenting blood on the air and his thoughts fixated on Liane and an all-encompassing desire to protect.

15

The second act started, but Liane kept feeling her attention wander. There'd never be another chance to see Isabella play Cyra in the Goddess' Veil, and yet she kept glancing over her shoulder, waiting for Erich to return. Where'd he go that took him so long? Should she have followed him rather than watched the play? Her gut told her she could trust him, but her brain had some lingering doubts.

They'd been seen together by the entire court, and that was enough to get the rumor wheel rolling. Now all she had to do was focus on her investigation, but the whole time she'd been trying to watch the opera, she'd felt his gaze burning her up, and she didn't hate it. Even though their arrangement was merely a means to an end, she found herself enjoying his company and grateful for his interventions.

She shook her head; she returned her attention to the opera. Isabella, playing the role of Cyra, sang to her sister, the Nameless Goddess, a mournful refrain begging her to turn away from the darkness that polluted her heart. As the tempo increased, their song turned to a battle as the sisters flung words at one another like knives. The pace continued to rise, reaching a heart-pounding conclusion as the curtain fell before the last act.

Silence stretched out as the orchestral accompaniment faded away, and for one fraught moment, they were all plunged into darkness. As the tension of the moment rose, drums beat steady like a beating heart, building back up as the curtains opened, revealing the final act when Cyra banished her sister beyond the veil to save the world from destruction. She'd seen this play enough times to have memorized it all by heart, but Isabella's performance was different, poignant, visceral, and raw. If only her thoughts weren't filled with Erich, she could better appreciate it.

The spotlight illuminated the stage, but it wasn't as she remembered. The backdrop of a rising sun was the same, but instead of finding Cyra preparing for battle, she lay on the ground, atop a puddle of spreading fake blood. Beneath the beat of drums, confused murmurs rippled through the audience. Standing up, Liane leaned over the edge of the balcony to get a better look. Isabella was lying very still, even as the first notes of her song began. Was this some new artistic interpretation to show Cyra's grief over having to banish her sister?

From the left wing, the actress playing the Nameless Goddess stepped out cautiously; she, too, was not singing. Her foot stepped in the fake blood, and she screamed, stumbling backward.

"Dear Goddess. She's dead!" the Nameless Goddess screamed.

"The moon shall rise and bring death to the sun worshippers!" shouted a voice from above the stage, echoing across the theater.

Liane searched the rafters and saw a shadowy figure leaping from beam to beam before scuttling down a setting backdrop and out of sight. Shock left her still and numb as it too seemed to have caught the entire audience off guard.

Then with a collective gasp, horror erupted in the audience. The conductor screamed from the orchestra pit. Fear rippled through the crowd like a rock thrown into a still pond. They turned at once and, like a wave, rushed for the door, trampling over each other in their panic.

On instinct, Liane looked at Heinrich. He was calm and seemingly unsurprised by the attack. This had been his plan. She looked where she'd last seen the killer. The guards would never catch him, not with a crowd of people rushing out of the theater. She contemplated jumping down and chasing him herself, but she'd likely break both her legs in the attempt.

"Liane, don't even think about it," Aristea warned, grabbing onto her arm. She pulled her away from the ledge and didn't let go.

The curtain partition rustled, and guards grunted. Mathias placed himself between the entry and them while Liane drew her dagger from the holster at her thigh.

"Why do you have a dagger?" Aristea asked.

"Is that what you're worried about right now?" Liane asked her.

Sidling up next to Mathias, they both held their breath. Whoever had killed Isabella could have done it to spark panic, and this might be the start of Heinrich's coup. Liane glanced back at him once more, and he stared back at her placidly. Mathias pulled back the curtain and then lunged forward, only to stop short when he spotted Erich struggling against their guards.

"Thank the Trinity, you're safe. I heard the screams and feared the worst," he said.

His eyes scanned her, as if checking for injuries. Why did he care? They hardly knew one another. He'd come looking for her in the woods as well. And even after that, she thought she had him figured out: a wayward prince, tangled up in the wrong crowd seeking a royal marriage, a convenient lie. Because there'd been dozens of suitors before him, she thought he was like all the rest. None of the others had shown any real concern for her, but this was the second time he'd come to her rescue.

"Let him go," she told her guards.

"No one can approach your majesties. Not until the empress gives us the order to stand down."

"They're right. Go with them. I'm satisfied knowing you're safe."

Her stomach flip-flopped. It was likely an act, but what if it wasn't? That didn't change anything. She'd made a vow, and she swore to keep it.

Guards encircled them and escorted them out. As they passed by Erich, she turned one last time, and he gave her a reassuring smile. Insulated by guards, she couldn't see the crowd as they pushed through, but she felt their fear, heard the panic in their voices as guards shouted for order. Outside the theater, the guards guided them into one of the many hidden passageways beneath the palace. No one spoke as their footsteps echoed against the stone floor and ceiling, rattling around in her skull. There'd never been a time in her life when they'd needed an emergency escape, but they were being escorted to their underground safe room.

As a girl, her mother had shown her the way there and taught her in case of an emergency, she was to stay calm, follow the guards, wait for news. Mother and Father had been in another box. Had they been escorted ahead of them, or had an assassin crept upon them while attention was on the terrified mob? Fear tightened her throat as they wound through familiar twisting passageways.

There were guards outside the door, and after their escorts exchanged passwords, they let them inside, where Father paced in the dimly lit room. When he saw them, Father pulled Aristea, Mathias, and her into his comforting embrace. Overwhelmed by fear, tears welled in Liane's eyes, and she fought them back, unwilling to let them fall. If Mother wasn't here and they'd been taken to the safe room, stars above... her stomach churned.

"Thank the stars above you're all safe," he said, squeezing them tighter.

"Where's Mother?" Aristea asked, voice trembling.

"I'm not sure; she stepped out right before the attack."

"Where'd she go?" Liane asked.

"The Avatheos summoned her," Father said.

Those words hung on the air, ripe with portent. Had he foreseen an attack and come to warn them too late? What if... what if...

"Mother has her guards; there's no need to worry," Mathias said, squeezing Liane's shoulder.

"As your older sisters, we should be the ones reassuring you," Aristea said, arms crossed over her chest as she stared at the door.

"You cannot shoulder all the kingdom's burdens." He wrapped an arm around Aristea's shoulder.

But if…

Liane looked over at Heinrich, anger and resentment threatening to boil over inside her. If she'd hesitated and he'd…

Clapping his hands together, Father said, "No need to worry. Your mother single-handedly defeated rebel armies; she'll be fine."

With muttered agreement, they huddled around their father. Aristea and Liane sat beside him, and Mathias sat at their back. Heinrich, sitting opposite them, accepted a glass of wine from their servant. When they offered Liane one, she refused, knowing it would sour on her tongue. She couldn't look at Heinrich without wanting to lash out at him, but she couldn't let go of her death grip on her dagger either.

Without windows or a clock, time distorted, and minutes stretched on like hours. No one spoke but for curt replies. Though they tried to distract themselves, all their eyes kept drifting back to the entrance. A sick, twisting sensation coiled in her stomach. Mother was competent with a sword and cautious, at times infuriatingly so. But Captain Rosen's fears of stardust's transformative abilities kept swirling in her head.

Cyra, please keep her safe, Liane prayed, eyes skyward.

When there was a knock at the door, everyone's heads turned, and, holding their collective breaths, they waited as guards exchanged passwords. The door creaked open, and Mother stepped in, hair frazzled but otherwise unharmed. They shot to their feet, swarming her as she threw her arms open, welcoming them into her embrace. The smell of her lilac perfume and the soft caress of her hand against her brow soothed Liane's troubled heart.

"Blessed Starlight," Mother said and, taking each of them in turn, planted a kiss on their foreheads before Father enfolded her in his embrace. They held one another for a moment, foreheads pressed against one another, neither speaking.

"These are grave times we live in," the Avatheos said.

Liane had focused on Mother and hadn't noticed him gliding in after her.

"What have you seen?" Aristea asked. It reminded Liane of how the Avatheos had pressed her to reveal her vision. She resisted the urge to look at him and instead stared at a worn spot on the carpet.

"Dark omens. Tonight, the bones showed me the crown and blood. We're on the precipice of another struggle for power."

The atmosphere shifted, and a prickle raced up her spine before radiating down her arms. Unwillingly, her eyes flicked over to Heinrich. He sat in their midst, calm and perfectly poised, a small, smug smile tugging at the corner of his lips. Liane gripped her dagger tighter, and Mother squeezed her free hand. Liane blinked at her. Did she suspect as well what Heinrich was plotting? Surely tonight had been a message to unsettle them before unleashing civil war on the capital.

"This was a warning. It wasn't an accident that their target was the singer playing Cyra," Father said.

"I fear war might be upon us," Mother said.

Liane held her breath, waiting for Mother to turn and point an accusing finger at Heinrich. But instead, Mathias surprised her by kneeling before the Avatheos, head tipped, palms upturned in supplication. What was he doing? Now wasn't the time for this; they had to stop Heinrich...

"Mathias...?" Mother said cautiously.

"I've made my decision. I'll go," Mathias said, his gaze focused on the Avatheos.

"I foresee a dangerous journey ahead, but Her light shall guide you," the Avatheos intoned as he made the sign of the star above Mathias' head.

"Mathias, what is he talking about?" Mother asked.

Mathias wouldn't turn to look at them but remained bowing before the Avatheos.

"I was going to wait and speak with you all before deciding, but tonight has made my decision. I'm going north to find a way to destroy the elves."

Mother made a strangled sound before covering her mouth with her hand. It was a suicide mission. No one who went beyond the border returned. If corruption magic didn't kill him first, then the elves would. Panic crested, rising like a dark tide. Why was he doing this now? The elves were always a threat. The real danger was sitting right there, drinking wine as if a woman hadn't just died.

"What are you talking about?" Liane cried.

"You heard them; they said the moon shall rise. The elves came here to send us a message. They'll never stop until they're destroyed." Mathias turned to face her, unshed tears in his eyes.

Liane shook her head to free herself of this madness before looking to Mother for help.

Her expression was fury carved in stone as she glared at the Avatheos.

"This is your doing. My son—"

"I saw it in a vision. He has been chosen by the goddess to pierce the heart of our enemies."

"I'm a man now, and this is my choice. For the good of the kingdom," Mathias said, grasping Mother's shoulder.

She shook her head, as if she would try and stop him, but no words came out. Father wrapped an arm around her shoulder, keeping her close. Aristea stood behind them, silent tears rolling down her cheeks.

Her secret burned in her chest, threatening to engulf her. These attacks weren't random elf attacks; they were part of Heinrich's plot. He'd staged this to confuse them and send them chasing ghosts.

"Don't you think it's strange the elves appeared now, after years of silence? How did they get into the palace? How did they know to kill the singer tonight? There's someone inside the palace, someone who would benefit from the chaos they attempt to sow." Liane turned to look at Heinrich.

"What are you insinuating, that I have something to do with this?" Heinrich said, without rising from his seat.

"I know about your bastard child and that you're plotting to overthrow the throne." The words burst out of her, and she was glad for it. She was tired of holding back, biting her tongue, and letting him hurt her family.

Her declaration sucked the air out of the room, and her family stared at her in stunned silence.

Aristea cleared her throat. "Liane, I know you're upset about Mathias, but you can't blame Heinrich for this."

"I saw the letters. His lover told him she'd given him an heir." Liane turned to face Aristea; she had to see the truth, or else he would keep hurting her.

"I wrote those letters," Aristea said.

Liane blinked. She couldn't have heard that correctly. "What?"

"The ones in the hidden beneath the false bottom of his desk drawer?"

Wrong. It couldn't be...

"You don't have to lie for him. I know he's working with the stardust smugglers. You don't have to make excuses for him."

"They're letters I wrote while we were courting. I was hopeful we'd conceive and mend the rifts in the kingdom through our union. But as more and more time passed, and it didn't happen, I became discouraged, and I burned the letters..."

Heinrich stood up and came over to grab her shoulders, bringing her close. Not in a comforting way, but possessively. Liane's skin prickled with anger as he gave her a smarmy smile.

"I managed to salvage it from the flames and kept the rest as a memento of our hopeful youth. When Cyra blesses us with a child, perhaps your doubts will be erased, Liane."

Aristea kept her head down, not meeting anyone's eyes in the room. Liane looked to her parents and brother, but no one would look at her. This was madness. How could they not see Heinrich manipulating Aristea in front of their very eyes?

"This isn't time for squabbling. We're stronger as a family, together," Mother said.

"Your mother's right. We can hope for the best, but we must prepare for the worst. Since the dukes are in the capital, I'll call a parliament meeting first thing tomorrow," Father said.

"We'll need allies outside the empire. I shall write to the southern country," Aristea said, sniffling slightly.

They chattered together, making plans for war against the elves, ignoring her and everything she'd said.

Mathias came over and pulled her into a bear hug, and against the top of her head, he said, "Don't worry, I'll be fine. I've gotten out of worse scraps before."

She pulled away and felt as if her head were full of cotton. They were doing it again, covering up what they didn't want to see. Mathias would walk into certain death, and they'd hold their fake smiles as Heinrich stabbed them in the back. She had to do something. But the small scrap of evidence she'd had was dismissed, and she was no closer to finding his mistress and bastard than she had been days before.

"And I think we should offer a marital alliance to Sundland as well," Mother said.

Liane's head snapped up. "You said who I married was my choice!"

"Aren't the two of you rather close?" Heinrich sneered.

"We've just met recently. I can't decide to marry someone so soon..."

"If we're going to war with the elves, then Sundland has the military power we need. Their support could mean the difference between winning and losing a war."

They'd turned her lie against her, but if she fought too hard against it, Mother would either force her to marry Erich despite her protests or find someone worse. By trying to accuse Heinrich outright, she'd tipped her hand too soon. If she had any hope of salvaging her investigation, she needed Mother to think her compliant.

"You're right; let's propose a marriage alliance between Sundland and us."

16

Fear gnawed at Erich's entrails as he watched Liane walk away and the dragon pushed against his bindings. He didn't think it would latch onto her quite so quickly, but what else could explain this madness that had overcome him? It wasn't like him to run headlong into danger. It wasn't his problem if she was besieged, or if an assassin waited for her in the shadows. Yet instinct had overridden common sense, and he'd rushed to her. This was how it started, wanting to protect. Then it transformed into possessive need, and in dragon form, hunger and desire were too similar. Never again.

He needed to focus. Get the sword, get out. After tomorrow, he'd forget they'd ever met. Eventually, the desire would fade...

"You'll need to come with us, your majesty," a palace guard said.

His empty hand twitched. They were asking nicely. No

cause for concern. But the dragon rolled, testing his bindings, attempting escape to follow Liane, and he tightened his hold, doubling the mental chains binding it. Flanked on both sides, he followed the guards down the stairs and into the entryway, where panicked groups of courtiers clustered, chattering, eyes rolling like nervous cattle. Their fear stank up the air and raised panic in him, clawing at the back of his throat. He hated this feeling; he was a cornered animal ready to strike.

"What is the meaning of this? Let us go!" shouted a red-faced lord, his clothing torn, likely in the stampede.

"Everyone must stay together for their own safety," a guard said.

"I heard an elf killed Cyra. Have elves gotten into the palace?" a woman shrieked.

"Please remain calm. There are no elves in the palace."

"Who would dare do such a thing?" another man shouted.

"We are investigating. There is nothing to worry about," they repeated their refrain.

A line of guards blocking the exit pushed the group forward, forcing them down a long hallway that spilled out onto the grand hall, and as much as he hated crowds, he stayed in the center. There it was safer to blend in. Doors closed behind them with an echoing clang. Erich's skin twitched as voices buzzed in his ears like swarming flies.

"I heard one was at the masquerade," muttered a woman.

"My servant says one of them attacked Princess Liane

during the hunt; that's why they took her to the temple," said her male companion.

The woman gasped. "What are Empress Eveline and the Midnight Guard doing if they cannot keep elves out..."

He hadn't seen who killed the singer, but he'd seen the man who'd attacked Liane. Not an elf, but a mere mortal. What made them assume it was the elves? Was it bias, or had it been the killer's intent? Whoever they were, they'd done it to incite panic. The crowd was already brimming with restless fear, and now they were kindling waiting for the match.

Pacing courtiers brushed against him, and he tensed, holding back the urge to lash out at them. If they didn't let him out soon, he might go mad. Surely, they wouldn't keep them here long, just long enough to calm the mania. It was too late to stop rumors from flooding the capital, but they could at least soothe the mob before they incited the entire city.

Doors opened at the far end of the room, and the crowd surged toward it, grasping at the guards as they entered. They pushed most of them back, with shields making a blockade as they selected ten people to leave. The optimist might have seen that and thought they were letting people go in groups, but being a pessimist, he suspected otherwise.

Unable to stand still, he paced the perimeter of the room, searching for an unprotected exit. Guards watched him; he felt their stares follow him around the room. Remain calm, he repeated his mantra. He was being conspicuous. Better to sit, wait and watch. A few courtiers rested on the double staircase, and there was room near them. If he sat down up there, he could survey the room.

He took a seat and watched the door that last opened. Minutes dragged on, and they didn't come back to release anyone else. When it did open, the original ten returned, and ten more were taken. One woman, tears streaking her white face powder, fainted in a man's arms. As he'd feared, they weren't letting them go; they were interrogating them. Not a problem; he'd endured torture and interrogation before. If he must, he'd use the allure to lie his way out of there.

Group by group, they took people out and then returned them. With each new group, the whispers grew louder, rippling outward. A young man broke away from a group at the foot of the stairs to whisper in an older man's ear, a few steps below Erich.

"They're using some stone. If it touches one of the corrupted, it will illuminate," the man said.

Ice coursed through his veins. A rune stone? A shaman he met in the eastern desert used it to test the magical aptitude of his apostles. They were extremely rare and impossible to deceive. If it were real, it would expose his corruption.

"You don't think the killer is here, do you?" a young woman squeaked.

"My gran is from the north, and she said elves can shape-shift. One might be hiding among us, in plain sight," replied the young lord.

They cast suspicious gazes around the room, and a few flicked in his direction. The last thing he needed was a terrified courtier pointing fingers at him. Humans didn't think when they were scared, and outsiders were easy targets. There were other loners, like himself, scattered across the hall, and it wouldn't take long before they gathered them all up for questioning. Erich shifted in his seat, debating moving, but it wouldn't make a difference while they were all trapped in this tinder box waiting to catch fire.

Someone from the group below him got up and made toward the guards. They'd turned on him quicker than he expected. Sizing up the guards behind him, Erich considered fighting his way out, and the dragon raised its head, stirring at the prospect of bloodshed. Beyond the guards was a window that looked out onto the night sky. He could try escaping out of it as he and Fritz had the night of the masquerade, but this time he wouldn't have Fritz's magic to help him.

A hand fell on his shoulder, and Erich spun around, raising his arm in a defensive gesture, and met Prince Mathias' grinning expression. He'd been so preoccupied with plotting his escape, that he hadn't heard him sneak up behind him.

"Can I speak with you a moment?" Prince Mathias asked.

Was he working with the Midnight Guards? Prince Mathias was at eye level with him, even standing a step below him, and much heavier than him. His wide stance meant he wouldn't be easy to knock over, and without using his dragon strength, he wouldn't want to fight a man with tree trunk arms bare-handed.

"Now seems like a strange time," Erich said slowly.

"Time isn't on my side, unfortunately."

"May I ask what can't wait?"

"Liane."

The Midnight Guards were behind Prince Mathias. There wasn't time for clarification. Better to trust and hope for the best.

"Lead the way." Erich gestured toward him.

Then turned to walk down the steps and the Midnight Guard blocked their way. Upon recognizing him, the guards bowed.

"Forgive me, your majesty. But we have orders to test all guests."

"I will personally vouch for Prince Erich of Sundland. If your captain has questions, direct them to me. Understood?" he commanded with a smile.

They bowed deeper and, with a hand clamped on his shoulder, Mathias led Erich out. Neither of them spoke as they strode down the empty hallway and into a private room. It smelled like Lord Endland's study: leather and cedar. When he was a boy, he and Lord Endland would sit by the fire together in squishy armchairs, drinking warm cider. It was one of those rarer moments in his life when he'd been at ease. The room had the same sort of feeling of comfort, but he wasn't safe, not while he remained cursed in Artria. Those memories were better left amongst the cold ashes of the fire he'd burned them in than let them leave him vulnerable. Erich frowned. He was in what appeared to Prince Mathias' office, but why had he brought him here?

"Nervous?" Prince Mathias chuckled.

"Not unless you think I should be?" Erich replied, relaxing his posture.

Mathias studied him for a moment.

"Please have a seat," he said, gesturing to a plush leather chair. After pouring two glasses of wine, Mathias offered one to Erich, and he took it with a muttered thanks.

"You wanted to speak to me about Liane?" Erich asked.

"I know you're not really courting my sister." Mathias rested his glass on the arm of the chair and met Erich's gaze unflinching.

Direct like his sister, but was he bluffing? Erich also set down his glass. Two choices lay before him: use his allure to assure Prince Mathias of his ardent desire for his sister, or tell the truth, knowing soon Erich would leave her and Artria behind. Without knowing his intentions, he wasn't ready to decide which route to take. It wasn't too late for him to toss him to the guards for testing.

"What makes you say that?" Erich said, deciding to call his bluff.

"I know my sister, and she's been too keen with you. Tonight, my mother proposed a marriage alliance between our kingdoms, and Liane agreed."

Did he suspect Erich's power, or was he too bluffing? Erich couldn't be sure. But Empress Eveline moved quicker than he anticipated. No matter. He'd be gone soon...

"Maybe I'm different."

"Are you?" Mathias arched a brow.

"Is this some attempt at scaring me away from your sister?"

"If you're easily frightened, you're not a good match.

No." He shook his head. "I don't know what scheme she's roped you into, and frankly, I don't want to know."

"Then what is it you want?"

"Before I ask, let me tell you a story." Mathias swirled his glass as he stared into it. "We don't like to talk about it. But yesterday wasn't the first time Liane's gotten lost in the forest. I was young when it happened, and I remember little apart from how scared my parents were and how she changed when she returned: burning up with a fever, saying the forest was calling her, that she had to go back and finish what they started... Crazy, right?"

"Fevered hallucinations," Erich said, taking a sip of his wine.

But he knew that wasn't it. Felt it in his bone and marrow. Erich tried not to appear too interested, but he thought of the dual-colored stag and its request to protect her, and tonight he'd run to her side without a second thought. Dangerous. Even if one of the ancients commanded it, she'd suffer with him at her side. He was poison.

Mathias studied him without speaking, and feeling the pressure of the growing silence, Erich spoke first.

"You're rather forthcoming with family secrets."

"Liane wandered into a corrupted place, and you took an arrow carved with runes for her. I think I can trust you with this secret." He winked.

Uneasiness slithered up his spine. He didn't want their trust or their secrets.

"What do you want?" Erich asked, growing agitated.

"Protect her, stay by her side, save her from the darkness closing in around her."

He should say no; he must say no. He never could do as he asked, even if he weren't here to steal their sword. But he saw the sincerity in Mathias' eyes, the palpable fear, and he couldn't help himself. He lied.

"I will."

17

Humidity rushed in as Liane opened her window, coating her in a thick, sticky heat, and a thin sheen of moisture wet her brow. Three days before the Sun Ceremony, which marked the start of summer, and she was already sweating before sunrise. Any other time she would have escaped her apartment and sought relief outdoors beneath a shady tree, but her self-imposed exile prevented it. The night before, when the family had said goodbye to Mathias, she'd refused to participate. He couldn't leave until she said goodbye. It was tradition.

A knock at the door disrupted her ruminations. It had to be Mathias. A part of her wished he'd change his mind and stay safely in the palace, but she'd known that was naïve. As a last resort, she'd ordered Luzie and the guards to turn away all visitors. She couldn't keep him in the palace forever, but she just needed to delay him a few more days, just long enough to prove Heinrich's guilt. The elves weren't what they needed to worry about. The danger was much closer to home.

Mathias knocked harder.

"Liane, I know you're awake," he said.

She didn't move and feared breathing would give her position away. If she didn't acknowledge him, it didn't count.

Mathias pretended to be brave, and he wanted to help, but rushing into certain death wasn't helping anyone. She couldn't let him do it. When he was a kid, he used to come to her to soothe his skinned knees and begged her to watch him practice with his wooden sword. She knew best, and he needed her to protect him from himself.

Knock. Knock. Knock.

Growing in urgency, louder and louder. Liane pulled her knees up to her chest. She was doing this for him. The beat sped up as he slammed his fist against the door over and over and over. A few minutes, a couple hours, and he'd give up for today. Delay his trip until he could convince her it was the right thing to do. But she'd never agree. She'd lost someone she'd loved before, and it tore her up inside. She couldn't lose him too.

Then the knocking stopped.

Liane stared at the door. He wouldn't leave.

"I'd prefer to say this to your face," Mathias said, voice muffled, but his sigh was audible. "I wanted you to know I've always looked up to you. No one is as strong and stubborn and amazing as you are. I love you, Liane. Take care of yourself."

A long pause. He was joking. That didn't count.

"It doesn't count!" she shouted.

But there was no reply. He hadn't even asked her before making his decision. She didn't know the Avatheos had asked him. Why hadn't their mother stopped him or Father or Aristea? They were all going to stand by while he died? Tears blurred her vision, and she tilted her head up to stem the flow.

"Very funny, Mat." Knock, please knock again, she begged the door.

But the knocking didn't resume, and a yawning silence stretched on in its wake.

Leaning out the open window, she looked down at the courtyard, praying she was wrong, and as the seconds turned to minutes, a small flicker of hope burned in her chest. He wouldn't leave; he wouldn't. He couldn't. She chanted the words repeatedly as if her own stubbornness might cast a spell over them both. Then a stable hand marched out with a black war horse, Mathias' horse. Liane's heart lurched. No. No. No. No...

She had to stop him. She rushed for the door and, by throwing it open, startled her guards. Then without explanation, she ran past them, her bare feet slapping on polished wooden floors. Down the passageway, she flew, and when she reached the stairs, she skipped steps, her feet hardly touching the ground. In the grand hall, she knocked over a servant carrying a pile of missives, sending them scattering across the marble, and she shouted a hurried apology before bursting out into the courtyard.

Yards away, the gate was closing, and Mathias passed through it. Each breath she took felt as if she were being stabbed, and even if she tried, she wouldn't have reached him in time. Liane's knees buckled beneath her as tears poured down her face. She was too late; he was gone, and she hadn't gotten a chance to say goodbye.

Mathias had changed. No, Mathias had grown. While she remained suspended in time, chasing ghosts of her past, he'd become a soldier ready to die for the empire. And what had she accomplished, after years of chasing smugglers and dealers... nothing.

"Liane, you're still in your nightgown." Mother knelt beside her and squeezed her shoulders.

Sobs wracked her body, but she didn't care. She was a fool, a pigheaded fool. Someone wrapped a coat around her shoulders, and she looked up, expecting another family member, but saw Erich instead.

"What are you doing here?" Liane asked, scrubbing tears from her eyes.

"Come to ask you for a morning ride," he said.

"I'm not in the mood."

"Maybe you should go with him," Mother said.

Liane blinked at her.

"You don't want to make the same mistake twice, do you?" Erich asked, extending his hand to her.

"What do you mean?"

"Mathias will wait for you. But not for long," Father said, coming over to put an arm around Mother's shoulder.

"Go get changed. You can't ride in your nightgown," Aristea added.

They'd all come out to say goodbye, ready to make sacrifices for the good of the kingdom, but more surprising was they'd plotted with Erich as well. She stared at him sidelong, not sure if she should be grateful or annoyed. In the end, she settled on grateful. If her family hadn't done this, she might never have seen Mathias again. Because of the nature of his mission, he had to leave in secret to not alert their enemies before he arrived.

Dashing the last of her tears, Liane headed back inside, where Luzie waited with her riding coat and boots. When she'd finished changing, she met up with Erich and her guards. He helped her into the saddle, and his hands lingered a little too long on her waist. Their eyes met, and a tingle raced up her spine as the lines between real and fake blurred.

Once they were in their saddles, Liane tried to push Erich from her mind: relegating him to a position similar to a guard, a shadow along her periphery. But as they rode through the stirring city and out of the northern gate, she found him impossible to ignore as her gaze kept coming back to him. Why had he offered to help, to strengthen their ruse, or to try and seduce her?

They crested a hill after leaving the city, and beyond, Mathias waited, standing beside his horse. Liane jumped out of her saddle and raced over to him, throwing herself into his arms as he crushed her in a rib-cracking embrace. She balled her hands into the fabric of his tunic, taking steadying breaths to calm herself, not wanting to fall apart in front of him.

"Promise me you won't do anything stupid out there," Liane said against his chest.

"I'm always careful, aren't I?" Mathias said against the top of her head.

"Says the man who frequently got caught stealing sweets from the kitchen."

"My stealth has much improved since I was six."

She snorted, and they pulled apart as she grasped his large, calloused hands, which swallowed hers whole.

"You're allowed to be happy, Liane. You don't have to hold on to the past anymore." He nodded his head toward Erich, who stood back a few feet with the guards and the horses.

"I am happy."

"He's a good man, and he'd be good for you if you'd give him a chance." She resisted the urge to look back at Erich. It wasn't as if she could tell Mathias it was fake. She didn't want him to worry.

"Never thought I'd be getting relationship advice from my little brother." She punched him lightly on the arm.

"I have a lot of sage advice to dispense. Next, we meet, I'll impart even more wisdom upon you." He tussled her hair, and she swiped at him, but he dodged her easily. When they were together again, she'd tell him the truth, and they'd laugh about it together. And she must believe he'd return; her fears for him were just that: fear.

In the stillness of the early morning, even the birds dared not make a sound. Mathias mounted his horse once more.

"Until we meet again," Mathias said with a half wave, and a crooked smile.

"I'm proud of you, Mathias!" Liane shouted as he rode away.

"How could you not? I'm rather impressive." He tossed over his shoulder.

She kept waving even as his back was turned, while he trotted down the road, growing smaller and smaller until he disappeared over another rise. Long after he was gone, she stayed rooted to that spot watching as the sun rose up on the horizon. After a while, Erich joined her, and they stood comfortably in silence together.

"I'm glad you decided to say goodbye. At times it seems easier not to, but it never is; it only gets harder the more time passes..." Erich said.

"Who did you leave behind? Family... or a lover?" Her skin flushed as soon as she asked. It was none of her business, but she couldn't help but be curious.

"My uncle, the man who raised me."

"Is he beyond the veil...?"

Erich shook his head. "Alive, but I haven't seen him in more than six years. We had a disagreement..."

There was more to the story he wasn't telling, but she thought she understood as her mind inevitably turned to Elias. She'd been so mad at him before he died, and by the time she'd come to her senses, it was too late to say goodbye. At times she wondered if the regret over that fueled her more than her thirst for vengeance.

From the corner of her eye, Liane studied Erich. Sunlight illuminated his tanned skin, catching the flecks of gold in his brown eyes and turning them molten. She should tell him about Mother's proposed treaty and end their fake relationship before it got out of hand. But the truth was, she still needed him. With Ludwig injured and assassins closing in, she was afraid to go alone.

Her investigation inside the palace had stalled, and there were answers to be found in the city. Mother wouldn't let her leave without cause, and seeing how they reacted the night before, finding evidence of Heinrich's plotting wasn't enough.

But she had the arrow, and if she could prove Heinrich had hired the killer, maybe then they'd believe her.

"I have a favor to ask," Liane said.

"And what's that?"

"Come with me to the guild district."

"Fancy doing some shopping?"

"No. There's someone I need to talk to."

18

She'd never met Master Maisel before that day. Typically, Ludwig did the information gathering. Small, gilded arrows gleamed on his lapel, denoting his role as head of the Fletcher's Guild, and the over-large peacock feather tucked into the velvet band trembled as he sat across from her.

"I must say, your majesty, your visit was unexpected. Normally you send your guard. What was his name again?" Master Maisel said as he removed his hat and uncovered thin, greasy strands of hair that failed to disguise his red, balding head.

When they'd started investigating stardust, they'd agreed to keep her identity a secret from informants like Maisel. Of course, someone known for collecting secrets would've figured it out, but she wasn't going to give him confirmation, not for free.

"I appreciate you seeing me on short notice," Liane said, hands folded in her lap, delivering her best impression of a poised princess, ignoring his remark about Ludwig.

"How can I be of service to your majesty?"

Liane set a jewelry box between them. She'd snuck back into the palace to retrieve it. As soon as she'd found the arrow, she wanted to meet with Maisel, but between the attack in the forest, and the opera last night, she couldn't easily escape. Alternatively, if she summoned Maisel, a notorious dealer of secrets to the palace, people would talk, and word would reach Heinrich. She'd already tipped her hand, and she was racing against the clock as it was. Heinrich had likely hidden his mistress and bastard as it were, but if she could link him to her assassination attempt, then even Mother couldn't look the other way.

Maisel leaned forward eagerly in his seat as she cracked open the lid and turned it to face him. The strange arrow sat atop a small fortune in jewels and trinkets. She hoped Maisel knew who had made it, and that the bribe would buy his silence. Liane had her own suspicions about the arrow, but she wouldn't say them outright. Proper princesses didn't know anything about corruption or forbidden magics.

"I'm looking to replicate this, and I've heard none are more skilled than you."

Bushy brows furrowed, he picked up the arrow to examine it with a small eyeglass. Turning it over, he traced his forefinger along the shaft, and the faded runic etchings, which no longer glowed.

"Where did you find this?" he asked, looking at her through the lens which comically enlarged his right eye.

"I found it in the forest."

"There's a rumor that an elf attacked you in the forest. Is it true?"

"There was an incident with a man sick with the withering, if that's what you're referring to," Liane said.

Let him chew on that for a while and hopefully distract from elf rumors. If the people knew what she'd seen in the ruins, it would incite panic. She still didn't know where the elves fit in with Heinrich's plan, but she wouldn't be the harbinger of chaos. She'd stop Heinrich before it came to that.

"I see." Master Maisel rolled the arrow between his thumb and forefinger.

"Would you be able to recreate it?" Liane prompted.

"I think we both know this cannot be made in the city." Master Maisel set the arrow back in the box and shoved it toward her.

"I thought you were the best. Perhaps I should have gone to Master Auerbach instead." Liane motioned to stand, and he threw out his arms to stop her.

"There's no need to be hasty!"

Liane sat back in her chair and fixed him with her stare. A bead of sweat dotted his forehead, and he fidgeted with items on the desk. He knew something but was afraid to say it...

"Is there something you can do for me then?"

"As I said, nothing I can do." He said, putting emphasis on the I, as his gaze shifted around the empty room.

Liane tossed a bag of geld onto the table to accompany the gems. "What do you know?"

"Have you shown this cursed object to the Midnight

Guard? Such a rare and precious object must fetch a handsome price."

Darkness blighted bastard. Through gritted teeth, Liane removed a gold chain with an emerald pendant from around her neck and laid it on the table as well.

Maisel licked his lips. "This much will buy my silence. As for the rest, I'd be honored if you commissioned a set of arrows and a bow."

"Consider it done." She would empty all her coffers if she must.

"The arrow is elven make, as I'm sure you know."

She didn't know, and her surprise must have shown on her face because Maisel's slimy smile broadened.

"Yes, I realized that. But how did a man get a hold of it?" she said, tapping the top of the table.

The corners of his mouth twisted up in a wicked grin.

"The Onyx Gang is able to get all sorts of things for a price."

Her stomach twisted. Did Maisel know all this time and hadn't told her or Ludwig? Why hold back the information? Unless he was being paid off as well...

"I'm aware of the Onyx Gang's dealings; honestly, Maisel, I'm disappointed you've not given me anything I don't already have. Perhaps I should go elsewhere after all." She reached for her bag of geld, but he stood up.

"Wait," he said as he stroked his thin beard, his eyes darting between the bag on the table and the door.

"Someone is paying off the City Watch to set the Onyx Gang free."

"I'm aware. Do you know who it is?"

"If I knew, then I'd retire to an island off Soccicio's coast."

"Then what do you know?"

He paced slightly back and forth, tugging on his beard, as if having a debate with himself or perhaps wracking his brain for information.

"Kroll Apothecary in the Velvet District. They've been using it as a front to sell drugs and other things. If you want to know who sold that arrow, I'd go there."

"Thank you, Master Maisel. I won't forget this," Liane said, snatching up her arrow for safe keeping.

She left his office, pockets lighter but with a proper lead. When she exited his office, Erich waited in the foyer of the guild building. He'd been surprisingly acquiescent, joining her on her little detours. She expected compliance from her guards, but Erich kept surprising her with his willingness to help.

"Get what you came for?" Erich asked, gesturing for her to step out the door first.

Her guards were waiting on the top stoop. They'd stop her if she suggested a visit to the Velvet District. It was a poorer district where seedy taverns and brothels flourished. Not a place for a princess. Ludwig would have followed her there with minimal grumbling, but her replacements weren't as willing. She'd have to find a way to escape them, and for that, she needed Erich's cooperation.

"There's one more place I need to visit. I hope that's all right..." she said.

"Princess, is this a ploy to spend more time together?" He smirked, and her insides flip-flopped traitorously.

"Don't flatter yourself. This is business, remember?" She turned away from him so he wouldn't see her blush.

They headed down the crowded Guild Street, her front guard carving a path through the pedestrians, and her rear guard covering them from behind. The Guild District emptied out onto Starlight Square, a central hub of the city. It was lined by inns and taverns and favored by pilgrims coming to visit the temple. With the Sun Ceremony days away, an influx of them made the square more crowded than usual. Barkers shouted, attempting to lure people in by offering good ale and meat pies. The chaos would have made for a convenient escape, but they were too far from the Velvet District, and her guards would catch up with her before she got very far.

Three roads led off of Starlight Square: Guild Street where she'd come from, Temple Street heading eastward, then Sun Marketplace to the south, where various shops and vendors sold their wares. A trickle of pedestrians wandered that way, looking to purchase trinkets and religious relics. It was the perfect escape route, crowded and lined by buildings and crooked alleyways she could escape through.

"Let's go here." Liane pointed down the lane.

"Then you do want to shop," Erich teased.

"I guess I do," Liane said as she took the lead, passing her front guard.

She misjudged her ability to push through a crowd. That, too, was usually Ludwig's job, and an oncoming pedestrian ran into her, knocking her into Erich's arms. He caught her with a hand at her waist, and warmth radiated from his touch, flushing her all over. With a cough,

Liane stood back up and smoothed the imaginary wrinkles on her dress.

"Thank you," she mumbled.

"Better be careful. Why not lean on me?" he said, offering his bent arm.

She shouldn't, but she did it anyway. Threading her arm with his, they perused shop windows together. They stopped in front of a bakery window, and as she eyed cakes dusted with sugar and jam-filled delights, she was tempted to go in and sample them. But she tore her eyes away and continued down the road until they passed beneath a swinging sign of a bookseller, one she frequented in disguise. They sold a salacious novel series about a woman forced to marry a wicked king that Liane adored. More importantly, though, their backdoor led to the alleyway and was her means of escaping her guards.

"Did you want to go inside?" Erich asked, nodding at the bookshop.

"You read my mind," Liane said.

Unlinking their arms, she went in first. Stacks of books, overflowing shelves, and piles on the floor, gave it a cluttered, cozy interior. It forced them to wander through the aisles one by one, Erich close behind her and one guard behind him. The second waited outside. The cramped bookshop was too crowded for them both to follow. In the farthest, dustiest corner, the smell of old books enveloped her like an old friend. If only she had time to wander about, picking up books at her leisure. But there wasn't time for pleasantries. As she pretended to scan the shelves, she eyed the door to the back room, waiting for her chance to make her escape. But Erich's scorching gaze followed her, making it impossible to sneak away.

"You're staring," Liane remarked without looking at him.

"You puzzle me."

Liane glanced over her shoulder. "Is that another line? Still trying to convince me to marry you?"

"Not a line, just an observation. You've dragged me across this city and beyond, and I've gone along willingly, and I'm wondering if you've enchanted me somehow."

She scoffed and rolled her eyes, but heat coiled in her stomach. To avoid looking at him, she pretended to be absorbed in hunting for a book, then she noticed the next installment in the Wicked King series on the top shelf. Standing on tiptoes, she reached for it, the tips of her fingers brushing it but failing to grasp it. Liane looked for a step stool, but before she could, Erich leaned past her. With one hand braced on the shelf, he pinned her between him and it. His chest was firm, and she imagined what it would feel like to run her hands over those chiseled planes. It should be criminal to be this handsome and untouchable. What cruel torture had she concocted for herself to make him off-limits?

Erich stepped back and handed her the book with a sultry smile. *Remember your mission, don't get distracted*, she chided herself.

"Thanks," Liane said as she took the book. She idly flipped through the pages, but her eyes kept flicking back to him. And how could she not? This close, she could appreciate every line of his square jaw and the molten gold flecks in his brown eyes.

"Now you're staring," he said.

"I'm wondering what motive you'd have to follow me around the city and beyond." She smirked.

Erich dragged his knuckles across her cheek, and her lips parted, head tilting upward. Against her better reasoning, she wanted him to kiss her, desperately. Maybe if they did, her curiosity would be sated, and he wouldn't be a distraction anymore.

Someone cleared their throat, and they snapped apart. The shopkeeper tutted as she came around the corner with a stack of books in her arms.

"Forgive me; I didn't mean to interrupt." The shop-keeper chuckled.

"You weren't interrupting anything," Liane squeaked, as she smoothed out her hair.

It'd worked out, because her guard turned around, presumably to give her privacy. If she could distract Erich next, she could sneak out the back.

"For just a few gelds, you can use the cozy spot in the back room." The shopkeeper winked at them.

"That won't—" Liane said.

"Thank you," Erich said, cutting Liane off. He pressed a few coins into the shopkeeper's palm.

Before she could protest, he tugged her into the fore-mentioned back room and slammed the door on the guard, leaving them alone. Shelves filled with worn books surrounded squishy chairs, creating an intimate space perfect for steamy trysts. Liane's heart stuttered in her chest.

"I thought we agreed to keep things platonic," Liane stuttered.

"We did. You need to get away from your guards, don't you?" Erich said, striding over to a shelf; he pulled on a book, and a hidden door swung open. "Seems the bookseller is a romantic, or maybe a smart business-woman. I can't tell which."

The flirting had been part of his ruse to get them back here, hadn't it? A niggling of disappointment twisted in her gut as her skin flushed with embarrassment.

"Why do this for me? You hardly know me," she asked.

"No one deserves to be locked in a cage," he shrugged.

There wouldn't be a better opportunity. While the guards stood watching, assuming they were necking, she'd sneak out to the apothecary and come back. Easy.

"I won't be long," she said.

"You don't think I'm letting you go alone, do you?"

She paused to consider his offer. She'd come this far thanks to his help, and it would be nice to have backup. But she still couldn't trust him completely.

"I'll let you come with me on one condition: you stay outside and don't ask questions."

"I wouldn't dare invade your privacy."

Their agreement settled; she ducked below the low-hanging doorframe and squeezed through the narrow hallway and out into a dingy alleyway. It connected with the street, which was crowded with shoppers. They joined the throng and headed southward toward the Velvet District. She'd been through the area enough times to know the back streets and alleyways by heart and led them through the maze of crowded buildings, which leaned upon one another.

They were nearly to their destination when she caught the attention of a couple thugs who looked her up and down menacingly. If Ludwig were there, he would have provided her with a change of clothes from her silk and brocade that screamed "rob me". Then when their eyes slid over to Erich, they seemed to lose interest, and she was glad she'd brought him along after all.

She found Knoll's Apothecary at the end of a street deep in Onyx Gang territory. Paint peeled off the sign, but Knoll's was still legible. Like most buildings on that street, it looked abandoned. Age had faded the exterior, and cobwebs gathered in its grimy windows. But when Liane tested the door, it swung open onto a silent crypt-like shop. Glassy-eyed creatures floating in murky liquid stared vacantly at her as she approached the dusty counter.

"Hello?" Liane said.

No response.

"I don't think anyone is here," Erich said from the doorway to the shop, nose crinkled as he peered into a murky jar sitting by the door.

"You're supposed to stay outside," Liane said.

"This place gives me a bad feeling. I won't ask about your business but at least let me stay close."

She should send him out; letting him get this involved was a risk. But she couldn't bring herself to dismiss him. The quiet and stillness had set her on edge as well. Then she heard shuffling footsteps coming from the back room behind the counter. The door was ajar, and leaning over the counter, she tried to peer through it.

"I think I heard someone. Wait here," Liane said to

Erich as she leapt over the counter. With her foot, she eased open the door, which creaked ominously. "Anyone —" Liane swallowed her words.

A trail in the dust marked the tread of the shopkeeper, but it had been disturbed; footsteps seemed to indicate a struggle. Inching closer, she found a man lying splayed on the ground, his throat cut and crimson blood stained his cream shirt. Stumbling backward, she crashed into a shelf, and an object near the top teetered before crashing onto the floor, releasing a putrid, acidic stench. Liane covered her mouth, but it did little to lessen the smell.

Erich rushed over to her, grasping for an empty sheath as he surveyed the scene before kneeling down beside the corpse and dipping two fingers into the blood.

"It's warm. This happened recently—"

A clatter of objects falling from a shelf cut him off, and Erich signaled for her to stand behind him before scooting around the shelf. Heart in her throat, Liane followed him and saw a fallen crate lying overturned on the ground. As Erich inched closer to investigate, it groaned and wobbled.

"Watch out!" Liane shouted.

Erich leapt out of the way before falling shelves and stock cascaded down where he'd been standing. A person wearing all black darted between shelves, hobbling toward the back door. Climbing over debris, she chased after them as they exited out onto the back alley. Their black hood and average height and build gave her no clues as to their identity, but she was certain they were connected to Heinrich. They turned the corner out of the alleyway, and Liane noted the pronounced limp of their right leg. She intended to follow the culprit, but a hand grasped hold of her shoulder. Liane spun around, hands raised to defend herself.

"Don't bother chasing him. A man agile on a bad leg isn't someone you want to fight," Erich said.

She didn't like it, but he was right, and seeing as they'd killed the apothecarist, Heinrich was already covering his tracks. Though she'd failed to capture him, she'd gained a critical clue. She had to find the limping killer, and she thought she knew where to look.

19

Dragging his lead feet up the townhouse steps, Erich sighed. That'd quite possibly been the longest night of his life. Or should he say day, as the midday sun burned down upon him. It'd been a full day since he'd left the embassy for the opera. If he weren't committed to his ruse, he would've denied Prince Mathias' request, and if he weren't a damned fool, he wouldn't have traipsed all over the city after Liane. As he reached for the door handle, it swung open and Erich, thrown off balance, stumbled over the threshold. Catching the door frame, he saved himself from landing face-first onto the marble tile.

"Welcome back, your majesty," the servant said in a monotone greeting. There were dark circles under his eyes.

"Didn't sleep either?" Erich asked. He'd spent a restless night in the palace, jumping at every creak of wood and footstep passing by. No one was being let out that night, and he'd been lucky enough to get a private room rather than sleep in the entry hall with the other guests.

"I was awaiting your return, your majesty," he said with a stiff nod.

Guilt struck him like a blow to the gut. He hadn't considered the servants whose job it was to greet him, in case he came stumbling in drunk late at night.

"Forgive me; I should have sent word," Erich said, rubbing a palm over his face.

"It is an honor to serve the future king of Sundland." He bowed his head.

A crawling, uneasy feeling skittered across his skin. He'd never go back to Sundland, even after he was cured. After they stole the sword tonight, he'd leave the city as fast as possible before rumors of him reached his father.

"Either way, you should get some rest now. I'll be in my room."

"You humble me, your majesty, but I must see your needs are met first. Is there anything I can get for you?"

Erich was about to refuse when the aroma of baking bread wafted down the hall. There hadn't been time for breakfast or lunch, and if he wanted to steal the sword tonight, he'd have to eat something and perhaps change his stained clothes. *A bath and a shave wouldn't go amiss either*, he thought, rubbing his stubbled chin. After tonight such luxury would be scarce. With the time he had left before sundown, he might indulge a bit.

"I'd like a bowl of warm water sent up to my room, and some soap, if you have it?" Erich said.

He'd use his dagger to shave, as he'd done on the road, no need to get too comfortable.

"I'll have it prepared straight away."

Pivoting on his heel, the servant strolled down the hall to do Erich's bidding. But before Erich could trudge up the stairs, Ivar appeared atop the landing.

"Your majesty! I was about to send the boy out to search for you!" Ivar said.

"As you can see, I'm perfectly fine, Ivar, just out late," Erich said wearily as he attempted to squeeze past him, but Ivar thrust out his arm, blocking him.

"While I am relieved to see you, I have an urgent matter to discuss." Ivar shoved a piece of parchment beneath Erich's nose.

Eyes blurred from lack of sleep; it took him a moment to comprehend. Skimming past the posturing, pomp, and flattery of formal correspondence, he skipped to the bottom.

I, Empress Eveline of Neolyra, propose an alliance with Sundland, sealed in good faith by the marriage of our children: Princess Liane Starweber and Prince Erich Ostrom.

At the bottom, Empress Eveline had signed in big looping letters and pressed a seal into wax, the Starweber twelve-pointed star. For a long moment, he stared at the words, trying to change their meaning. Liane assured him it was all pretend, that nothing would be formally announced. Did she know and fail to tell him? But how could she have when they'd spent all morning together...

There was still time. Royal marriages took months of negotiation, dowries must be agreed upon, and allegiance terms settled. By sunrise, he'd be gone, and this mess would be behind him. Father might hear rumors of his appearance, but he'd never catch him.

"Toss it into the fire," Erich said with a fake yawn.

As he stretched his arms over his head, he pushed Ivar out of his way to ascend the stairs.

"We cannot simply disregard this offer. The empress will be expecting a response," Ivar's voice rose, squeaking a bit.

"Isn't it your job to handle these sorts of things? Let them know we will take it into consideration, and there are many offers I am considering."

"You've been seen courting Princess Liane. This isn't someone like Greta who you can discard at your convenience."

Erich flinched. He deserved that, but it didn't change his mind either. Suppose they were to marry after he'd been cured, and he chose to reclaim his title. There was no guarantee he wouldn't pass on this curse as his mother had to him.

"Can't I?" Erich said, giving Ivar a savage look.

Ivar didn't flinch, and instead, he puffed up his chest.

"I had hoped you'd come to your senses, but it seems you're determined to refuse your destiny until the end?" Ivar asked. His tone had shifted from a groveling supplicant to a disappointed father.

"It isn't my destiny but a burden my father wishes to foist upon me. I will not take it, and I will not become him."

"Duke Mattison is on his way to Artria. If you refuse the empress' proposal, he'll take it."

Erich's fist clenched. Duke Mattison was old enough to be Liane's father and a sadist who'd delight in breaking her. But still... he couldn't get involved. Though the thought of leaving her to an uncertain fate made the dragon roll inside him, fighting to break free, he tightened the chains around it. His survival was all that mattered. Knowing Liane, surely, she'd find a way to avoid it.

"How long before Mattison gets here?" That's all that mattered, avoiding his uncle.

"A few more days. He'll be here to celebrate the Sun Ceremony."

Good enough. He'd be long gone by then.

"Then he can have her."

"Lord Endland would be ashamed if he saw you now. Running away like a coward. He thought better of you. And for a moment, I thought you might choose the good of Sundland over yourself. If you walk away now, then all he did for you would be for nothing."

The insult cut to the marrow because it was true. He was a shadow of the man he'd envisioned as a boy. Endland took him in, raised him as a son, with the vision of making him a great king. Despite the darkness which lived inside him, Erich thought he could be good. But after a few months at the palace and everything good and bright within him turned to shadows. Father recognized the power inside him and twisted it to his own ends, and what scared him more was he enjoyed it. The control, to make those that hurt him suffer. This potent concoction of darkness and power was too dangerous in the hands of a ruler, and even if he were cured, the shadow would always remain, a reminder of what he might become if tempted.

"I cannot fulfill his dreams or yours. I'm sorry, Ivar. I'm not the man you thought I was."

Erich went to his room, where a bowl of water and a bar of soap awaited him. But he didn't deserve such a luxury, nor did he have the patience to shave. His mood soured, and his appetite was ruined. He was feeling restless and eager to get moving on with his plan. First, he had to meet up with Fritz and make plans to steal the sword. Before he left, he wanted to get his dagger. Kneeling on the bed, he ran his hand along the gap where the bed met the wall until he brushed against a bundle of fabric. The space was tighter than he realized, and he had to tug it free, and in doing so, the fabric unraveled, flopping it onto the bed inscription side up.

"The strongest man knows his greatest weaknesses," it said.

Lord Endland had gifted it to Erich on his sixteenth birthday, right before he'd left for court. Back then, he thought his greatest weakness was being born dragon cursed. Erich picked up the dagger and traced his fingers along the words. All of Endland's hopes and ambitions for a greater Sundland had gone into Erich. But given a choice, the wickedness in his blood won out. Erich turned it over and shoved it back into the sheath at his hip.

Ivar was standing at the bottom of the steps when he exited his room.

"You're leaving again. But you've only just returned," Ivar said.

"There's something I have to do," Erich said.

Not waiting for Ivar's response, he walked out the door. If he lingered, Ivar would have offered him a ride in the carriage or tried to convince him to reconsider marrying Liane. But on a day like today, walking would expend his restlessness and soothe the dragon. Head down, Erich walked against the current of pedestrians flowing up the hill toward the Temple of Sol and made his way southward toward the Velvet District.

The further he got from the temple, the fewer people there were until he was alone walking the filthy streets of the Velvet District for the second time that day. Not far off the main road, he found the tavern and inn that Fritz told him about: Moonlight Tavern. The squalid main room was mostly empty apart from the grizzled, one-eyed woman behind the bar. She watched him with her good eye as she cleaned a dented pewter glass with a stained towel.

"Drink?" she asked in a gruff voice.

"I'm here for Fritz," Erich said, hand resting on his dagger.

"And you are?"

"His friend."

"Didn't know he had any. Been staying here near a year, and you're the first to come calling," she said before spitting into a bucket.

A year hiding in this dump, disguising his identity, perhaps fearing death at every turn. How could he stand it? Why had he done it? From what he glimpsed of the elf's power, he should've been able to transform rocks into geld or something and at least stayed in a nicer inn. Or stolen the sword on his own long ago.

"Can you tell him Erich is here to see him?"

"Do I look like a messenger? Go up the stairs and tell him yourself, he's in room three."

"Thanks," Erich said.

Stairs creaked as he climbed, and the worn carpet stank of stale vomit. Delightful. Four doors faced into the hallway, and room three's door number was rusted and crooked. Erich rapped on it with his knuckles and, while waiting for a response, scanned the empty hall. As far as he could tell, the remaining rooms were empty. Good thing because he didn't want to risk anyone overhearing their conversation. Fritz opened the door a crack, his pale face and wide eyes filling the gap.

"Oh, wasn't expecting you; come in," he said as he opened the door wider.

"Shouldn't your visions have told you?" Erich replied, eyes skimming the cramped room.

Apart from the cot, which occupied half the space, the room was bare and lacked any personal effects. If the bartender hadn't mentioned it, Erich wouldn't have guessed Fritz had been living here for almost a year.

"It doesn't work like that, I'm afraid. The All-Mother grants visions as she sees fit, and not everything I see comes to pass," Fritz said as he closed the door.

"I guess there are limits to your powers then." Not that he cared or believed in that sort of thing. He'd agreed to work with the elf because of the cure, not because of some prophecy.

"Have a seat. I'd offer you some ale, but it tastes like piss." Fritz chuckled, his back to Erich. Fritz flitted about the room, making the bed, and straightening things that weren't crooked. Was he nervous? Did he have something to do with what happened last night? After things settled, he'd heard about how the killer claimed the kill for the moon: more commonly known as the Nameless Goddess. The same goddess the elves worshiped.

"There was a murder at the palace last night. Know anything about it?" Erich said.

Fritz stood very still. "Is that why you're here?"

"I don't care about what happens to some singer. But I do care about getting the sword and my cure. If there's an added complication I need to know about, I want you to tell me now."

"I don't know if they're involved, but I've suspected for a while that my people have been supplying the drug you call stardust."

"Are they going to get in the way of us getting the sword?" In the end, that's all that mattered.

Fritz turned to face him, his eyes lacking pupils, glassy gray and shifting between a dusty purple to midnight blue.

"There is a prophecy among my people that foretells the end of days; as the dragon star rises once again, they fear the golden sword in the wrong hands will unlock the great calamity. Balance must be restored before it's too late; night will become day and day become night, the dead will rise, and all the world will burn."

Fritz shook his head, and his eyes went back to normal though they were unfocused as he clutched his forehead.

"Is that a yes?" Erich said, hand clenching onto his pommel. These sorts of things would have been better said when they'd first made their agreement.

"My people are angry, after what the humans have done to us." Fritz clenched his hand into a fist as he stared out the window, which faced the wall of the next building. "I came here and spent nearly a year trying to stop the prophecy, but I fear some of them are growing impatient and have taken more drastic measures."

Now that he knew what he was up against, there was even more reason to get the sword and get out of town.

"My timing couldn't be better then. I've got news: the sword is being transported from the palace to the temple tonight."

Fritz didn't react, just kept staring at the window, standing very still.

"Then we'll meet outside the palace at sunset?" Erich replied.

Fritz turned to him, piercing him with that unsettling, ageless stare. "Yes, I'll see you tonight."

20

L iane tapped her fan on her knee as she consulted her list of potential assassins. Few courtiers fit the killer's description: lean, agile, yet walking with a limp. According to a priestess she'd questioned, Duke Schatz had a bad case of gout, which caused a limp, but his gut also hung over his belt buckle. Luzie pointed her toward Count Harig, whose war injury left him relying on a cane to walk, but after seeing him snoozing on a bench like a sunning cat, she doubted he could be as agile as her culprit. Besides not matching her killer physically, both suspects lacked the most crucial piece: a connection to Heinrich. Both candidates had supported her mother during the rebellion.

That left one name on her list: Lord Sommerfeld. He was born with a clubbed foot and matched the physical description of her killer: young and hopefully agile. Liane had met him once years ago but didn't remember much about him apart from his limping gait and that he was one of Heinrich's hangers-on. Lord Sommerfeld's father had sided with Heinrich's during the rebellion and been executed for his treason. Not only did he match the description of her killer, but he also had a motive as well.

After crossing the first two names off her list, Liane had searched the palace for Lord Sommerfeld and found him outdoors enjoying a picnic with a group of courtiers she didn't recognize. Liane sat down on a nearby bench, fanning herself as she spied, envying her target's shady spot. To investigate properly, she'd need to get closer, but she couldn't walk up to them without reason. But when she imagined herself hunting an assassin, she didn't think the hardest part would be talking to people... If she were Aristea, she would've charmed them with her wit, and Mathias would've jokingly asked Lord Sommerfeld if he were the killer. But she wasn't her siblings. No one saw her as herself; they either pitied her illness or wanted to get closer to advance their own political agendas. Some men had even seduced her to that end. Older and wiser now, it was why she refused permanent attachments. You couldn't be disappointed if you didn't let people get close to you.

"What are you staring at?" Ludwig whispered in her ear.

Liane spun to see Ludwig's bemused expression.

"Damned Darkness, Ludwig, you scared the life out of me."

"You look alive to me," he said with a wry quirk of his lips.

"Suddenly, you're a comedian, I see." Liane struck him lightly with her fan as he chuckled.

She'd missed this; she'd missed him. Proving Heinrich was a traitor was harder without him. She'd never realized how much she relied on him until she tried to do it all herself.

Lord Sommerfeld and his companions glanced in their direction. Great. Now what? Should she approach them and say what...? Hello, I was just wondering if you've killed anyone recently? Liane shook her head.

"How would you approach that group?" Liane nodded to the courtiers, who pointedly looked away.

"Are you asking me how to make friends?" Ludwig asked.

"I don't need friends. There's something I need to find out..." she trailed off. The truth had nearly spilled out of her unthinking. It was natural for her to conspire with Ludwig. If she told him, he'd want to help, but he should be focused on recovering.

"What lead are you chasing?" Ludwig asked.

"Nothing, it's nothing. Like you said, I'm trying to make friends, that's all," Liane cleared her throat.

With a furrowed brow, Ludwig scanned Lord Sommerfeld's group. He knew without her telling him what she wanted.

"I don't recognize most of them, but that's Lord Sommerfeld. He controls a strategic province across the mountains. Surprising to see him at court again."

Her heart thumped in her chest. Had her hunch been right?

"What makes you say that?" Liane asked

Ludwig glanced around the garden. Sommerfeld and his companions weren't watching them anymore, but she could see from the way their heads were tilted in her direction that they were listening. Leaning in close, Ludwig whispered in her ear.

"Heinrich attempted to seduce Sommerfeld's wife, and when he found out, he confronted him... As you might imagine, Heinrich didn't like that and sent him into semi-exile to the countryside."

Was getting back into Heinrich's good graces enough to kill for? Liane looked closer at Lord Sommerfeld. He had a round soft face and hands and appeared far and away from a killer. But appearances could be deceiving, and he was back at court...

"Perhaps he's back to make amends with Heinrich...?" Liane prompted.

"Doubtful, Heinrich doesn't forgive and forget easily."

"But what if Heinrich asked him to do something? Wouldn't he forgive him then?"

"What have you heard?" Ludwig asked.

Liane chewed on her bottom lip and avoided his gaze. Anything she said would be a blatant lie or exposing what she knew. But she could trust Ludwig; they'd fought side by side all this time. Liane couldn't do this alone, not balancing her fake engagement and keeping Heinrich unawares at the same time. Captain Rosen had told her to keep it secret, but she could trust Ludwig; she should have told him long ago. And looking at Lord Sommerfeld, she was starting to have doubts she could find this assassin without his help. Heinrich might have hired anyone, some servant perhaps. If that were the case, there were hundreds of them in the palace. She couldn't possibly investigate them all in the next couple of days.

"I thought you promised to stay out of trouble," Ludwig said when she didn't answer.

"It finds me!" Liane said, forcing a laugh when curious glances were cast their way. "Love, that is. I figured it was time," she said, using her fake engagement as bait to distract the courtiers.

"I heard about the engagement. Should I be congratulating or consoling you?" Ludwig asked.

They couldn't talk there, not with so many listening ears. Liane stood up and gestured for Ludwig to follow, and they headed down a winding path deeper into the garden, away from the crowds. Ludwig's limp slowed their progress.

When she found a secluded spot facing the Midnight Tower, Ludwig sank down beside her, groaning and rubbing his injured right leg. He'd gotten it because of her, while trying to protect her. If she told him the truth, he'd rush back to work too soon, and if he was permanently crippled as a result, she'd never forgive herself. But he wouldn't walk away without answers. He'd already suspected she was hunting a new lead.

"What have you been up to since you went on leave?" she asked, trying to make small talk.

"Changing the subject, I see? You're on to something. Don't try and hide it."

She tugged at a loose thread from her sleeve, avoiding his questioning gaze. "If I tell you, promise me you won't intervene."

"What's going on?"

"I think Heinrich is plotting treason."

Ludwig scoffed. "The man is a cheater and arrogant

scum, but he's not foolish enough to try and take on your mother, not with Cyra and the church backing her rule."

"What if he had someone powerful backing him?" Liane asked.

"Whose more powerful than Cyra?"

Liane swallowed hard past a lump in her throat.

"The elves?" she practically whispered the word.

Ludwig was quiet for a long moment, not moving and not speaking. Liane stood up and paced in front of him.

"Someone powerful is funding the stardust smugglers, getting them out of jail. Selling it to the nobles!" Liane said, the words spilling from her mouth filling the silence.

"Clearly, someone with influence is connected to the elves and the stardust. But Heinrich, what does he have to gain?"

"The crown, the empire. Isn't it obvious?" Liane threw out her arms to make her point.

Ludwig stood and put his hands on her shoulders. "Listen, I know you hate him for what he did to Aristea. But you can't accuse a man of treason for the sins of his father."

Liane clenched her hand into a fist, and a gap widened between them. Of all people, she thought Ludwig would believe her. And if he doubted her, maybe she was wrong. What if she had been blinded by her own anger and resentment and missed some vital clue?

"You're right. Forget I said anything. It was a silly notion." She shook her head.

"Look, I know I said some things I regret, and I don't want you to feel obligated to solve this alone... We'll eradicate stardust together, even if it takes years. We're in this together." His eyes flicked past her as he spoke.

"Something wrong?" Liane asked. Glancing over her shoulder, she saw Captain Rosen headed in their direction.

"I think I should go lie down; my leg is aching," he said, rubbing his leg. But he wouldn't look straight at her, and all the color had drained from his face.

Before she could stop him, he hobbled away from behind, his uneven gait reminding her of something... Captain Rosen's warning rang through her head: trust no one. But that wasn't possible. This was Ludwig. When elves attacked the smugglers, he'd searched for survivors. He despised Heinrich as much as she did; he wouldn't work for him. And yet watching him from behind, the resemblance to the killer was uncanny. A pit of dread settled in her stomach, but she shoved her unease down long enough to smile at Captain Rosen.

"Captain Rosen!" Liane greeted, her voice over-eager. She needed to rein it back in, or Captain Rosen would be suspicious.

"Your majesty," she said with a tight bow. Her hawk-like gaze followed Ludwig, then snapped back to Liane. She wasn't free of her distrust either. "It's fortunate we ran into one another. I've been meaning to speak to you. Any new developments?"

Liane's heart lodged into her throat. "Nothing yet. But if I hear anything, you'll be the first to know."

"Be sure you do. I'd hate for another incident like last night to happen." Her dark, shrewd eyes pierced Liane as if she saw through her lies.

"I will," Liane said, choking on the lump in her throat.

Then with a bow, Captain Rosen departed, leaving Liane trembling with cold despite the heat of the day. Ludwig wouldn't betray her; he couldn't have betrayed her. She'd prove it. Ludwig was in the barracks this morning and couldn't have been in the city killing the apothecarist.

Spinning around, she turned to her guards Aayden and Simon, who'd just come onto watch. "Was Ludwig in the barracks this morning?" she asked.

They shared a look. "I was training the new recruits. Did you see him, Simon?" Aayden asked.

"I was out..." Simon said, rubbing his neck.

There were other soldiers in the barracks; surely they'd seen him. Not willing to believe her worst fears, she headed there and a found group milling about outside, laughing and gambling with bone dice. They jumped to attention, bowing to her as she approached.

"Your majesty," they said in unison.

Heart pounding in her ears and her mouth dry, Liane wet her lips.

"Do you know Ludwig Wildner?"

"Your majesty's head of the guard, of course, we do," said a guard.

She focused her attention on him, latching on as if he were a lifeline.

"Were you off duty this morning?

The guard shifted uncomfortably. "I was, your majesty. I was playing dice with some other guards who were as well."

"Was Ludwig among them?" she asked.

He furrowed his brows in confusion. "I thought he was on leave...?" He turned to his companion for confirmation.

"Yes, that's what I heard. He went into the city this morning to visit family who came for the Sun Ceremony."

Her stomach dropped. Ludwig had no living family. They'd all died in an elven raid when he was a boy.

"Are you sure?" Liane asked.

They frowned and scratched their chins, avoiding her gaze.

"Yes, I'm certain. I don't want to get a fellow guard in trouble. But I wouldn't lie to your majesty," the guard said.

Ice crashed through her veins. It couldn't be true, but from his build to his ability Ludwig fit the description of her killer...

21

"Just for a little while," Liane said, hands pressed together as she stared hopefully at Luzie, who avoided her pleading eyes by gazing at the ceiling.

The idea that Ludwig was a killer was unimaginable, but she had to talk to him, alone, and get his alibi before Captain Rosen questioned him. And to do that, she needed Luzie's help sneaking out. Luzie's strawberry blond locks and shorter, stockier frame weren't a perfect match for Liane's fiery-red hair and tall thin body, but in the dark and wearing a maid's uniform, she could move around the palace without being questioned. But Luzie stubbornly refused to cooperate.

"I made an oath to protect you from harm. This is the opposite of that. There's still an elf on the loose, for stars' sake!" Luzie shouted.

"There is no elf, and besides, they won't think to attack a palace maid."

Luzie frowned at her, hands on hips. "We don't know for certain."

"What if I swear I won't leave the palace grounds?"

"If Ludwig were with you, I wouldn't protest but wandering those tunnels alone in the dark... What if you fall and break your neck? Or worse things, I don't even want to imagine..."

"It's Ludwig I want to see," Liane said, latching on and hoping it would be enough to convince her.

Luzie narrowed her eyes. "Then why not summon him to your rooms?"

She'd caught her. Luzie didn't usually question her whims, but then again, there'd never been danger this close to home before.

"I can't do that, and I can't tell you why not. But I will, soon. I promise!" Liane grasped Luzie's arm and squeezed.

"Does this have something to do with stardust?" she asked, still not looking directly at her.

Luzie had lost her mother to stardust around the same time Elias had died. When it was new, and its effects not entirely understood. Their mutual grief and desire for vengeance had drawn them together. And it wasn't technically a lie to say this was related. After all, if she proved Heinrich was helping the gangs distribute it, then it would stop the flow.

"It is."

Her expression softened as she sighed. "One hour, and if you're gone longer than that, I alert the guards."

"Two, just to be safe. Actually, let's make it by curfew," Liane said. Outside her window, the setting sun cast pinkish-orange light over craggy mountain peaks. If Ludwig wasn't at the barracks, she'd have to wait until he returned. But he'd have to come back before curfew. Guards were only allowed out and about if they were on duty, and even then, they needed to be in pairs.

"Fine," Luzie said, shaking her head.

"I will make this up to you. I promise," Liane said, throwing her arms around Luzie's neck; she squeezed her tight.

"Free the city of stardust, and I'll be satisfied," Luzie said.

Their agreement made, Liane went behind the changing screen and shed her gown, exchanging it for Luzie's uniform. After she put it on, Luzie pinched and cinched the too-big dress in place, and for the finishing touch, Luzie removed her bonnet and placed it on Liane's head, tucking fiery-red strands under it. When she was done, Liane examined herself in the mirror; the front of it dipped dangerously low, threatening to expose her chest while the skirt hem hit shin length. If anyone looked at her too closely, it'd be obvious she was wearing a stolen uniform, but it'd have to suffice.

"That's as good as I can get it," Luzie said, standing back to admire her work.

"Thank you, truly." She gave Luzie one more fierce hug.

Eager to be on her way, Liane pulled back the tapestry to press the sunburst molding that opened the hidden door. It swung inward and revealed the darkened passage.

"Please be careful," Luzie said, handing her a chamberstick and flickering orange light, illuminated rough-hewn stone walls.

"I'll be back soon," Liane said as she closed the door behind her.

Darkness pressed in around the halo of candlelight as she descended the steps. She didn't need much light to guide her and soon found the abandoned collapsed tunnel which connected with forgotten passages to other parts of the palace. Holding up her light, she found the gap in the debris before setting down her light to squeeze through. When she was on the other side, she reached through the hole and brought the candle over.

On the other side, it opened out onto a short hall ending at a cellar where wine barrels aged. Liane opened the cellar door and peered out and found it empty, then she scurried along the servant's passageway and out into the gardens.

Out in the open, she walked slowly but intently, clutching a blank piece of paper that served as her errand should anyone stop her and ask. But at that time of night, most of the servants were rushing to finish their tasks before curfew and didn't give her a second glance.

Rows of tall pines lined the gravel path leading to the barracks: a multistory, stone building built against the palace walls. Clusters of guards stood around talking and laughing, their faces illuminated by the braziers they gathered around. Among them, she recognized a few familiar faces, and not wanting to reveal herself, she hung back in the shadow of a tree debating how to best approach. If she were recognized, they'd march her back up to her room.

"Here to meet someone?" a guard asked, startling Liane.

"Oh no, I was just passing by," she said, lowering her voice, and tilting her face away from the man, just in case.

The guard nudged her shoulder. "You don't have to pretend. Got a sweetheart? Who is it? I'll call him out for you."

"Well, I was hoping to see Ludwig. Do you know him?"

"Ludwig, huh?" he said, as if such a request surprised him.

Liane chanced a peek out of the corner of her eye as the guard surveyed the barracks.

"Isn't that him there? Looks like he's headed out." Liane followed the line of his pointing finger and saw Ludwig limping away from the barracks. "Were you love birds planning on meeting up? Don't stay out too late. Don't want to get caught after curfew now, do you?" He chuckled as he strolled away.

Liane waited until the guard was out of sight before chasing after Ludwig and was about to call out to him when he diverted from the gravel path and walked deeper into the twilight garden beyond, toward a gazebo where a servant in palace double star livery paced. They were one of Aristea and Heinrich's household. Pulse drumming in her throat, she watched Ludwig read a note the servant handed to him. His shoulders tensed, and then, with a curt nod, he walked away, coming in her direction. She ducked behind a bush and held her breath as he walked by.

Where was he going at this hour, and what had been

in that message? Though it felt wrong to doubt him and to spy, her gut told her to wait and watch. Keeping a safe distance, she followed him until he strolled through the palace gates. Curfew wasn't far off, and it wasn't like Ludwig to head out late at night. If she followed him, she might see what he was up to and maybe even find a chance to talk. But leaving the palace broke her promise to Luzie... Nibbling on her thumb, Liane debated her options. She had to prove Ludwig's innocence. Turning on her heel, she followed him out of the palace.

A GIBBOUS MOON rose in mocking defiance against the bright blue sky. Even with sunset hours away, the eye of the Nameless Goddess peered past the veil, reminding Erich of another impending change. For too long, moon cycles had swung above his head like a guillotine's blade. Tonight, if he were successful, he wouldn't have to fear it again. With time, he might even learn to appreciate its radiant beauty as poets and artists seemed to. Tearing his gaze away from the horizon, Erich resumed his scouting mission. After meeting with Fritz, he'd returned to the palace to survey potential locations for an ambush. There were multiple routes they might transport the sword along, the most obvious being the main road which connected both temple and palace together. It was direct and easily defendable, but it also had the added complication of heavy foot traffic, which at peak hours could provide cover for Fritz and Erich. That was assuming they didn't wait until past curfew to move it.

Making a mental note, Erich followed the road parallel to the palace. Walls encircled it, and from the tops of the ramparts, guards patrolled. From up there, they'd have a view all the way to the temple. Crossbows couldn't reach that far, but if they were seen from above, they'd call for reinforcements, which shortened their window of opportunity. Towers marked the corners of the palace wall, and from there, the road branched in two directions: one down a smaller back street, and another down a narrow alley. Glancing down the street, he saw it rolled downhill, between rows of townhouses. The other branch followed the southern wall of the palace ending at a small gate where a man and donkey cart waited.

A guard greeted the man before inspecting and letting him inside. It must be some sort of utility gate, where supplies were delivered. If this street joined up with Temple Street, then he might have found his route. Back-tracking, Erich followed it down the hill as it looped around, emptying out back onto Temple Street. If he were trying to transport an important artifact, Erich would have taken the less direct but secret route. The most glaring flaw was the number of niches and alleyways where ambushers could hide, leaving the convoy exposed. If he were the Midnight Guard, he'd wait until after curfew bells and move it directly and armed to the teeth.

There were too many variables to be certain what they'd choose. And guessing meant picking the wrong one. And there wasn't time for near misses. He had to be certain. Tonight he could not fail.

Returning to the palace square, Erich waited for sunset and Fritz to arrive. Pedestrians leaving the palace flowed past without a second glance. In these upper districts, no one thought twice about a well-dressed man standing on a street corner. But as the moon grew brighter and light dimmer, his impatience grew. Long shadows crept across the cobble, and Erich started to pace. Lamplighters came around, pressing flame to wick, and the haunting yellow glow of lamplight mixed with the dying light of day. The flow of pedestrians reduced to a trickle, as the last rays of golden sunlight sank below the tops of buildings. Where was Fritz? He hadn't changed his mind, had he? His plan wouldn't work without a diversion, and Erich couldn't be in two places at once.

The shadow of a nearby lamp flickered strangely, warping and contorting, then it sprouted arms and a head. Blinking, Erich rubbed his eyes, but the object grew, coalescing into a figure who approached him. It solidified into Fritz, who grinned at him in greeting. A few stragglers strolling past didn't look twice at the elf as he waved to Erich. It was as if they hadn't seen him at all.

"How did you do that?" Erich asked him.

"Can't you step out of shadows?" Fritz teased.

Erich shook his head. Whatever elven magic he used, that could be an asset to them tonight. No use in questioning it.

"Either way, you're late. I need you to create a diversion at the main gate, drive them to the southern gate, where I'll be waiting to ambush them. Then we'll—"

"I'm late because I had a vision," Fritz said, his voice solemn. But something about his tone made the hairs on the back of his neck stand on end.

"I hope you saw us successfully retrieving the sword," Erich said.

Fritz's eyes were glowing golden as he gazed past Erich and into the distance. "You were standing at a crossroads, and a voice whispered: 'remember your promise.' Does that make any sense to you?"

Snapping back to the present, Fritz regarded him with an inquisitive gaze. Before leaving for Sundland's court, Erich had promised Endland he'd stay true to himself and become a great king. But Erich had reached that crossroads long ago and made his choice, and there was no turning back now. Then there was the promise he'd made to Prince Mathias, to protect his sister, but that had been a lie. There was no turning back now. Once he had the sword, and his cure, there would be no reason to stay in the city or to ever think about Liane again.

"It was a false vision: I don't make promises."

Fritz frowned. "That's unfortunate..."

"We don't have time for prophecies; there's a job to do, remember?"

"You're right. I'll set up the diversion, as you said." But Fritz seemed uncertain.

There wasn't time for second guessing, the moon's changing waited for no one, and only a few days remained before the next full moon. Either he got this sword, or he left the city before the next change.

"No second guessing," Erich said.

Fritz nodded, and his form shifted, becoming a stranger with blond hair, blue eyes, short and stout. If he hadn't seen him change, he never would have guessed it was him.

"I know what needs to be done. I'll see you later." With a wave, he jogged toward the palace gates.

They parted ways, and Erich strolled down the road, finding a spot in an alleyway where he could see the gate and stay hidden among the shadows. Time dragged on as they waited, and his mind wandered, remembering things better left forgotten. Endland wanted him to be a righteous king, the sort who'd marry a princess like Liane, save her from arranged marriages with men like his Uncle Duke Mattison. But he never could be that man; it was why he left it all behind. Fritz was wrong. He'd already chosen his path at the crossroad, and he couldn't look back. With time, Liane would become like others he'd walked away from, a distant memory. The thought made the dragon twist in his gut, but more surprising was his own regret.

Pushing her from his mind, he concentrated on the steady trickle of courtiers exiting the palace as he drummed his fingers on the hilt of his dagger. A limping figure headed toward him, and Erich pulled back into the shadows. The gait and build were unmistakably the killer from the apothecary. *What was he doing in the palace? Was Liane in danger?*

No sooner did the thought cross his mind, than a woman emerged after him. At first glance, she appeared to be a maid, then a breeze kicked up and tore the bonnet from her head, freeing her bright-red hair. His stomach dropped as he watched her scurry down the street after the limping man. He turned away. It wasn't his business if Princess Liane chased a killer through the city streets after dark. The sword, the sword, the sword. That was all that mattered.

The dragon rolled in protest, clawing and biting at the chains that held him. His stance was clear: protect Liane. But at any moment, Fritz would launch his diversion, and Erich would need to be ready to ambush the convoy. But as moments stretched on, his thoughts kept circling back, and the dragon within him refused to calm. Liane couldn't be seriously risking her life, for what? Erich stamped his foot on the ground and paced back and forth, the dragon's restless energy transferring to him.

There wouldn't be a better chance. But he was also quite certain the convoy would leave after curfew. That meant he had at least two hours to follow Liane, make sure she was safe, and return before that happened. The dragon calmed within him, seemingly in agreement with his plan. Groaning, Erich dragged his hands through his hair. He must be the world's biggest fool, but he followed after Liane.

22

Keeping to the shadows, Liane tracked Ludwig as he limped between dilapidated buildings lining the Velvet District. When she accidentally kicked a rock across the cobble street, Ludwig spun around, and Liane pressed her back against a wall, hiding from him on instinct. What was she doing? This was Ludwig. He'd never hurt her, and yet her heart thumped in her chest as she listened to his footsteps recede. Poking her head around the corner, she spotted him turning down a crowded street lined with brothels and taverns. Knowing Ludwig, he knew he was being followed, and either she revealed herself or turned back.

Because she'd come this far, she had to know the truth and darted out after him. The street was crowded, and when she tried to shout to Ludwig, her voice was overwhelmed by the cacophony of patrons and barkers attempting to lure them in.

Through the crowd, she watched as Ludwig turned

down a narrow alleyway and rushed to catch up. But when she rounded the corner, it was empty ending at a single nondescript door and Ludwig nowhere in sight. Seeing as there was nowhere else to go, she concluded he must have gone inside. A single lamp swung above the door, casting orange light onto Liane as she knocked firmly upon it. A slat slid open, and a pair of hooded eyes peered out at her.

"Password?" they said.

Password? What could be the password? "Uh, you see..." she fumbled.

"Silver Tongue," Erich said.

Liane spun around to Erich. What was he doing there?

"That's not it." The man started to slam the slat shut, but Erich jammed his hand through the gap.

"Are you sure about that? Bosch told me it changed to Silver Tongue." He moved closer to the hole, meeting the man's gaze.

The bouncer's eyes turned glassy. "Silver Tongue was yesterday's password, but knowing Bosch, he'd make that kind of mistake. Come on in then."

The door swung open, unleashing music and loud drunken voices from within. Lamps dangling from the ceiling could barely permeate the haze of smoke around the room, let alone give her a good look at the people inside.

"We run into one another again. I didn't take you for the seedy back-alley club type," Erich said as he gestured for her to enter first.

"I'm not," Liane said as she passed by the brusque door guard.

As she entered the main room, a blanket of warmth enveloped her, accompanied by the sickly-sweet scent of burnt sugar that she'd come to associate with stardust. She'd heard of stardust dens. Ludwig wouldn't let her step foot in them, saying it was best she didn't see. At first, stardust created euphoria in its users: they were faster, stronger, and smarter than they'd been. Some swore it made them luckier, and judging from the wide-eyed, pinpoint pupils of the patrons sitting around the gambling tables, they felt much the same. What they didn't know was once the euphoria started to wear off, it ate away at their energy, hollowing them out until they were nothing but a creature of craving, obsessed with stardust and caring for nothing else, not eating, not sleeping, not their loved ones... They ended up like the patrons lying strewn across beds and benches at the edges of the room, eyes staring sightlessly at the ceiling.

Now she understood why Ludwig forbade her from coming here. Everywhere she looked, she saw Elias staring back at her. Gaunt hollowed-out eyes and pallid skin stretched over bones. It made her stomach churn and made her want to run out the door, but she was frozen in place.

"Then it's a good thing I showed up when I did," Erich said.

"You're not going to ask what I'm doing here or try and convince me to leave?" Liane asked, tearing her gaze away from the blank-eyed addicts.

"Would you, if I did?"

"No."

"Then let's just say I'm here to watch over you."

She should send him away, but the smell, smoke, and memories made her sway on her feet, and her head swim. Erich put a bracing hand on her lower back and led her to a nearby empty table. He didn't seem like the type to use stardust. For those who used it long enough, symptoms started to show up in the color of their skin and in their erratic behavior. But she'd overlooked them in Elias too. Liane shook her head. Best not to compare the two. Whatever good fortune brought him here, she wasn't going to question it.

They sat down, and a gaunt serving girl came around to offer them refreshments, which Erich politely declined. He sat with his back to the room, giving her the chair, which allowed her to survey it inconspicuously.

Elias was dead, but she'd get revenge for him... But she couldn't continue her investigation with Erich watching her...

"Do you frequent these sorts of places?" Liane asked, drumming her fingers on the table. Ludwig had to be in here somewhere, but why, was he chasing a lead he'd kept from her?

"Only when impulsive women lure me there."

"Then you followed me." Her eyes flicked back to him, studying him a moment. Had it been careless to put her trust in him?

"I saw you sneaking around wearing clothes that weren't yours. Can you blame me for being curious?"

Across the room, boisterous laughter echoed, and a familiar mocking tone caught her attention. Head swiveling toward the direction, she saw Heinrich seated at a card table with his usual pet lords. A buxom blonde bounced on his lap, dragging a pile of silbern and geld toward him. She tossed her head back in throaty laughter, as Heinrich buried his head into her ample chest. Liane clenched her hand into a fist. She'd found Heinrich's mistress.

She half rose from her seat, ready to confront him, when she noticed Ludwig hovering at Heinrich's shoulder with his back against the wall. Liane sunk back into her chair to watch. Ludwig had come to meet Heinrich? Surely, he was trying, as she was, to uncover his plot. But then why had he deterred her from investigating? Was he worried she'd get hurt? That'd never stopped him before... Doubt crept in, and she tried to shake it away.

Heinrich rose, excused himself, and signaled for Ludwig to follow before heading up to the next floor. She had to know what they were talking about, and as she stood to follow as well, Erich grasped her forearm, tethering her in place. Liane glared down at him.

"You can't just rush in, or you'll be seen," he said.

There wasn't a reason to trust him. The logical thing to do would be to say goodbye and chase after Ludwig herself. But as Erich's large hand wrapped around her wrist, she felt the cracks inside her widening. She was angry and impatient, and he was right. She'd moved without thinking once, and Heinrich had thwarted her; she couldn't rush in without a plan this time.

"What do you suggest?" she asked.

"Follow my lead."

With his help, they inched across the room toward the stairs, but on their way, they stopped at card tables, and even lingered by the bar. Their progress was agonizingly slow, but she trusted Erich's plan. When they reached the foot of the stairs, at last, she heard voices.

"I can't live off scraps of affection forever, Henny," a woman whined.

Erich thrust out his arm, blocking Liane before she was seen. From around his impressive bicep, she saw Heinrich, his back to her, and the woman from earlier standing outside an open room door.

"Haven't I given you enough? An apartment in the city, jewels, and new dresses," Heinrich said sharply.

"I hate having to sneak around. You said you'd make me an empress. How much longer do I have to wait?"

"Shh," he hissed. "We're in public."

"There's no one here but the spy," she said in a cajoling voice as she reached up to stroke his cheek.

Heinrich slapped her, knocking her to the ground, and Liane inhaled sharply. If Erich hadn't been in her way, she would have rushed up the stairs and slapped Heinrich herself.

"Remember your place," Heinrich spat.

Erich's hand clenched into a fist, and this time it was Liane who had to grasp onto his arm to hold him back, even though she'd very much like to see him punch Heinrich. She pulled him toward her, and his body caged her against the wall, the muscled planes of his chest pressing hard against her breasts. Her gaze flicked up to his stubbled chin, his firm lips. Now wasn't the time, but her body reacted to his proximity anyway with a churning heat that made her breath catch. His molten brown eyes flicked down to meet hers, and for a moment, everything else melted away. His lips were dangerously close. If she leaned forward...

A door slammed, and the woman stomped past them, sniffling pitifully. When she was gone, Liane slipped out from under Erich's grip and cleared her throat. Neither of them spoke for a moment. Then, certain the coast was clear, Liane cautiously climbed the stairs to press her ear to the door the woman had just exited.

"The job is done," Ludwig said, his tone cold and detached.

What job? The apothecarist? Then Heinrich had ordered it?

"And is everything in place for the Sun Ceremony?"

"It is."

"But there's something you're not telling me," Heinrich drawled, and Liane clenched her fist, fighting the urge to knock the door down and catch him in the act.

"You're mistaken."

"Ludwig. You don't want the truth getting out, now do you?" Heinrich dragged out each word, his tone that of an adult scolding a child.

Liane's heavy breathing echoed back at her as she pushed harder against the door. Ludwig wouldn't betray her; he wouldn't, he couldn't.

"It's inconsequential."

"That's for me to decide, isn't it?"

Her heart thundered in her ears, and a part of her wanted to run away, to pretend she'd never doubted Ludwig, that this had all been a bad dream. But the other side of her needed to know and wouldn't let her feet move.

"Liane suspects you."

Heinrich's laughter echoed through the room as a cold chill ran down Liane's spine. This had to be a dream, a horrible nightmare. She stumbled backward, the contents of her stomach pushing at the back of her throat as she teetered, nearly tipping over. Erich caught her around the shoulders, steadying her. Ludwig was supposed to be her best friend, and he'd betrayed her to Heinrich, of all people. Had she ever really known him? a voice whispered at the back of her mind.

Erich guided her back down the stairs and back into a secluded corner at the rear of the club, her thoughts a swirling vortex of anger and betrayal.

"Are you alright?" Erich asked, his brow furrowed with concern.

Pain and anger lodged a lump in her throat. Erich, a relative stranger, had shown her more compassion and more reason to trust than her supposed best friend. She shook her head. There must be some misunderstanding, some piece she'd missed. But try as she might to find a motive, she couldn't think of a reason.

"No. I'm not." A sob caught in her throat, and she pressed the heels of her hands against her stinging eyes. She wouldn't cry. Now wasn't the time, and it didn't change anything. Heinrich was plotting something to do with the Sun Ceremony.

"What do you want to do? Should I escort you back to the palace?" he asked.

Pushing aside her personal feelings of betrayal, she assessed the situation rationally. If she went back to the palace now without proof to turn over Heinrich, no one would believe her. She couldn't hand over Ludwig, which meant she needed some other evidence, something irrefutable.

"I want to make Heinrich pay," Liane bit out. Saying the words aloud bolstered her confidence. And a plan started to spin in her mind. If she could win over Heinrich's mistress and find his bastard child, then maybe that would be enough to prove his motives at least.

Liane scanned the tavern for the blonde and found her sitting at the bar with a friend, applying a cloth to her red face. When she approached, both women looked up at her with narrowed eyes.

"Mind if I sit down?" Liane asked.

The woman and her friend glanced at her up and down, lips curling into a sneer at her ill-fitting servant's uniform. Her temper already close to the surface, Liane gritted her teeth to keep from exploding with impatience and anger. That wasn't going to win her any favors.

"Ladies," Erich said, sliding into the seat Liane had indicated.

She glared at him, silently questioning him with her eyes, but he winked at her and angled his body toward the two women. They both looked him up and down with open appreciation, lust-filled gazes darkening as they lowered their lashes. The blonde dropped her cloth on the counter and tossed her hair over her shoulder. A twist of jealousy pierced Liane's gut.

"How can we serve you?" the brunette purred. She reached across to touch Erich's arm.

"I was hoping you could answer some questions for

this fine lady here," Erich addressed the blonde, while gesturing to Liane.

"I suppose it depends on the question." She didn't look eager to answer.

"I overheard you talking with Prince Consort Heinrich, something about making you empress," Liane said, cutting right to the heart of the matter.

The woman tensed as the color leached from her face, making the slap mark on her cheek stand out vividly. "I don't know what you're talking about."

"There's nothing to fear; you're safe." Erich grasped her hand and squeezed, drawing her gaze to his.

Like a flower wilting in the summer heat, her eyes softened, and her shoulders relaxed.

"I'm Henny's favorite. His wife can't give him what he wants, and I make him feel special, powerful. He's going to get rid of her soon, and he promised when he's emperor he'll make me his empress if I can give him a son." The words tumbled from her mouth, as if some dam had been broken.

Liane looked to Erich for confirmation; he'd heard it too. "And have you given him a son?" Liane pressed.

A small frown creased her brow. "Well, not yet, but we will soon. I'm sure."

"But he has a son, doesn't he?"

"He's tried with a lot of ladies. There's rumors that he's impotent..." she said with a sly look at her friend.

If that were true, then it would be impossible for him to have a bastard child. And maybe Aristea was telling the truth about those letters. But it didn't change the fact that he was plotting something during the Sun Ceremony.

"Do you know what's going to happen during the Sun Ceremony?" Liane pressed the blonde.

She shook her head, frown deepening even further. "I don't."

"I think she's telling the truth," Erich said.

Liane sighed in frustration. Not nearly enough. But it was the closest she had to answers. At least she had the woman's confession that Heinrich promised to make her empress. It wasn't much but better than nothing.

"Would you be willing to come to the palace tomorrow and tell your story?" Liane pressed.

"I dunno..." She trailed off, frowning.

"That or I tell the City Watch what I heard you say about being made empress. That could be considered treason," Liane added. Thinking a threat would ensure her cooperation.

Her face paled as she looked from Erich to Liane. "You're lying."

Erich cupped her chin, turning her to look into his eyes. "You must help. The fate of the kingdom depends on it."

Her shoulders relaxed once more as she nodded. "Alright. I'll do it."

A knot of tension unraveled in her chest. She'd done it. She had some proof of Heinrich's treason, not much, but better than nothing at all.

"Meet me at the palace gates after third bell," Liane said, meeting her eyes once more to make sure she knew she'd make good on her threat.

Just then, a deep, echoing boom rang through the room, and all heads swiveled to the door.

The bartender cupped his hands around his mouth and, in a bellowing voice, said, "You heard that, last bells. You lot get out!"

Curfew was upon them, and she had to get back to the castle.

23

The room erupted in chaos. Gamblers scooped up their winnings, and bouncers traveled from bed to bed, rousing the inebriated from their stupors, forcing them out the door. A rush of patrons stampeded the exit, and Erich, on instinct, placed himself between them and Liane, pinning her to the bar.

"I have to get back before last bell." The color had drained from her face as panic settled over her features.

His window of opportunity was closing as quickly as the bottleneck of bodies rushing the exit. But he couldn't abandon her now, and besides, he was heading back toward the palace himself. Getting out the front door was out of the question; they'd only waste time or get in a scuffle trying to exit. Running a hand through his hair, he surveyed the emptying tavern. There must be another way. One of the women they'd been talking to tapped him on the shoulder.

"There's a back door; follow us." She pulled up the bar and allowed them behind it.

"Let's go," he said, tugging Liane behind him.

In the storeroom behind the counter, crates of liquor sat in neat piles around a back exit. The two women went out first and out into a dingy alleyway that connected with the crowded street. Patrons spilled out of taverns and brothels, seeking shelter before last bell. Using his shoulder like a battering ram, Erich pushed a path through for them, but progress was painfully slow, and on the main streets, there would be others rushing to get inside before twelfth bell. If they walked from this distance, they'd never make it back in time.

They needed a ride, but the Velvet District was too narrow for carriages, and others who'd had the same thought as him, were rushing for the three carriages waiting at the end of the street. Picking up the pace, Erich practically dragged Liane behind him as he watched the first and second drive away. The third remained, but a few drunken patrons stood between it and them. They were nearly there; he could smell the scent of horse and see the craggy lines in the carriage driver's face. But before he could climb inside, another couple beat them to it, slamming the door in his face, and Erich watched as the last one drove away.

Warning bells rang, rattling him down to the bone. A quarter till.

"We'll have to run," Liane said, meeting his gaze with a confidence that surprised him in its sincerity.

"I was thinking the same."

With a playful smirk, she ran ahead of him, weaving

through the crowds of drunken patrons stumbling their way back to homes and inns. The City Watch was already out on patrol, scooping up unconscious users from the gutter.

Despite the urgency of their situation, he felt strangely light. Worries about the evening faded away as Liane sharpened into focus. Her red hair snapped like a banner behind her as her giddy laughter ripped from her throat as they ran up Temple Street against the flow of pilgrims while the curfew bell tolled.

The palace was in sight, when Liane skidded to a halt, her excited laughter dying on the wind. The palace gates were closed, but the bells continued to ring. Ten minutes until curfew.

"They closed the gates early?" Liane frowned, her shoulders tensing.

Fritz. It must have been his diversion. Erich cursed himself. As far as Fritz knew, Erich was in place. Trinity above, don't let him be too late. But he couldn't leave Liane standing here.

"Why would they close the gate?" She huffed, pacing back and forth, her red brows pinched together.

A patrol of City Watch marched their way. They were rounding up stragglers already, and they'd lock them in prison too if he didn't find her a place to stay. Just imagining her locked in that filthy cell overnight, being petitioned by some unsavory character, made his stomach clench.

He could take her to the ambassador's townhouse. It wasn't far from here, but then Ivar might try and meddle, or worse, think Erich was sincerely going to consider marriage. The alternative was one of the many nearby inns. If he bought her a room for the night, then she could return to the palace come morning, and he'd find Fritz and salvage this ill-planned evening. Just one more short detour, then he'd be back on track.

"There's no use in wondering. Let's find somewhere to take shelter before curfew. Or else we'll end up in a cell together." Erich nodded toward the guard moving ever closer.

"Has that happened to you before?" Liane asked.

"There was once this fiery redhead who thought I was a criminal…" Erich teased.

A flush rose to her cheeks.

"It's getting late, and the inns will be packed." She marched away, and despite the urgency of the situation, Erich chuckled to himself as he followed her.

They headed back the way they'd come, stopping at inns closest to the palace, but each one they tried was full. With days remaining before the Sun Ceremony, the inns were bursting at the seams, and there weren't any beds. Minutes ticked by, and with each rejection, Erich felt the noose tightening around his neck. Maybe they'd wait a few minutes after curfew, to ensure the roads were clear. Maybe Fritz hadn't set off a diversion already… maybe not all hope was lost.

After numerous failed attempts, they were near the end of Palace Street, where the inns were shabbier but not as bad as the Velvet District. The grizzled innkeeper who greeted them was covered in scars. Not exactly a luxurious establishment but shelter was shelter, he supposed.

And they had one room available, unlike every other inn they'd tried.

The innkeeper took his time removing the keys from the hook, and Erich tapped his foot impatiently as he waited to escort her up to the room. He'd see her inside, say his goodbyes and run like the wind back toward the palace. *It might not be too late*, he told himself.

The room was at the end of the hall, and a suspicious dark stain stretched from the bottom of the door to the carpet. Erich tried not to think about what it was as he opened the door. It was tiny. A small single bed took up half the space, and a leaning nightstand sat beneath a calcium-crusted window. Liane stepped inside and wrinkled her nose but voiced no complaints. Not exactly accommodations befitting a princess. But at least one step up from a cold jail cell floor.

"You'll be safe here until morning," Erich said and held out the key for her to take.

"You're not staying?" She blinked at him in confusion.

"There's only one bed. It wouldn't be appropriate. I'll head back to the embassy—" His words were cut off by the echoing bong of the final curfew bell. Walk out now, and he'd be rounded up by City Watch. Not that he was concerned about that. He'd already planned on staying out past curfew. The problem was, Liane didn't know that. He hesitated in the doorway; his reasonable explanation dashed.

"Looks like you're stuck here with me." She turned to face him, and there was something in her gaze, fear and hurt, that he couldn't turn away from.

Erich closed the door behind him. Damn fool that he

was. He'd stay just a little while until she'd settled. A few more minutes couldn't hurt, could it?

Luzie was going to kill Liane. About then, guards would be combing the palace in search of her, and when they realized she was missing, she'd really be in trouble. It could be worse; she could have been arrested. Arms wrapped around her torso, Liane stood in the center of the room. If she stretched out her fingertips, they would touch both walls, and brush against the corded muscles of Erich's arm. No. Best not to let her thoughts stray in that direction.

Searching for something to focus on and seeking a diversion, but no matter what she did, her attention kept returning to Erich. And how could it not? His presence seemed to fill the space. It always did, but now there was much more of it and less space between them. But with his back to her, she was free to study his broad shoulders, muscled torso, and taut rear. Liquid heat pooled in her stomach, and the hairs on the back of her arms stood on end. Turning, he caught her staring, and her face burned with the rest of her, and she spun away, embarrassed.

"Do I make you uncomfortable?" he asked.

Yes. No. Yes... Her eyes flicked up to meet his smoldering gaze, which sent a tingle racing down to her toes. But not in the way he meant.

"No!" she said a bit too loudly, then clearing her throat, she said, "What gave you that impression?"

"You look strung tight as a bow string. If it would put you at ease, I can sleep out in the hall."

"That won't be necessary," Liane said, a little too quickly, waving her hands in front of her. To stop herself from doing it more and look like a mad fool, she slammed them down at her sides. It was not that she intended to seduce him; that would be a disaster. But she didn't want to be alone, and she couldn't deny her attraction to him... the entire night had been a disaster.

Her and Erich's relationship wasn't real, but it was his strong arms that braced her when her world crumbled around her. She didn't want to think about Ludwig, and it was easier to forget if she were distracted, conveniently, a very tempting one was watching her intently.

Clearing her throat, she said, "Wine?" She hoped, offering up the cheap wine sitting next to stale bread and sweating cheese, might be enough to calm her nerves.

"I'll pass," he said with a crooked grin.

"Bit of a wine snob, aren't you?" she teased to dissipate the rolling tension that swelled between them.

"Let's say I have particular tastes." His gaze flicked over her, brushing past her exposed collar, igniting a scorching heat that pulsed through her veins.

She wanted to sit down, but the room lacked chairs, and the only place to sit was the bed. If she sat down, would that give him the wrong signal, or the right one? Then Erich sat down first, removing the debate entirely.

"Would you like to sit as well? I promise I don't bite." He patted the mattress next to him.

She imagined his teeth grazing her skin, nipping,

sucking. No. *Get those thoughts out of your head*, Liane chided herself. It'd been too long since she'd taken a lover. That was why her thoughts had turned lustful...

"I'm fine standing," Liane said, hating how her voice croaked.

Erich's eyes flashed with humor. Did he know the effect he had on her and was enjoying making her squirm? Well, he didn't realize how stubborn she could be. She wouldn't give in to this impulse because that was all it was.

"Are you planning on standing there all night then?"

"And what if I am?"

He shrugged. "Suit yourself. You're missing out, though, this mattress not only smells of must, but it's rock hard."

Laughter gasped out of her throat, too throaty and eager.

Erich leaned back on the bed with a smirk, and as he did, the fabric of his shirt gapped open, revealing a dark patch of curly hair on his chest. She imagined running her hands through it, as she straddled his waist, grinding... No.

Maybe she should have that glass of wine after all. Liane poured herself a generous glass before gulping it down; sour wine coated her tongue, doing little to sate her thirst.

"Thirsty?" he asked with an arched brow.

"I'm a fast drinker."

"There's more pleasure to be found in savoring, the aroma, the taste..." His eyes were heavy-lidded as he regarded her, his big, kissable lips parted.

They weren't talking about wine, were they? Liane licked her lips. She hadn't felt this awkward with a man since her first time with Elias... At times, her mission fulfilled her; her purpose gave her reason and helped keep Elias' specter from her nightmares. While revenge fueled her, sometimes, when she closed her eyes at night, she'd see his hollow, drug-induced gaze begging her for justice. At times she could chase it away, bringing in different lovers to try to fill the gaping void of loneliness inside her. Sleeping beside someone, after sometimes disappointing sex, she'd feel a little less alone, but it was always temporary. It always came back, and then she'd seek comfort again.

That night, she felt that same ache clawing at her insides, and Elias' face would haunt her as she closed her eyes. She'd drawn the line with Erich, thinking he'd be a distraction from her mission. But the longer they spent together, the more she wondered about him. Wanted him. And needed to cross the line, to forget, and to feel for once.

Standing at the edge of the bed, Erich looked up at her, his gaze wary. Kneeling over him, she straddled his torso, and he shifted beneath her, rising up, so their faces were inches apart. His warm breath fanned over her face as he placed a broad hand against her waist, neither pushing nor pulling but waiting for her to make the next move.

"What about our arrangement?" he breathed against her.

"To hell with it."

When Liane kissed him, he opened his mouth,

inviting her in, his tongue warm, soft, hungry as his hand glided up her back, grasping the nape of her neck and deepening their kiss. It stoked the flames of desire within her, pulsing down to her core. Then he pushed back lightly, breathing heavily. Liane leaned back.

"Why did you stop?"

"I shouldn't."

He hadn't shoved her off him, but there was something holding him back. An uncertainty shimmered in his eyes.

"Do you want to stop?" She motioned to climb off him, but his hands grasped onto her waist, fingers curling in the fabric of her skirt.

"Don't," his voice rasped.

"Do you want me?" Liane asked, breathless, waiting.

"Very much."

"Then you can have me. Is that what you want?"

"I do."

He pulled her down to him, and their teeth clashed together in their urgency, wanting to be closer, needing to be closer. As his rough hand grasped her waist, he lay back, cupping her rear as liquid heat pooled in her stomach, radiating outward. Never had she felt starved, desperate, and satiated all at once. Was it magic, the wine she'd drank? No. She'd never been more sober in her life. All she knew was she wanted more of him, all of him and now. His erection pressed against her thigh through the fabric of his breeches, and she ground against him, desperate to feel him—all of him, inside her. She needed him now, like a woman starved.

Interrupting their kiss, Liane reached between them,

tugging at his breeches to free his shaft. It sprung loose, and she curled her hand around it, reveling in the feeling of soft velvet gliding over hard. Slick with desire, she hitched up her skirts and guided him inside her, gasping as he bucked forward and thrust into her. They stayed like that for a moment, and in the candlelight, flecks of gold in his brown eyes flashed as he watched her. Sparks danced across her skin, heightening all sensations, and burning up within her, desperate for release. Erich, too seemed ready to burst, as a guttural growl escaped his lips. His hands fisted into the fabric of the comforter, until she started rolling her hips, riding his length as cresting waves of pleasure brought her higher and higher.

Then his hands were on her, running up her sides, cupping her breasts through her ill-fitting dress as she moaned and moved faster and faster. Stars danced in her vision as waves of ecstasy washed over her. As they both climaxed, she uttered a string of unintelligible words before collapsing onto the bed beside him. She couldn't recall a time a man had ever made her feel this way before.

Both spent, they lay on the bed beside one another, panting and sweat drenched. Erich brushed a strand of damp hair away from her face, surprisingly gentle. And while her lust had been sated, her need for human comfort hadn't, and she snuggled up against his chest. She'd lay here for a moment. Just enough to not feel so lonely, and when she was in his arms, that gnawing sadness disappeared. Instead, she felt comfortable, and at ease. It wasn't long before exhaustion overcame her, and she slipped off into a dreamless sleep.

24

Strong arms encircled Liane, fitting her body against his as if it were made to. It felt nice. Safe. Warm. Erich's breath fanned across the nape of her neck, tickling her, and she unconsciously squirmed, pressing her rear against his erection. Desire warmed her belly, spreading down and sending tingles racing over her limbs. Usually, once was enough, but it seemed their rushed, but impassioned coupling hadn't assuaged her hunger. They did have all night; perhaps this time, they'd take it slow and explore one another's bodies thoroughly.

As she rolled over to face Erich, morning light burned her bleary eyes, and she blinked at the tattered curtains hanging in the window. They'd slept together in this tiny bed all night? That was another first.

Then realization struck her like a bolt, and she sat upright. The Royal Guard, City Watch, and Midnight Guard were all likely searching for her right now. She tossed off the covers and jumped out of bed, startling

Erich, who grasped for his dagger attached to his discarded belt on the floor. Weapon in hand, he stood next to her, eyes darting from door to window as if he expected someone to burst in any moment. But when he found nothing, he lowered his weapon to his side and stared at her with a slow blink of recognition. Liane giggled at his tousled hair, mussed clothes, and lack of pants. Then her eyes drank in his muscled thighs, brushed with dark coarse hair.

"Are you always this excitable in the morning?" she asked, gaze lingering below his belt. The damage was already done; she may as well enjoy herself before returning to the palace...

"Morning? We slept until morning..."

"Apparently. Shall we order breakfast first or skip to dessert?" Her tongue darted out to wet her lips.

"I've got to go," he said, dashing her hopes as he tugged on his trousers.

It felt as if he'd dumped a bucket of icy water over her, extinguishing her ardor. "That's good. I need to get back to the palace anyway," Liane said, clearing her throat, but he didn't seem to notice her as he threw open the door and stomped out into the hall, leaving her alone, again.

What a fool she'd been to think he'd be different. Once he'd gotten what he wanted, the caring, protective man she'd met dissipated, transforming him into yet another faceless lover. She should have maintained her rule.

No attachments. No regrets.

~

A CURE HAD BEEN within Erich's reach, and he'd let it go; for what? Recklessness wasn't like him, and when he'd woken up surrounded by the rosewater scent of her skin, her body pressed against his, he'd wanted to stay. Even as he walked away, it lingered in his clothes, and the dragon rolled beneath his skin, demanding he return. Erich growled and ran a hand through his disheveled hair, which hung loosely, instead of its tight maintained knot. She'd done this to him, found a single loose thread in his resolve, and unraveled him. He shouldn't have gotten entangled with her from the start. The dragon would destroy her. Its desire only turned to madness and its obsession her executioner. But last night, he'd let it take over and given into its impulse because he wanted her too. But it may have cost him everything.

Erich reached the top of Temple Street in record time and stopped to survey the stream of passersby. Guards were at the palace gates per usual, without a hint of discord. Had Fritz gone ahead with the plan without him and failed? Or had he fled the city with the prize in hand?

Foolish as it was, Erich stalked the perimeter of the palace, hoping beyond hope he'd find Fritz waiting in the shadows for him. But as the sun started to rise on the horizon, it became apparent he was gone, and Erich had indeed lost his chance. He'd gambled it all on the sword and lost. Mere days remained before the next full moon, hardly enough time to get away from civilization, hunker down, and wait out his transformation. Before that, he'd have to return to the ambassador's townhouse, tail between his legs, and beg Ivar for supplies for the journey. Pathetic.

And then what?

He felt the yawning loneliness of his life stretch out before him. For a moment, he'd allowed himself to hope for a future free of the change, but it seemed he was doomed to forever wander this earth alone and hated.

"Back at last, I thought you'd never return," Fritz said.

Erich turned, scanning the sunlit alleyway where he stood, and then Fritz stepped out from a sliver of shadow against the building.

"Did you get it?" Erich asked, a faint ember of hope rekindling inside him.

"You chose your path at the crossroads," Fritz said cryptically.

Erich flinched at the jab. "You're right to blame me. I let the dragon lead me when I shouldn't have."

"Last night would never have worked, the transport was disrupted by an uproar in the palace, and soldiers were swarming the streets. It was postponed until first light instead and was heavily guarded. But I managed to follow them, and I know exactly where the sword is being kept inside the temple and how to get it."

The knot of guilt unraveled slightly, but not much. He couldn't have foreseen such a complication, but with the transport completed, he had two choices: either enter the temple and risk being caught or walk away and give up on a cure.

"I'm in. What's your plan?"

"Meet me at twilight at the temple steps; I'll explain everything then."

～

AFTER GIVING ERICH A HEAD START, Liane headed back to the palace. It was better they didn't see one another again; it would only lead to more awkwardness. And besides, now that she had the evidence she needed, the fake courtship wasn't necessary. When she reached the gates, she greeted the guards on duty: a man and woman she did not recognize.

"Morning, I'm sure you're surprised to see me here. It's a long story," Liane said casually and attempted to slip past them.

The guards thrust out spears, blocking her path.

"No one is to enter the palace, today," the woman said crisply.

Liane blinked at them. In all her years of sneaking in and out of the palace, she'd never had trouble sneaking back in. The gate guards knew her by now and typically let her pass with an indulgent shake of their heads.

"I think you're mistaken. I'm Princess Liane. I was out overnight, but I'm back now. Surely Mother sent out a search for me..." unless Luzie hadn't followed through on her threat and kept her leaving the palace a secret.

"I hadn't heard of a missing princess, had you?" the man asked, scratching his chin.

"I didn't." The woman hadn't taken her eyes off Liane and scanned her up and down, lingering on the too-short hem of her borrowed uniform. "Nor do I know princesses who pretend to be maids."

Liane tugged subconsciously at the hem of her dress but quickly straightened her shoulders. She didn't have time for this. She needed to get inside and get changed before her witness arrived.

"Who's your superior officer?" Liane challenged, meeting their skeptical gazes with an arrogant tilt of her chin.

"Lieutenant Rothman."

She recognized the name, as she did with most officers of the gate, and felt confident. He'd vouch for her.

"Bring him here."

The woman nodded to the man, and he hurried inside in search of the lieutenant. A few seconds later, they returned with the ruddy-faced lieutenant in tow.

"Princess Liane!" he exclaimed. Then to his subordinates, "What are you doing? Let her majesty in."

They fumbled over one another in their rush to step aside.

"I didn't realize you were out in the city this morning, or I would have left word with the gate guard. Forgive me, Princess."

"It's fine. But why are the gates locked down?"

"Haven't you heard—" he cut off as a unit of soldiers marched past. Midnight Guards. They were swarming the palace, patrolling all quarters. More than they'd been since the opera singer's murder. A prickle ran down her spine. Had something else happened?

"We better get you inside," the lieutenant said with a pitying look at her.

Liane's stomach clenched as a thousand horrific scenarios played out in her mind. Were Mother or Father hurt? What about Aristea? By the stars, she'd never forgive herself if her family was harmed and she wasn't there to protect them.

"What happened?" Liane asked.

He shook his head. "I shouldn't say. I don't truly know the details myself."

"My family?"

"Safe and accounted for..." he trailed off. "Does the empress know you were outside the palace walls? Because by our report you were indoors at last check. Your maid assured us..."

Then Luzie had covered for her. She deserved all the gold in the royal vaults for being a steadfast friend.

"I won't tell her if you won't," Liane said, trying to tamp down the fear churning in her gut.

The lieutenant visibly relaxed, but they walked the rest of the way back to her apartment in tense silence. When they arrived, her guards were surprised to see her on the wrong side of her door and stepped aside to let her in. Inside, Luzie was sobbing, and Liane rushed over to her, fearing she'd been injured. She turned to Liane with a tear-stained face, but seemingly unharmed.

"Oh, your majesty," she wailed.

"Was someone hurt? The guards mentioned a lockdown, but they wouldn't tell me why..."

"That's not it." She sniffled, dabbing at her running nose. "It's Ludwig!" she cried harder. Her next words unintelligible.

A cold chill ran down Liane's spine. "What about Ludwig, was he hurt?"

She grasped Luzie as shuddering sobs wracked her body and took a deep breath to calm herself as she waited for Luzie to collect herself enough to speak.

"He was arrested last night; they say he'll be executed

for treason. But Ludwig couldn't do such a thing! He loves his empire; he wouldn't plot treason."

The statement struck Liane like a blow to the stomach. She'd doubted Ludwig, but she wasn't willing to turn him over. Then who reported him? She stood to pace. With time and distance, she could see a bit clearer, and she was certain it was Heinrich's doing. Somehow, he'd coerced Ludwig to work with him, to hurt Liane. And he must have been the one to turn him in for treason, perhaps to cover his own tracks.

She had to talk to Ludwig, get his side, and explain it to Captain Rosen. Without warning, Liane threw open her doors, startling her guards for the second time that morning. They chased her as she stormed down the hall, out into the garden, and across the courtyard to the midnight tower.

A pair of guards blocked the entrance to the tower, and she marched straight over to them.

"Let me in. I demand to see Ludwig," she said.

"No one can see the traitor. Not even you, Princess," the first guard said, with a sympathetic look. They all knew and pitied her, but she didn't need their pity; she craved justice.

"Either you'll let me in, or I force my way in."

They shared a look, doubting her ability to do just that. Anger rose in her, flushing her skin. If she wasn't careful, she'd break out with a fever. When they didn't move, she lurched forward to shove her way past them, but they caught her by the shoulders and gently pushed her back. What resulted was an awkward standoff between her guards and the Midnight Guards. Both parties watching the other warily. If she asked them, would her guards fight their way inside for her? If it were Ludwig, he would.

"Do not make this difficult, please," the second guard pleaded.

Liane huffed in frustration.

"Then do as I ask, as I will not ask again."

"We cannot, captain's orders," replied the first guard.

"Let her in," Captain Rosen said, opening the door from behind them.

They snapped to attention, bowing slightly for Captain Rosen, who stared at Liane with an inscrutable stare. Liane stared back, not ready, or willing to back down.

"Ludwig is innocent," Liane told her.

"I think you should talk to him." She stepped aside to allow Liane in.

"Thank you," Liane replied and strolled past her into the tower's interior.

Captain Rosen personally escorted her through the door at the far end of the circular room. A spiral stairwell led down, lit by torches that flickered orange light on dark stone. An inhuman roar echoed up from the bowels of the tower and sent a chill racing up her spine.

"Keep close; this is not a place for a princess," Captain Rosen said, her hand resting on the hilt of her sword as they descended the stairwell into darkness.

Their footsteps echoed off the walls, and apart from her panting breaths, that was the only sound for a very long time. It was colder beneath the ground. The walls were slightly damp to the touch, and the deeper they went, the louder the rumbling growl became. After several flights, they stopped on a landing where a guard sat at a desk. He jumped to attention, saluting Captain Rosen. The stairs went further down from that, and Liane suspected that's where the growling was coming from, but she dared not ask more about it.

Captain Rosen greeted the desk guard before removing a keyring from her hip and unlocking the door with one of the large iron keys. The door swung outward and revealed a hall lined with cells on both sides. Most were empty, except the one in the center. Ludwig sat inside it, his knees drawn up to his chest and his back to her. Liane gripped the bars tightly, as if she could bend them by sheer will and set him free.

"Ludwig!" she said, but his name came out as a strangled gasp, guilt over doubting him choked her.

"You shouldn't be here," he said, without turning to face her.

"I shouldn't? Ludwig, you're behind bars; they say you've committed treason."

"I've done all they said and more. I've done awful things."

A hand clenched around her heart, and she wanted to deny it.

"Don't say that. I know you, you're a good person..." she started to say.

"But I did." He rose to face her; his eyes were haunted and vacant. "I've killed people." In the dim candlelight of his cell, his face was gaunt and menacing.

Her throat clenched closed; she couldn't breathe properly, and her back prickled as warmth spread out from her scar tingling to the tips of her fingers. This must be a nightmare, one she'd wake up from any second. Ludwig wasn't capable of violence.

"I know Heinrich made you do those things; tell me everything, and I'll make sure he's punished. I know he's plotting something with the elves..."

Ludwig clenched his hand into a fist and stared at it. "What does the prompting matter when it was by my own hand?"

"Why? Tell me why and I can fix it."

Ludwig shook his head. "What does it matter the reason? You'll never find proof of what he did. He's too powerful, has too many connections..."

"I can stop him. We're going to get revenge for Elias, remember?"

Ludwig lowered his hand to his side. "I thought I could change things, but I was wrong. I'm rotten to the core, and he used my own wickedness to get what he wanted. People like me don't win; there's no justice."

"We can; we're so close." Liane reached through the bars, fingers grasping, hoping if she could just touch him, he'd see reason.

"I've been using stardust. It's too late for me."

Her knees turned to jelly as she crashed onto the floor. "You're using? How?"

Ludwig wouldn't face her. "At first, I wanted to find answers, figure out who was pulling the strings at court, in the City Watch. But they wouldn't trust me, so I took it once, and that led to another and another. It made me powerful, impossibly so. I could do anything despite fatigue or injury. And stranger yet, I didn't wither like others, and my quirks led me to Heinrich; by then, it was too late, and I couldn't stop..."

Liane glanced at his injured leg. That was who killed the apothecarist on a bad leg. Suddenly he was in front of her, standing at the bars of the cell, grasping them. Liane jumped back, startled, and then regretted it at the shame in his expression.

"I—" He choked on his words. Frowned and then tried again. "I wanted you to see me. I wanted you to hear."

Liane blinked in confusion, then realization slowly dawned on her. Last night at the club, Ludwig had known she was following him. He'd led her there.

"What do you know?"

"Ca—" he choked. "T—"

Perspiration covered his brow, as he slumped onto the ground, head in his hands.

Something was keeping him from talking, but what could stop him? What more did he have to lose? He was already in prison. Unless it wasn't fear that was holding him back, but magic.

Ludwig clenched the bars until his knuckles turned white as he looked at her, trying to convey some message with his eyes. Heinrich was plotting something during the Sun Ceremony. Stardust was giving Ludwig and perhaps others special powers... A coup. It had to be; he'd always resented his place second to Aristea. He'd been trying to conceive an heir... Her stomach churned at the thought. But that didn't explain where stardust fit in to his plot...

"We need to talk," Captain Rosen said.

"Can't you see he's innocent?" Liane said.

"He's already confessed to killing the opera singer and plotting with elves in a coup. We cannot strike those confessions from the record, not when a member of the royal family has already made the accusations."

Ludwig looked at Liane with a stricken gaze before turning away. Words would never be enough, not if Heinrich had pointed the finger first. She had to hope her witness was enough to turn the tides and save Ludwig.

With resistance, Liane left Ludwig in his cell and followed Captain Rosen up the stairs and back to her office. Less than a week ago, she'd been summoned here after being discovered in the ruins. It seemed lifetimes away. Captain Rosen offered her a seat, and Liane's legs practically collapsed under her after climbing so many stairs.

"I have evidence now. I found Heinrich's mistress. She'll confess to their affair and maybe we can question her, find proof of Heinrich's involvement somehow..." Liane said, the words spilling out of her but even as she said it, she knew it wasn't enough. His mistress had already told her she didn't know anything.

Captain Rosen didn't react to her words at all and instead stared out the window which faced the mountain range behind the palace.

"Do you know why I asked you to help me find the traitor?"

"Because you suspected my guard?" Liane prompted. Feeling bitter and angry at Heinrich, at Ludwig, at Captain Rosen for using her like a pawn.

"No. Because you are not swayed by Heinrich's charms like the rest of court."

Liane snorted. "Heinrich is far from charming."

"Isn't he? Why else would Princess Aristea stay with him, despite his infidelity? Why does your empress side with her son-in-law over her daughter?"

"Do you think I know?" Liane snarled.

"You're not listening!" Captain Rosen turned to face her at last. Her expression carved from marble as her voice rose scolding Liane, and partially quenching the flush of impetuous anger that had flared in Liane. She felt like a single raw exposed nerve. If Captain Rosen didn't get to her point soon, she might explode again and lose her chance to save Ludwig.

"Then what do you want from me!" Liane asked between clenched teeth.

"We're not sure how but Heinrich is using some forbidden magic or stardust to bend the court to his will. You heard it from Ludwig: some people it gives power to, but you alone seem to be immune to Heinrich, as am I, but I cannot stop him as my hands are tied. But more importantly, your ability seems to neutralize his hold; somehow, if you can convince your family, then my men and I can do the rest."

Liane sank back into her chair as she processed the words, and a hand squeezed around her heart. It was magic all along; that's why Aristea stayed, why Mother believed him despite his obvious lies.

"Why are you telling me this now?"

"Because I wasn't sure I could trust you. This power is

dangerous, and you can never be certain who might be under its influence."

She took another shuddering breath. Then she'd have to convince her family, and some way, somehow, break the spell. Maybe if they were confronted with his mistress, it would jolt them. And if Liane was wrong... Liane shook her head. It'd have to be enough because the alternative was unthinkable.

"I think I have a plan."

"Good, there isn't much time. Whatever he's planning, it is happening on the solstice. I fear there are others like Ludwig, who've gained power from the stardust, and he'll use them as his soldiers. I can have my men on alert, but I'd rather the problem be neutralized before then."

Two days. She'd have to stop him before then.

<h1 style="text-align:center">25</h1>

With the threat of rebellion hanging over her, Liane was more restless, hot, and sweaty than usual as she paced, waiting for Heinrich's mistress to arrive. If the woman didn't show, she'd have to find another way to convince her family. She was about to give up when she noticed a lone figure surveying the gates with uncertainty. She cautiously approached and trembled as if the slightest breeze might send her running in the other direction. Before she could change her mind, Liane rushed to greet her.

"I've been expecting her; let her through," Liane said to the guards, hoping to wave the woman through without the usual search. There wasn't a moment to waste.

"Yes, Princess. But first, we must inspect her for weapons," the guard said, his tone slightly annoyed.

"Princess?" the woman gasped, color draining from her face as she looked at her wide-eyed.

"Yes, yes. Hurry up," Liane said to the guards, tapping her foot as she waited for them to make certain the woman wasn't a threat.

When they were finished, she stepped out, eyes lowered to the ground.

"You didn't mention you were a princess..." the mistress said, eyes lowered as if she feared looking directly at Liane.

"That's not important right now. There's someone you need to speak with." She grabbed her by the wrist and pulled her toward the palace.

When they entered the grand hall, courtiers cast strange looks in their direction, which Liane ignored. With the Sun Ceremony mere days away, the palace was bursting at the seams with visitors, and it made bringing a guest inconspicuously impossible. Not that it mattered anymore. Heinrich knew she was onto him, and as long as she got to Aristea first, he couldn't do anything else to hurt her.

She found Aristea in the hall of entertaining, holding court with a few foreign dignitaries visiting for the Sun Ceremony. Not wanting to make a spectacle out of an innocent woman by dragging her into the middle of the room, Liane left her by the door, promising to return for her before approaching Aristea. She had to push her way through the crowd until Aristea noticed her and motioned for them to make way.

"We need to talk," Liane whispered in her ear.

"Liane, now isn't the time," Aristea said with an unflappable smile. Then to the woman speaking, she said,

"Lady Beltrod, you were saying." She gestured to the woman Liane had interrupted.

The woman wrinkled her nose at Liane for her interruption, but Liane ignored her.

"It's urgent," Liane said, not bothering to whisper this time.

"Even so," Aristea said out of the corner of her mouth.

"There's someone I need you to meet." Liane pointed to Heinrich's mistress, who was standing in the doorway to the hall, eyes large and round and mouth agape as she took in the gilded ceilings and painted murals on the wall. When several heads swiveled to look at her, she stood up straighter and rolled her shoulders back. Liane snapped her attention back to Aristea, who was flushed for a brief moment, before her courtier's mask slid back into place. With a few muttered excuses, she stood, grasping Liane by the elbow and guiding her out of the room.

"You follow," Aristea said to the woman in a tone that was not to be disobeyed.

They took shelter in the closest, empty room, and Aristea slammed the door behind them. Not since they were children had Liane seen her this angry. At times when she was frustrated at Liane for not listening, she'd fly into a rage and stomp and growl. When she turned to Liane in that moment, she was reminded of the tantrums Aristea used to throw.

"What are you thinking bringing Heinrich's mistress into the palace?" she seethed.

Liane's mouth hung open, and she struggled for words for a moment. "You knew?"

"Of course, I knew. Do you think I'm a fool?" Aristea

hissed, "Now take her out of here before anyone else sees." Aristea shook and wouldn't look at the woman directly, but her skin flushed red, making her golden hair illuminate softly.

"I didn't bring her here to humiliate you. I brought her here to prove to you Heinrich is plotting treason."

Aristea's eyes flashed. "This again?"

"He framed Ludwig, and he's been controlling you with magic! We must stop him before he stages a coup during the Sun Ceremony!"

Aristea's face softened, and her clenched fists uncurled as she shook her head. She was getting through to her; for a moment, she saw confusion cross Aristea's expression as she struggled to comprehend. Then her eyes glazed over, and she shook her head.

"Liane, you look flushed. I know the news about Ludwig upsets you, but this sounds like another hallucination." Aristea reached out to cup her cheek, but Liane knocked her hand away.

"Why won't you listen? Heinrich is never going to be faithful, and he's never going to give you an heir because he's impotent," Liane said, slinging harsh words she wouldn't otherwise in hopes it broke whatever hold Heinrich had over her.

It did the opposite, however, and Aristea's expression was carved from stone. With a sharp inhalation, she said, "I know Heinrich isn't perfect, but neither am I. If I can't give him what he wants and needs, it's worth it to let him find joy in other women," she said the words as if by rote. Then turning to look at the mistress, their eyes met, and the woman bowed lower, dropping to her knees and trembling like a leaf. "Go. I wish you no harm but leave the palace," Aristea said, sounding suddenly very tired.

The woman jumped up as if struck by lightning before scuttering out of the room. Liane watched her go, a knot of dread twisting in her stomach.

"Then this is it? You'll trust his word over mine?" Liane said, her temper getting away from her.

"This isn't about trusting him more. You're feverish and not in your right mind…"

Liane shook her head. Aristea was a lost cause, and she couldn't convince her; she'd have to go to Mother directly. Liane stormed out of the room, without another word to Aristea.

As she ran down the hall, her scar throbbed. Despite her protests to Aristea, she felt a fever brewing, and it made her sluggish, and putting each foot in front of another started to feel like running through mud. But there wasn't time to waste. Up the stairs and around the corner, she headed for Mother and Father's personal quarters. When she arrived, she threw open their chamber door, surprising Father, who was being dressed by his servant.

"Where is Mother?" Liane asked, bent over, and panting for breath.

"Liane, you're flushed. Is something wrong?" Father said, waving away the servant.

She shook her head, but Father grasped onto her shoulders, and she leaned into his grip to keep standing upright. Concern marred his face as he pressed the back of his hand to her forehead. "You're burning up with a fever. We need to summon the Vice Premier."

"It's nothing, just a little hot out. Now, where is Mother?" Liane bit out. Why did they all treat her as if she were made of glass, as if she might break at the slightest touch? Ever since the accident, they'd treated her this way, and she was sick of it. For once, couldn't they just listen to her?

"Take a seat. I'll have my servant bring you some iced wine."

She couldn't sit down and sip wine; urgency thrummed through her. If she sat down, she might not have the strength to stand again. It felt as if everything was about to crumble around her.

If Mother wasn't in their chamber, she must be in the hall hearing the day's petitions. Ignoring her father's pleas, she jogged out and passed by her guards, who'd just caught up. And when she ran past groups of courtiers, they pinned themselves against the walls to avoid being bowled over. Whispers followed her. There'd be rumors of her crazed episode for weeks to come, but she'd endure it if she could find Mother and convince her.

A line of petitioners stood outside the double doors of the audience chamber, and Liane passed them up, ignoring their grumbles of protest. Mother sat at the center of the room, beneath vaulted ceilings and frescos of Cyra riding on clouds. Behind her, a painted sun rose, the beams seeming to burst out from her. The Dukes of Parliament, who flanked her on the benches to her left and right, muttered as Liane approached.

"Liane, we're in the middle of a hearing." She looked more confused than angry; it was a start, at least.

A man kneeling in front of her mother, clutching his feathered cap, glanced in uncertainty between them.

"This can't wait," Liane said breathlessly.

Mother stood, splaying her hands on the table in front of her. "What is so important that it can't wait?" she asked.

"Heinrich is plotting treason and framed Ludwig for it."

Audible gasps rippled through the room, as dukes and clerks alike shuffled in their seats. Apart from that, no one spoke as Mother stared at her with cold, hard eyes. No one else dared to look at her directly.

When no one would speak, Liane presented her case.

"I've been investigating stardust for years now, and I've realized it has properties beyond our comprehension. In most users, it eats away at their bodies, before eventually killing them. In others it makes them stronger, gives them abilities we've never seen. And now I know why. It is being provided to Heinrich and the gangs by elves, and he's using it to build an army of super soldiers, and he'll use it to stage a coup!" Liane was gasping for breath by the time she was finished.

"That is a serious accusation," Mother said. At least she wasn't trying to dismiss her entirely, like Aristea had.

"Then you'll arrest him?"

Mother shook her head slowly. "We've heard all this evidence already. Just last night, Prince Consort Heinrich led the raid, which uncovered the Onyx Gang's lair. He found documents linking them to elven traders and exposed a spy in our midst: Ludwig."

Her vision blurred, and she struggled to stay upright.

"That's not true, he framed Ludwig. Heinrich is—"

The room spun around her, and Liane grasped onto the back of a nearby chair to stand upright. In a moment, Mother was around the table and embraced her to prevent her from tipping over.

"You're burning up. It's another fever. Someone call the Vice Premier!" Mother shouted.

She felt as if she were sinking, being dragged down into mud that covered her face starving her of oxygen. She wanted to argue and fight for Ludwig, but the sound of wings beat in her ear, and over her head, she thought she saw a raven peering down at her with golden eyes from the ceiling. The inky-black of its feathers seeped outward, leeching color from the fresco.

"On the longest day, the sun shall rise, and the end becomes the beginning." The words echoed inside her brain, rattling around in her skull. She blinked and sunbursts burned behind her eyelids.

Searing pain radiated out from her back. It felt as if she were burning, set aflame by invisible fire, and the only thing keeping her from slipping into oblivion was Mother's arms, her last link to reality, but even that started to slip through her fingers. She was falling, tumbling endlessly through black oblivion with no end in sight.

26

Waiting for the damned summer sun to set had nearly driven Erich out of his skin, or perhaps it was because the dragon was too close to the surface. As evening approached, it grew emboldened, making his emotions volatile and unpredictable. Normally when the moon was this full, he was alone in the woods, and he didn't have to fear accidental discovery. That day, rather than risk exposure to Ivar and his household, he'd spent the entire day in the city dodging pilgrims, and now his nerves were raw, and his jaw ached from clenching it. As he approached the temple, a stream of pedestrians flowed down the temple steps; their long shadows stretched out behind them, creating monstrous silhouettes, and the air smelled like smoke. Great gray plumes rose behind the temple, muddying the orange and pinks of the twilight sky. Until the solstice, they'd burn non-stop in Sundland; the sky barely lightened in the summer months, and such practices weren't necessary.

Then it struck him, he'd never see another solstice in his homeland, and his mood soured more. Best not to think of it. He must focus on the task at hand. He couldn't afford another distraction. Someone tapped Erich on the shoulder, and he spun around to see Fritz grinning at him.

"Ready?" Fritz asked.

"Not traveling by shadows today?" Erich asked.

"Even I won't risk gaining their attention." He nodded toward a couple of Midnight Guards standing alert at the base of the temple steps, watching the flow of pedestrians going in and out.

Erich knew they weren't there to oversee pilgrims, but instead, they'd doubled the normal guards from the last time he'd been there. He just hoped Fritz had some elven trick up his sleeve to get them inside, undetected.

"You're not as fearless as I thought," Erich said, tearing his gaze away from the temple.

"Little late for doubt, isn't it?" Fritz said, as if reading his mind.

"Only if your plan is strolling in past those guards in broad daylight."

"Like I said, I'm not that reckless. They're not typical humans..." his gaze lingered on the guards but didn't expand on the thought.

Erich was tempted to ask him more, but he feared the answer and held his tongue. Whatever they were didn't change his need, and it was too late to turn back now.

"Then what are you thinking?" Erich asked.

"Follow me." Fritz strolled past the temple steps, and down a nearby alleyway.

A large open space encompassed the temple and, at its perimeter, buildings. Shops, mostly selling souvenirs and relics, crowded in. A river that the city had been built up around ran along one side of the temple, and along its soft banks, there were no structures. Fritz led him to the river's edge, and they walked along the sandy shore for a while, as luxury merchant townhouses overlooking the river loomed above them. They were nearly a block away from the temple, when Fritz stopped to kneel by the water's edge.

"Did you get turned around? We're nowhere near the temple," Erich remarked

"Do you see it?" Fritz pointed at the side of a nearby retaining wall.

Squinting, he could make out iron bars against what appeared to be some sort of sewer grate. He was going to make them climb through sewage again. Erich started to shake his head, then stopped. If they got through this damned night alive, he'd be cured, and what was one last time climbing through sewage to be free at last?

Erich waded into the water, which was surprisingly shallow. It hardly came up to mid-thigh, but Fritz didn't immediately follow him.

"What's the holdup?" Erich asked him.

"You're not going to argue?" Fritz asked, eyebrow cocked.

Erich shrugged. "You haven't steered me wrong before."

"It's almost as if you trust me."

"Don't get ahead of yourself."

Fritz laughed and waded in after him. The sun was starting to set now, and away from the perpetual burning braziers of the temple, darkness descended quickly. Which was for the best, cause then he couldn't get a good look at the chunks floating by in the water. The water was up to his waist by the time they reached the grate, and Erich could see it had already been snapped apart like brittle twigs. Apart from where it broke, the metal looked new without corrosion, and he concluded Fritz had come early to make way.

Fritz climbed up into the man-sized hole first, then turned to offer Erich a hand up, even though he was twice Fritz's size and just as likely to pull him back down. Erich grasped the edges of the gap and pulled himself up, his feet slipping in the sludge pouring from the grate. It took him a moment to stabilize his footing. Once he got inside, he couldn't stand up all the way and had to stoop over as he wiped thick slime onto the dry part of his tunic. He'd have to burn it all later; the stench would never come out. His eyes adjusted to the darkness, and he realized the pipe they were standing in was very old, seemingly carved from the stone with thousands of chisel marks.

"Where I'm from, pipes like this carry warm air to heat homes and buildings," Fritz explained. "It would have gone to houses that were here before, but those routes are closed now, but the one leading into the temple is still open."

"How do you know it's the same here?"

Fritz touched a marking in the wall, worn and covered

in grime. But when his finger brushed over it, a rune faded briefly in the dim light.

"A warming enchantment, faded into nothing now. But the tunnel is full of them, and the temple is the only building that remains from before the fall." For a moment, Fritz's eyes glowed gold, reminding him that his companion wasn't human.

Without another word, Fritz headed down the tunnel, footsteps splashing softly, and Erich pushed away questions about the temple and tunnel's origins. As Fritz said, the tunnels branched in many directions, some collapsed, others slanting upward and dripping sludge. Every so often, he felt a prickle of magic and found some half-eroded rune carved into the wall. As curious as he was, the pungent odor stinging his nostrils kept him moving, and they traveled deeper. They'd taken several turns, his back ached from stooping, and he was starting to fear they'd never escape those infernal tunnels when Fritz stopped suddenly.

"That's our way up," Fritz said.

That one didn't have sludge oozing down it, a small mercy. Bracing their legs on the sides, they shimmied up as the incline grew steeper, and by the time they reached the top, Erich's legs and arms were trembling with exertion when Fritz stopped and pressed his hands against something. Stone scraped seconds before light poured into their tunnel, and Erich blinked in the sudden light. Fritz climbed out first, and Erich a second later.

It brought them to what appeared to be a washing room. Large steaming vats sat on ashen coals, and lines of linen crisscrossed the room covered in dangling wet robes, dripping onto the flagstone. Though the fires beneath the vats weren't lit, a lingering heat remained. Beyond the hanging clothes, neat piles of folded robes and sheets lay on a table.

"We can't walk around smelly and leaving muddy footprints giving us away," Fritz said, tossing Erich a set of priest's robes.

"Couldn't you have found a vent that led directly into where they're keeping the sword?" Getting into costume and sneaking around might be the elf's thing, but Erich preferred the more direct route.

"They're too smart for that, I'm afraid. That tunnel collapsed long ago."

Shedding his clothes, Erich yanked on the robe, which was a bit too small for his bulky frame, the sleeves cutting off above his wrist, and squeezed his biceps. Fritz's robes, on the other hand, fit him perfectly.

"You've done this before, haven't you?" Erich asked, curiosity getting the better of him.

"It's important to know your enemy," Fritz admitted, flashing him a grin beneath the priest's veil.

He wondered how much time the elf spent in this temple, investigating the cracks and crevices, flushing out their secrets. When he'd run into him in the infirmary, he thought it was a one-time exception, but perhaps he'd been here more times than Erich realized.

Pulling down his own veil, he was surprised it didn't block his vision as he feared. By some clever invention, the layers of sheer fabric stopped others from seeing his eyes, but he could see out without much obstruction. The discovery left him unsettled. Though he didn't worship the goddess Cyra, it felt sacrilegious to uncover one of the mysteries of their temple.

"Now, keep close, walk slow, and don't talk to anyone," Fritz instructed.

Erich nodded his head. He knew what he was here for. The muscle. Fritz never needed him to steal the sword; he was a security measure. If anything went wrong, he was there to ensure they got out alive.

Fritz guided him out of the laundry, up a set of stairs, and down a corridor that ended at the door opening onto a wider hallway. When he was certain there was no one there, they stepped out. As they turned a corner, two priests approached from the other way. Without speaking, Erich and Fritz bobbed their heads in greeting, and the priests returned it without a second glance. Once they were past them, Erich let go of a breath he'd been holding. They'd passed the first test. Now to get the sword.

Down the second set of stairs that ended in a long, darkened passageway, Erich felt a prickle of magic race up his spine. Double doors, taller than him, blocked the passage, and more surprising were the runes burned into the wood. He didn't recognize any of them, but he presumed they made the wood impervious to burning or prevented break-ins.

"The church banned the use of runes," Erich said, hand hovering over the markings. They were charged with magic that warmed him, like the brush of an animal against his palm.

For as long as he could remember, he'd felt a sort of kinship to the markings; they drew him instinctively in ways he could not explain. But just as someone cursed as he was by corruption, he'd learned to fear them as well. Erich withdrew his hand, but Fritz did not share his hesitation and pressed the flat of his palm against the runes. They glowed beneath his touch, shifted along the wood, circling around him like eager hounds. He'd never seen that before; it was as if they were alive.

"For the same reason, they've gathered up seers and magic adept to their cause, for their own gains," Fritz remarked, his concentration focused on the door.

"What do you mean—" Erich started to ask, when a high-pitch whine filled the room. It was coming from the door.

"Damn. I set off one of the triggers. Cover me; I need to focus to disarm it." Fritz put his second hand on the door, and runes started to swirl, faster and faster, blurring together, creating several concentric rings before closing in around his hand, and when they touched Fritz, he hissed in pain. The runes started inching up his arms, then their colors shifted to red, then to blue, and back to gold.

The colors pulsed, swirling and mesmerizing, and Erich had to tear his eyes away to not get pulled into them as well. Hand on his dagger, Erich ran to the end of the hall, ears pricked for any approaching footsteps, but it was hard to hear anything with the screeching door in the background.

Fortunately, or rather unfortunately for Erich, he didn't need to hear because two priests burst into the hall. When they saw him, they hesitated just long enough for Erich to launch himself at them and knock them both unconscious with two swift strikes to the tops of their heads. They crumpled onto the ground, and Erich dragged them out of sight. He didn't want their unconscious bodies to alert the next wave, and he felt certain there would be more. And the next one might be Midnight Guards.

"How's it going?" Erich shouted over the alarm.

Dots of perspiration dampened Fritz's forehead, and the runes were off his arm and back on the door, more purple and quivering but in place. Then with a gasp, they turned blue, and Fritz stumbled back, panting for breath as the screeching stopped. With the alarm disabled, they'd likely bought themselves a little time, but not much. The entire temple would be on alert. Fritz got back to his feet and threw open the doors of the vault, and stepped inside. Erich turned his back to keep watch.

"Uh, Erich," Fritz called from inside the vault.

"Problem?"

"Huge."

Erich turned and found Fritz, holding the Golden Blade.

"We got the sword; what's the problem?" Erich asked, eyes darting down the hall, not taking long to look at their prize.

"That's the problem. I don't feel any magic coming from this. It should be imbued with the goddess' essence, but it's just dead metal."

A stone settled in his stomach. A decoy? Then they'd come all this way for nothing... Erich rushed over and took it from Fritz, but he knew it was true as soon as he grasped it. He felt nothing at all, no call of the ancient, no wellspring of magic welling up in response to his. Footsteps thundered down the hall, and if they wanted out with their lives, they had to get out of there before they were cornered.

The problem was the only way out was toward them. They ran back the way they came and stopped at the top of the stairs, their path blocked by three Midnight Guards. The dragon reared its head, nostrils flaring and leathery wings flapping against his ribcage. There was no getting away without a fight, and if he unleashed the dragon's power, he could win, but it meant exposing himself.

"Do it," Fritz said as if reading his thoughts.

Erich unleashed one of the chains holding back the dragon, and, with one link free, he was greedy for more. It tugged at the rest of its bindings, fighting him for control, but he held back, not ready to unleash his full power. Despite his inner struggle, strength pulsed through him, burning in his veins like poison. When a guard swung a sword at him, he caught it in his hand. It sliced his palm, and blood dripped from his hand, but the wound was already healed. Erich bent the tip of the sword in his hand, and the Midnight Guards' eyes widened in terror.

Pulling out his dagger from its sheath with his free hand, he twirled through them, slicing with superficial cuts enough to wound and disarm but not to kill. Blood splattered onto the pure white of his priest robes as the guards crumpled to the ground in front of him. The scent of blood and the rush of the fight was going to his head, and the dragon roared, hungry for fresh meat. Erich knelt down, grasping the front of a man's shirt, bringing him close, his nostrils flaring.

Fritz grasped onto his shoulder, pulling him back, and it brought Erich to his senses.

"What are you waiting for? Let's go," Fritz said, not mentioning Erich had been seconds away from tearing out a man's throat.

Erich blinked at the chaos he'd unleashed, felt the dragon pull loose, and he slammed the chains back again, holding tighter than before. Then they ran. It would take too long to go back through the tunnels, and if they were cornered, they couldn't fight properly, so they bowled over pilgrims leaving the temple late and down the steps.

Erich ran hard and fast, until his heart felt like it might burst. He had to get out of the city. Now that the Midnight Guard knew he was corrupted and worse, that he'd gotten a taste for blood. If he stayed in Artria, he'd be a danger to himself and others. But to get away safely, he needed Ivar's help.

27

Liane woke with a gasp and sat up straight in bed. She blinked past blurry eyes at the shifting light and shadows around her. It took a moment for the room to come into focus, but as her bedroom solidified around her, she noticed Mother sitting at the edge of her bed, clutching a cold cloth in her hand. As a child, Mother often dabbed at her forehead to help soothe her as the fevers raged.

"I think your fever's broken, but you should rest some more," Mother said, in a low, soothing voice.

"How long was I out?" Liane asked; her mouth was dry and her throat scratchy.

"An afternoon and the night."

Liane pressed her fingers to her throbbing temples. Typical of her fevers, her head was pounding, and her back ached, accompanied by an itching, burning sensation spreading out from her spinal column. The rash would linger for days, but at least there wasn't a massive black crow staring at her from the corner of her room. She'd been hallucinating again, but these past few times felt more real than usual... She shook her head; there wasn't time; the fever had already robbed her of what little she had.

"Heinrich is going to attack during the Sun Ceremony," Liane said, infusing all the confidence she had into that single statement.

Mother smoothed the blankets and wouldn't look her in the eye.

"It was a bad dream, darling. You'll see when you feel better," she said.

"It wasn't a dream." She tried to grab Mother's shoulder, but her grip was weak, the fever had sapped her strength, and her arm trembled with the effort of holding it up.

Mother gently removed her hand before sandwiching it between hers with a sigh. "Enough, Liane."

"He's put you under a spell that I'm immune to. He's twisting all your minds with some diabolic magic, and planning to overthrow the throne." The words spilled out of her like an overflowing cup, and the same urgency flared in her skin, making her skin warm.

"When do the lies stop?"

"I'm not lying; you're just not listening!" Liane shouted in exasperation.

"You've been lying to me for years; how can I hope to trust a word you say?" Mother said, using a stern tone she rarely used on her.

Liane's mouth opened and closed, like a fish out of water.

"What—I—" she choked on the words. Shame colored her cheeks, and Liane stared at the bedspread; she'd been caught.

"I knew you were sneaking out of the palace playing vigilante with Ludwig, and I looked the other way because I thought it would help you move past Elias. But considering certain revelations, I fear I was wrong. What if he'd hurt you?"

"Ludwig would never hurt me. Heinrich framed him!" Liane started to protest.

"Not, Ludwig. Prince Erich—or whatever his real name is…"

Liane blinked with confusion; what did Erich have to do with any of this?

"I was going to tell you about Prince Erich, but I had to find proof."

"Then you knew he was a fake prince all along and didn't say anything." Mother looked at her aghast, one hand clutching her chest.

"A fake… but…"

Ice coursed through her veins and turned her stomach. She didn't know anything about Prince Erich and had entered an agreement with him thinking she had the upper hand, but he'd been lying to her all this time. She wrapped her arms around her torso, feeling dirty and used.

He lied to her about everything.

Mother squeezed her hand. "I was fooled as well until Duke Mattison came to the palace. When I mentioned Prince Erich, he told me that the real Prince Erich went missing six years ago and is presumed dead. Whoever that man was, he's an imposter."

She thought she was going to be sick as she slumped back down onto the bed.

Mother tucked her in up to her chin.

"Rest a while." Mother planted a kiss against her forehead.

"Where is he now?" Liane asked as Mother walked toward the door.

She looked sad for a moment. "The City Watch is on their way to arrest him now. He'll never be able to hurt you again."

As Mother walked out of her room, Liane sat in the silence and knowledge of Erich's betrayal. Then she shoved it aside. In the end, he would be another of an endless string of disappointments, and she would forget him because she had to. But it didn't lessen the sting, not one bit.

THE PRIEST'S robes were too conspicuous, and Erich had discarded them not long after leaving the temple, in favor of a pair of pants and tunic he'd stolen from a washing line. They were too small and slightly damp, but better than the alternative. He'd taken the long way back, not wanting to bring trouble to Ivar's doorstep, and his thighs and arms were chafed by the time he arrived at the ambassador's townhouse, reeking of sewage, and sweat, and wearing stolen clothes. But at least he felt confident the attempted theft of the Golden Blade couldn't be traced back to him. He'd spent all night leading the guards on a chase through the city, leaving false leads along the way.

As he stumbled through the door, the servant, accustomed to strange arrivals, simply crinkled his nose and suggested a bath. Erich trudged upstairs to shed his stolen clothes as a pair of servants filled a pewter tub with boiling water for him. As he undressed, his muscles cramped, and he grit his teeth against the pain. Any time the dragon was unleashed outside of the full moon, it depleted him. It was good he hadn't lost full control, or he might be curled up in a ball, writhing in pain. As it were, he'd be feeling the aftereffects for days. Precious time he needed to escape the city and seek shelter for the full moon.

Tomorrow night. One day to get out.

Once the bath was filled, Erich sank into the warm water, letting it ease his aching, tired muscles. Dirt muddied the water, and the tub had to be changed three times before it ran clear. And when it did, Erich dismissed the servants to allow himself a few moments to soak and regain some of his strength. Head resting against the rim of the tub, he stared up at the ceiling. If he could get official papers from Ivar, he could leave the city with minimal hassle, and from there, maybe he should head north to the feral lands. If the elves were anything like Fritz, they'd accept him as he was, or at the very least, he wouldn't be a danger to them.

Erich held up his hand; he'd almost killed an innocent man in cold blood tonight. Maybe he didn't deserve a cure; perhaps there was no changing him from the monster he was deep inside. With a groan, he ran his palm over his face.

Someone knocked at his chamber door. The bath water was cold anyway, and so he climbed out and pulled on the clean tunic and breeches, before going to answer the door. All the while, the knocking grew more persistent, and when Erich threw the door open, he wasn't surprised to see Ivar on the other side, face flushed.

"Thank the Trinity, you're here. You're being summoned to court."

Ivar shook his head, and his gaze darted down the stairs where the palace messenger presumably waited.

Erich ran a hand along his jaw. "I don't have time for that; I need to leave the city today. I'll be headed back to Sundland." He figured it was easier to lie to Ivar about his reasons than try and coerce him.

For a moment Ivar perked up. "Does that mean?" Then Ivar's expression fell. "We'll arrange for that after you've been to the palace... There's a small problem..." Ivar leaned in, whispering the last part.

They couldn't have found him this quickly. He'd been careful to make sure he wasn't followed...

"Ambassador Gunderson, what is the delay?" said a guard in palace livery. Not a Midnight Guard as he'd feared, but no more reassuring.

"Nothing, we were getting ready to go." Ivar glanced down at Erich's bare feet. "His majesty was about to put on his boots and join you. If you'll give us but a moment."

"What is the meaning of this?" Erich asked, taking on a hardly-used tone of royal impatience.

"It's been reported that someone is impersonating the lost Prince of Sundland."

"According to who?" Erich asked.

"The King of Sundland." The man held up a document, imprinted with the three-headed dragon, the Sundland royal seal.

The document looked real enough, but Father couldn't have known he was here in the city. There was no way a message could have gotten there and back in time. Erich looked to Ivar. "What is the meaning of this?"

"Duke Mattison arrived in the city earlier than expected. I wanted to tell you, but you've been missing for days," Ivar said under his breath.

His uncle, who'd be the next king if Erich were to disappear, permanently. He doubted he'd vouch for his identity if he were brought into questioning. Or at the least, leave him locked in a dungeon long enough for his identity to be exposed. Whatever the outcome, going with these guards was out of the question.

"You'll need to come with us until everything is sorted." The guard reached for him.

Instincts kicked in, and he rolled his shoulder to avoid his reach before swinging up and catching him in the jaw. The guard stumbled back as Erich drew his dagger and slashed at the man behind the first, clearing a path down the stairs. Bare feet slapping on the wood floors, he ran through the foyer. Two more guards were waiting outside with a carriage, presumably meant to transport him to the palace. Erich feinted toward them, before turning and running down the street.

"Stop that man, in the name of Empress Eveline Starweber!"

But the pedestrians on the street simply jumped out of the way, perhaps more fearful of the crazed look in his eyes. He'd known he shouldn't have claimed his identity again; he just never expected it to catch up with him so soon. Swerving, he headed down a nearby alleyway, leaping over refuse to scale a fence. The dragon stirred, flapping leathery wings, close to the surface as the full moon approached and emboldened by the taste of freedom from the night before. But Erich resisted the call of that power. He wouldn't kill unless he had to, and he already felt its hunger stirring.

For now, the palace guards simply thought he was a fraud, but if they made the connection between him and the corrupted from the temple, he'd be sent to the Midnight Tower, never to escape. Erich ran down a narrow alley and onto a busy street, where he slowed his pace, as to not draw attention along the crowded market street. He dared not look over his shoulder to check if he was being followed but marched forward despite the odd looks from passersby, who noticed his bare feet. They gave him a wide berth, probably assuming he was insane, and it left him exposed. And when a trio of palace guards rounded the street corner, they spotted him straight away.

Reverting his course, he ran in the other direction. This time the crowds worked against him and slowed his progress as the guards shouted for him to stop. Fear burned in his chest. Was this the end? Did all his struggle and sacrifice lead to this moment, where he would be executed as a fraud? After all this time, would his uncle's damned meddling be his undoing? A gap between buildings appeared on his right, too small to be considered an alley. He squeezed into it and discovered it ended as a sheer solid wall. No more running; it was either fight or die.

Spinning around, he faced the guards as they approached, weapons drawn. Erich grasped a hold of the chains binding the dragon. If he unleashed him, he'd survive, but there would be blood. Could he live with that on his conscience? Did he want to live, having chosen corruption over humanity? The thought made him hesitate, and they closed in.

"Psst."

Despite his better judgment, Erich's eyes flicked in the direction of the sound.

Impossibly, Fritz's head poked out from the shadows, one hand held out to Erich. Without thinking, he took it, and Fritz yanked, pulling him in. Instead of colliding with a solid wall, he was tumbling, falling through a void of darkness. Stars reeled around him, flashing by like comets, spinning, and spinning, until his eyes danced with flickering lights. Then he landed hard on cold rubble, blue sky reeling overhead, and broken marble pillars towered over him. It took him a moment to let his brain catch up with his eyes.

Meanwhile, Fritz lay panting beside him, beads of sweat plastered his dark hair to his forehead.

"That was a close one," Fritz said.

Erich sat up, grabbed his dagger, and stood, turning in a slow circle expecting to find the guards upon them and the city around them. But they were somewhere he'd never seen before but felt the faint prickle of magic.

"Where are we?" Erich asked and kicked a rock to make sure it was real.

"A forgotten place," Fritz said, sitting up. His dark eyes skimmed the surrounding ruins.

"How did you do that?"

"Elf secrets."

Erich stared at him, not sure if he'd gone mad or should be grateful he saved him.

"What was that place?" If Erich closed his eyes, he thought he could still see the stars reeling, the suns burning out and dying.

"The rift. We're not supposed to carry others through it. But I couldn't let them take you. I see why they say not to. I feel like I've been kicked in the ribs." He grabbed his side and inhaled deeply.

"Why do that for me?" Erich asked, studying the elf. After failing to get the sword, he thought he'd seen the last of him.

"I brought you into this. I couldn't leave you to take the fall."

Erich stood up and wouldn't look at Fritz as he crossed his arms over his chest. Scanning the horizon, he could see the edge of the city cresting over the hilltop. He'd gotten out alive, by some miracle.

"I wouldn't have blamed you; I was foolish for hoping there was a cure."

"There's no shame in having hope. It's what keeps us fighting," Fritz said, resting his hand on Erich's arm.

After leaving his old life behind, he'd freed himself of

attachments. No friends, no lovers. But seeing as Fritz had risked his life and for Erich, he might have to reassess that decision. And if he were living another life, he might have told him as much.

"Where will you go from here?" Erich asked.

"I'm not going anywhere," Fritz said, his gaze returning to the horizon.

"But the sword was a fake."

"What we found in the vault was fake. The sword is here, and I know it. I saw you in my dreams, and you led me to the sword, and thanks to you, I'm closer than I've ever been."

"How can you be sure? Because from where I'm standing, you've not done much."

"Because before I met you, I hadn't had a vision in a year."

Erich was silent for a long moment, and Fritz continued staring out at the horizon. "Seeing the future is a tricky thing. We can never be certain what actions will change the flowing course of fate. A year ago, I saw the sword's wielder, a human, a woman. It was something we'd long feared. At first, the elders thought Empress Eveline was the one, but none of the prophecies have come true yet. But they draw closer. We can feel it in the widening of the rift..."

Wind rustled over the ruins, picking up dust and whispering words that made the back of his neck prickle with magic. Erich waited for Fritz to continue.

"I disagreed with the elder's interpretation of my dream and saw the coming of the wielder as a sign of hope. I thought if I could get the sword to her, she could heal the rift and restore balance. But the elders have already decided to destroy it, and so I came here hoping to stop them by getting the sword first."

"You said it yourself; visions are tricky. What if you're wrong?"

"Fate branches infinitely, each choice creates new paths, and we are at yet another set of crossroads. I've decided not to leave, not without the sword."

"Don't you care for your own life?" Erich thrust a hand in the direction of the city. "They'll kill you if they find out what you are."

"It is living that makes us fear death," Fritz said, glancing up at Erich. "You fear the great unknown. But the future is unknowable, even by someone like me. I see nothing but possibilities, and you will stand at many crossroads before the end; this is another."

Erich's hands hung loosely at his sides. He felt like a coward to walk away now. But what other choice did he have? To go back was death. There was nothing left for him there. Then Liane flashed through his mind. He regretted not saying goodbye and leaving her as he did, but it was for the best, wasn't it?

"I can't go back, so I suppose this is goodbye," Erich said and thrust out his hand to shake.

"You never know; our paths might cross again." Fritz shook his hand.

But Erich knew it was better if he was gone, where he couldn't hurt Liane or anyone else. If only his heart and the dragon could agree.

28

Liane stood with arms outstretched as the seamstress tugged on the hem of her Sun Ceremony gown. It had been finished over a week ago, but Liane had summoned her to make one last alteration: a slit up the side. Without the support of her family, and not knowing what Heinrich had planned, she wanted to be prepared for anything, which meant easy access to the dagger she'd have strapped to her thigh.

"How about now, your majesty?" the seamstress asked with a hint of venom in her tone. She'd argued against damaging the dress, and the short notice making last-minute alterations just before they left for sunrise rights, but when Liane had threatened to make the cut herself, she acquiesced.

Cold, silken fabric glided across her heated flesh as she jutted out her leg to test it. Turning her leg in the mirror, she imagined her dagger strapped there and nodded with satisfaction as she pulled back her leg. The fabric fell back into place, disguising the opening between layers of fabric. The seamstress did excellent work.

"Thank you, it's perfect," Liane said.

The fitting finished, she went behind the screen to take off the gown and allow the seamstress to make the final alterations. It was nearly finished, and once she was dressed, they'd head out on the procession to the temple. As the seamstress stepped back to make last-minute adjustments, Luzie came over with a tray of cold fruit and chilled wine.

"You must have read my mind," Liane said, reaching for the glass of wine and holding it with one hand and fanning herself with the other.

The sun hadn't even risen, and she was already burning up. The Vice Premier advised against her participating in the ceremony this year, but Liane had insisted. She'd need all her strength to get through the day, though, and she couldn't risk her fever spiking again. The cold drink slid down her gullet, not providing the relief she'd hoped for, but not deterred, she popped a piece of fruit in her mouth and savored the juices.

Luzie pressed the back of her hand against Liane's brow.

"You're burning up. Should I call the Vice Premier?" she asked.

Liane shook her head. "It's hot in here. Open up the windows, would you?"

"I already did, remember?"

The curtains were drawn back, and she couldn't see much past the gloom of early morning darkness. She wished she could drop herself into a tub of ice, or better yet, go deep into the mountains and swim in an icy mountain river, but without having that as an option, she'd just have to endure.

A sudden knock at the door ripped her from visions of cool escapes, and Luzie hurried over to answer. She'd hardly opened the door when Heinrich came striding into the room, already dressed in his gilded Sun Ceremony doublet and hosen.

She glared at him. She wasn't counting on seeing him this early, and her dagger wasn't within reach. "What are you doing here?" she spat, eyeing the spot on her night-stand where it was hidden.

"Cordial as always, Liane. I take it from your temper; you've heard the news." A slimy smile curled the edges of his mouth.

She resisted the obvious bait; had he seriously come here to gloat over Erich? Was this his attempt at putting her off balance?

"Get out of my room," she snarled, pointing at the door.

Ignoring her, he picked up a sun pendant from among the accessories laid out on her dressing table and ran his thumb across the surface of the pearl inlays, drawing out the moment.

"Sweet, innocent, naïve Liane. You really didn't know, did you?" he said.

She wouldn't rise to the bait and engage with him, though she was tempted to stab the point of the sun pendant into his eye.

"I asked you to leave," she said through clenched teeth.

He turned to face her. A smirk curling over his face. "I came here with a peace offering."

"What?" It left her teetering, stumbling to find something to say. Of all the things she expected from him, it wasn't this.

Heinrich tutted. "We've never gotten along, but I thought we could come to an understanding. I'm not the villain you've made me to be."

"The evidence says otherwise," Liane seethed. The thrumming in her back grew stronger, turning into a crashing beat in her ears.

His smirk slipped for a quick moment but was quickly replaced.

"You don't want to make an enemy out of me, Liane." His voice was low, threatening, and deadly.

"And you shouldn't underestimate me."

He laughed, throwing his head back as if she'd said something truly hilarious. "Don't regret those words later." And then he walked out, leaving her with a pounding headache and a clear determination: she was going to kill him.

As the Sun Ceremony celebrated the power of the feminine, it was customary for the women of the family to lead the procession, which wound its way down Temple Street away from the palace. Mother at the forefront, wore her golden sunbeam crown draped in a golden veil that covered her face, and behind her, Aristea and Liane, acting as goddess handmaidens, wore midnight blue and silver, to represent stars in the night sky. The Sun Ceremony celebrated the longest day of the year, when Cyra's power was at its peak, and she was reborn in fire and sunlight.

Liane, too had armed herself for battle. Because she didn't know what to expect from Heinrich, she tried not to let his threats rattle her and focused on getting to the temple. Pilgrims and citizens alike bordered the street, bowing low as they passed. Their pace was agonizingly slow, and though she'd done this same trek countless times since the age of sixteen, she never remembered it being quite this arduous and taxing. Halfway there and her back throbbed painfully, and each step became a test of will as she put each foot in front of the other, trying her best to keep in time with Aristea.

Sunlight lined the tops of the mountains, but not quite cresting, and a hush hung over the normally bustling city, punctuated by the occasional cough and the subtle shuffle of clothing. Her heartbeat thrummed in her ears, timed with the aching pulse in her back. Almost there. She could do this. Fortunately, her silver veil hid the beads of perspiration on her brow from the crowd gathered, but if she exhausted her energy getting to the temple, how would she stop Heinrich during the ceremony?

Don't think. Just walk, she told herself.

By the time they reached the temple steps, the first rays of morning sun lightened the sky, turning it a ruddy orange.

She searched the crowd for movement, her body tensed and ready for attack. A line of Midnight Guards held them back, clearing the steps for their approach. Liane noticed Captain Rosen among them, and when their eyes met, she nodded in Liane's direction. She was counting on her.

Two rows of priestesses flanked the steps ascending upward to the topmost platform where the Vice Premier and the Avatheos waited, Golden Blade in hand. As Mother mounted the stairs, her long train dragged behind her, rippling like molten gold. Brazier light reflected off the thousands of small reflective stars sewn into the fabric, and light ricocheted across the temple's façade. Gasps and whispered prayers followed as the crowd pushed in, tears pouring from their eyes. For those who'd never been to the city before, it must have seemed like looking upon Cyra herself.

Each movement and gesture was planned down to the most minute detail to enrapture the people. At midday, during the ceremony's apex, Mother would glitter and dazzle even more, as if Cyra had stepped down from the heavens to walk among mortals. But before that, there were hours of prayer and ritual to get through. Maybe Heinrich would interrupt the ceremony and spare her a long and arduous litany of prayers. She could only hope...

As her mother drew nearer, the Avatheos held out the Golden Blade for her to take, and her mother knelt with hands outstretched in offering. It was said Cyra forged the blade from the fire of stars and used it to sever night from day and bring life and light to the world. Mother would use it in the ceremony. As Cyra's representative on earth and in spirit, she would banish the dark. She'd seen the same ritual performed a thousand times before, every year but one: the year the fevers had started, she'd been stricken and confined to bed.

Liane closed her eyes, pushing back the memory. But a phantom heat crawled over her skin, spreading outward like a rash across her body, or maybe it was the after-effects of yesterday's fever. Sweat rolled down her brow, and she resisted the urge to reach under her veil to wipe it away. She needed to focus. Heinrich and Father were standing at the bottom of the steps; they'd followed at the back of the procession. Liane's eyes narrowed on Heinrich, waiting for the slightest twitch of his hand or some signal he would give to his hidden allies in the crowd.

Nothing stood out to her as abnormal. Mother had the sword, and the Avatheos stepped aside. For a moment, she felt his gaze upon her as he stood near Mother. Had he noticed her inattention and was displeased? Liane's stomach twisted, as if a live fish were inside her gut doing summersaults. Mother lifted the sword skyward, and sunlight glinted off its surface, bursting outward in a dramatic display and blinding Liane. As she closed her eyes to block it out, it got brighter and brighter. It felt like direct noonday sun was on her skin, and she felt hot and itchy as if she were crawling with ants.

Beating wings echoed in her ears as a tingling sensation spread out across her skin, leaving her feeling light-headed and uneasy. The fever hadn't left her. It was coming back with a vengeance as she feared, and she swayed on her feet.

But it wasn't like the usual fever; it felt more intense: less of a burn and more a warm feeling that somehow detached her from herself as if she were floating away from her body. Was she hallucinating again? A giant raven, the size of a man, sat atop a nearby rooftop and swiveled its head from side to side as it regarded her, blinking a single, bright golden eye.

"Today, on this longest day, we greet the sun which banishes the darkness," the Avatheos intoned, his voice slicing through the silence and sending a jolt down her spine. In fact, it felt as if someone had dragged a knife down the middle of her back.

The nauseous feeling intensified, and the burning intensified as a buzzing sound rang in her ears. The warmth that pulsed through her began growing stronger and stronger. The raven opened its mouth to caw. *I can't be sick; I have to stop Heinrich.*

"It begins!" the raven croaked before taking to the sky.

Gasping, she bit down to stifle a cry of pain as the Avatheos continued his litany.

"I invoke the goddess who severed the darkness bringing us light," the Avatheos said.

"With this blade, I vanquish the darkness and rebuke the Nameless Goddess and those who serve her," Mother replied.

A pulse and the knife dug deeper. Liane whimpered, wrapping her arms around her body, instinctively curling inward to try to protect her organs.

"I call upon the stars that guide us."

"I answer her call and promise to guide my people into the light."

A beat of drums echoed in her head over and over. It drowned out the sound of everything but the Avatheos, who was glowing a bright, brilliant light that burned her eyes but from which she couldn't look away either.

"I entrust myself to the goddess' power which guides me." The Avatheos' voice rang in her ears as if a bell had been struck. But the sound did not fade; it grew louder and louder and felt as if it would split her open down the middle.

"Cyra, we thank you for the gift of sunlight, we praise you for delivering us from darkness, we give ourselves to your power," Mother replied.

Everything burned. She was being roasted from the inside. Suddenly she felt a whoosh and a pop, and something exploded out of her. And the pain stopped.

Liane opened her eyes and found herself enveloped in soft, glowing light. She blinked a few times, her brain struggling to comprehend its source. Because it was coming from her, from her skin, she was glowing. Horrified and mesmerized, she overturned her hands, examining them with mild horror and fascination. She'd never had a hallucination quite like this before.

Then she turned to look at the crowd, and all eyes were on her. The ceremony had stopped, and Mother held the blade loosely at her side. Before she could try and comprehend, they began to fade, ripple, and distort as if she were looking at them through water. Blinking didn't improve the vision; it only warped more until she was kneeling beside a pool of water, and when she looked up, the two-tone stag was staring at her with his dark and light eyes.

"The end is the beginning and the beginning is the

end," the same echoing voice which spoke to her in the woods said.

"What does that mean?"

"It begins and ends with you," he said.

Then everything seemed to whoosh around her; the light retreated, pulling back and slamming into her chest and leaving her breathless. The temple steps came back into focus, and the stag and pool were gone.

Liane toppled over, head cracking on the temple steps, and through the fog of light around her, she thought the world looked dimmer as if she'd absorbed the morning light around her. There were no clouds in the sky, but the rising sun seemed diminished somehow. The glowing skin was gone, and so was the pain, even the pain in her back, which ached even on good days. Footsteps rushed toward her, and shouts surrounded her.

Mother's face swam in her vision as she cried out her name.

"Liane! Liane!" But it sounded a thousand miles away, as if she were calling out to her from somewhere else. Someone lifted her up into their arms and carried her past the threshold of the temple steps.

This couldn't be happening. She tried to protest, but her tongue was thick in her mouth, and she couldn't form words. They carried her through the pews of the chapel and past the statue of Cyra, whose cold, impassive stare looked down at her from her pedestal, but there was a brilliant glow behind her head, as if it were a halo of light. Liane blinked as Cyra's face transformed into that of her mother's, brows pinched with worry.

"Bring the Vice Premier here straight away," she shouted.

Images flashed through her mind, memories she thought were dreams brought back into vivid detail in her mind. Then her eyes fluttered closed, and she was lost for a time in the past.

A voice roused her from bed. Rubbing sleepy eyes, Liane sat up straight and blinked into the darkness.

"Come, it's time," it said.

As a child, she knew no better and kicked off her blankets to follow its command. They were staying at the summer hunting lodge, and back then, she didn't have guards at her door. She padded out of her bedchamber and into Mother and Father's room, where they were sleeping. The sword was waiting, glowing faintly in the moonlight.

"I've been waiting for you, Liane," the sword spoke to her, but she didn't question it because she'd been dreaming of it for weeks before.

And when she grasped the hilt, she felt its magic coursing through her, but it didn't hurt; it felt warm and familiar.

"Now to the fountain. Hurry, there isn't much time," the sword urged her.

Shockingly all the guards outside were sleeping, and there was no one to stop her from wandering off into the forest alone. The dual-colored stag was waiting for her at the forest's edge, blinking at her passively with its mismatched eyes. Then it bound away, leading her on a chase. She chased after it without tiring and without pricking her bare feet on the bramble. The sword kept her safe. After a long while, she wasn't sure how long, she came to the edge of the fountain. The water was dark and deep, and the edge green and golden, bursting with life. She knelt beside it and gazed into that dark, bottomless void, and the cosmos stretched out before her as the golden sword glowed again in her hand.

"Don't be afraid. It's time. Step into the water," the voice said.

Liane stood up, one foot hovering over the edge, and dipped her toe in. The water crept up, grasping around her leg, tugging her down, holding onto her like a warm embrace. Then she heard shouting, and her concentration broke.

Mother. She was worried about her.

"We must finish," the sword urged. "Do not look away. It is almost complete."

But Mother was crying and shouting her name. She couldn't avoid the call. She turned to see her mother in her nightgown and coat running toward her. As soon as she looked away, pain seared through her, burning her from the inside and roasting her alive. A deep cut sliced along her back, and she became nothing but searing pain.

She dreamed of that night again, in more painful detail than usual. That was when the fevers started, and she'd first hallucinated. Liane thought she must have only dozed for a moment, but when she opened her eyes, she was lying beneath a blanket of stars. Was she back in the forest or falling through that endless void in the pool of water? No. She realized she was staring up at a domed ceiling painted to look like the night sky, inside the temple. What about Heinrich, had he made his move? She had to warn someone. But she was too weak to move or even raise up the thin blanket off her body.

Voices murmured around her, but she could not quite make out what they were saying, and it took all her concertation to make out the words.

"The goddess' chosen has revealed herself. She's the answer we've been seeking, and you've kept her from us."

"You're wrong. Liane can't be her chosen one," Mother said, her voice tight and terrified.

Chosen, for what…? Then she thought of her dream and the sword speaking to her, but it couldn't be real. It was just a dream.

"You should've told me the moment you knew," the Avatheos' voice snapped like a whip crack, echoing across the room and bouncing back at them.

"I saw too many paths to be certain. In some, the princess married and lived a long, happy life, and in others, I saw her falling to the darkness, raising the dead to command. There was never certainty," the Vice Premier replied coolly.

"Your love for the child clouded your judgment. I thought more of you. Now go. I will decide on a punishment for you later."

Rolling her head to the side, Liane saw the Vice Premier bow her head and back out of the room, leaving the Avatheos and Mother. With their backs turned to her, neither of them had realized Liane was awake. They wouldn't have kept speaking candidly if they knew.

Mother paced restlessly, in a way that she'd never seen before. She always seemed calm, unflappable. Right now, the lines around her mouth were pulled taut, and her hair was frizzed and messy. Certainty landed on Liane's chest, with a horrid crushing feeling.

"Why have you kept the truth from me?" the Avatheos said.

Liane wanted to ask her the same question.

Mother stopped pacing to face the Avatheos. "She was a child. Much too young to be burdened with such purpose, especially one whose fate was uncertain."

"I dreamed of her at her birth, born beneath the dragon star. I knew the time was coming. And on her thirteenth birthday, I dreamed again and wrote you, but you denied it. Now she is twenty-six. You've delayed us by nearly three decades. Your selfishness could have destroyed the kingdom, the continent!"

Mother didn't answer, and Liane wanted to shake answers from her. If these dreams were real, if the hallucinations weren't hallucinations. Then... then... Every thirteenth year, there was a thirteenth month. Liane had been born in one of those years. They were considered bad luck years, but she'd never taken it seriously until now.

"If you had a child, you'd understand..."

"All children of light, I love as if they were of my flesh. And the goddess has entrusted me to protect them all. This is why Liane's gift shouldn't be hidden. You did not stand in the way when Mathias chose to walk into darkness. Why would you keep Liane from her destiny?" the Avatheos asked.

"You manipulated him in the same way you manipulated me! He never should have gone just as I shouldn't have made that deal..."

"And lost your kingdom to darkness. We all must make sacrifices."

"You can't have her; I won't let her become your sacrificial lamb."

Her stomach squirmed, and she wished she had the strength to speak out, to ask questions, but it felt as if her lips were glued closed.

"That is for her to decide, isn't it?"

A tense silence followed, and neither spoke for a long moment as a cold stone settled in her stomach. What did Mother mean by sacrifice? What hadn't they told her all this time?

"Fear not, child of light, the goddess will protect her chosen. As she has protected and guided you. For now, let her rest. She has a long road ahead of her."

They left the room, and Liane's questions went unanswered. For a long time, she lay with her eyes closed, listening and hoping they'd come back. A thousand questions rattled around in her mind. Hidden power and secrets she could only imagine. But none of that mattered right now. While she'd been lying unconscious in bed, Heinrich might be making his move.

Sitting up took more out of her than she anticipated, and her head swam as she kicked her legs out over the side of the bed. She tried to stand up and quickly fell back down onto the bed a second later. Then the door opened, and a veiled priest walked in carrying a tray of something aromatic. If she couldn't stop him herself, she had to warn someone.

"Prince Consort Heinrich—" she croaked, but couldn't form words as her throat burned.

"The Avatheos ordered you to drink this," they said in a gravelly voice, offering her the cup, ignoring her statement.

Liane took it on impulse.

"I need to warn you someone is going to steal the Golden Blade. Tell the Avatheos and the others before it's too late."

"You need to drink," they said in reply.

Liane frowned.

"Didn't you hear me?" It took too much effort to argue, and her head pounded.

"Drink." His voice was deep and scratchy, not the usual melodic and soothing voice of a priest.

It seemed strange, but she drank the tonic; maybe then he'd listen. As soon as it touched her lips, she smelled something vaguely familiar though she couldn't quite place the odor. As the priest waited for her drink, she chugged it down in one gulp.

"Now, will you listen to me..." Her words slurred, and the room swam around her.

Her thoughts grew sluggish, and she tried to cry out but couldn't find the words. As she reached for something, anything, she tilted over, back onto the hard mattress. The priest came closer, and as he stood over her, she caught a glimpse of his scarred face beneath the hood. *That wasn't a priest at all,* she thought before darkness took her.

29

On the road, Erich hardly slept because it left him vulnerable. Try and rest in the wrong place, and he'd wake up with a highwayman's knife at his throat. As he left Artria behind, he walked all night, the buzzing fear of his near capture and the impending full moon driving him to put as much distance between him and the city as possible. But as it so often did, exhaustion forced him to stop and rest just before sunrise. What little sleep he got was fitful, thanks to the restless forest.

Wind whistled through the trees, like a whisper. "Erich..." it called.

His eyes flew open, and he stared at the dawn-lit forest. All was suddenly still. The rustling had stopped, and a prickle of magic caressed his skin. It raised the hairs on his arm and the back of his neck.

"Erich." The voice was closer now, as if someone had whispered it in his ear.

He made a slow turn as he took in his surroundings, then a white blur darted past the corner of his eye, and he pivoted toward it, dagger held out in front of him. Not that it would make a difference against the powerful magic being he sensed.

The dual-colored stag pawed at the ground, nostrils flaring. A normal stag could be territorial, especially in the rutting season, but it was far past then, and besides, this wasn't a normal stag.

"Would you turn your back on your vows?" it spoke in his mind.

A shudder rippled through him.

"I don't know what you're talking about."

"We chose you as her protector, and you agreed. Now she needs you, and you've run away."

Erich's stomach lurched, and the dragon stirred, arching its back as it filled the space within him, threatening to break through his human shell.

"I made no such promise."

"Your actions speak otherwise," the two-toned stag said. Its mismatched eyes seemed to peer into his very soul, stripping it bare and laying it on the forest floor between them.

"She's better off without me. I'll only cause her harm." He looked up to the rising sun, one day before the full moon. Tonight.

"The wielder needs your help to draw the blade."

Erich shook his head. Ancient being or whatever, he was wrong. The darkness in his soul would only corrupt her, and if it didn't, then the dragon would consume her. As if it read his thoughts, it raised its head to scent the air, teeth bared.

"I don't even know where the sword is. I couldn't find it." The excuse felt paltry when talking to something as ancient and powerful as the stag.

"It's inside her."

"Inside her," Erich echoed, feeling like a fool. "What does that mean?"

But before he could get clarification, the stag disappeared. He spun around again, half expecting it to be hiding in the shadows as Fritz often was, but it was gone leaving Erich with more questions than answers.

He couldn't go back. It had taken him all night to get this far, and on foot, by the time he got back, it'd be hours before sunset, and the transformation would happen no matter his determination. And yet...

Someone grasped his shoulder, and Erich grabbed hold of it, twisting it behind their back before pressing his blade tip against Fritz's bobbing throat.

"It's me." Fritz gasped, hand up in the air.

"What are you doing here?" Erich asked as he lowered his weapon.

How'd Fritz known where to find him? Perhaps in the same way the stag did. Erich realized there was still a lot to learn about magic.

"I had a vision." Fritz's eyes were silvery as moonlight and unfocused as if he were still seeing beyond time and into some distant future.

"Did the stag speak to you too?" Erich asked, gesturing toward the place where the stag had just been.

"You saw Aolois as well?"

"If you mean the dual-colored stag, then, yes."

Fritz practically vibrated as magic spread from him in thick black tendrils, arousing the dragon's interest as he watched him pace.

"Then I was right; our fates are intertwined. In my vision, I saw the moon and the sun colliding. At the time, the elders thought it meant the end of days, but I knew it couldn't be. Why did I not see it before? It all makes sense now..."

"Maybe for you..." Erich scratched his head. All this talk of prophecy and visions wasn't adding up for him.

Fritz turned to face him, his eyes bright golden and rimmed in silver, his gaze bottomless, ageless. As if the cosmos wheeled behind them, seeing beyond time and space to futures upon futures that he might only imagine.

"You and Princess Liane were always destined to meet. You who carry the blood of dragons, and she the sword's wielder... why did I not see it before? Together you can restore balance." He threw out his arms, and the shadows around him darkened, coalescing into a shimmering starry sky haloing his body.

"What does Liane have to do with any of this?" His throat tightened around her name, as he thought of their final parting and the stag's warning. Erich cleared his throat. "The stag mentioned the sword was inside her. What does that mean exactly?"

"The sword chooses its wielder, and during the ceremony, they are bonded. Something must have gone wrong to prevent the union, and it fused with her body to protect them both. We assumed they hadn't met, but this changes everything! We must get the sword before it's too late!" Fritz started pacing again.

"What are you suggesting? We kidnap her or...?" Getting a weapon out of the city was one thing. But smuggling a princess, that was quite another. And he wouldn't consider the second option.

Fritz stopped in front of him, grasping him by the shoulders. His pupils were the size of pinpricks, bouncing back and forth as he studied Erich's face. "There's more that I haven't told you yet."

"And what's that?" Erich asked warily.

"I went to find her after I realized, but by the time I arrived at the temple, I was too late. She'd started to awaken, and she was kidnapped from the temple. My people know what she is, and they'll kill her to stop the union."

"Take me back there. Pull me through your rift or whatever you have to do," Erich said.

Fritz shook his head slowly. "It's too far. It only works in short distances, and besides, even if I could, I'm already weakened from doing it once, and if I tried again, there's no guarantee we wouldn't get caught in-between."

His chest tightened as the dragon roared, clawing, biting, and fighting to break free. It took all his self-control to not give in to it, and let the madness take hold. If he transformed into a dragon, he could fly to her and rescue her, but he was just as likely to kill her in that form. Erich took a step back from Fritz, trying to regain his composure. But one thing was certain, he must return for her. He'd hold back the dragon until then; he had to.

30

The overwhelming stench of fish coated Liane's mouth, making her empty stomach churn. Whatever they'd given her hadn't worn off entirely, and her mind felt fuzzy. She blinked at salt-crusted walls and tried to sit up, but discovered her arms bound behind her back, tethered to her ankles. In the corner, boxes and crates reached the ceiling, and tattered fishing nets were pulled taut by a barrel ready to tip over. Beyond that, a door to goddess knew where.

Then it hadn't been a dream; she'd been kidnapped from the temple. *Stay calm*, she told herself. Panicking wouldn't save her, but her heart galloped in her chest anyway, and her muscles were as weak as a newborn kitten's. When she struggled against them, she only ended up panting for breath and exhausted from her effort.

Thumping footsteps approached, and Liane tensed in anticipation, eyes trained on the door as it swung open. Niklas strolled in with a greasy smile. How ironic, after years of chasing him and his gang, he had her tied up.

"Morning, sweetheart. Did you sleep well?" he said as he crouched beside her.

"Your accommodations are terrible," Liane tried to snipe back, but her voice was strangled and raspy. Not as intimidating as she hoped.

"I finally caught the pesky fly that's been buzzing around me all this time." He grabbed her chin and turned her head from side to side.

That was all she'd been to him? A pest? She'd given blood, sweat, and tears to destroy him, and dealers like him. And what would he do with her now that he had her? If he wanted to kill her, he could have done so back at the temple. Taking her meant he had something bigger in mind. A cold chill ran over her body. Did this have something to do with the glow and the secret power Mother had kept from her? But she couldn't let Niklas see her sweat.

"That's funny; I was just thinking how I'm going to squash you like the roach you are."

"You talk a big game; you won't be so cocky after they're done with you."

"What are you going to do with me?" She hated the way her voice trembled as she asked.

The slow smile that curled his lips made her stomach squirm.

"I'm not going to do anything. But who knows what those elves want? All I know is they were willing to pay handsomely to have you. I'd hate to be in your shoes, being handed over to those sadistic fucks." He cackled as a cold chill rippled down her spine.

What did the elves want with her? Then it hit her; it wasn't her but whatever her connection to the goddess' blade was. She didn't even fully understand it. What was the word the Avatheos had used? Wielder... whatever that meant, the elves wanted her, and she had to get out before they arrived.

"Why don't you cool off a while? They only arrive at sunset, so we have all day to wait." Niklas stood and walked out of the room, leaving her alone with her tumbling thoughts.

She struggled fruitlessly against the ropes once more. Not that she thought it would change anything, but she refused to lie still and wait for the elves to come to take her.

Then a tingling sensation swept over Liane's body. Sweat dewed on her forehead, another fever was brewing. No. A soft glow cast shadows onto the boxes around the room. Had there ever been fevers, or was it unexplained magic wreaking havoc on her body? The fevers always accompanied strong emotions, and right now, her fear seemed to have awoken it again. This time instead of just burning up, she was illuminating. Now that she knew what it was, could she try and harness it?

Liane concentrated on the raw skin where the ropes chafed her skin, and in doing so, the heat intensified there until a burning smell filled her nostrils. A second later, she felt a snap and her arms broke free. Burned pieces of rope slid off her wrists which had been rubbed raw by the coarse fabric. Sitting up, she unraveled the last of it wrapped around her ankles. She stared numbly at the shimmering luminescence as it faded back into her skin.

Magic. She had magic. The scar on her back throbbed. That was connected too, wasn't it? When she got out of here, Mother would have a lot to answer for. But first, she'd have to find a way out.

Feeling was returning to her limbs, and she tested her dexterity by flexing her fingers and stretching out her legs. She still felt weak, but she managed to pull herself up on a box enough to stand before taking a few wobbling steps. Confident she could walk, she studied her hands next. Apart from casting light and burning ropes, what else could she do? She wasn't sure where to start with trying. Better to not rely on it and use what skills she'd always had.

First of all, she needed to know what waited for her on the other side of the door? Taking a deep breath, she pushed away her fears and inched toward it. She cracked it open and peered out into the large storehouse on the other side, filled with barrels of salted fish. That explained the horrible smell. Niklas and three other men sat in the center of the room, their backs to her, absorbed in a card game. They'd dragged a barrel over and set a piece of wood on top, making a makeshift card table.

Four gangsters against her. She'd won against worse odds... with Ludwig to back her up. She brushed against her thigh and discovered they hadn't taken her dagger. That was the advantage of being underestimated, she supposed. So, it was one dagger and her against four gangsters. It wasn't ideal, she must admit. Liane shook her head and closed the door.

If she had any hope of winning, she needed to separate them to take them out one by one. Then she noticed the precarious stack of boxes by the door and crafted a plan. Picking one from the top of the stack, she carefully pulled it down. The pile tottered before settling again. Inside were a few jars of pickled fish. Extracting one, she flung it down, shattering it.

Blood thundered in her ears like the beating of wings as she took a place behind the stack. She prayed Cyra would favor her, and they'd come to investigate. They might just as likely assume it was nothing and continue their game of cards. Or they'd all come at once, and her plan would fail.

Footsteps approached, and Liane rested her hand on the hilt of her dagger, holding back from drawing it as she pressed a shoulder against the stack.

The door swung open, and a thug poked his head in. Noticing her gone, he turned back to shout, "The princess is gone!"

Blighted Darkness. She could do this. Her hand tightened on the dagger, and multiple footsteps stomped on the stairs, racing toward her. Double blighted darkness.

"You sure?" someone asked just outside the door.

"Pretty sure."

Liane held her breath. Come inside, just another step. A little closer.

As he took a step past the threshold, she shoved the pile of boxes and crates, sending them cascading onto the thug, pinning him beneath their weight. Perhaps crushing him, she didn't stop to check.

Fortunately, the door swung outward, or she would

have been trapped inside. The second man climbed up over the rubble, losing his footing as he scrambled to check on his friend. And when his back was turned, Liane snuck up behind him and stabbed him in his side, where there were no bones or muscles to slow her jab. Hot blood poured over her hand as he turned, looking at her wide-eyed. Horror at what she'd done sunk like a stone, and she let go of her dagger still in the man's side, as she stumbled backward into a third man who grasped her by the hair and dragged her out of the room.

"You little bitch!" he snarled, tugging her down the stairs where Niklas was waiting.

Niklas strode toward her, thunder in his gaze.

"How did she get out?" he asked.

"I don't know, but she stuck Heiner, and he looks like he's bleeding out..."

"Call a healer. I'll take care of her," he said, grabbing hold of her arm. He twisted it behind her back as she cried out in pain.

But it wasn't the rough grip of his arm that terrified her. It was the bright, hot fire burning through her veins as if she were made of molten fire, turning her vision red as something whooshed in her ears. Then a bright flash burst from her. Enough to startle Niklas into letting her go and obscuring all their visions. Blindly Liane scuttled away, as the men screamed about their burning eyes.

A few feet away, she spotted a pair of double doors; the crack between them exposed the daylight on the other side. If she got out, she could find the City Watch, get help. Taking her chance while her captors were still inca-pacitated, she ran full tilt for the door and had nearly reached it when it slid shut in front of her, flung closed by invisible hands. Liane skidded to a halt before crashing into it. And then tugged on it, but it was shut tight, and her body was too weak to pull it open.

Behind her, someone laughed, high and sinister, as they grasped a hold of her arm, spinning her around to face them.

"Where do you think you're going?" Heinrich said, with a leering smile.

Pure adrenaline and hatred fueled her, and she launched herself at him, clawing at his skin like a ferocious animal. But before she could even land a hand on him, he tossed her aside with a flick of his wrist, sending her flying across the room and crashing into a barrel of salted fish. Her head cracked against it, and stars danced in front of her eyes.

Heinrich strode toward her, his eyes glowing unnaturally blue. How had he done that, with what power? It couldn't be real; it had to be some sort of nightmare. And yet. And yet... Captain Rosen had warned her about the power of stardust, the superhuman strength. Liane never imagined it'd be Heinrich taking it. She tried to rise again, but invisible hands grasped her arms, pinning them at her sides, holding and pushing her down to the ground. She squirmed against them as Heinrich loomed over her.

"You can't escape, don't exhaust yourself trying," Heinrich said as he crouched down in front of her, leaning in close enough that she could smell his thick cologne that made her gag and under it something sweet, like burnt sugar. Stardust. Her suspicions were confirmed.

"You've let yourself become corrupted, for what? You'll never win against my mother."

"I haven't corrupted anything, Liane. I am returning to the way things are meant to be. Magic is my birthright. All I'm doing is claiming what's mine, like the crown your bitch mother stole from me."

Her eyes widened. "Stardust is poison; it kills people."

"It kills the weak, like your stableboy. What was his name? Lewis?"

"Elias," Liane snarled. Hearing his name on his lips only fueled her anger more.

If only the power that flooded through her before came to her aid, but all she felt was cold. No magic burned in her veins now.

"That's right. Elias. Peasant scum aren't meant for this power. They cannot begin to understand it. But those idiots have given me valuable information. When I am emperor, those with the gift will rise above the weak and powerless."

"You're a monster."

"Only the strong should survive," Heinrich said. "That's how I know you're not worthy of your power. That much magic inside you... wasted..." He grabbed her chin, his nails digging in her flesh; the hunger in his gaze disturbed her. Twisted and perverse. She imagined he'd drink her of all the magic in her veins, if he could.

"Then why kidnap me if you think I'm beneath you?" she asked.

"Because that's what the elves want. Short-sighted fools that they are. They'll drain every drop of blood out of you, carve out your bones, and burn you to ash before scattering you to the four corners to make sure the power inside you stays forgotten."

Her eyes bulged. He was lying; he had to be, trying to scare her or confuse her. She felt his words slide over her like a slimy tentacle, probing at her mind and evoking images. She shoved the tentacle out, and Heinrich stumbled back for a moment. Again, a smile grew on his face as if he'd proven something to himself.

"You've never been susceptible to my influence, not like the rest of your family. It's why I wanted to give you one last chance, before handing you over. You could be an asset to my new kingdom, much better than your sister."

"I'll kill you for what you've done."

Heinrich laughed again, hollow and without humor. "Oh, Liane. When I'm done with you, you'll wish you were dead."

She was opening her mouth to challenge him when she felt something like a thousand knives being stabbed into her body all at once, and all she could do was scream.

31

Vines and moss covered the cave's entrance, just like most of the ruins, but unlike the rest of the rune-carved columns and cobble, this spot pulsed faintly with magic, weak enough had it not been the day before a full moon, he might not have sensed it. The dragon felt it, and arched its long sinewy neck, twisting and reaching for it in hopes it could latch onto the power stored there. Erich pulled its bindings tighter, but they were starting to fray as the sun sank lower in the sky.

"This is your way back into the city?" Erich asked.

They'd spent most of the day on the return trip, and all the while, Fritz had assured him he had a way in. Erich wasn't sure what he'd expected, but an ominous tunnel on the outskirts of the city wasn't it.

"It's a hollowed-out vein. In ancient times it would have flowed throughout the city, but now it acts as a sort of underground tunnels system."

He'd read about the veins of magic and thought they

were nothing but stories. On closer inspection, however, there were no tool marks in the stone or any indication of how it'd gotten there. Whether it was magic or other natural causes that created it, it didn't change the fact that it made him uneasy. Erich didn't like being underground, the suffocating darkness of no sky, no light. Not exactly a friendly atmosphere, but at least it wasn't a sewer.

"If you knew these tunnels existed, why not use these to get in and out of the palace?" Erich asked.

"You don't think I tried? They wouldn't let me. They're hollow now, but they're still imbued with power. Most of it's dormant, but what remains sentient is feral and scared. It won't obey just anyone... I thought... well, anyway. I am certain they will listen to you."

Could rock have feelings, or was it the magic that was alive and aware? Either way, he looked at the mouth of the cave, at the yawning jaws of a monstrous beast, and a shiver of uncertainty snaked its way up his spine.

"What makes you so certain?" Erich asked.

Fritz had magic, not twisted corruption eating away at him bit by bit, like Erich. What would make it obey him over the elf?

"Because it has to," Fritz replied cryptically and motioned for Erich to step inside.

It was either try the tunnels, or risk sneaking over the city walls. The latter was a known danger, while the former... Erich shook his head. There was no use turning back, and so he stepped into the darkness, and as he did, he felt the magic flutter around him, like thousands of butterfly wings. He stood very still, letting it scent him as a nervous dog might. After a few seconds of standing still, the air settled, and he felt a sensation he might have called a sigh. Had it come from a human mouth? It released a warm burst of air that fanned across his face pleasantly.

"I guess they like me?" Erich asked Fritz.

Fritz nodded and lit their makeshift torch. Guided by its flickering light, they made their way deeper. They hadn't gone very far when the pathway branched in two directions.

"Which way do we go?" Erich asked him.

"It's your choice; it chose you." Was that a hint of bitterness Erich detected in his tone? Fritz continued, "Last time I tried, the tunnel ended at a sheer drop into darkness, and when I tried backtracking, I ended up in the dark for hours before stumbling out where I'd started from."

It still made no sense to him why the tunnel would choose him—insane as it was to think a tunnel would have feelings—but he didn't have time to question it. Erich picked the tunnel to the left, which led them to what seemed like a never-ending labyrinth of twisting corridors and endless splitting pathways. Without the sun overhead, it was impossible to say what time of day it was, but Erich felt daylight diminishing as the dragon slithered out of his grip, pushing closer and closer to the surface. It was always eager, but more so today than ever before. It had fixated faster on Liane than anyone else he'd seen, they had to find her before sunset, and he became a threat to her.

Then their feeble torch started to sputter, and worse

yet, he thought he recognized that boulder with veins of golden minerals; they'd passed it several turns back. Had they been going around in circles? Perhaps Fritz was wrong, and he wasn't meant to do this. Maybe the tunnel lured him down here to wander in the dark until he died. Well, before that, he would transform, and he hated to imagine the dragon in this tiny space; his neck hurt just imaging it.

Their torch faded, flickered, and then extinguished.

"You said I was the one to lead us through here," Erich said with a hint of sarcasm in his tone. Words echoed around them; without the ability to see the wall around them, it felt as if he were standing in an empty void of complete darkness.

"Maybe it's not you but the dragon that needs to lead," Fritz seemed to surround him, his voice echoing off the walls came from all directions at once.

"And kill you when I lose control?" Erich snapped.

"You have more control than you realize," Fritz remarked.

Sighing, Erich dragged his hand through his hair. This was madness, complete and utter insanity. He couldn't control the dragon, apart from keeping it contained. Erich breathed in and out, steadying his breath in the way Lord Endland had taught him. It had been years since he'd intentionally harnessed the dragon's power at his father's behest. It'd been building for years, small incidents, like tiny cuts, to prove his loyalty and his worthiness as an heir, despite the curse his mother gave him. Then Father had demanded he unleash the dragon to punish a traitor. Father wanted to let him live as an example. But once wasn't enough for the dragon, one taste of his blood, and he became the dragon's obsession. And when the full moon rose, the dragon killed him and his family.

The next day he'd left Sundland behind. Father would have cleaned up the mess, which only made it worse. He couldn't be the noble king Endland envisioned him to be. He was like his father: a monster. But while he was down here in the dark debating his next move, Liane was somewhere above ground in need of him. Saving her wouldn't change what he'd done, nor would it change him. But he couldn't let another death weigh on his conscious.

Listen here, Erich addressed the dragon.

Deep down, he felt it stir, lifting its head and its nostrils flaring.

I'm going to let you loose but only to find Liane. Understand?

Protect. Her. The words rumbled through his mind. That was likely the closest thing to an agreement he was going to get. Erich exhaled and let go of one chain, then another, the rest he held in check, preventing the full transformation. Power tingled across his skin; his senses were suddenly more aware, more acute, and he smelled magic in the air, a heady scent that brought with it an insatiable hunger.

With the dragon's vision, the darkness faded, and he could see Fritz, the shimmering silver aura surrounding him, and his luminous golden eyes staring straight at Erich. The dark had never been a problem for the elf, had it?

"I see you took my advice." Fritz smirked.

Erich shook his head and turned away from Fritz,

ignoring his teasing. Inhaling the scent of sunshine and something else he couldn't quite pinpoint. It was faintly reminiscent of stardust but not as potent. Squinting in the gloom, he saw a shimmering path winding through the tunnel. Something told him that's the one he should follow.

They headed down the tunnel, turned a corner, and he noticed a gap in the rocks. When he stepped through, it opened onto a massive room; the impossibly high ceiling supported black and white pillars, and on the floor a mosaic of the interlocking sun and moon. Fritz's gasp echoed back at them as he walked reverently toward the center of the room.

"What is this place?" Erich asked, his voice reverberated across the walls making it sound foreign to his own ears.

"One of the lost temples of the Divine Twins. I thought they'd all been destroyed," Fritz said in a hushed whisper, as he turned slowly in place, taking in their surroundings.

There wasn't much time to marvel at it, but as they passed through the hushed space, Erich craned his neck to take in the domed ceiling painted with constellations, and the sun and moon split in half at the center. It reminded him of the two-toned stag.

A hallway connected with the temple room, and they followed it out. Time seemed to stretch out. Minutes felt like an eternity, and doubt began to creep in. The dragon was being suspiciously obedient and hadn't turned to attack Fritz nor fought for control of his body.

Then the end of the tunnel started to lighten, and he

smelled the sea. Erich quickened his pace, and as the scent grew stronger, he ran, eager to be out of the darkness and gloom but closer to Liane. Orange light illuminated the end of the tunnel, as he threw himself forward, stumbling out onto a rocky shore. It let out along a small cove along the coast, and gulls reeled overhead, crying mournfully as they flew out across the sea toward the setting sun. Not much time was left before the final tether holding back the dragon would be severed.

A horn blew and drew his attention to his left. Scrambling over rocks, he got a better vantage point of his location and saw the nearby harbor. The wind carried the scent of fish, salt, and beneath it, magic and stardust. He followed the trail, down the outcrop and toward the dockyard where boats were being loaded with goods. The smell of magic was getting stronger, and then he smelled something that angered the dragon, and he had to hold on tight to keep it from bursting free. It was fear. Liane's terror. Erich clenched a hand into a fist.

Fritz came to stand beside him and shaded his face against the setting sun as he surveyed the numerous buildings.

"She could be in any one of these buildings," Fritz remarked.

And he'd investigate every one of them if that's what it took. Desperation flared in his chest as he threw open warehouse doors, weaving through barrels and stacks of crates being loaded onto ships. With each failure, panic rose like a wave threatening to crest over him; the dragon rolled, growing overeager, being let loose of that final chain. If he weren't careful, he'd lose control here in the center of the dock, killing innocents and failing to save Liane or worse, hurting her in a haze of madness. But where was she? He couldn't find her among the muddle of scents and sounds on the dock.

A foghorn blew again, rattling around in his ears, but beneath it, he heard something else: Liane's scream. It ripped through him, and the dragon roared in reply. All his senses sharpened, narrowing in on her as he pinpointed her location and raced down a narrow alley to a warehouse at the far end of the dock. Two scarred men blocked the entrance, and as he rushed toward them, they brandished cudgels in a failed attempt at intimidation. He hardly paused, knocking them both over with a quick punch to the gut, and they doubled over, allowing him access to the warehouse door.

Erich threw the door open, and his vision narrowed, focusing on Liane writhing on the floor and Heinrich standing over her with a malicious gleam in his eyes. Erich's vision turned red as he rushed toward him; his feet seemed to hardly touch the ground. Erich grasped Heinrich by the neck, squeezing, and his eyes widened with shock as he tossed him aside like refuse.

Then he knelt beside Liane, cupping her cheek, scanning her to assess her injuries. Her breaths were short and pained. Seeing her this way made his blood boil, and the dragon clawed to be freed. He cradled her in his arms, caressing her face and praying to the Trinity she'd open her eyes. For a moment, the world slowed down, and he held her close; even the dragon quieted inside him. Then after a few heart-rending moments, her eyes fluttered open, and she blinked up at him.

"Erich...?" she croaked.

"Shh. You don't have to speak," he said, brushing damp hair from her face.

Her hand caught his wrist. "Why... what are you doing here?"

A simple question with a complicated answer. She probably thought he'd lied and used her. Where did he even begin to explain? From the moment they'd met, she captured his attention and when he imagined her in danger, his insides felt as if they were being pulled out, hung, and smoked like sausage. They just met and he'd move heaven and earth to protect her.

Before he said anything, someone drove a knife into his back. With a roar, he stood to see Heinrich striding toward him, too far to have cut him, and yet he felt the wound bleeding. Heinrich was bleeding too; blood ran down his chin from a split lip. The bastard was more resilient than he had thought.

Erich set Liane down and placed himself between her and Heinrich, the dragon's power thrumming in his veins. He'd love to rip the bastard apart, limb by limb, but before he could, an invisible hand struck him in the gut, knocked the air out of him, and his knees buckled.

He tried to get back up, but invisible hands held him down, as Heinrich's lackeys had done in the forest.

"Now, doesn't this feel familiar? You on your knees, and me over you." Heinrich smirked.

Erich growled, more monster than man in that moment. He'd tear his throat out.

"As you can see, I don't need others doing my dirty work now." He tossed Erich's words back in his face as he wrestled against the invisible bindings. "Now, let's see what you've been hiding."

Tendrils prodded at his consciousness, pressing at the edges, trying to worm their way in. He hadn't felt anything like it since he'd left Sundland, not since Father. He didn't know others had this quirk. Erich slammed his mind shut, locking out Heinrich as Father had forced him to learn. But a smile was spreading on his face.

"I knew there was something not right about you. What are you?" He kicked Erich in the chest, knocking him onto the ground before pressing a boot to his neck.

"More powerful than you'll ever be," Erich snarled.

This close, Heinrich reeked of burnt sugar and corruption magic. Whatever had given him this power, it was temporary. Some token or object he was drawing from. That's why he hadn't noticed it before. Fortunately for Erich, borrowed magic burned hot and potent but fizzled out quickly. He just had to endure until it did. Then Heinrich ground his boot against his neck as his vision turned black and stars danced behind his eyes.

"You are nothing but the scum beneath my boot," Heinrich said.

"Stop!" Liane shouted.

"Silence. I'll deal with you in a moment." He flung out a hand, and Liane's lips were slammed shut.

But not only that, her nostrils too. Her face was turning blue as she clawed at her neck, trying to breathe.

"Unleash your hold on her; she'll suffocate." Erich's frantic gaze darted from Liane to Heinrich.

"Don't tell me what to do, worm."

Liane thrashed and clawed, growing increasingly

desperate, but Erich couldn't get loose of Heinrich's grip, even with the dragon mostly untethered. The dragon was writhing, bucking, and biting, fighting to the surface as Erich's vision turned red. The last burst of dying light flooded into the warehouse, and he felt it sweep over him like a cold breeze as wings beat in his ear. Erich let go of the last of the bindings holding the dragon back and grasped a hold of Heinrich's ankle with a scaled fist. There was no more holding back now.

32

Liane was dying. She couldn't breathe, and the edges of her vision were turning black. It also explained why when she looked, Erich's body stretched like fresh caramel, his skin turned scaly, and spiny ridges tore through his shirt. A lack of oxygen could explain the long serpentine tail that burst out of his trousers, swinging wildly back and forth. Just when she thought she'd pass out, the invisible hands clamping her mouth shut let go, and she gasped for air, holding her burning throat. Distantly she heard horrified screams, but Liane couldn't tear her eyes away from Erich's long sinewy neck turned back to meet Liane's enraptured gaze. She was both horrified and amazed at his transformation from man to beast. No, not a beast. A dragon. A real one.

He towered over her, piercing her with molten, gold eyes, filled with an impossible human intelligence. All her life, she'd heard stories of the corrupted: monsters that would tear her flesh from her bones given a chance. And that was if she was lucky. The unfortunate ones were turned into creatures like them. But as he lowered his head to her, she didn't feel compelled to run; instead, she reached out to touch him. He rested his reptilian head against her palm, and taking her other hand, she cupped both sides of his snout, staring into his soulful, golden eyes. Warm breath fanned across her face, enveloping her in a cocoon of safety and warmth. Erich rumbled low in his throat, a sound akin to a purr. His tail whipped behind him, knocking over heavy barrels of salted fish, scattering them. The strength in his tail was likely strong enough to shatter every bone in her body, and yet she was more reminded of a puppy. She laughed lightly at the absurdity of the thought.

"A dragon! I knew you were hiding something, but I never imagined this!" Heinrich cackled.

She had almost forgotten he was there and spun to place herself between Erich and him. But there was no hiding his bulking form; at his full height, his head brushed against the high ceilings. If Erich's secret was revealed, the Midnight Guard would kill him surely. She had to protect him, somehow. Erich growled, and the sound vibrated through her chest, and across from them, Heinrich faltered in his slow approach. Fear was in his gaze for the first time, but then a manic smile replaced it.

"I'll skin your lizard hide and mount your dragon head on my mantel," Heinrich said, thrusting an arm toward him.

Liane felt a blow of an invisible force thrust toward her, knocking her off her feet and flattening her to the ground. While it didn't knock Erich off his feet, he reared back, roaring loud enough to shake dust from the ceiling. Pushing against invisible hands, he clawed at the air, and Liane, seeing the rage burning in his gaze, rolled out of the way to duck behind a nearby barrel for safety.

The ground shook when Erich came crashing back down, and Heinrich wobbled, losing his footing. With another roar, Erich lunged for Heinrich, closing the space between them in a blink, and in response, Heinrich threw out his arm, sending a barrel of salted fish careening toward him. It crashed into him, scattering fish and spraying brine but didn't slow Erich down.

Heinrich weaved through barrels trying to escape, as Erich stalked behind him, knocking aside the barrels in his way. The stench of fermented fish was overwhelming, and Liane covered her mouth with her sleeve to stop herself from gagging. She lost sight of them in the chaos, and while she was distracted, Heinrich snuck up behind her and pressed a dagger to her throat.

"Make a sound, and I'll slit your throat," Heinrich whispered into her ear, as he dragged her toward the door.

She had no choice but to obey, knowing he'd make good on his threat. Erich's back was to them, smashing barrels and whipping his tail, clearing out any hidey-holes Heinrich might have crawled into. Heinrich tensed, presumably terrified of Erich's wrath, and while he was distracted, she attempted to squirm free, but his dagger scored her flesh, and a rivulet of warm, sticky blood ran down her throat.

Then Erich froze, nostrils flaring; he turned toward

them, stomping over barrels, cracking them beneath his claws as Heinrich pressed the knife closer.

"Come any closer, and I'll kill her," he snarled.

Erich huffed, twin clouds of cold vapor rising from his nostrils as he bared his teeth in a menacing growl. Heinrich inched backward and grasped behind him for the door. As soon as it slid open, he yanked her out onto the dock while Erich roared, following them out. The sun had set, and a full moon rose against the twilight sky.

Screams of terror echoed in the night as dockworkers and merchants caught sight of the dragon. Heinrich couldn't possibly beat him and instead was trying to lure him out into the open, where the Midnight Guard would do his dirty work.

"Leave, Erich, I'll be fine," Liane shouted.

But Erich's gaze was trained on her, stubbornly following, blind to danger. Maybe in this form, he was blind to human reason, lost to animalistic urge. How long before the Midnight Guard found them? With their magic and training, they were meant to take down creatures like him. They'd kill him without a second thought.

She had to do something, but what? She tried to envision the magic creating a burst of light, but there was nothing, not even a tingling warmth. If it couldn't save her, then she'd have to use something else. Taking a deep breath, Liane shoved backward, catching Heinrich in the solar plexus. His hand jerked, and bright pain lodged in her throat, and blood poured down her front, but he also loosened his grip. Liane ducked as Erich launched into the air, pinning Heinrich to the ground with a sickening crunch.

Liane turned away but heard Heinrich's guttural screams before the wet popping sounds silenced him. She clamped her hands over her ears, stomach heaving, fearing to look and see Heinrich's fate.

It took a few seconds before she could find the courage to look. Heinrich was unrecognizable, a bloody, pulpy mess, his blood spread out across the dock, dripping between planks, leaving a dark stain. She'd hated Heinrich, and his death was essential to save her family and the kingdom, but she took no pleasure in his demise. Just shameful relief and regret.

Erich had done that... He'd done it to protect her... but why? After a week of pretending, a single night together, none of it felt like reason enough. But she also knew from the moment they'd met she'd felt undeniably drawn to him, even now his muzzle dripping with blood, Heinrich's blood. She did not fear him. Illogically, impossibly so. All her thoughts were on protecting him. Helping him escape the city before he was discovered... She took a faltering step toward him, a thousand questions on the tip of her tongue.

"You don't fear him?" a man said from beside her.

She startled and turned to gaze into his molten gold eyes, so like Erich's but different somehow.

Unlike the rest of the sailors and dockworkers who'd run in fear, he didn't seem afraid or surprised; in fact, he seemed almost oblivious to the dragon. His strange golden eyes were trained on her. He turned his head, and she noticed the tip of his pointed ear poking out from beneath the curtain of ebony hair. An elf. Liane recoiled and instinctively put a hand against Erich's long neck, seeking his protection, and he rested his serpent-like head on her shoulder. Was he one of the elves Heinrich wanted to sell her to?

"Don't come any closer," she said, taking another step back.

"I'm a friend, Liane. You do not need to fear me," the elf said, hand outstretched.

"How do you know my name?" Shards of ice ran through her veins, and she was thankful for Erich's bulking security because she was completely without weapons. But Erich didn't seem concerned as he didn't lunge or move to protect her. Could she trust the elf? What if he was under the elf's command? Liane shook herself; that couldn't be true.

"I dreamed of you long ago, though I didn't learn your name until recently. The All-Mother has chosen you to restore the balance and wield the blade, and I've come to teach you how to use it."

A strange, irrational part of herself wanted to grasp a hold of it. If a dragon had come to her defense, could an elf explain these powers she'd known nothing about until this morning? But Heinrich had told her they wanted to kill her... and everything she knew about elves was they were corruptors, wielders of dangerous magic.

Shouting proceeded the thundering of booted feet, and Liane turned to see a regiment of Midnight Guards rushing toward them, led by Captain Rosen. Fear spiked in her veins as Erich reared up and his large, leathery wings splayed out behind him. They arrayed themselves in a circle, weapons drawn and pointed at Erich. The elf put himself between her and the Midnight Guard, drawing a dagger and holding it in front of himself.

"They won't hurt me," Liane said to him. "You should worry about yourself."

Erich roared, hissing menacingly at what he perceived as a coming threat. Without thinking, she thrust herself between them, arms splayed wide.

"Don't hurt him; he's not a threat. He protected me..." Liane said to Captain Rosen, her unwilling gaze flicking toward Heinrich's mashed corpse.

Captain Rosen looked over; her expression was impassive.

"That is a dragon, Princess. A monster formed by corruption. Step away so we might protect you."

"Only if you promise to not hurt him."

Captain Rosen shook her head and said something out of the corner of her mouth to an archer beside her. He raised his weapon and pointed it toward Erich's head.

"No, you can't—" But before she could even finish her protest, they shot something toward him, catching him in the shoulder.

Erich reared back again with a pained shriek, and when he brought his feet down again, the dock shook beneath her, threatening to crack.

"Go, you have to fly," Liane shouted at Erich.

His golden eye met hers, and she saw the resistance in it, then she shoved, hard. Despite his bulk, she felt force behind her hands, and in her ears, she heard the beating of wings. Hesitantly, he took flight, rising in the sky, neck craning back to watch her.

"Go," she shouted, as she tilted her head skyward. Liane watched Erich as his silhouette faded against the bright light of the full moon.

33

Erich's head pounded as if he'd indulged in too much ale. It was typical after a change, as was the taste of blood in his mouth and the maddening itching, caused by his reformed flesh from dragon scales. Returning to human form, his skin always felt too tight, as if the dragon were wearing his human skin. For now, it slept, sated for another moon's turn. It was easier to bind it, lock it down deep in the furthest reaches of his consciousness. Groaning, he sat up and pressed the heels of his hands to his burning eyes.

The night before was a blur, coming back to him in fragments as the dragon's thoughts were flashes of images. Liane's face was foremost among them. Her eyes wide with wonder and surprisingly trusting. He tried to sift through memories of her, to ensure he hadn't harmed her. Then he remembered through the dragon's eyes as she embraced him. Foolish woman. What had held the dragon back? Somehow, impossibly, she'd broken through and tamed him at his most dangerous.

Then why did his mouth taste like blood? Erich clenched a hand as flashes of Heinrich's death flittered through his mind. Though he'd deserved what he'd done to him, he didn't relish in taking human life.

A forest of tall pines surrounded him on all sides, a dragon-sized indent on the ground, where he'd fallen asleep at sunrise. Midday sun burned overhead. If he didn't cover up soon, his skin would burn from sunlight. Tattered shreds of his clothes hung around his naked body as he stood and shaded his eyes against the bright light, which illuminated the tops of a mountain range. The opposite side of the mountains behind Artria. He must have flown all night. It explained his aching muscles. But how had he escaped the city and made it here? Those memories were blurrier, harder to translate from dragon to man.

"Awake then?" Fritz asked.

Startled by an unexpected greeting, Erich turned to see Fritz looking away and thrusting a bundle of clothing toward him. Erich took it without a word, and the elf sat back down beside a small campfire to poke at smoldering kindling yet to catch.

"I'd have dressed you, but I figured you'd rather do it yourself," Fritz commented, the back of his neck burning red.

"How did we escape the city?" Erich asked.

"Help me with the fire. I was never good at lighting these," Fritz said without looking up at him and without answering his question.

Sighing and knowing the elf would tell him in his own time, he knelt down and, cupping his hands, blew on embers until they caught. The flames licked at the dry wood, rising higher, turning into a small fire. When he was satisfied it would keep burning, he looked to Fritz for an explanation, but he was still avoiding his gaze as he scraped scales off some trout.

"Liane?" Erich prompted.

"Safe."

"And I—"

"Turned into a dragon in front of her," Fritz said.

"What aren't you telling me?" Erich asked.

Fritz skewered two fat trout and set them over the fire without speaking. Then watched the first cook for a few long minutes before pulling it off the fire. One side looked charred while the other undercooked. And Erich, needing to do something with his hands and not wanting to eat charcoal fish, set the second piece further from the flame, hoping it would cook more evenly. Transformations left him ravenous, but even he couldn't stomach burnt food.

Erich cleared his throat, to give Fritz a hint to continue.

"There's too much to recount," Fritz looked tired, haggard. The dark circles smudged under his eyes made him look like he hadn't slept in months.

"Give me the short version then," Erich growled.

"You killed the prince consort, the Midnight Guard arrived, and Liane compelled you to run and saved your life. But she remains in the control of the Church of Sol, now with awakened powers and to be used as their weapon and an even bigger target on her back, should they reveal her nature. I think that about sums it up."

"What do you mean? If she's with the Church of Sol, can't they protect her?" Erich said.

He hadn't stopped to consider what Liane's power might mean to the church but seeing as they'd been gathering up all traces of it or destroying it for centuries, it came as no surprise that her power would interest them. But with the Midnight Guard and the might of the church protecting her, she'd be safe, wouldn't she?

"Corruption is like a hydra; cut off one head, and three more pop out," Fritz said as he turned the fish over to cook the other side.

"You're talking in circles again."

He sat back on his heels and met Erich's stare. "The Avatheos intends to destroy all dark magic and my people using the sword. And that's why they want her dead. But light cannot exist without dark; if either succeeds, it will awaken chaos and the end of the world..."

"Then we go back and rescue her—" Erich stood as if it were as easy as marching back into the capital.

"It's too late; the course of fate has already changed. We cannot stop it," Fritz said, looking dejected. "Had I realized the truth sooner, I might have prevented this. I could have convinced her to leave before her power awakened but now that the Avatheos knows, he will not give her up easily. And they'll keep her closely guarded; there won't be another chance."

Liane's face floated to mind, her brows pinched, as she'd sent him away. She'd known they wouldn't let her go, and to stay beside her was a death sentence. But the dual-colored stag knew and sent her to him for a reason, and if he believed in things such as fate, he might have thought this was all meant to be.

He'd never intended to get involved. All he wanted was a cure. Maybe he couldn't be freed of his curse, but this power he feared had saved her, and it could do it again. It was time he stopped cowering in the shadows. Even if it meant walking into certain death, he'd do anything to protect her. At least then, this curse had some meaning, some purpose other than destruction.

"What will the Avatheos do with her?" Erich asked.

Fritz sighed and leaned back on his hands, head tilted upward to the sky. "They'll likely take her to Basilia to train and mold her into the perfect weapon. Why?" His gold and silver eyes turned to Erich, pinning him in place, perhaps guessing what he was about to say.

Erich held out his hand to Fritz. "There's still a sword to steal, and you still owe me a cure."

34

Days had passed since she'd helped Erich escape, and, in that time, she'd slipped in and out of exhausted sleep plagued by fevers. Priestesses came into her room, plying her with foul-smelling tonics, and changing out her cold cloths. It reminded her painfully of the early days of her fevers, right after she'd fused with the sword.

Mother sitting at her bedside, head sagging against her chest, slumbered. Liane's fever had broken just before sunrise, and she'd dared not wake her. She must be exhausted. Had she even slept over the last few days? Liane wasn't even sure how many days it'd been. From her fuzzy memories, it must have been at least three, perhaps more. Instead of waking Mother, she lay in the silence, letting her thoughts tumble over one another, like stones in a fast-moving river, as sunrise crested the mountains. She watched sunlight creep across her bedroom floor, then crawl over her comforter. She wanted to go outside and tip her face skyward to soak in the rays. But she could hardly lift her arms from her sides. So, she reached for the coming sunbeam, but when it touched her, it burned, and Liane yelped and retracted her hand. If indirect sunlight burned her, would she be unable to go outside ever again? What curse had this sword put upon her?

Her shout woke her mother, and she lunged to her feet, her golden, gray-streaked hair falling around her shoulders in a tangled mess. Her hands floated above Liane as if she feared to touch her, as if she were made of glass that might shatter at the slightest touch. She'd been like this once before, the morning after the first forest incident.

"What's wrong? Are you in pain? Should I call for the priestess?" Mother wrung her hands together, her eyes scanning Liane from head to toe.

Liane shook her pounding head, which turned out to be a mistake because it only made her headache worse. They needed to talk, and she wouldn't do it lying down, but when she attempted to sit up straighter, Mother reached out to stop her.

"Don't move too fast; you're not strong enough yet." Mother looked at her with a pleading gaze.

"Why didn't you tell me?" Liane said, grasping Mother's hand to keep her from pulling away. No more secrets.

Mother's shoulders sagged as she sat on the edge of the bed with her back to Liane. But she hadn't let go of her hand, which she held onto with a vice-like grip.

"You don't need to worry about that right now; focus on healing."

"I think I deserve answers, don't you?" Liane said it calmly, but a storm was raging inside her. She wanted to give Mother the benefit of the doubt before she cast judgment, but she was unreasonably angry. She needed to scream and bite and kick. All this time, she thought she was sick, but there was something inside her, and she never knew...

"I always knew I wasn't the wielder of the sword, just a temporary guardian," Mother began.

Liane inhaled sharply but held her tongue.

"I was desperate when I called upon the ancients for their help. I shouldn't have, but I wanted to save the kingdom, and the Avatheos assured me it was my destiny. If I knew then the cost, I would have found any other way... but I cannot change the bargain I struck. To save the empire from my wicked uncle—Heinrich's father." She stuttered on the name, and their eyes met for a moment before Mother turned away once more.

For a moment, she saw the guilt in Mother's gaze, and knew it hurt her to realize how wicked Heinrich was. They'd all been deceived by him, and she could forgive her for that. What was harder to forget was the lifetime of secrets she'd kept. Mother sighed, inhaled, exhaled, and then continued.

"I waited for the sword's wielder for years and had the new Vice Premier consult the stars in anticipation. Then they chose you. My bright, shining star." She turned back to Liane and stroked her forehead affectionally. And despite her anger, Liane found comfort and solace in the action. "I knew if I told the Avatheos, he'd take you to Basilia to train. He'd have stolen you as an infant from my arms. Your Father and I discussed it, and we agreed to wait until you came of age, and when the time came, we'd let you choose. The ancients might have marked you, but I wanted it to be your life."

"What changed?"

Mother lowered her eyes to the comforter. "The night you were summoned, I woke in a panic, and like a woman possessed, I rode out to the place where it all began. I never intended to interfere, but as I saw you about to walk into that strange fount of corruption, I acted without thinking and called out to you. All I saw was a bright flash of light, and then you were lying on the ground, burning up with a fever. I thought the ancients had taken back the sword, and stricken you with fevers to punish me..." She shook her head, tears rolling down her cheek. "I did this to you, cursed you, I thought. I never knew the sword fused with you, not until you began to glow at the ceremony..."

A numb throb answered in her back as anger and relief warred within her. All this time, she thought there was something wrong with her, that the goddess had cursed her with fevers and a bad back, but in reality, the sword was inside her all along.

"I could forgive you when I was a child. I could under-stand your fears. No one wants to lose their newborn, but I'm twenty-six, past the age for kind lies. You never gave me a choice; you would have let me live forever thinking I was broken!" Heat flared in her cheeks; as her voice rose with each word, a faint glow covered her skin in golden light.

Mother recoiled, eyes wide and terrified. It wasn't a

lack of choice; she feared her, feared the power inside her, and something inside Liane broke. Tears flowed down her cheeks as her body shuddered with her own grief. At the life that could have been, at her own self-loathing all this time. Mother reached for her tentatively, offering comfort, and Liane leaned into her, grasping a hold of her, seeking reassurance as a child does in the embrace of their mother. She was angry at her for the lies and the secrets, but she loved her too and couldn't seem to reconcile between the two parts of her.

Sniffling, she pulled back, and Mother cupped her cheek, brushing away her tears. "Liane, I love you, and I know I should have told you a long time ago. There's no good excuse for what I did. But I hope you can find some way to forgive me..."

"I think I need to be alone for a while," Liane said.

Mother, for her part, didn't protest but stood up and headed for the doors, leaving Liane in silence and her thoughts storming. Where did she go from here?

35

Recovery was slow and painful. Liane languished in bed, tended by silent priestesses who treated her with a sort of hushed reverence. Guests came and went, giving her a vague semblance of normalcy. First, her father came to sit by her bedside. Not speaking much, but she knew he wanted her to forgive Mother and him. And it wasn't that she didn't; she'd be a hypocrite not to. She'd been lying as well, pretending with Erich. But her reality had been shattered, and she needed time to process.

Apart from him, Luzie was in and out delivering news of the outside world: Ludwig had been released from prison and absolved of treason. Without Heinrich to back them, all known stardust smugglers had been caught and were being tried for their crimes. Corrupt magistrates and wardens were being held accountable for their part as well. The vengeance she'd so long sought was being done, and yet she felt hollow.

Not long after Luzie delivered news of Ludwig's release, he came to visit her. He wasn't limping as much anymore, and when he walked in, she jumped out of bed and flung her arms around his neck, despite the priestesses' protests. Liane dismissed everyone from the room and led Ludwig over to a nearby sofa, where they sat with their hands linked together. She studied his gaunt face. His cheeks were hollowed, and his eyes sunken. It reminded her of Elias toward the end, and she feared the worst.

"You've lost weight since you were in prison, weren't they feeding you?" she said, knowing full well it was stardust withdrawal.

"You don't have much of an appetite when you think you're doomed to die," Ludwig teased as he ran a self-conscious hand through his hair.

The thought sobered her. Ludwig had nearly died, would have if Heinrich had succeeded, and so would she had Erich not come to her rescue. She'd tried not to think of him much; it was better she forgot, but each time, she cast him from her thoughts, her mind wandered back to him. His deep golden eyes, his hands on her waist, and his lips against her. She'd never been able to thank him, and likely wouldn't ever see him again. *And that was for the best*, she tried to tell herself.

"Any news of Erich?" she asked cautiously.

Ludwig shook his head. "We haven't heard anything. There's no trace of him or the elves."

No news was good news, she supposed. But while Erich was safe, the threat of the elves lingered. They wanted her, and even with Heinrich gone, there were bound to be other greedy men or women willing to sell her to them. And now more people knew about her than before; she would constantly be in danger.

They spent the rest of their visit catching up, and before she'd let him go, she made Ludwig promise he'd resume his place as a guard only after he'd healed from his injuries and his stardust addiction.

Aristea came to visit her last, and for many days Liane worried she was upset with her for Heinrich's death. When she finally came to visit, she was wearing the black widow's veil. Traditionally worn for a year after the passing of a husband. But Heinrich had been posthumously declared a traitor and was denied burial in the royal crypts. Seeing Aristea wearing it made her blood boil; even after he'd been exposed, she'd dared come here in full mourning for him.

"You're wearing the veil for a traitor?" Liane snapped, half rising from her seat as Luzie showed Aristea in.

"I don't have excuses to give you," Aristea said quietly with her shoulders curled inward, and her head bowed.

"He tried to torture and kill me. He was going to sell me to the elves and probably kill you and Mother to steal the throne."

"I know."

"And yet you still love him enough to mourn him?" Liane asked.

"I shouldn't cry for him." Her voice broke. "I always knew he was a wicked man, and yet I stayed with him. Even as he cut me into smaller and smaller pieces. I told myself it was to protect the family, even as he hurt me, and made me second guess my every thought. But Liane, when I heard he was dead, I was relieved, and I hated myself for that. I should have been strong enough to walk away before that..."

After five years of marriage, her husband was dead, and Aristea was free. But Liane realized it wasn't for him she was grieving, but the life that should've been, for the sacrifices she'd made to keep peace in the kingdom. Liane's anger dissipated like the morning mist, and Liane opened her arms to let Aristea in.

"You were strong, and you don't need to blame yourself. He was the one who was wrong to hurt you. There's nothing to feel bad about," Liane said.

Aristea fell into her arms and grasped fistfuls of Liane's nightgown as she pressed her head against her shoulder. "Liane, I'm sorry. You were there to defend me, and I—"

"I know," Liane said, rubbing circles into Aristea's back.

They held onto one another for a long time until Aristea's crying abated. She sat back, and her sheer black veil revealed her tear-streaked face. And for the first time in a long time, they talked as sisters, slipping back in time when they were girls with nothing else to concern them but petty court gossip and the like. By the time they were done talking, their eyes were puffy from crying, and Liane's mouth hurt from smiling.

"I don't know how else to bring this up. But we got a letter from Mathias. He's heading for the border. I wanted you to know before you heard it from someone else."

Her heart clenched to hear those words. But she knew he'd made his decision to protect the empire, and she also realized even with Heinrich gone, the dangers remained. She'd been so focused on her own goals she hadn't stepped back to see the bigger picture. She couldn't protect Mathias or Elias, for that matter, but what purpose did she have now? Liane curled a hand against her chest; even now, she felt the faint flickering of power deep in her belly. Mother hadn't stolen her choice; she merely delayed it. Like Mathias and Aristea, she was willing to do anything to protect her family.

"He's going to be alright," Aristea said, squeezing Liane's shoulder, resuming the role of protective older sister once again.

Aristea had already shouldered too much; Liane couldn't force her to endure it all. And then Liane saw a bit of why her mother had done what she did. Misguided as it was, she tried to protect her. And then Liane was hit with sudden clarity.

The next day, the Vice Premier gave her permission to leave her room. After weeks locked away, and her skin still sensitive to the sun, she could think of only one place she wanted to go: the library. It was there she'd sought escape in her invalid youth.

Her guards trailed her as she slowly walked down the hall, and courtiers she passed moved out of her way, staring at her with wide-eyed stares. They muttered when she turned her back, and she imagined they were speculating on whether she'd glow again. Liane ignored them because they didn't matter.

When she reached the library, she inhaled the scent of books before perusing the shelves to find a familiar favorite. Book in hand, she curled up into a chair away from the windows and lost herself in fictional adventures. But it wasn't long before her attention started to drift.

Erich was never far from her thoughts, and while she fantasized about running off into the forest in search of him, she suspected he was long gone. Twice as much time as she'd known him had passed since then, but memories of him refused to fade. Would she be forever trapped by this longing for a man she could never have?

"Something troubles you, child of light?" the Avatheos' sonorous voice rippled over her, and Liane stood up to bow to him.

Back bent in his own bow, he shuffled toward her, and her skin prickled at his approach, glowing faintly. She realized now that her magic responded to the Avatheos in a way she couldn't explain. But then again, there was still so much she didn't know about her magic. She'd wanted to ask him, but it seemed presumptuous to summon the head of the church on her own whim.

"I should be the one bowing to you, not the other way around," he said, still stooping before her.

Liane stood awkwardly, not sure what to say. "Surely not," she blurted and cringed at her outburst. A thousand burning questions churned within her, and that was what she started with?

"You've been chosen by the goddess to wield her divine blade."

"How can you be sure I'm chosen, and this wasn't all a mistake?" Liane asked, still not convinced this wasn't all a huge cosmic joke.

A small smile curled the Avatheos' lips. "Your arrival has long been prophesized across generations. I knew you were coming, felt the power in you but couldn't be certain until the ceremony when the magic was awakened."

"What am I even supposed to do?"

The Avatheos stepped closer, and the tingling sensation increased, sparking along her body until she felt as if she were electrified.

"Surely you can feel it, the spark in your soul. You were destined to cleave the dark, as Cyra once did. You must end The Corruption once and for all."

"Where do I start? Just one light display, and I was left feverish and weak," Liane said, shaking her head. But despite her protests, there was a deep burning desire to do more. And the Avatheos' words stoked it like an ember waiting to ignite.

"That will improve with training. Come with me, to Basilia. There other priests and I can teach you how to harness your true potential."

This was it, the feeling of longing, the lack of purpose in her life that had shadowed her all her life. This was the moment she had been waiting for.

"When do we leave?"

~ The story continues in Dragon's Temptation ~

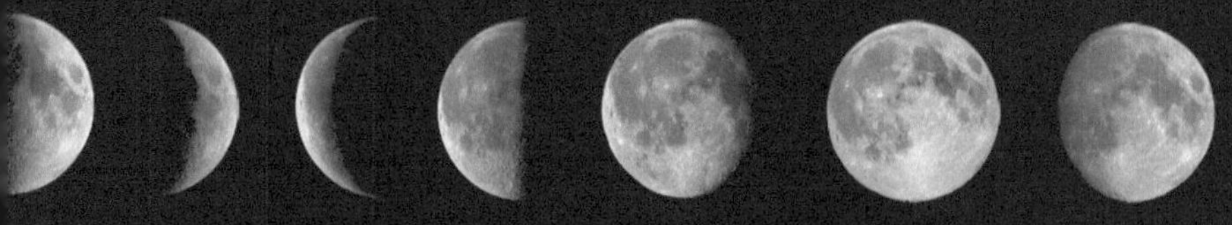

GUIDE TO NEOLYRA

NICOLETTE ANDREWS

CAST OF CHARACTERS

ROYAL FAMILY

Alexander Holt Starweber—Father of Liane
Appearance(s): Empress Ascending, Dragon's Deception
Aristea Starweber—Older sister of Liane; heir to the throne of Neolyra
Appearance(s): Dragon's Deception
Eveline Starweber—Mother of Liane; Empress of Neolyra
Appearance(s): Empress Ascending, Dragon's Deception
Heinrich Meisner Starweber—wed to Aristea Starweber
Appearance(s): Empress Ascending (referenced), Dragon's Deception
Liane Starweber—second princess of Neolyra
Appearance(s): Dragon's Deception
Mathias Leopold Starweber—grandfather of Liane; former emperor; Eveline's father **(deceased)**

Appearance(s): Empress Ascending, Dragon's Deception (referenced)

Mathias Alexander Starweber—younger brother of Liane; son of Alexander and Eveline; prince of Neo

Appearance(s): Dragon's Deception

Theresa Starweber—grandmother of Liane; Eveline's Mother **(deceased)**

Appearance(s): Empress Ascending,

Viznent Meisner—former Duke Meisner, traitor who led uprising against Empress Eveline **(deceased)**

Appearance(s): Empress Ascending, Dragon's Deception (referenced)

PALACE HOUSEHOLD

Catarina—Empress Eveline's head maid; married to Falko

Appearance(s): Empress Ascending

Elias—Liane's childhood best friend (deceased)

Appearance(s): Dragon's Deception (referenced)

Falko—Head of Royal Guard

Appearance(s): Empress Ascending, Dragon's Deception

Gunnar—Master of Stables

Appearance(s): Empress Ascending

Levi—Head Attendant

Appearance(s): Empress Ascending

Ludwig Wildner—head of Liane's guard; Liane's best friend

Appearance(s): Dragon's Deception

Luzie—Liane's head maid

Appearance(s): Dragon's Deception
Aayden—Liane's guard
Appearance(s): Dragon's Deception
Simon—Liane's guard
Appearance(s): Dragon's Deception

COURTIERS

Duke Licht—Duke of Licht; Liane's suitor; friend of Heinrich
Appearance(s): Dragon's Deception
Frey—General; Emperor Mathias's best friend
Appearance(s): Empress Ascending
Duke Holt—Ruler of Ronnenmond; Alexander Holt's relative (father in empress ascending older brother in dragon's deception)
Appearance(s): Empress Ascending, (referenced) Dragon's Deception (referenced)
Duke Friesigner
Appearance(s): Empress Ascending
Duke Visscher
Appearance(s): Empress Ascending
Duke Kretschemer
Appearance(s): Empress Ascending
Dance Mistress Eleanor—Dance teacher to Aristae and Liane
Appearance(s): Dragon's Deception
Duke Schatz—Gout sufferer; Duke of Parliament member; Empress Eveline Ally
Appearance(s): Dragon's Deception (referenced)

Count Harig—courtier; Empress Eveline Ally
Appearance(s): Dragon's Deception (referenced)
Lord Sommerfeld—courtier; former Heinrich ally
Appearance(s): Dragon's Deception
Lady Beltrod: courtier

CHURCH OF SOL

Aolois—Two toned stag; godling of twilight/balance created by the divine twins.
Avatheos—Leader of the Church of Sol
Appearance(s): Empress Ascending as a Vice Premier; Dragon's Deception as Avatheos
Cyra—Sun Goddess; One of the Divine Twins
Appearance(s): Empress Ascending, Dragon's Deception (referenced both times)
Church of Sol—primary religious organization on the continent
Divine Twins—First two deities born to the All Mother
Appearance(s): Dragon's Deception (referenced)
Golden Blade—Cyra's divine sword that she used to sever night from day.
Appearance(s): Empress Ascending, Dragon's Deception
Nameless Goddess, the—Moon Goddess; one of the divine twins
Appearance(s): Empress Ascending, Dragon's Deception (referenced both times)
Sun Ceremony—Summer solstice in Neolyra celebrated by invoking the sun through ritual led by the leaders of the Church of Sol

Appearance(s):Dragon's Deception
Vice Premier—Secondary rank in Church of Sol beneath the Avatheos
Appearance(s): Dragon's Deception, Empress Ascending (different Vice Premier)

MIDNIGHT GUARD

Captain Rosen—head of midnight guard; first woman head of the guard
Arne—midnight guard
Fynn—midnight guard

OTHERS

Warden Oswald—corrupt warden of the Atrira's prison
Appearance(s): Dragon's Deception
Fritz—an elf seer
Appearance(s): Dragon's Deception
Elyon—an elf
Appearance(s): Dragon's Deception
Niklas Ehrle—Leader of the Onyx Gang
Appearance(s): Dragon's Deception

SUNDLAND

Anja Endland Ostrom—former Queen of Sundland; Mother of Erich (Deceased)
Appearance(s): Dragon's Deception (referenced)

Arnfast Ostrom—Duke Mattison; Erich's oldest paternal Uncle

Appearance(s): Dragon's Deception (referenced)

Erich Ostrom—Were-dragon; Heir to Sundland Throne; Son of Harald and Anja

Appearance(s): Dragon's Deception

Freya Ostrom—Queen of Sundland; Erich's Stepmother

Appearance(s): Dragon's Deception (referenced)

Harald Ostrom—King of Sundland; Erich's Father

Appearance(s): Dragon's Deception (referenced)

Ivar Gunderson—Ambassador of Sunland in Neolyra

Appearance(s): Dragon's Deception

Greta Gunderson—daughter of Ivar

Appearance(s): Dragon's Deception (referenced)

Oskar Ostrom—Duke Ericson; Erich's youngest paternal Uncle

Appearance(s): Dragon's Deception (referenced)

Theo Endland—Lord Endland; Erich's Maternal uncle & mentor

Appearance(s): Dragon's Deception (referenced)

COUNTRIES/ LOCATIONS

Ageless Sea—sea separating Xi'an and the continent
Artria—capital of Neolyra
Basilia—religious capital & central home of the Church of Sol
Gauldeen—province in Porroque famous for its wine
Guild Street—guild locations
Imperial Square—Artria's city center
Neolyra—Empire and largest power on the continent
Palace Street—street leading to the palace
Porroque—western coastal country known for its cheese
Rift, the—Space between the real world and the veil, used by elves for short distance quick travel
Soccicio—coastal southeastern country on the continent
Starlight Square—city square that intersects guild street
Sundland—land locked, northeastern country on the continent
Temple Street—street connecting with Church of Sol

Xi'an—large continent to the south of the continent. Known for their clever alchemists and their unusual experiments.

Velvet District—pleasure district of the city holding gambling dens, brothels, and drug dens aplenty.

TERMS & DEFINITIONS

All Mother—mother of the divine twins (Cyra and the Nameless Goddess)

Ancient(s)—godlings of lore, created by the divine twins at the dawn of time.

City Watch—city guards

Corruption, the—a cataclysmic event that destroyed light magic, and altered magical beings turning them into corrupted.

corrupted—anyone who is tainted by corruption magic.

corrupt magic—infected magic

chimera—creatures born from corrupt magic.

Eternal Light—the afterlife

Feuerster—monsters formed from embers and living flame.

Hunters—non-church sanction corruption hunters who sell their parts on the black market.

Midnight Guard—specially trained by the church of sol to hunt corrupted

Onyx Gang—an organized crime group who sells stardust.

Oracle—someone who can see into the future by reading signs in the stars and in runes and casting bones.

Ruins, the—the remnants of a lost civilization

Runes—magical markers, their uses forgotten

Valley of Darkness—the place the dead pass through on their way to Eternal Light

Veil, the—barrier separating life and death

Veins—source of magic.

Warped Mages—someone who uses corruption magic and corrupted creatures, like Chimera.

Trinity—three form goddess, (seen as maiden, mother, crone,) worshipped by Sundlanders

Wicked King—A series of salacious novels about an arrangement marriage between a woman and an evil king.

Acknowledgments

Words cannot encompass the gratitude I feel upon releasing this book. Even before I set fingers to keyboard, this story has been burning a hole in my heart. From conception to publication, it has been an indulgence, one I wasn't sure would please anyone but myself. Not to be dramatic, but this book saved me from a dark pit of despair in which I feared I'd lose my love of writing for good. I'm not sure if this book would be possible without my tribe of supporters.

First, I must heap praises upon my husband, Drew, who acted as my sounding board and gave me quiet encouragement as I wrestled with this manuscript. Even as this book's production dragged on, his encouraging words and support helped me power through the tough parts. Then there is my best friend Nicole who always believes in me, even when I don't believe in myself. I will learn not to argue with her one day. (She knows what I'm talking about). Kat, my amazing editor, continues to go above and beyond for me, helping to untangle my messy grammar.

I mentioned in my dedication, but this book wouldn't be possible without Kickstarter. I had an idea and a dream, and my readers showed up in a big way, helping me create something I've always dreamed of. Thank you for believing in me and this book and helping Dragon's Deception become everything I hoped it would be.

Yuki: A Snow White Retelling

Okami: A Little Red Riding Hood Retelling

Diviner's World

Duchess (Free)

Sorcerer (Free)

Diviner's Prophecy

Diviner's Curse

Diviner's Fate

Princess

Witch of the Lake Series

Feast of the Mother

Fate of the Demon

Fall of the Reaper

About the Author

Nicolette is a native San Diegan with a passion for the world of make believe. From a young age, Nicolette was telling stories whether it be writing plays for her friends to act out or making a series of children's books that her mother still likes drag out to embarrass her with in front of company. She still lives in her imagination but in reality she resides in San Diego with her husband, children and a couple cats. She loves reading, attempting arts and crafts, and cooking.

You can visit her at her website: www.nicoletteandrews.com or at these places:

facebook.com/nicandfantasy

twitter.com/nicandfantasy

instagram.com/nicolette_andrews

amazon.com/author/nicoletteandrews

bookbub.com/authors/nicolette-andrews

goodreads.com/nicolette_andrews

pinterest.com/Nicandfantasy

tiktok.com/@nicandfantasy